Praise for
Monica Burns

"Burns doesn't disappoint!"
— **RTBOOKreviews**

"Monica Burns writes with sensitivity and panache."
— **Sabrina Jeffries, NYT bestselling author**

"powerfully done…the scenes between Tobias and Jane
mesmerized me. I loved it."
— **Joey W. Hill**

"No one sets fire to the page like Monica Burns."
— **eCataromance**

"Definitely recommended reading."
— **The Romance Studio**

The Rogue's Countess

By

Monica Burns

Table Of Contents

Dedication

For Laura Polito Mceleney.
Without her, it's unlikely anyone would be reading
this book.

Chapter 1

May 1895

Moonlight draped a pale shroud over the garden landscape as Phoebe descended the wide stone stairs leading into Lord Montjoy's gardens. Behind her, the music spilled out of the ballroom. It followed her as she moved deeper into the large decorative gardens that extended away from the mansion.

The further away from the house, the softer the music became until it faded to a mere whisper. Despite the heat of the day lingering in the garden, it was a welcome respite from the crowded ballroom and its stifling heat.

She had deliberately waited until Alfred was engrossed in conversation with his latest mistress and several of his friends before she'd dared to venture out into the garden. If Alfred had realized what she was planning, he would have stopped her, which meant her efforts to save her dearest friend would fail. Failure meant Lawrence would pay a far greater price than any humiliation or pain Alfred could inflict on her.

In the almost six years they'd been married, her senses had become dulled to Alfred's drinking, philandering, and cruelty. She'd learned to step outside of herself when he rutted on top of her, but it was much harder to insulate herself from his verbal tirades. Those she tried to avoid at all costs. It was so much easier if she didn't incite his anger.

Tonight had been one of those rare moments when she'd failed to keep her wits about her. It had been a long time since she'd spoken without thinking in Alfred's presence. Instinctively, Phoebe's hand reached up to touch the back of her head. Her scalp still stung from where Alfred had pulled viciously on her hair earlier this evening.

From the beginning of their marriage, her husband had never shown her kindness, and her inability to give him an heir had made things worse. After her second miscarriage, Alfred accused her of having taken steps to rid herself of a child. It was the farthest thing from the truth, A child would have made life more bearable, and his cruel words had made her lose her tongue.

Alfred had become enraged when she'd declared he might be the one responsible in the matter as well. She'd pointed to his drinking, which usually made him impotent when he shared her bed. The moment the back of his hand had hit her cheek, she'd learned a hard lesson. It was the first and only time he'd actually hit her, but Phoebe had never made the same mistake again until tonight.

It was only when Alfred was between mistresses that Phoebe ever had to dread him entering her bedroom to demand his conjugal rights. It was why she'd been surprised to see him enter her room earlier. He had only recently taken up with his latest paramour, and she'd been too bewildered to think twice. Before she could stop herself, she'd questioned his reason for being in her rooms. Normally, Alfred inflicted pain with cruel words. In his inebriated state, he'd tried to slap her. When she'd darted out of the way, the only thing he'd been able to grab hold of was her hair. She winced again as the memory seemed to make her scalp sting worse.

The garden path darkened as the row of trees lining the pebbled walkway blocked the night sky. Ahead of her, she could see where the path broke outward to encircle a small fountain illuminated by the moon. As she left the trees' shadows, she sat down on one of the white marble benches situated around the ornamental structure to wait. Lawrence would be here soon.

Soft voices echoed nearby as other guests sought a more intimate setting. It wouldn't be difficult for her and Lawrence to convince someone that they were having an affair. Rumors of a liaison would simply be seen as the result of a longtime friendship. Alfred would most likely beat her for daring to cuckold him, but it didn't matter. News of her alleged affair would save Lawrence from prosecution. Phoebe frowned as she recalled how frantic her friend had been when he'd visited her that morning.

Phoebe had just finished pouring a cup of tea when Lawrence had called on her. Although clearly upset, her friend had managed to wait until the door had closed behind Bateman before speaking.

"I'm done for, my pet," Lawrence exclaimed in a hoarse voice as he kissed her cheeks in greeting, then turned away to pace the floor like a caged animal. Her friend was rarely rattled, but his manner was that of a hunted man.

"What's wrong?" she exclaimed softly.

"I was careless." One hand shoving its way through his blond, wavy hair, her friend prowled the room with a dark and grim expression. "I wouldn't be in this damnable position if I had simply used my head."

Even despite his obvious fear, Lawrence still struck a dashing figure. With his firm, full mouth, long, sooty eyelashes, and crystal blue eyes, women in the Set always vied for her friend's attention. It wasn't simply his looks that caused a stir. He was witty, charming, and kind. Although, as far as mothers were concerned, it was her friend's title and money that was the true attraction. Already wealthy in his own right, as the future Earl of Linshal, Lawrence stood to inherit a great deal more once his father was gone.

Yet, none of those things were what made Phoebe adore her friend. As an American heiress, her father had bought her a title. It wasn't something she'd ever asked for or wanted. In fact, she would have preferred to simply wait to fall in love with a man who loved her as well. But her father had been adamant that only a husband with a title was good enough for his daughter.

Worse, he had made no effort to be discreet about the fact he was hunting for a husband suitable for his daughter. While her dowry had not been something to sneer at, it had been less than substantial to secure her a duke or earl. Her father's blatant and often uncouth efforts to gain her a title were why many of the Marlborough Set had always viewed her with disdain. Alfred's bombastic, often drunken behavior only exacerbated the situation. Nor did her husband's low standing on the social ladder in terms of land and wealth.

The first few social events she'd attended after her wedding had been nothing but haughty condescension and outright snubs. It was at one of those affairs that Lawrence had witnessed several women snub her. He'd immediately charged to her rescue and introduced her to members of the Set who had willingly included her in their circle.

From that moment forward, she and Lawrence had been best friends, and over the years, the bond they had formed was akin to that of brother and sister. Although Alfred disliked Lawrence, her husband knew Phoebe's friend opened doors all the way up to the Prince of Wales himself. Doors that would have remained closed to them without her friendship with Lawrence.

It was a social power Alfred was keenly aware of, and she was certain it was the only reason he'd never forbidden her to discontinue her friendship with Lawrence. It was a fact for which she was grateful as Lawrence was the only person she could confide in completely. Her friend had placed his trust in her as well.

"Come sit down and tell me what's happened." Phoebe patted the cushion beside her on the settee. Like an obedient child, Lawrence sat down next to her.

"It's Coombs. He saw Anthony and me leaving the Boulders club together," her friend rasped. "He's denounced me as a sodomite to several of his friends."

"*Dear Lord.*" Phoebe stared at him in heartfelt dismay.

Almost from the beginning, Phoebe had known Lawrence was different from other men. It didn't make her love him any less. She'd always believed Lawrence was who he was simply because it was the way God and nature had made him. Now he might be punished for the fact, and the thought horrified her.

"Ever since the bastard lost all that money to me when my mare beat his stallion at Newmarket, he's had it in for me." One hand rubbing his forehead, Lawrence leaned forward to stare at the rug beneath his feet and shook his head. "Now he's determined to ruin me, or worse, have me locked away."

"Are you certain he saw you with Anthony?"

"Yes," her friend said with a dark note of dismay in his voice. "He didn't say a word. He just smiled, and I knew he wouldn't simply turn his head away as someone else might have." A shudder ripped through her friend, and Phoebe wrapped her arm around his shoulder.

"Surely there's something we can do to discredit Coombs so others think he's simply trying to make trouble."

"I've been up all night trying to think of something. Anthony has already left for France, and I can't think of any other alternative for myself."

"No, there has to be another way." Phoebe shook her head in protest at the thought of losing her closest friend.

"I don't see how, my pet." Her friend released a harsh breath. "My money might keep me out of Newgate, but the scandal…Father's unwell, and it will devastate him."

"We will not let it come to that. We're going to find a way to stop Coombs," Phoebe said with a firmness she didn't feel. "And I find it reprehensible that Anthony deserted you so easily."

"He didn't desert me." Lawrence rebuked her with a gentle glare before standing up to pace the floor again. "He pleaded with me to come with him."

"And you chose not to leave because of your father."

"If the scandal doesn't kill him, Phoebe, learning the truth from someone other than me would."

"Then you're going to tell him?"

She eyed her friend with sympathy. For years, Lawrence had debated whether to reveal his lifestyle to his father. The two men were close, and the thought of his secret destroying that relationship tormented her friend. On more than one occasion, Phoebe had encouraged her friend to tell his father the truth.

She'd suspected the old earl already knew his son's intimate relationships were not with those of the female persuasion. The fact that Lawrence's father never pushed his son to marry made Phoebe believe he already suspected the truth. Her friend jerked his head in a positive response.

"I have no choice," he said grimly. "Coombs would take great pleasure in telling Father if I don't tell him myself."

"He loves you, Lawrence. That won't change when you tell him the truth."

"Perhaps. But he will be devastated, nonetheless."

Phoebe nibbled at her lip as she contemplated her friend's predicament. He was right. Even if Lawrence's father had already guessed his son's secret, the earl would most likely still be upset by the news. It was one thing to ignore the possibility of a truth and something altogether different to be confronted with the reality of it.

No matter who told the earl that his son's lifestyle was outside society's boundaries, it would still distress the old man. She liked Lord Linshal a great deal and despised the thought of him being hurt by scandal. Phoebe released a soft sigh.

"If only fate had been kinder to us both. If you'd not been in France for all those months, Father was prowling

London in search of a title for me, things might have been different," she said wistfully.

"Husband and wife." A look of sadness crossed his handsome features as his mouth twisted in a slight grimace. "It would have been the perfect solution for both of us, would it not?"

"Yes."

Phoebe nodded in agreement. It wasn't the first time she'd thought of what might have been. If they had been married—she drew in a sharp breath at the idea that flitted through her head. There would be a price, but she would willingly pay it to save her friend.

"You don't have to tell your father. No one has to know," Phoebe said in a resolute voice. "There *is* a way to make Coombs look like he simply wants to cause trouble."

In quick succession, puzzlement, hope, and protest swept across Lawrence's face as she'd laid out her plan. He'd immediately dismissed the idea, stating no one would believe what she was proposing. Unfaltering in her determination to help her dearest friend and protect his father, Phoebe countered all of Lawrence's arguments until he'd reluctantly agreed that it might work. It took her only a few minutes more to convince him that tonight was as good a chance as any to stop Coombs.

The only drawback to her scheme was Alfred's reaction. She knew her husband would be furious at the thought of being cuckolded, but a part of her wanted a moment of vengeful satisfaction for all Alfred had put her through since they'd been married.

Water splashed quietly into the stone basin from the fountainhead behind her as a shrill, feminine laugh nearby made Phoebe tremble with trepidation. Where was Lawrence? She'd dropped several hints to Lady Lydia that she had an assignation in the garden. The woman was an infernal gossip, and Phoebe knew the woman would be watching her like a hawk to learn who her lover was. If they were to be caught in each other's arms when Lady Lydia stumbled upon them, Lawrence needed to arrive soon.

Had he rethought his decision and decided not to follow through with her idea? If Lawrence thought for even an instant that Phoebe would suffer Alfred's wrath, her friend wouldn't meet her as they'd arranged. No sooner had the question slipped through her mind than a heavy tread on the gravel path made her jerk her head toward the sound.

Relief swept through her at the sight of the tall, masculine figure walking through the shadows in her direction. Only a short distance away, she heard another couple talking. When he hesitated, Phoebe leapt to her feet. She refused to let Lawrence rethink her proposition, and the presence of another couple nearby would help propagate the notion that they were involved.

"You came," she exclaimed, making her voice loud enough to carry, but still inviting as if she were greeting her lover. Rushing forward, she launched herself into her friend's arms and pressed her lips to his. It took only a split second for her to realize her mistake.

The body she'd flung herself against was hard and solid. Lawrence was not a weakling, but this man was a rock by comparison. Stunned, Phoebe stood braced against him and struggled to comprehend the error she'd made. The stranger's lips held the warmth of sunshine on a summer's day as his mouth moved gently against hers. Still disoriented, Phoebe didn't pull away as his kiss sent a pulse of heat through her.

Unlike Alfred, this man didn't crush her mouth beneath his. He made no attempt to dominate. Instead, the stranger's lips teased and cajoled a response from her with disturbing ease. Dear Lord, she needed to stop this insanity. She was a married woman.

Laughter drifted through her head with bitter mockery. A financial arrangement was not a marriage. She was nothing more than chattel. A pound of flesh for Alfred to rut with like a common whore when he was without a mistress or a whipping boy when he was angry.

The warmth of the stranger's mouth was a tantalizing caress that sent her senses reeling. Unable to move, her protest died in her throat as muscular arms pulled her deeper into his embrace, and a hot tongue gently pushed its way into her mouth. Despite the fire in his kiss, the stranger's touch was gentle, tender, almost.

His fingers stroked her cheek in a way that made her feel as though she were a beautiful jewel. No one had ever kissed her like this before. This was a sweet seduction that offered a promise of pleasure, not a cold, painful act of humiliation. With a shudder, she jerked her head backward and away from his incredibly sensual lips.

"Forgive me," she choked out as she stared up into gray eyes that were almost silver in the moonlight. "I thought…thought you were someone else."

"A mistake I'm happy to forgive." The words were a sinful, velvety caress across her senses, and she trembled as his fingers trailed their way along the curve of her exposed shoulder to the edge of her sleeve.

"Perhaps…if you would release me."

"Is that what you really want?" The quiet question sent another tremor rippling through her.

"I don't understand."

Phoebe's heart fluttered like a frantic bird in her breast as something foreign swept over her. She could tell he felt it, too. It was a fierce and fiery sensation that she knew was desire. Incapable of pulling away from him, she tried to keep breathing as his fingers caught her by the chin, and his thumb rubbed across her lower lip in the lightest of caresses.

Every inch of her was on fire, unlike anything she'd experienced before, and she realized she wanted more of his touch. The thought made her suck in a sharp breath of surprise and trepidation. This man was dangerous not only to her senses, but to everything she'd come to accept as her lot in her life with Alfred.

"Most women would have protested quite vigorously the moment they realized their mistake." The silken whisper layered her skin with a frisson. He lowered his head and brushed her ear with her lips. "And yet, you seemed quite content to remain in my arms."

"That's not true."

It was a lie. She knew she should have put several feet between them the moment she'd realized he wasn't Lawrence and certainly when he'd returned her kiss. She didn't know why she hadn't done so already.

"You're not a very good liar," he murmured with obvious amusement as he bent his head to tease her lips in a hot kiss. "You're still in my arms."

Wild excitement washed over Phoebe at the playful caress. Quivering, she closed her eyes and breathed in his masculine scent. Brandy, leather, and pine poured over her senses as his mouth nipped at hers. It was a heady sensation. Tantalizing.

"I am not about to struggle with you like a damsel in the arms of a cad," she snapped as she saw his amusement. "I am waiting for you to release me."

"Another lie?" he chuckled. It was a pleasant laugh, unlike Alfred's malicious one. The stranger's gentle humor declared he was teasing her. "I think you enjoyed kissing me, and I think you'd like me to do so again."

"I would *not*," Phoebe gasped as she stared up at him in dismay. Another lie, but she could hardly admit the truth.

"Very well then," he said with a wicked smile. "I won't stop you from fleeing."

In the next instant, his arms were no longer wrapped around her, and he took a small step backward. The loss of his warmth stunned Phoebe. It was as if she'd been abruptly thrust out into a cold and bitter winter day. She didn't move. She couldn't. When she didn't try to escape, he reached out to stroke her cheek with his forefinger.

"I wonder if you know how lovely you are," he murmured as his finger grazed its way across her bottom lip once more in a sensual stroke.

Phoebe flushed at his compliment. She knew she should run back to the sanctuary of the ballroom as fast as she could, but logic was swiftly overruled by her desire to stay. His kiss was the first intimate touch she'd ever experienced that hadn't involved some form of cold humiliation. It was impossible to deny his touch had stirred a longing deep inside her. A yearning for something more in her life, if only for the briefest of moments.

"I…" She shook her head as she struggled to describe what she was feeling.

He closed the narrow space between them once more, but didn't touch her. Instead, he bent his head, his warm breath feathering its way across her ear lobe.

"Have you never been properly kissed, sweetheart?"

"I don't know what you mean," she said with a catch in her voice. His mouth nibbled at her ear. The sensation sent shock waves rippling through her.

"Your kiss is reticent, almost innocent," he murmured with the merest hint of puzzlement. "It's as if you've never been kissed before."

The stranger's observation made her throat close up with emotion. What he'd said was true. Phoebe couldn't recall a single instance when her husband had kissed her as this stranger had done. Alfred's touch had always been a cold, painful assault on her mouth. It had always created a sickening feeling in the pit of her stomach. This man's kiss was the first taste of pleasure she'd ever known.

"I am no stranger to a man's bed, if that's what you mean," she said in a tight voice as images of Alfred rutting over her like a pig filled her head.

"Then it was a poor lover who left your mouth tasting so delectably untouched." His mouth singed hers for the briefest second as he kissed her lightly. "You might be acquainted with a man's bed, but whoever he was, it's obvious he left you longing for something more."

She drew in a sharp breath at the way he'd seen into her soul so easily. He kissed her again. The caress sent her heartbeat skidding out of control. Pleasure tingled its way down her spine as she leaned into him and reveled in the fire of his touch. Everything faded away as she experienced something she'd only dreamed about.

The stranger pulled her close once more, and her mind reeled as her mouth eagerly parted for him. His kiss connected her to him in a way that made her forget everything, but the way his touch heightened her longing for something that had never been within her reach until now. Common sense tried to push its way through the mist of pleasure enveloping her, but it was smothered by the honeyed languor flowing through her limbs.

From deep inside, the years of longing for a lover's gentle caress welled up to engulf her. Held hostage to the sensations gripping her, she willingly allowed herself to drown in a whirlpool of arousal and need. Blinded to everything but the taste of him, she explored his mouth with a fervor that stunned her. In response, his lips broke away from her mouth and down the side of her neck.

White heat skimmed over her skin, and her head fell back as his mouth nipped at the side of her neck and moved downward. A fraction of a second later, his tongue slid hot and wet into the valley between her breasts. It was a decadent caress that pulled a low moan of pleasure from her. It made her crave something even more intense and intimate.

Desire washed over her at a frightening speed, as somewhere in the back of her mind, she realized exactly what she'd been missing from her marriage bed. Wild and erratic, her heartbeat pounded loudly in her ears as molten heat streamed its way through her belly, down to the sensitive spot between her legs. The rush of warmth there tugged a small cry from her as she shuddered against him.

"Oh, please, I…please. I want…" she gasped.

In a bold move that made her heart thud violently, she stroked him through his trousers. He jerked at her caress, then pulled her tighter, trapping her hand between them until his erection pressed deeply into her palm. A shudder rippled through her at the thought of him inside her while a small voice cried out a warning. Desire silenced the soft cry. A dark growl rumbled in his chest. The sound reverberated against her lips before he lifted his head to stare down at her.

"I think it best I let you return to the ballroom before I lose control completely," he rasped.

Desire blazed in the depths of his gray eyes as he stared down at her. It was clear he was attempting to be a gentleman, despite the heated caresses that had already passed between them. The fact that he was unwilling to push his advantage said a great deal about the kind of man he was—a man who was honorable enough to forego acting on his carnal needs.

This was a man who would be a considerate lover. He would never take without giving in return. The knowledge sent a pulse of stark need streaking through her. If only for this singular moment in time, she wanted to experience a lover's touch without revulsion or dread.

"I don't want to return to the ballroom," she whispered and impulsively tugged her head down to his.

All she wanted was to feel alive—to revel in an ecstasy she'd never experienced in her life. His mouth spoke of passion, but his touch was gentle as he stroked his fingers along the curve of her neck.

There would never be another moment such as this, and every second was a gift she would cherish. This brief interlude would be a memory she would summon whenever she was faced with the harsh reality of her daily life. It would remind her that someone had once touched her gently and passionately. She would remember that for a few brief moments, she had been more than an object used to satisfy the base physical needs of a man.

The spicy scent of him filled her nostrils. He smelled clean, strong, and powerful. Every part of him overwhelmed her senses until desire violently stripped her of all reason. She didn't protest as he guided her off the path into the darkness of the foliage that lined the path. Instead, she went willingly, frantically as her body demanded something she'd never experienced before, but she still recognized it. The cool night air nipped at her thigh before a large hand seared her skin. From deep within her, an unexpected passion rose inside her until her mouth was clinging to his. Long fingers tangled with hers as they worked the buttons on his trousers free.

Seconds later, his heavy weight was in her palm, and with inexperienced fingers, she ran her hand over his thick, hard length. The touch made him groan before his hand slid up her thigh to reach the heat of her center. He rubbed lightly against her sex, and she jerked. Her breaths hot and rapid, she thrust her hips forward.

"Oh, please. Now. I need to feel…" Her words trailed off into a low moan as he increased the pressure to the small nub of flesh between her legs.

There was no right or wrong, only this moment of human connection that promised to fulfill her in ways she'd yet to realize. His hand forced her to wrap her leg around his waist, and in the next breath, he filled her with a mind-numbing thrust that pushed her over the edge of an abyss.

Almost as if he knew what her reaction would be, his mouth swallowed her cry of intense pleasure. Hard and fast, he stroked her body with his. A pitched sensation grasped her insides until she felt her body tighten around him. Her spasm drew a dark growl from him as he increased the speed of his thrusts.

Suddenly, a wave of fire engulfed her, then skimmed its way across her skin and downward to the apex of her thighs. White-hot heat raced through her blood until it tightened her insides and convulsed with an intensity unlike anything she'd ever experienced.

Her cry of ecstasy was silenced by a passionate kiss. Beneath her hand, his heartbeat pounded a fierce rhythm against her palm as he possessed her at a blistering pace. A second later, he buried himself deep inside her and throbbed against her with a ferocity that matched her own climax. Ever so slowly, the rasp of his harsh breaths and Phoebe's frantic ones slowed to normal.

Reluctant to give up the power, warmth, and comfort of his touch, she clung to him. She wanted this moment to never end. She didn't want to leave the tenderness of his embrace or give up the brief moment of contact that said she was alive inside. This stranger had pulled her deepest desires up from the depths of her soul until she'd been blind to everything except the sensations holding her prisoner.

Gray eyes smoky with the remnants of desire met hers, and she wanted to drown in the warm steel of them. Strong and rugged, his features spoke of a strength that was as much physical as it was emotional. It was impossible to tell if his hair was black or dark brown in the dim light, but it was his gaze that hypnotized her. It was the first time she'd consciously studied his face. She'd been so consumed by an overwhelming need to connect with another soul, it wasn't until now that she'd truly looked at him.

His mouth twisted in a slight smile, almost as if he could read her thoughts. With obvious reluctance, he retreated from her. The tip of his finger traced the curve of her bottom lip in a sensual invitation. It made her ache for him all over again. What would it be like to spend one night after another in this man's bed? Phoebe drew in a sharp breath.

Dear God, what had she just done? Horror held her rigid as the full extent of her folly took shape in her mind. She'd lowered her personal standards to that of her husband. Not once during her marriage had she ever contemplated having a liaison with any man. The thought had been unthinkable. Not because she feared Alfred, but because she possessed little except her self-respect. Something she'd surrendered to a stranger in a few brief moments.

It didn't matter that Alfred meant nothing to her, that he was cruel to her, or that he had a string of mistresses. She'd lowered her standards to that of her husband. Guilt and shame lashed through her with a violent shudder. Phoebe avoided looking at stranger, and quickly stepped aside to shake out her skirts. With trembling fingers, she tried to restore her appearance, all too aware of the lock of hair brushing her shoulder that would be difficult to pin up.

"Here, let me," he said in a deep, husky voice.

Phoebe stiffened as he turned her around and proceeded to repair her hairstyle and brush off the back of her gown. Somewhere in the back of her mind, she experienced gratitude for the fact her dress was a midnight blue. The color would hide any dirt left behind from her wild, rash behavior.

When he'd finished, the hands glided across her shoulder and down her arm while his mouth nibbled at the curve of her neck. It was a lover's caress, and she struggled to fight the powerful urge to lean back into him, but guilt held her in check. With a jerk, she pulled away from his touch and spun around, struggling desperately not to give in and stay.

"I…I must go," she breathed.

"First, tell me why." It was a gentle command, but a command nonetheless.

"Why?" Phoebe pressed her hand against the base of her throat as if she didn't understand his question. It was a pointless gesture. She knew precisely what he was asking. She shook her head with a sense of helplessness. "I…needed to feel…"

"Desirable." He finished her statement, but it wasn't the right word.

"No," she whispered. "I needed to feel human. To feel alive."

He stared at her for a long moment, and his intense scrutiny made her look away in embarrassment. A warm hand stroked her cheek, and somewhere in her tumbled thoughts, she ached at the thought she would never feel alive again. The knowledge jolted painfully through her, and she fought to stave off tears of self-pity.

"And do you feel alive now?" The soft question made Phoebe draw in a deep breath as she looked up at him.

"Yes." *So alive that I shall never forget you.* Her throat tightened as she remembered the reality she had to return to.

"I want to see you again."

His soft words made Phoebe jump, and her heart stopped for a full beat before it resumed. For a fleeting moment, she almost said yes. She wanted to feel him touching her once more. She wanted to feel alive over and over again. Shame washed over Phoebe at the thought. In one swift stroke, she'd failed to save Lawrence as well as sacrificing her principles.

Where was Lawrence? He should have been here by now. Phoebe peered into the shadows of the garden path, willing her friend to appear. When he didn't, she looked back at the stranger. An odd glint flashed in the silvery gray of his eyes as he lightly touched her cheek. A knot formed in her throat. How could her plan to help her dearest friend have gone so terribly wrong with something that felt so right?

# Chapter 2

"I want to see you again."

Gideon ran his thumb across her lower lip. There was something fragile and vulnerable about her. It was an emotion he was certain she rarely showed to anyone. Hesitation swept across her beautiful features, and he thought she was about to say yes. Intense disappointment sailed through him when she shook her head vehemently.

"*No.* It's impossible."

"Nothing's impossible," he said firmly as he caught the faint hint of another accent threading its way under her English accent. It was undefinable, but he ignored the thought. "Tell me why you won't let me see you again. Are you married?"

The moment the question passed his lips, a voice in the back of his head clanged as loudly as the bells on a fire wagon. Gideon had made it a rule never to indulge in liaisons with married women. He'd restricted himself to widows and courtesans. Now, for the first time in his life, he was considering setting aside his principles to see this woman again. A powerful surge of emotion pumped its way through his blood and told him to do whatever it took not to let her go.

"Tell me."

Instantly, she retreated a step at his softly spoken command. As she darted backward, Gideon quickly reached out and caught her arms in a gentle grasp to keep her from fleeing. A shudder rocked its way through her body and into his. *Christ Jesus*, she was terrified. He jerked away from her. The last thing he wanted to do was frighten her. Was her husband a brute? Was that why she kept glancing over her shoulder as if terrified someone would find them together?

Shame made her turn away and nodded. Gideon's heart sank as she confirmed the truth. He'd been desperately hoping she was a widow, even though instinct had told him otherwise. Gideon knew he should simply walk away, but he couldn't. Instead, he caught her chin in his fingers and tipped her head upward.

"Does he beat you?" he demanded roughly. Surprise made her flinch before she shook her head.

"I have learned not to give him any reason to do so," she whispered. Again, Gideon noted the muted rhythm of something foreign in her voice that made him wonder if English was her natural language. He dismissed the thought as he focused on her. She pulled free of his light hold of her chin and turned her head away. Fury flooded his limbs at the thought of someone hitting her. A man who hit a woman deserved to be beaten until they were one breath away from death.

"Please, you must let me go."

"Let me help you." For a split second, Gideon saw her waver as she debated his offer, then shook her head.

"You cannot," she whispered.

"I *don't* believe that."

Frustration sailed through him as he watched several emotions flash across her features. Confusion, dismay, shame, and fear. It was the fear that gnawed at his gut. Gently, he cupped her cheeks and forced her to look at him once more. She stood frozen in front of him before she pulled away with a sharp movement. Gideon saw her swallow hard as if something had lodged in her throat.

"What happened….it was a mistake," she whispered.

"You're *wrong*."

Although he spoke softly, there was a ferocity in his voice that made her draw in a sharp breath. She denied his statement with a shake of her head, but the anguish he saw in her convinced him that she'd experienced the same bewildering connection between them that he had. Loud cries echoed in Gideon's head, demanding he prevent her from leaving. He had no explanation for his reaction to her or why it was so imperative he should not allow her to leave.

Silence filled the space between them, and he released a harsh breath of frustration. She suddenly took a step back and extended her hand as her expression became polite yet distant. It was as if she'd crawled into a shell where no one could see anything except a woman of serene composure.

"I must go before…I trust the remainder of your evening will be an agreeable one." There was an absurdity to her words that angered him.

"*Damn it to hell,*" he muttered as he caught her smaller hand in his. "At least tell me your name."

"It's best we remain strangers. What happened here was a moment of madness," she said firmly, but he could see the despair engulfing her despite her matter-of-fact manner. In the shadows, her beautiful eyes were soft and luminous, and a grunt of frustration made him tighten his fingers on hers.

"And if we meet in the future?"

"We will act as if we've never met before."

"Do you really think it possible either of us can forget what passed between us?" he said tersely.

"We must, and if we should meet again, I'll have your word as a gentleman. You'll act as though we've never met." When he hesitated, a look of determination made her lips thin with resolve. "Your *word.*"

Gideon shook his head in protest at the sharply spoken demand. At his silent objection, she grew still as a small animal facing danger. It was impossible to tell if it was a fear of him refusing to abide by her demand or something else that caused her to remain unmoving in front of him. The urge to pull her close and simply hold her until her fear receded twisted his gut.

"Don't ask me to—"

"*Your word,*" she demanded.

One idea after another crashed through his head with a desperation he didn't understand. Every possible argument he could think of to make her change her mind was useless. The moment her lovely mouth thinned with determination, Gideon accepted the fact there was nothing he could do except agree to her request.

Resignation slid through him as he slowly turned her hand over in his and pressed his mouth to the inside of her wrist. A small shudder rippled through her at the touch, and Gideon breathed in the soft, sweet smell of roses. It was as if she'd picked the most fragrant of the flowers in his garden and brushed them across her skin. He slowly lifted his head, and their gazes locked as, with great reluctance, he nodded.

"You have my word," he bit out.

The air between them vibrated with raw tension. Relief flared in her gaze before guilt and shame replaced the stark emotion. Her vulnerability returned as she tugged her hand out of his to take two quick steps away from him. Without thinking, Gideon immediately followed, then stopped as she stretched out her hand as if to hold him at bay.

"*Please,* please don't make this even more difficult for me than it already is." The plea in her voice sent a bolt of awareness through him. She was as reluctant to leave him as he was to let her go. His throat closed, and it became difficult to breathe.

"If you have need of me in the future—"

"I shall not," she said with resolve, despite the bleakness reflected in her voice.

Then, with a sharp inhalation of breath, she spun around and hurried back along the garden path leading to the ballroom. Gideon took two strides forward as he started to run after her, but his mind brought him to an abrupt halt. He'd given his word to her. To break it would only cause her pain.

The moment his mysterious enchantress disappeared around the bend in the path, his anger and frustration exploded in a vicious gesture. As the side of his fist slammed into the rough bark of a nearby tree, he grunted at the lack of satisfaction the resulting pain gave him. It was doubtful he would find someone at this late hour to join him in the ring. Even if he did, it still wouldn't be enough. He needed a brawl.

What the devil had just happened to him? One minute he'd been on his way to meet Lady Westerly for a brief moment of pleasure, and in the next, he'd found a passion unlike anything he'd ever experienced in the past. From the first moment she'd thrown herself into his arms, it had been difficult to let her go. Who had she come out to the garden to meet? A lover?

Gideon found that difficult to believe, even though she'd flung herself into his arms with a breathless greeting. While the note of relief in her voice had been distinct and poignant, almost as if she'd been greeting a friend and not a lover. He was also certain it was the first time she'd ever come close to having a liaison. It had been easy to see her horrified reaction as the reality of what had happened registered with her. She'd lost all her inhibitions in his arms, and her shocked dismay convinced him that he was the first man who'd touched other than her husband.

Every visible emotion she'd displayed told him she'd been appalled at having lost control of her senses. Yet despite her obvious shock of having made love to a stranger, he firmly believed she'd not wanted to leave him any more than he wanted to let her go. With every caress and touch of his hand, she'd responded to his touch like a violin did at the hands of a virtuoso. She'd held nothing back, and neither had he.

The realization stunned him. It was the first time since

he'd been witness to Edith's shallowness that he'd broken his vow. An oath he'd made to never let another woman cause him to lose his head. But the bewitching creature he'd held in his arms for just a short time had done exactly that. All of his liaisons had been physically satisfying, but not once had he allowed himself to feel anything more than gratification and pleasure in a lover's arms.

The moment a woman indicated she wanted more from him, Gideon ended the relationship. Although he'd remained friends with one or two of his past lovers, his feelings for them were that of friendship and nothing more. All of that had changed moments ago. Not only had he broken his firm rule never to cuckold another man, but he'd also broken the promise he'd made to himself. Not since Edith had he forgotten everything but the woman in his arms.

Still dazed by his lack of discipline where his sweet enchantress was concerned. Gideon headed back toward the ballroom. Gideon knew he should at least seek out Lady Westerly and express his regrets, but he was in no mood to pander to the woman after what he'd just experienced. Everything about his mysterious temptress had thrown him off balance. Something Edith had never done where he was concerned.

Gideon's stride was long and fast as he returned to the house. He'd agreed not to recognize her if they met again, but she'd not extracted his promise not to search for her. In the back of his head, he heard a voice reminding him that she was married. If he'd known that before he'd made love to her, would it have made a difference? The resounding no echoing through his head emphasized how deeply his mystery lover had affected him.

As he strode up the steps leading onto the patio outside the ballroom, Gideon paused outside the doorway to study the guests from his position in the shadows. Despite his hunger to catch another glimpse of her, the sea of people made it impossible to find her among the throng. Resigned as to his ability to find her easily, he muttered a vicious oath beneath his breath.

The heat of the ballroom pressed into him as he walked through the French doors leading into the house. No matter which direction he turned, he still couldn't see her. Had she left the ball to avoid meeting him again? A low chuckle on his left caught his attention, and he jerked his head toward the sound.

The sight of Sebastian Rockwood, Earl of Melton, smiling at him renewed Gideon's hopes he could be able to find her. Sebastian was someone everyone sought to know. The Reckless Rockwoods, as the Set called them, knew almost everyone in polite society. An introduction would at least give him the opportunity to enjoy her company, even if he never had the chance to feel her in his arms again.

"You look extremely frustrated, Gideon. Who is she?" His long-time friend arched an eyebrow at him as the two of them shook hands.

"I don't know." At his reply, Sebastian's eyebrow rose higher. A small smile touched the Earl of Melton's lips.

"Perhaps she's all too aware of your reputation where the ladies are concerned."

"No," he snarled at his friend's jest. "We've never met before tonight."

"Are you certain?" Sebastian frowned in confusion. "That's highly unusual. What is her name?"

"I don't know. She wouldn't tell me," Gideon ground out his reply between clenched teeth as he looked around the room, searching for his mysterious enchantress. "But there was something different about her voice."

"Something *different*? If I didn't know better, I'd say you were beyond enamored with this mystery woman." There was a touch of amusement in his friend's voice, and Gideon shot a fierce glance in Sebastian's direction. A somber look immediately darkened his friend's features.

"What does she look like?" Sebastian asked in an apologetic voice. "I'll help you find her."

Gideon quickly described his elusive enchantress, and with a nod, Sebastian joined him in the search. The two of them studied the room in silence for several moments before a soft feminine laugh floated through the air toward them.

"The two of you look as though you were searching for something that's impossible to see." At the light-hearted teasing in the Countess of Melton's voice, Gideon turned to greet Sebastian's wife. With great effort, he forced a smile to his lips while he carried the hand Helen offered him to his mouth to brush the air over her fingertips.

"Good evening, Helen. How are you?"

"Quite well, thank you." The countess tipped her head to one side and eyed him with curiosity as he resumed his search of the crowded ballroom. "Are you looking for someone?"

Gideon didn't answer Helen as he saw the woman he was so desperately wanted to see again. Indecision barreled through him. Now, what was he to do? A man he vaguely recognized suddenly appeared at her side, and she took his arm as he guided her toward the exit. Gideon jerked his head in the couple's direction.

"There, Sebastian. At the main entrance to the ballroom. Do you know her?"

"No, I'm afraid not." The earl turned his head toward his wife. "Helen, are you familiar with the lady standing close to Lady Montjoy?."

"The pretty woman in the midnight blue gown?" Helen asked quietly. A quick glance in her direction revealed the Countess of Melton's perplexed look. Gideon jerked his attention back to the man and woman at the ballroom exit.

"Yes," he said in a tight voice.

"That's Viscountess Helstone."

"The woman just about to go out the door?" Gideon bit out as he watched his enchantress.

"Yes," Helen said with a nod. "She's one of the American heiresses that took London by storm last year. I believe she married the viscount a few months after she arrived."

"Are you certain?" Gideon asked with a growl as his gut suddenly tightened. "She sounds as if she's from the Continent and grew up with an English governess."

"That is most likely the result of her attending *Le Manoir*. I imagine they did their best to remove any trace of her American accent," Helen said with a sympathetic note in her voice. "The school is renowned for their students marrying well."

Gideon grew rigid at Helen's explanation, but his attention never wavered from Lady Helstone. It wasn't simply his failure to recognize the faint hint of an American accent beneath the aristocratic notes of the viscountess's sultry voice that angered him. What enraged him the most was that she'd married a title. The anger crashing through him made his muscles knot painfully throughout his body. For a second time, he'd played the fool to a woman who'd married for social position.

"I've heard that it's a very unhappy marriage," Helen said with a note of sympathy in her voice.

"No doubt." Gideon turned away from the woman he'd broken his own rules for and to see Sebastian's eyebrows arched in puzzlement. With a shake of his head, Gideon's jaw locked with tension as he bowed in Helen's direction.

"Helen. Sebastian. If you'll excuse me, I'll bid you goodnight."

Before his friends could say a word, Gideon turned away and made his way to the exit. There was a brawl with his name on it somewhere in town.

Chapter 3

Five years later
April 1900

"Y ou look lovely, dearest."

Constance Rockwood Blakemore, Countess of Lyndham, forced a smile to her lips as she met her baby sister's gaze in the full-length mirror. Louisa's dismay was obvious as she stared at her reflection in the cheval glass mirror inside Madame Sabine's shop.

"Doesn't she look lovely, Helen? Patience?" At Constance's silent urging, Helen Rockwood, the Countess of Melton, quickly nodded her head.

"You look beautiful as always, Louisa," Helen said with a smile despite the hesitant note in her voice.

Standing to the left of her sister-in-law, Patience released a small noise, and Constance wasn't sure whether it was suppressed laughter or a sound of disagreement. Louisa tipped her head slightly to see the reflection of the Mistress of Cairnlarich in the mirror. The hat Patience wore had a netted veil she'd pulled down to cover her scars. It made it almost impossible to determine what she was thinking. When their middle sister remained silent, Louisa whirled around and frowned at her sister.

"Well, Patience?"

"*You* are beautiful, but all those flowers, ruffles, and bows make you look like a wedding cake, and *you*, dearest, are the bride, *not* the cake," Patience said firmly. "If you wear that gown, you're quite likely to appear as a figure of fun in Currer's next serial installment."

Patience's words made Louisa stiffen in horror as she spun about on her heel to study her appearance in the mirror once more. Her younger sister's mention of the Currer Chronicles made Constance start slightly. The biweekly serial had turned the Set on its ear in recent months as P. Currer had slyly taken aim at various members of the peerage by including them in his stories.

A work of fiction, the author's characters were based on actual members of the Marlborough Set. Although names were changed, there was little left to doubt in the reader's mind as to who the author was poking fun at. The skill and precision with which Currer lampooned the antics, scandals, and behaviors of the peerage was an amusing read until one was on the receiving end of the author's mighty sword of ink. With a brief glare in Patience's direction, Constance turned her head toward her baby sister, a placating smile on her lips.

"I find it highly unlikely Mr. Currer would mention a wedding dress," Constance said firmly with a shake of her head in her attempt to reassure Louisa. "The man has a great deal of fodder to draw from, given the recent antics of Lord Barrington and his latest mistress."

"We are *not* the Reckless Rockwoods without justification, Constance. I truly think we're living on borrowed time in escaping evisceration by the man's wicked pen."

Patience defiantly tilted her head as she disagreed with the eldest of the three sisters. It was impossible to read Patience's features through the netted veil, but the Mistress of Crianlarich's bearing emphasized her irritation. Constance knew her sister's dissent was not without merit. The Rockwoods *had* been lucky to date when it came to being singled out in Currer's serial.

"It's true. I had fully expected Currer to target Percy for threatening to thrash Lord Sproats last week." Louisa lent her voice of support to Patience. At the mention of the viscount, Patience's posture became one of fierce anger.

"Our brother was well within his right to dress down the man. Sproats's comments were crude and deeply insulting to Rhea," Patience snapped. "It's a small wonder Percy didn't pound the man into the ground, and he would have without any trouble at all."

"And if Rhea hadn't displayed such grace under pressure, our brother might easily have found himself in Newgate." Constance glared at her middle sister before she sighed. "But I agree. Percy was well within his right to threaten the man for his insulting advances toward Rhea. I'm simply grateful she insisted on returning to Green Hill House the next day."

"Well, *we* might remain untouched by Currer's caricature of the Set, but some of our friends have not." Anger flared tightened Louisa's mouth. "Look at how Gideon has been taken to task in recent months."

"For heaven's sake, he's a grown man," Constance bit out through clenched teeth. "His reputation for breaking hearts is well-established."

Currer's droll, doubled-edged word-play had recently made the Rockwood family friend, Gideon Lethbridge, Earl of Chelmsford, the latest character in the Currer Chronicles. As one of the Set's most eligible, yet elusive, bachelors, the earl had been mocked in the latest serial. Now, Patience had dumped oil onto the fire by suggesting Louisa might be mentioned in the next edition of the satire. As Louisa stared at her image in dismay. Constance quickly stepped forward to wrap an arm around her younger sister's shoulder.

"We'll have Madame Sabine find a way to fix the dress."

"The wedding is in two weeks, and she hasn't finished half of my trousseau," Louisa said in a voice filled with panic. Mortification caused her to shake her head as she was obviously struggling not to cry. "Patience is *right*. I *do* look like a wedding cake."

"You could walk down the aisle in rags, and Ewan would still find it impossible to look at another woman. The man is blinded by his love for you." Constance smiled with encouragement. "I'm certain Madame Sabine can fix this gown. We *all* know the woman will move heaven and earth to keep her most devoted *and lucrative* client happy."

"I agree wholeheartedly. Madame Sabine would fight the hounds of hell to ensure you're happy." Helen, who'd remained silent until now, smiled with confidence at her youngest sister-in-law. "I know how high your dressmaker bills are. Sebastian is constantly muttering his frustration every time he sees the latest bill from Madame Sabine."

"But it's not *his* money he's spending," Louisa replied as a cheerful grin replaced her dismay.

"A fact I remind him of whenever he expresses his disgust and outrage at what your dresses cost," Helen replied with a laugh. "That and the fact he promised never to begrudge you a dress bill again for helping him rescue me from Lord Templeton."

The mention of those frightening events more than ten years ago caused a shadow to sweep across the countess's face. Louisa quickly stepped forward to clasp her sister-in-law's hands and kiss Helen's cheek with great affection.

"My brother is fortunate to have a wife who patiently listens to his complaints." Then, in the next second, a mischievous smile curved Louisa's lips. "*But* even if he had listened to me to begin with, he still would have been forced not to begrudge my fashion vice."

Laughter followed Louisa's mischievous remark. Satisfied things were on an even keel for the moment, Constance turned away, intent on finding Madam Sabine. The seamstress could weave magical gowns that almost equaled Monsieur Worth but at far less a cost. If Sebastian knew how much a gown by Worth costs, he would be appalled.

Constance's dressmaker bills were rarely as high as her

younger sister's. In fact, Lucien had remarked on more than one occasion he was glad she didn't have her sister's extravagant tastes. But the bill from Monsieur Worth last year had put Lucien in a state of shock. It had been an impulsive purchase, but the moment she'd seen the gown, it had been impossible to resist.

She'd excused her extravagant purchase based on needing a new gown for Helen's and Sebastian's anniversary ball. She'd also been seven months pregnant with Isabel, and Monsieur Worth's creation had emphasized all her best features while cleverly hiding the true size of her expanding girth. She bit back a smile as she remembered her husband's outrage when the bill had arrived.

His anger had been short-lived when she'd modeled the gown that had arrived with the invoice. Instinctively, he'd realized she'd been feeling like a large cow, and the dress had bolstered her spirits. Her husband had then demonstrated he would always find her beautiful.

The soft swish of the curtains that hid the inner confines of Madame Sabine's workshop pulled Constance out of her musings. A woman emerged from the back of the shop carrying several bolts of material with her chin pressed into the one on top to manage her load better. As the clerk set the material down on the counter, Constance stepped forward to capture her attention.

"Pardon me, would you please tell Madame Sabine that Lady Westbrook needs to speak with her about her wedding dress?" The moment the woman looked at her, Constance stiffened with surprise. "*Lady Helstone.*"

The woman flinched at Constance's soft exclamation before she shook her head vehemently. Cheeks flooded with a rosy color, the woman cast a furtive glance around the shop.

"I'm sorry, my lady, but my name is Mrs. Hodges."

At the woman's denial, Constance stared at her in disbelief and tipped her head to one side to study the woman's features more closely. A sliver of doubt made Constance frown. It had been over two years since she'd last seen Lady Helstone. The viscountess had disappeared from society after her husband had been shot and killed by his mistress.

Even with the spectacles the woman wore and her hair pulled back in a severe bun, Constance would have wagered a heavy sum that the woman was Lady Helstone. Every physical attribute was still visible despite the severity of the woman's appearance. The only thing that seemed off was the woman's cultured English accent. There wasn't even a hint of the American dialect, but then several years at boarding school and time in the company of the Marlborough Set could be the reason for that.

"Forgive me, but the resemblance is uncanny." At Constance's observation, a wry smile tilted the woman's lips upward as if she were enjoying a private joke.

"So I've been told, my lady. Even Lady Helstone has remarked on our similar likeness." The woman's ironic amusement vanished as Mrs. Hodges glanced over her shoulder at the curtain, hiding the workshop behind her. It was almost as if the woman was frightened someone might hear their conversation. "Let me find Madame Sabine for you, my lady."

Constance frowned as the woman vanished through the curtains in search of the dressmaker. The woman was lying. She was certain of it. Even though the woman's quiet voice held no trace of an American accent, Constance knew an excellent finishing school would have seen to that. The more she thought about it, the stronger her conviction became that Mrs. Hodges and the Viscountess Helstone were one and the same. But why? What in heaven's name would make Viscountess Helstone deny who she was, let alone work in a dressmaker's shop?

Constance paid little attention to gossip, but news of Lord Helstone being shot and killed by his mistress during a lover's quarrel wasn't a tidbit one quickly forgot. Even though it had been more than two years ago, the scandal had been in the news for months. The trial had been a spectacle, with Helstone's mistress pleading self-defense and subsequently being acquitted. Constance's focus drifted toward the bolts of cloth the woman had set down on the counter.

With just one touch, the *an dara sealladh* might tell her something about Mrs. Hodges. The gift of sight and royal blood of the Stewarts had flowed in her mother's veins, making Constance and her siblings far more unique than most people realized. Except for her brother Sebastian, all of her siblings had varying strengths of the *an dara sealladh*, but it wasn't something they openly put on display.

While Lucien supported her assisting those who actually came to her for help, he objected strongly to Constance taking it upon herself to help people who didn't ask for her assistance. She winced. Lucien didn't just object to her interfering without someone's permission. He was vehemently opposed to her meddling in the affairs of others, particularly when it involved matters of the heart. If he were here now, he would drag her out of the shop to prevent her from satisfying her curiosity. They seldom argued, but when they did, it made her feel awful.

Constance winced slightly as she remembered the argument they'd had two months ago in front of the family. The memory made her debate walking away from the counter, but a whisper in the back of her head protested strongly. Of course, the *an dara sealladh* might not even show her anything at all. This last thought ended her indecisiveness.

In a leisurely fashion, Constance walked along the counter and stopped in front of the material Mrs. Hodges had brought out from the back of the shop. As if she were merely examining the bolt of silk, Constance ran her hand over the spot that still bore the slight indentation from Mrs. Hodges's chin.

Constance drew in a deep breath and waited. After more than a minute, she released a sigh of frustration. It seemed she would have to accept Mrs. Hodges's story, after all. Constance slowly turned away from the counter and saw Madame Sabine at Louisa's side, exclaiming with horror at the dress. She was about to rejoin her sisters when the bell over the shop entrance jingled. Constance turned her head toward the door to see Lady Wrotham walk into the dressmaker's shop. The moment the marchioness saw Constance, a wide smile curved the older woman's mouth.

"My dear Constance, how lovely to see you." Lady Wrotham hurried forward to clasp Constance's hands in hers in a warm greeting.

"It's wonderful to see you as well, my lady," Constance said as she bussed the woman's cheek.

"How is the dowager? I heard she had taken ill a month ago."

"Grandmama is recovering nicely. We're fortunate she was in town when she became ill. She wanted to return to Lyndham Keep, but Lucien was adamant she remain here with us. He indulges her, *and me*, quite often, but this was one occasion when he refused to be swayed by Grandmama's protests."

"And how *is* that devilishly handsome husband of yours?"

Amusement sparkled in the older woman's gray eyes. The marchioness had been a friend of Aunt Matilda's for years, and Constance had accompanied her aunt to Lady Wrotham's house on numerous occasions. The woman had buried three husbands, and Constance had always marveled at the woman's indomitable spirit enduring so much grief over the years. She wasn't sure she would be able to find such strength to go on if anything happened to Lucien. An image of her husband filled her head, and she smiled at the marchioness's question.

"Other than experiencing frustration with me from time to time, Lucien is quite well. And you?"

"Desolate," Alva sighed with obvious frustration. "My secretary decided to run off to Gretna Green and marry a schoolteacher, so I decided a new dress would cheer me up."

"I'm so sorry. How long had she been with you?"

"Almost six years. It has come at a most unfortunate time too." The marchioness released another sigh. "The charity ball for St. Catherine's is little more than a month away, and Lydia's skill with numbers made her invaluable. I placed an advertisement in the Times this morning, but I fear finding a new secretary will prove quite difficult."

The marchioness's voice became a distant sound as the *an dara sealladh* pulled Constance down into a familiar darkness. Like a theater curtain being pulled open to reveal the stage, she found herself standing in a cold, uninviting room. A shiver skimmed through her as the chilly air slid across her skin. Twilight filtered through a small window, but it barely illuminated her surroundings.

Small fragments of charred wood were scattered about in the hearth, which made Constance believe there had not been a fire in the hearth for some time. The bed in one corner appeared less than sturdy, while a table was pressed against the opposite wall. A ladder-back chair was angled away from the table as if someone had left their place with great haste. Against another wall was a wardrobe. It was a bleak room filled with the weight of defeat.

The emotion eased slightly as a soft glow on top of the table caught her attention. The light surrounded a stack of papers, but it shone brightly on the name written on the top sheet. P. Currer. For some odd reason, the light engulfing the papers was as if a ray of hope had found its way into this grim, dreary room. Behind her, a door creaked open, and she turned toward the sound. She barely had time to register Mrs. Hodge's coming entering the small lodgings when she was hurtled forward into a well-lit room where smoke created a haze in the air.

Her brothers, Percy and Sebastian, were seated at a card table with their friend, the Earl of Chelmsford, and another man. Although she couldn't hear what they were saying, her brothers were grinning like cats who had swallowed a handful of canaries. In a split second, she was standing behind the patriarch of the Rockwoods. Sebastian pointed toward the pile of banknotes in the center of the table as Gideon shook his head in disgust.

A movement to her left caught Constance's attention. The sight of Mrs. Hodges moving to stand beside Gideon took her by surprise. As the woman reached out to touch his cheek, Mrs. Hodges's appeared overwhelm with confusion, longing, and another emotion that puzzled Constance. It was almost as if the woman were experiencing guilt.

Suddenly, she heard a quiet sound that she recognized as laughter. Constance jerked her head toward Percy, who was grinning with triumph as he reached toward the middle of the table to collect his winnings. As he did so, the bank notes dissolved into a mist to become a sheaf of papers.

Constance instantly recognized the papers as she watched the last sheet fall onto the stack with a soft light shining down on the author's name, P. Currer. With amused resignation, Gideon shrugged in defeat. With a wry twist of his lips, the earl dropped his cards onto the baize-covered tabletop. The cards fell downward in slow motion, and the *an dara sealladh* threw her back into the present.

The transition was more abrupt than usual, and she swayed on her feet. Immediately, a firm hand cupped her elbow, and she recognized Patience's soft voice expressing concern. Incapable of responding, Constance struggled to maintain her balance.

The *an dara sealladh* always left her drained emotionally and physically for a short period, but this time it was more debilitating than usual. Everyone in the family experienced different physical reactions when they emerged from their visions. They were all well-acquainted with the signs of the *an dara sealladh* as well as each other's unique type of after-effects from their visions.

Normally she was seated when she emerged from her visions, but this time she was deeply grateful for Patience's firm grip as her sister wrapped her arm around Constance's waist. If not for Patience, she was certain she would have collapsed to the floor. As the remnants of the *an dara sealladh* faded away, Constance opened her eyes to see Alva, her sisters, and Madame Sabine gathered around her with varying levels of concern and understanding on their faces.

"My lady, you must sit down," Sabine exclaimed in a low voice as she glanced at several customers in the shop. Constance rejected the suggestion with a small wave of her hand, but the dressmaker dismissed her silent response. "I insist. My office has a comfortable place for you to rest."

"I don't think—"

"You're going to sit down, Constance," Patience said quietly. "If you could see how pale you are, you wouldn't argue. Now come along."

Surrendering to Madame Sabine's and Patience's insistence, which Helen's and Louisa's quiet voices reinforced, Constance nodded her consent. In short order, she was seated in a comfortable chair in Madame Sabine's office in front of a cheery blaze in the fireplace. Once the dressmaker was satisfied Constance was comfortable, Sabine excused herself to resolve the problem of Louisa's horrendous wedding gown. Patience was about to sit down opposite her, but Constance waved her hand in protest.

"No, I'll be fine. Helen will need your support to help keep Louisa calm," she said with a small smile.

"All right," Patience nodded, then grimaced behind her veil evident. "The dress is most assuredly a disaster. It's nothing like what Louisa described."

"Well, for heaven's sake, do *not* mention the Currer Chronicles to her again." Constance eyed her sister sternly. "I have no doubt Sabine will manage to make that disaster of a dress into something superb, even if the woman has to make a completely new gown."

"I think it will be a new gown entirely," Patience said dryly before her demeanor changed, and she bent over to rub her hand over Constance's back in a soothing gesture. "But I'm not sure I should leave you alone. You were dreadfully pale. If I wasn't so certain you'd experienced the *an dara sealladh*, I would have thought you on the verge of morning sickness—"

"*Heaven forbid!* It's been less than seven months since I had Isabel," Constance exclaimed as she remembered how difficult her daughter's birth had been. "I'm not ready for another baby so soon, even though I know Lucien would like to have a son. He's not said so directly, and until he does, I have no intention of broaching the subject with him.."

"All right, but *do not move* from that chair. If you were to have another—"

"I doubt that will happen, but I promise not to move until I'm certain I'm fully recovered."

She smiled at Patience, who studied her for a moment from behind the veil hiding the burn scars she'd suffered during the deadly fire at Westbrook Farms three years ago. As if satisfied with Constance's answer, Patience gave her a quick hug and headed toward the door of the dressmaker's office. Her sister had almost reached the exit when Constance called out to her.

"Oh, Patience, I *would* love a cup of tea. Would you ask Mrs. Hodges to bring me a cup?"

"Of course."

"And Patience, see to it that it's *Mrs. Hodges* who brings me my tea."

"Mrs. Hodges?" Her sister stiffened slightly as she looked over her shoulder at Constance.

"Yes, Mrs. Hodges."

"If you're thinking of doing what I think you are, have you forgotten what happened two months ago when Lucien—"

"Go, Patience. I am already feeling much better, and I can only feign distress for a little while longer." Constance frowned and waved her hand at her sister.

Although she couldn't see her middle sister's arched eyebrows, she knew Patience was eyeing her with more than a hint of concern. The family had all been privy to her terrible argument with Lucien when he'd learned she had advised Lady Reigate to reconsider accepting Lord Shively's proposal. With a shake of her head, Constance glared at her sister for questioning her.

"I really *could* use that cup of tea, Patience."

With a sharp nod, her sister hurried out of the room. Left alone with her thoughts, Constance pushed the thought of Lucien's disapproval aside to contemplate her vision. Whether Mrs. Hodges was Lady Helstone or not, the woman was living in squalid circumstances.

The conditions would be heart-wrenching for anyone, whether they were a member of the working class or the nobility. However, Constance knew such poverty for a noblewoman was highly unusual. What had reduced Lady Helstone to such a penniless state?

Constance remembered the woman had been one of the American Dollar Princesses who'd arrived in London seeking to marry a title. All of those brides had brought substantial dowries to their marriages. It made little sense as to how the woman could be penniless upon Helstone's death. She frowned as she contemplated what she'd seen in her vision.

As always, the *an dara sealladh* had revealed only bits and pieces of the story, and everything she'd seen was too jumbled to make much sense of it. The most puzzling thing was Lady Helstone appearing at Gideon's side. It was quite likely she'd met the earl, but the expressive emotions on her features as she'd reached out to Gideon indicated a relationship far closer than simply acquaintances or even friends.

There had been something intimate about the woman's manner that made Constance feel as if she'd intruded on something deeply personal. Despite its lack of clarity, the *an dara sealladh* had convinced her of two things. The woman calling herself Mrs. Hodges was living in squalid conditions. Two, the woman was also connected to P. Currer and Gideon somehow. Whatever had brought the woman to such circumstances, Constance was determined to help the woman if she could. She even had a solution to make it happen. The question was whether Mrs. Hodges and the marchioness would like each other.

The soft sound of china rattling outside the room broke through Constance's thoughts. As the soft clatter echoed through the air, Constance turned her head to see the woman calling herself Mrs. Hodges enter Madame Sabine's office with the tea Constance had asked for. As the woman set the tea tray on the side table on her left, she avoided looking at Constance.

"Do you require anything else, my lady?"

Instead of answering the woman's question, Constance reached out to pour a small amount of milk into her cup, then added tea. She didn't look up, but it was easy to sense the rising tension in the woman.

"Do you know who I am, Mrs. Hodges?" Constance took a sip of her tea as she looked up at the woman over the rim of the delicate teacup.

"Yes, my lady."

"And do you know anything about me?" When the woman didn't answer, Constance released a sigh and gestured toward the chair opposite her. "Please sit, Mrs. Hodges."

"I cannot, my lady, I have—"

"I insist," Constance's head tipped to one side in a silent demand the woman do as she'd asked. The woman was clearly ready to dart from the room, and Constance released a soft sound of exasperation. "Madame Sabine will not question you as I shall explain you did so under protest."

The woman didn't move, and Constance sighed. Setting her teacup and saucer on the tray, she shook her head.

"You leave me with no choice but to stand as well."

"*Oh no, my lady.*" The genuine concern in Mrs. Hodges's voice was reflected in her sudden look of dismay. Although she showed a distinct reluctance to do so, the woman sank down into the chair opposite Constance.

"Thank you. Now then, let me ask you again. Do you know anything about me other than my name?"

"I have…I have heard rumors."

"Would you please elaborate on that statement?"

Mrs. Hodges hesitated at the softly spoken command for a moment before she straightened in her chair and a worried frown her brow.

"It's rumored you can talk with the dead."

"The rumors are true, although my family and I are discreet about our abilities."

Constance winced at the half-truth. The Rockwoods had earned their reputation for impulsive behavior justly, and their unique talents had added to their sometimes reckless behavior. Pushing the thought aside, Constance picked up her teacup again.

"While there are a growing number of Rockwoods who possess the ability, I am the only one who does consultations with those seeking to reach out to lost loved ones. However, even those are by referral."

"If you have a message from beyond the veil you wish to share with me, I've no interest in hearing it."

Bitterness threaded its way through the woman's voice as her chin tipped slightly upward in defiant disdain. Startled by the woman's reaction, Constance took another sip of the beverage that was still hot.

"I received no message to pass along to you, but there's one thing the rumors appear to have left out. I also have the ability to see things from the past as well as what the future might hold."

"I don't understand." Mrs. Hodges drew in a sharp breath. Although her features were serene and unreadable, behind the spectacles she wore Constance saw the woman's trepidation.

"I sometimes see things about people I meet. People such as yourself."

"*Me?*" Although her countenance remained unreadable, the woman's body language conveyed her apprehension. Her back was ramrod straight as she sat rigidly in her chair while her hands were clasped tightly together in her lap. "I'm uncertain what your…experience might have revealed about me, but I doubt it was anything of significance."

"I confess my vision was confusing on several points, as is often the case." Constance shrugged her acceptance of how the *an dara sealladh* worked. "But I *do* know you're not Mrs. Hodges, are you, Lady Helstone?"

The observation was a gamble on Constance's part, but what little doubt she had was laid to rest at the woman's reaction. Dismay and resignation furrowed Lady Helstone's brow as turned her head away. It was only for a brief instant before the noblewoman lifted her head in a regal, almost defiant, movement to look at Constance without remorse.

"You are correct, my lady." Constance quickly set her teacup down on the tray at the woman's response and leaned forward in her chair.

"But why?" she asked with avid curiosity.

Anger darkened Lady Helstone's countenance, and Constance immediately regretted not holding her tongue. It had been a rude, impertinent question. Remorsefully, she reached out to touch the woman's hand. The woman quickly jerked away from the touch as anger and possibly even fear furrowed her brow. Clearly, the woman had heard a touch was enough to trigger the *an dara sealladh*.

"Forgive me. That was terribly rude," Constance said softly as she drew back from the woman. "In addition to our gift of sight, every Rockwood is somewhat reckless when it comes to acting or speaking without considering the ramifications."

The woman nodded sharply in response to Constance's apology. The cold anger on her oval-shaped features faded, but her outrage was still apparent. Constance winced with self-reproach.

"I truly am sorry, my lady. My curiosity was prompted out of concern for you and my desire to help." The remorse in Constance's voice made Lady Helstone relax slightly as she nodded.

"Your ladyship is kind, but I have no need of assistance, despite anything you…anything you might have seen."

"What I saw were lodgings with a fireplace that hasn't seen a fire in days. A bed that looks as if it will fall apart the moment someone lies in it, a small chifforobe, a table, and a chair," Constance exclaimed with indignation at the description. "It wasn't fit for the working class, let alone a noblewoman."

The woman paled slightly, but she reveal nothing as to what she was thinking. If anything, the woman exuded a quiet strength as she stiffened her shoulders in silent indignation.

"And once again, my tongue has given offense," Constance sighed quietly at her inability to guard her tongue. She was fortunate Lucien wasn't within earshot, or hellfire would rain down on her head. "Forgive me. It was not my intent to cause you discomfort. It's simply that my family is familiar with the hardship of others, and we always do our best to help those in need."

"If your rash nature is indicative of the rest of your family, then I understand why the Set refers to your family as they do."

A wry smile touched Lady Helstone's lips as she looked at Constance, and a small flash of amusement danced in the woman's gaze. Relieved the viscountess was willing to excuse her behavior, Constance released the breath she'd been holding.

"You are most gracious in forgiving my insulting manner, not once, but twice."

"Your comments reflect concern for my welfare, and I appreciate your kindness in doing so. However, as I've already said, I have no need of assistance."

Constance frowned with frustration. It was obvious the woman thought Constance was offering her charity. She needed to tread lightly if she wanted to ensure Lady Helstone understood it wasn't charity but an opportunity. Whether the noblewoman's decision to seize upon the chance to improve her living circumstances was her choice.

Based on her observation in the past few minutes, Constance was certain Lady Helstone would work well with the marchioness. The real question now was whether or not the woman possessed the skills the marchioness required. A quick glance at the woman's hands revealed she lacked the usual calluses on her fingers that most seamstresses had. So that begged the question as to what she did for Madame Sabine.

The question of why sent a dozen more questions thundering through Constance's head, but she managed to bite her tongue. As she took another drink of her tea, a soft laugh echoed out of Lady Helstone. The sound make Constance jerked her head toward the viscountess to see a small smile curving her lips.

"It truly is a struggle for you not to ask questions, isn't it?"

"I confess it is far more difficult than most people realize," she sighed with exasperation as the woman's smile of amusement broadened.

Constance smiled in return. She liked Lady Helstone. In fact, she was certain they would become great friends, especially if she was correct in thinking the viscountess was meant to be with Gideon.

"Then, I shall put you out of your misery and tell you that I do Madame Sabine's books."

"Her bookkeeper," Constance murmured as she remembered Lady Wrotham bemoaning the loss of her secretary and the woman's skill with figures.

"Such as it is."

"How long have you been working for her?" Deliberately, Constance turned her head away from Lady Helstone and reached for the teapot to freshen up her cooling tea.

"More than two years."

The response made Constance swallow a gasp of dismay as she remembered Lady Helstone's impoverished circumstances. The viscountess's words triggered several questions in Constance's head, which immediately triggered more. That meant the viscountess had been employed by Madame Sabine shortly after Lord Helstone had been shot and killed. The timing was not lost on Constance. What had happened to make the viscountess's finances so dire? Helstone had been a brute, but the viscount's death should not have changed Lady Helstone's financial situation. If anything, her husband's demise should have given the woman a great deal more freedom than most women enjoyed.

Images of the papers she'd seen in her vision popped into her head. As if the mental pictures were a puzzle falling into place, she drew in a quick breath. P. Currer. If she remembered correctly, Lady Helstone's first name was Phoebe. Given her vision, it was not much of a leap to think the woman was the Chronicles author. Working in Madame Sabine's shop was the perfect place for gathering the latest gossip that the woman could use in her satire. The question was, why? Without thinking, Constance tipped her head to one side and stared intently at the other woman.

"Tell me, Lady Helstone, are you acquainted with the Currer Chronicles?

Chapter 4

Phoebe struggled to control her rising panic as she stared at Lady Lyndham for a long moment. If anyone else had asked, Phoebe would have interpreted it as a simple query as to whether she was familiar with the Currer Chronicles. But this was the Countess of Lyndham, a member of the Rockwood family. A woman who could see what others could not.

As their gazes met, Phoebe saw the countess's astute expression. Whatever the woman had seen had convinced her that Phoebe was connected to Currer. It changed everything. This was precisely why she'd never mentioned any of the Reckless Rockwoods in her serial.

She'd heeded the rumors, and it had obviously been a wise decision on her part to avoid any mention of them. Not that the Rockwoods had actually done anything in recent memory that deserved to be scorned at the hand of her pen. Phoebe folded her hands in her lap and prayed her anxiety wasn't visible.

"I think everyone in London is well-acquainted with the Currer Chronicles, my lady."

"I meant, do you know the author personally?"

The question only strengthened Phoebe's conviction that the countess knew she was the author of the Currer Chronicles. At the time of Alfred's death, his heir had thrown her out of the house her dowry had bought. Her father's poor business sense had ensured all her money went to Jasper Wakefield. Although she knew her father had thought the money would pass onto his grandchildren, he'd failed to consider the possibility she might not have children. Perhaps worst of all, her father had failed to negotiate an annual stipend for her in the event of Alfred's premature death. The end result was that she'd lost her home with no annual stipend, which had left her penniless.

It was a harsh reality Phoebe had been forced to deal with the minute the new Viscount Helstone had ordered her out of the house that was now his. If Lady Lyndham had seen her current lodgings in her vision, then the countess had most likely seen something that suggested Phoebe was connected to the author of the chronicles.

She blew out a small breath of quiet resignation. It was pointless to deny her association with the serial. She could only hope the countess would keep Phoebe's involvement a secret.

"I know the author quite well. I'M P. Currer." Her quiet reply caused Lady Lyndham to jerk slightly as if Phoebe had surprised her with such a direct response. Unable to help herself, she smiled with amusement at the countess's astonishment. "Your reaction suggests you expected me to deny it."

"Well…yes," Lady Lyndham said with a light-hearted laugh while a frown of puzzlement furrowed her brow. "I did."

"I've learned over the last two years to choose my battles wisely. I know when to fight, when not to, and when to surrender."

"A wise woman, indeed," the countess said with another laugh as she set her teacup on her tray. "And quite clever, I might add. The entire Set hangs onto your every word while hoping they're not the ones being placed under the microscope next."

"Do you intend to out me as the author?" she asked with bated breath.

"*Of course not!* The repercussions would be quite severe." The countess exclaimed in an appalled voice as she shook her head vehemently. "If you chose to return to society, it would be a painful experience. The Set can be as vicious as a rabid dog. I would never subject you, or anyone else for that matter, to such a painful verbal flogging."

"I am well-acquainted with the Set's taste for blood, and I have no wish to reenter their midst so they may inflict more wounds." Phoebe bit out through clenched teeth as she remembered the people who'd been unkind to her from the moment she'd been introduced to London society.

"When it comes to the Marlborough Set drawing blood, we agree, which is precisely why I know already we shall become close friends."

"Friends, my lady?"

"Absolutely. I think you're quite clever, have a wonderful sense of humor, and you are kind. *that* I know from your willingness to forgive my transgressions earlier. In fact, I insist you call me Constance."

Stunned by the offer of friendship, she stared at the countess in amazement. Although Lawrence's women friends had welcomed her into their inner circle, none of them had ever made any effort to befriend her as Lady Lyndham was doing. Not only that, but the countess had said they would become close friends. The woman barely knew her. How could she possibly know that? A second later, Phoebe realized how ridiculous the question was given the woman's talent.

Still bemused by the countess's cheerful declaration, she couldn't think of a reply. Out of the corner of her eye, Phoebe saw a movement in the doorway. She turned her head to see the woman who had escorted Lady Lyndham into Madame Sabine's office. Tension flooded Phoebe's body. Had the woman heard her confession? As the woman walked toward them, the countess leaned forward and patted Phoebe's hand.

"You have nothing to fear. My sister, like my other

siblings, might be reckless occasionally but would never betray a friend." The gentle reassurance in the countess's soft words made Phoebe relax slightly.

"Are you feeling better, Constance?"

A netted veil made it difficult to see the woman's features, and Phoebe suddenly realized Lady Lyndham's sister was the Rockwood who'd been badly burned in a terrible fire. She'd heard the tragic story about how the woman had barely survived the deadly blaze that had cost two family members their lives. Her heart went out to the woman.

"I am feeling much better," the countess replied as she waved her hand in Phoebe's direction. "Patience, have you met Lady Helstone? Phoebe, may I present my sister, Lady Patience MacTavish, Mistress of Cairnlarich."

"How do you do, my lady," Lady Patience nodded politely at Phoebe. For a fraction of a moment, Phoebe thought the woman was on the verge of saying something else before she turned toward Constance. "Madame Sabine says she intends to create a new gown for Louisa."

"A new gown?" Constance asked as she arched her eyebrows slightly.

"Apparently, Sabine assigned one of her new apprentice seamstresses to make the dress, and the woman mixed up two different patterns to create that monstrosity. Sabine was as horrified as we were."

"Oh dear, I hope the poor woman isn't dismissed."

"Louisa made it clear to Sabine that she would never shop here again if that happened."

"And will everything be ready in time for fittings?"

"Sabine said there was more than enough time to create a new dress and finish the rest of Louisa's trousseau. She's clearly not willing to lose a client as faithful as Louisa."

"Good, I was worried we would leave here with her in tears."

"Our little sister is all smiles at the moment, but she's

quite eager to return to Melton House. Apparently, Ewan is arriving on the afternoon train from Stirling. But she asked that I make certain you're well enough to go home."

"I am completely recovered." Lady Lyndham smiled at her sister as she stood up, and Phoebe rose as well. "In fact, I was just about to invite Phoebe to tea tomorrow before you arrived."

Speechless once again at the countess's generous nature where she was concerned, Phoebe shook her head. She couldn't possibly accept the invitation. While she had no regrets that she was no longer a member of the Marlborough Set, accepting the offer of tea was foolish. Heaven only knew what would happen if Lady Lyndham had another vision. Not to mention the fact she had an obligation to Madame Sabine. Phoebe shook her head.

"That's very kind of you, my lady—"

"Constance, please." Lady Lyndham gently chastised her as she reached out to take Phoebe's hands in hers and squeezed them in a gesture of friendship. "I'll see to it that Madame Sabine does not object."

"I really don't—"

"I refuse to take no for an answer, Phoebe. Shall we say tomorrow at three o'clock? Lyndham House on Park Street in Mayfair." The countess smiled merrily and didn't give Phoebe the chance to express any objections. "I look forward to seeing you again."

Still smiling, Lady Lyndham slipped her arm through her sister's, and the two women walked out of the room before Phoebe could gather her wits and refuse the woman's invitation.

The next afternoon, Phoebe was still trying to

comprehend how she'd managed to find herself stepping out of a hansom cab onto the sidewalk in front of Lyndham House. She paid the driver, then slowly climbed the steps to the wide front stoop and its impressive door. Phoebe glanced down at her gown and winced. She'd only had time to pack a few dresses before Jasper had tossed her out and into the streets. Of all her day gowns, this dress looked the least outdated.

Why hadn't she simply sent a note with her regrets? The thought tugged a wry smile to her lips. When it came to the Countess of Lyndham, she was relatively certain the woman would not have allowed her to escape so easily. Phoebe had no idea why the countess had invited her to tea, but she would express her thanks after a reasonable length of time and take her leave.

She inhaled a deep breath and tried to settle her nerves as she tugged on the doorbell handle. In seconds the door opened, and a butler invited her into the house. Phoebe was in the middle of removing her hat and gloves when a door to her right opened to reveal the Countess of Lyndham. To Phoebe's surprise, she saw a glimpse of relief flit across the woman's lovely features. The countess quickly crossed floor of the main entrance to greet her warmly. A welcoming smile curved her mouth as the countess caught Phoebe's hands in hers and gave them a light squeeze.

"Phoebe, you're here at last. I was worried you might send word you were unable to come," Lady Lyndham exclaimed as she linked her arm with Phoebe's and gently moved them toward the room she'd emerged from.

"I almost did, my lady," Phoebe replied as she winced slightly at her confession. A frown of disapproval furrowed the other woman's brow.

"I really do insist that you call me Constance, as I fully intend to call you Phoebe," she chided Phoebe in a firm, yet gentle voice. In the next breath, the countess smiled with exasperated amusement. "And *do not* let my brother Percy convince you that I prefer Connie. He knows I can't abide the name. But I am so happy you came. I would have been deeply disappointed if you hadn't."

"Then, I'm delighted I've not spoiled your afternoon." Phoebe laughed. The sound surprised her. It had been a long time since she'd found anything to laugh about, let alone smile. But, in the course of the past two days, the countess had managed with ease to make Phoebe laugh.

"Indeed, I would have been quite put out if I had been forced to come fetch you from Madame Sabine's clutches." The countess laughed.

As they entered the salon, Phoebe saw four women sitting around a low-level tea table. Trepidation swept through her, and Phoebe came to an abrupt halt. She recognized the Marchioness of Wrotham, and the woman pouring tea was Lady Lyndham's youngest sister. The two older women, Phoebe didn't know. At a light touch on her arm, Phoebe jerked her head toward the countess.

"You are among friends, Phoebe." With a reassuring smile, Lady Lyndham gently pulled Phoebe across the room. As they reached the small group, all four of the women smiled a welcome. Constance gestured toward the oldest of the four women, seated in a chair close to the fireplace with a shawl wrapped around her shoulders.

"Grandmama, this is Lady Helstone. Phoebe, may I present the Dowager Countess of Lyndham." Before Constance could turn away, the older woman arched her eyebrows slightly as her bright-blue gaze skimmed over Phoebe in an assessing manner.

"Helstone? Are you married to that blackguard Helstone?" The question was blunt and to the point, but the kindness echoing in the dowager's voice took the sting out of the words.

"No, my lady, I was married to Alfred Wakefield. Jasper

Wakefield is the new Viscount Helstone. One Helstone was more than enough for me," Phoebe said as she instinctively straightened her posture, fully prepared for a set down. The dowager countess stared at Phoebe in astonishment before she laughed boisterously.

"*Now*, I understand why my granddaughter took to you so quickly, my dear." The older woman winked at Lady Lyndham. "You have the same backbone my Constance here has, which is why I made sure she married my grandson. She was just the thing the boy needed to keep him on his toes."

"You know quite well, Grandmama, that no one can make Lucien do anything he doesn't want to do." Constance smiled and shook her head. The dowager raised her eyebrows at her granddaughter-in-law.

"And you know good and well the amount of sway you have over him, Constance. The boy would move heaven and earth for you."

"And I for him," Constance replied as she stepped forward and kissed the elderly woman on the cheek.

Constance turned away from her grandmother to continue with the introductions. With a sweep of her hand, she gestured toward a plump older woman seated next to the marchioness.

"Aunt Matilda, Lady Wrotham, this is Lady Helstone. Phoebe, may I present Lady Matilda Stewart, my aunt, and her good friend, the Dowager Marchioness of Wrotham. And my sister, Louisa, soon to be the Countess of Argaty, is the one pouring the tea."

"I'm delighted you could come, lass," Constance's aunt exclaimed in a soft brogue as she smiled warmly at Phoebe. "I know Constance was worried you might send your regrets."

As Constance guided Phoebe to a nearby chair, Lady Stewart leaned forward to pour a cup of tea.

"Louisa, fix Lady Helstone a plate of those cress sandwiches Cook made. Add one of those scones as well, while I pour the lass a cup of tea." The Scotswoman said firmly.

"If anyone wishes to know how your nieces came to be so strong-willed, one need only look to you, Matilda," Lady Wrotham said drolly before she smiled at Phoebe. "How are you, my dear Lady Helstone?"

"I am well, thank you. I hope you are in equally good health." Phoebe said quietly as she sat down in a chair next to Constance and accepted a cup of tea from Lady Stewart.

"Do you know each other?" Constance asked in obvious surprise. She stared at first Phoebe and then Lady Wrotham.

"We do." The marchioness smiled with genuine pleasure before a contemplative frown crossed her still smooth and youthful features. "Although I don't believe we've seen each other since the…"

The dowager marchioness's immediately shook her head in remorse. A knot threatened to close Phoebe's throat, but she smiled at the older woman. It was obvious from the woman's dismay she'd not intentionally meant to refer to Alfred's death and subsequent scandal.

"It *has* been a long time since we last met, my lady. I am flattered that you would remember me."

"Nonsense. I remember you well," Lady Wrotham said with a relieved smile. "Lord Linshal's son introduced us as I recall. How is that young man?"

"Unfortunately, Lawrence and I lost touch after he went to the Continent. I've not seen him in almost five years."

The words made Phoebe's heart ache. She'd stopped writing to Lawrence two days after Alfred's death. If Lawrence had known Jasper had thrown her out of Helstone Place, her friend would have jeopardized his own safety to come to her aid. She loved Lawrence too much to let him take such a risk. Instead, she'd written him a letter that she was leaving London and didn't know when she would return.

It hadn't been a lie so much as a way to make her dearest

friend not worry about her. In a sense, she *had* left London, at least the London she'd been a part of for several years. The sound of Lady Stewart speaking to the dowager marchioness pierced her thoughts, and Phoebe focused her attention on the conversation.

"Have you heard from Lady Alice recently, Alva?" Lady Stewart asked the dowager marchioness.

"I went to Edinburgh to see her and the baby two months ago." The dowager marchioness beamed. "Thomas had grown so much since I saw him over the holidays. Alice is supposed to come to London this fall for a visit."

"That sounds lovely, my lady," Constance said with a smile as she looked in the dowager countess's direction. "I know Grandmama loves when the children visit Lyndham Keep. She says it livens the place up with all the ruckus Jamie and Imogene make. "

"I enjoy it very much," the dowager countess said with a smile before her lips thinned with annoyance. "That is when my grandson sees *fit* to let me return home."

"Didn't I just say that no one can make my husband change his mind when he's made a decision?" Constance arched her eyebrows and smiled at the older woman before looking at Phoebe. "She's still put out with Lucien for overruling her about returning to Lyndham Keep when she was ill last month."

"Harrumph." The noise of discontent made everyone laughed as Constance shook her head at the dowager countess, which earned her another sound of discontent. With another laugh and a shake of her head, Constance turned to look at the dowager marchioness.

"Have you found someone to replace your secretary, Lady Wrotham?"

"Unfortunately, no. I interviewed two applicants this morning, but neither of them had any experience managing accounts," the marchioness said with a worried frown.

"I'm sure ye will find someone tae help ye, Alva." Lady Stewart reached out to pat her friend's hand in a comforting gesture.

"Are you looking for someone skilled in bookkeeping, Lady Wrotham?" Louisa asked as she set aside her plate with its half-eaten scone.

"Yes, but I need the individual to act as my personal secretary as well." The marchioness sighed. "I'm afraid I shall be forced to ask Gideon for his help. I love my son, but he will no doubt find me a curmudgeon of a woman."

"Then, we must find someone before you are forced to ask him for help," Louisa declared emphatically. "We are all quite fond of Gideon, but I think Constance would agree with me that he can be rather domineering at times."

"Dear heavens," Lady Wrotham said with a gasp of amusement. "I thought I was the only one to think he has a propensity to be arrogant on occasion."

"I know someone who might suit you," Constance said quietly.

Lady Lyndham leaned forward to set her teacup and saucer on the table in front of her chair. As Constance reclined back in her seat, Phoebe saw her new friend looking at her. The countess's expression said she expected Phoebe to speak up. With a sharp shake of her head, she eyed her new friend in consternation. The determined set of her mouth indicated Constance's resolve to have her way, and Phoebe wanted to bolt for the door. She should never have come today.

"You do?" Lady Wrotham's question was filled with hope as she waited for Constance to continue.

"Yes, although I think she might see someone recommending her for a position as charity."

At Constance's reply, Lady Wrotham set her teacup and saucer on the table. Although Louisa promptly refilled the teacup, the woman didn't pick it up. Empathy furrowed Lady Wrotham's brow as she nodded her head.

"That is something I know far too well. Matilda knows how difficult it was for me to ask for help when my father died. If not for her and Robert, I don't know what I would have done," Lady Wrotham said quietly as she smiled at Matilda in obvious gratitude. The Scotswoman immediately reached out to pat her friend's hand.

"Aye, I remember all too well. Peter Sutton was a dishonorable blackguard with no redeeming qualities. What sort of man throws his niece out of her home?" Lady Stewart's features were dark with outrage, and the rest of them inhaled sharp sounds of dismay.

All too aware that her gasp of horror had rung out perhaps the loudest, Phoebe quickly took a drink of her now tepid tea. Out of the corner of her eye, she saw Constance turn her head to watch her for a moment. Alarmed by the woman's penetrating look, Phoebe focused on the teacup in her hand that shook slightly as she witnessed the countess's determination.

Was this why Constance had invited her to tea? Had her vision shown the woman how Jasper had tossed Phoebe out into the London streets without a penny to her name? Had her new friend hoped Phoebe would find a common bond with the marchioness?

She quickly dismissed the idea. Constance had been almost as startled as Phoebe when Lady Stewart had revealed what had happened to Lady Wrotham. The marchioness covered her friend's hand in a silent expression of gratitude for the Scotswoman's umbrage on her behalf.

"But if my uncle had been an honorable man, I would never have met Alexander, which means I would never have had Gideon," Lady Wrotham said with a wistful smile before she laughed. "The dowager grand duchess once told me after Alexander and I had been married for several years that she'd been worried I would outmatch her stubborn nature by refusing her demand that I serve as her companion. I think even then, she knew Alexander and I were meant for each other. Alexander and Gideon inherited the woman's steely determination."

Lady Wrotham laughed again as she shook her head in amused resignation. Across from the countess and her aunt, Louisa sighed with delight as she stirred the tea in her cup. Her features had taken on a dreamy expression, and Lady Wrotham laughed.

"I can see now why Matilda has always said you are a romantic at heart, Louisa," the dowager marchioness said, still smiling.

"I plead guilty," the younger woman said with a laugh before her dreamy look returned. "They say yours was a love match and that he had to fight his father fiercely to marry you."

"He *did*. According to his grandmother, their shouting matches echoed like volleys at the battle of Waterloo. Alexander was third in line to the duchy, and he refused to let his father dictate our happiness. In fact, if it had not been for the dowager grand duchess, we would never have had our ten years of happiness. The woman was a force to be reckoned with until the day she died. It nearly killed her when Alexander died."

Lady Wrotham's sadness was stark and poignant as she focused on a spot over Louisa's shoulder. It was obvious the woman was thinking of happier times. The marchioness's sorrow was made Phoebe's heart ache for her. The woman had clearly lost a great love. As if aware she was the object of fascination, she emerged from her private retrospection and smiled at Louisa.

"I would love to hear more about your romance," Louisa said with a note of pleading in her voice.

Clearly eager to hear more, the younger woman leaned forward with a look that encouraged Lady Wrotham to tell more of her story. Phoebe couldn't help but hope the woman would do so. The marchioness laughed at Louisa's eagerness to hear more.

"Alexander was one of the dowager grand duchess's favorite grandchildren, and she was determined to see him happy. The moment the woman weighed in on the matter, Alexander's father gave way. She always said it had taken her less than fifteen minutes to secure our happiness. Alexander said an hour was a more reasonable time frame. It was *quite* the scandal at the time. Although when I married Thomas little more than a year after Alexander died, that was almost as great a scandal."

The dowager marchioness's mischievous smile died and her sadness returned. Phoebe admired the woman for her perseverance. Before her own scandal, she'd heard of the death of the marchioness's first husband, and gossip had said Lady Wrotham had been grief stricken.

"Although, when Cornelius died less than a week after we were married this past Christmas, the gossip was dreadful. I don't know which was worse, the rumors I had done something to hasten his death, or the appalled gasps when they learned I would not go into mourning. I loved Cornelius dearly, but we were married for only a few days, and I know he would have approved of my rebellious decision not to wear black."

As Phoebe listened to the dowager talk about her past loves and losses, she marveled at the woman's strength. It made Phoebe ashamed of all the times she'd pitied herself over the years for her own hardships. In sharing her memories of the past, Lady Wrotham had demonstrated her strength of character in overcoming the worst obstacles that life could put in one's path.

It was impossible not to admire the older woman. Many people would have become bitter and morose when confronted by so much loss. In fact, she felt ashamed of her own moments of bitterness as she'd listened to Lady

Wrotham's story. The marchioness released a small noise of irritation.

"Forgive me. I have become maudlin." Protests filled the air, and the dowager marchioness waved her hands to silence them. The mischievous smile returned to her lips as she looked at Constance. "Now then, Constance, you were saying you knew of someone who might be suitable to act as my secretary."

"I do, but as I said, I think this individual believes I've taken up their cause as a charity case, which isn't true. I happen to like her very much."

"Then, you *must* introduce me to her so I can persuade her that pride goeth before a fall."

Beside her, Constance coughed, and Phoebe turned her head to look at her. The countess arched her eyebrows imperiously. It was an obvious indication that if Phoebe didn't speak up, Constance would. With a grimace of annoyance, she was forced to acknowledge the woman was determined to befriend her. Not only that, but she was also equally set on seeing Phoebe ensconced in the role of Lady Wrotham's private secretary. She glared at Constance for a moment, but the woman merely smiled with satisfaction as if knowing she'd won their battle of wills.

"I believe what, Lady—" The sound of Constance clearing her throat in a warning manner made Phoebe tighten her mouth for a moment before she continued. "It appears *Lady Lyndham* has decided to take me under her wing and believes I would be suitable for the position."

Beside her, Constance uttered a sound of frustration and annoyance while the dowager marchioness gasped in surprise. A quick glance around the tea table said Constance's family was equally astonished. Phoebe's cheeks grew hot as she saw the other women staring at her in amazement. Embarrassment tightened her muscles as she quickly set her teacup and saucer on the table in front of her. Determined to escape being placed under the microscope, she stood up.

"I must be going. Thank you for a lovely tea, Lady Lyndham," she said coolly as she set her tea cup and its saucer down on the table. Chagrin and regret visible on her face, Constance stretched out her hand as if she realized her meddling had been a serious miscalculation on her part. For a moment, Phoebe experienced the need to reassure the woman that she was grateful for her efforts in offering to help. Phoebe immediately chastised herself. If she did so, the countess might see that as an incentive to continue her efforts to help Phoebe.

"Please don't leave, Phoebe. I'm sorry for any discomfort—"

"Constance Rockwood Blakemore. Did nae Lucien warn you about meddling in the affairs of others?"

"Yes, but—"

"Ye are fortunate Lucien is nae at home," Lady Stewart snapped as Phoebe headed toward the door.

When she reached the main hall, a maid appeared to retrieve Phoebe's hat and gloves. She quickly tugged on first one glove and then the other as she walked toward the front door. She had almost reached it when Lady Wrotham's voice rang out quietly in the foyer.

"One moment, Lady Helstone."

The imperious note in the dowager marchioness's voice made Phoebe instinctively come to a halt. When Lady Wrotham didn't say anything else, she slowly turned around, knowing the woman was waiting for her to do so. She'd expected to see pity, but there was only curiosity and appraisal as the marchioness studied her in silence. Still feeling vulnerable, Phoebe lifted her chin.

"Yes, my lady?"

"It just occurred to me why I've not seen you for such a long time. Am I correct in assuming your husband's cousin forced you to leave Helstone House?" Lady Wrotham's question made Phoebe's fingers tighten around her purse as she debated what to tell the woman. When she didn't reply, the marchioness's arched her eyebrows with a demand that Phoebe answer the question. "I wish to know the truth, Lady Helstone."

The woman's voice was stern and inflexible, and Phoebe's heart sank. Humiliation crept through her as she nodded, then bowed her head. Lady Wrotham uttered a scathing word in reference to Jasper before she took a step toward Phoebe.

"My dear girl. I think you already know how much I understand what you must be feeling at the moment," she said gently. "It is difficult to receive help from others, but the most courageous of individuals are the ones who accept assistance despite their reluctance to do so. Will you not help *me?*"

Startled by the question, Phoebe stared at Lady Wrotham in surprise. The dowager marchioness's words conveyed a compassion and understanding few people would have shown her. The woman had deliberately veiled her offer to help Phoebe by claiming she was the one in need of assistance.

A warm, kind smile curved the dowager marchioness's lips, but her silent plea for help was evident. A fleeting thought whispered through Phoebe's head as she tried to remember where she'd seen eyes of the same color. Before she could isolate the memory, Lady Wrotham caught Phoebe's hand in hers.

"I truly do need help. I love my son, but I *know* without a doubt, Gideon's choice will be either a curmudgeon or a busy body. I can abide neither. I think we would do well together, and despite Constance's misstep, I trust her instincts."

As Phoebe studied the woman for a long moment, she saw no pity, only compassion. Swallowing hard, she pushed her pride aside and nodded her agreement. The relieved smile curving Lady Wrotham's mouth as the woman squeezed

Phoebe's hand made her realize the marchioness's plea for help was genuine.

"Thank you, my dear." The woman's kind look was quickly replaced with a no-nonsense expression. "Now then, I need you to start right away. I am afraid I've made a terrible mess of the charity's books in the short time since Lydia left. I would not be surprised if it takes you weeks to correct the damage I've done."

"I doubt it is quite that bad," Phoebe said with a small laugh. "But I must give Madame Sabine some form of notice. I do not wish to leave her without someone to handle her accounts."

"You are thoughtful as I knew you would be. I shall call on Madame Sabine and make arrangements for an immediate replacement."

"Oh, but—"

"I was one of her first customers. Sabine will be more than happy to accommodate me, especially when I offer to pay for a new bookkeeper." The dowager marchioness waved her hand in a placating but dismissive manner. "Now then, I am something of a workhorse, and I have a tendency to work late into the night. So I think it best you move into Chelmsford House."

"*Chelmsford House?*" Phoebe struggled to keep the horror out of her voice as she stared at the dowager marchioness in dismay. Her heart began to pound frantically as she remembered how she'd mocked the Earl of Chelmsford in several recent installments of the Currier Chronicles.

"Yes, I live with my son when I'm in town. Although my stepson has invited me to stay at Wrotham Place whenever I wish, I prefer Chelmsford House. Abner and Miriam are very kind, but I have little in common with them. Gideon is in Holland at the moment, so the two of us will be well-settled in our routine by the time he returns."

As Phoebe remembered how unflattering her depiction

of the earl had been in her serial, she realized she'd agreed too hastily to the dowager marchioness's offer. From the gossip she'd overheard at Madame Sabine's, the man had not been happy with her caricature of him as a Lothario who danced from one woman to the next like a bumblebee did flowers. If he were to discover who she was—Phoebe's mouth went dry at the possibility. Before she could think of a reason to retract her acceptance of the marchioness's employment, Lady Wrotham tucked her arm into Phoebe's and pulled her back toward the salon.

"Come along now, my dear. We must put Constance out of her misery. The poor woman was distraught at having caused you pain."

With another gentle tug on Phoebe's arm, Lady Wrotham pulled her back into the salon. Deep in the back of her brain, she heard a voice cry out a warning, but she'd already agreed. Drowning out the word of caution was another voice that said she would no longer have to choose between food or coal for a fire.

That was something Phoebe had done for months now when she received her first payment for the first installment of the Currer Chronicles. She had been determined to go cold and hungry if necessary rather than dip into her savings. Every farthing she earned from the serial was set aside to purchase a small cottage in the country. She only had a few more months before she would be able to escape the city altogether, at which time P. Currer would vanish into the mist from whence he'd come.

She would simply have to do her best to stay out of Lord Chelmsford's path. For the past two years, she'd walked right under the noses of the Marlborough Set. Surely it wouldn't be any more difficult to do the same where the earl was concerned.

Chapter 5

Gideon Lethbridge, Earl of Chelmsford, rubbed the back of his neck to loosen stiff muscles as the carriage turned onto Curzon Street. The trip home had been longer and more arduous than he'd expected. His conversation with Willem Ruigrok at his tulip farm in De Zilk had caused him to miss the passenger steamer out of Amsterdam yesterday.

Usually, he didn't find traveling exhausting, but with no seats available on the passenger steamer for two more days, he'd been forced to take passage on a cargo ship to the port of London. The amenities on the steamer were few, and the Channel had proven to be a rough journey. He couldn't remember a time when he'd ever been more ready to sleep in his own bed than now.

Despite the fatigue he was suffering now, missing the passenger steamer had been well worth it. His conversation with Ruigrok had been insightful, and the bulbs the expert horticulturist had sold him were unique to the man's farm. The tulip grower's advice about the proper storage of the bulbs was certain to go a long way with the bulbs he already had. It meant his small tulip bed in the orangery would hopefully produce enough bulbs to plant in the garden at Lethbridge Farm. Ruigrok had indicated that his bulbs would last up to six years with the right care, which would provide him with new bulbs to plant for years to come. The carriage rolled to a halt in front of Chelmsford House, and Gideon stepped out of the vehicle. He looked up at the coachman and nodded.

"Thank you, Jeremy," he said as he started toward the front door, then suddenly stopped and turned to the driver. "Oh, please tell Brown I'll be riding a little late tomorrow morning, say ten o'clock. I imagine Xerxes will be unruly but have him saddled him all the same."

"Yes, my Lord. Mr. Brown hired a new stable hand who has been exercising Xerxes. I don't think that horse will be any more difficult than usual," Jeremy said with a cheerful grin.

"Should I look to my laurels when it comes to the beast?" Gideon arched his eyebrow at the young coachman with a small smile. The man shook his head and grinned.

"You have nothing to worry about at all, my lord. Myers was thrown the first time he tried to ride the horse. Xerxes has never thrown you because he knows you're the master."

Gideon laughed at the driver's words and waved him on his way as he climbed the steps to the front door. It opened before he reached the top step. Removing his hat and gloves, he handed them to his butler.

"Welcome home, my lord."

"Thank you, Pendleton. Is her ladyship still up?"

"Lady Wrotham is in her sitting room with her new secretary."

"New secretary? What happened to Miss Smithers?"

"She dashed off to Gretna Green with her young man shortly after you left for Holland."

"And how did my mother find…never mind, I'll ask her myself." Gideon waved his hand as he headed toward the staircase.

His mother could be the most exasperating creature, and yet she had the kindest heart of anyone he'd ever met. It was difficult for her to refuse someone's help when they asked for it. The charity ball for St. Catherine's was a perfect example. He'd told her not to give way to Lady Gresham's pleas, but she had anyway.

Gideon could only pray that whomever she'd secured as a personal secretary didn't turn out to be someone who preyed on the goodwill of others. Determined to ensure someone hadn't taken advantage of his mother's kind heart, his weariness vanished, and he climbed the stairs two at a time. When he reached the second-floor hallway, he strode quickly toward his mother's suite.

The sound of laughter echoed behind the closed door to his mother's rooms as his knuckles rapped on the wood. His mother called out for her visitor to come in, and he turned the doorknob to enter her room. Another peal of his mother's laughter filled the air, along with a laugh he didn't recognize. The door swung wide to reveal an elegant room decorated in rich jewel tones of blue and gold. As he crossed the threshold, he saw his mother reclined on her chaise lounge with a woman seated next to her. The stranger's head was bent over a folded newspaper in her lap. His mother leaned forward and shook her head in protest.

"No, Phoebe, I'm certain that's a description of Lord Pickward. It sounds just like the odious, pompous man." The moment he cleared his throat, his mother looked in his direction and uttered a cry of happiness. "*Gideon.* You're home."

Before he could close the distance between them, Lady Wrotham was on her feet and hurrying across the floor toward him. He chuckled as he welcomed her hug and kissed her cheek.

"I take it you are glad to see me."

"Of course, I am, my darling boy. I hope your business ventures were successful."

"Quite. I decided to invest in a new shipping line that will ferry passengers and cargo back and forth from London to Amsterdam." Gideon smiled with satisfaction at having made what he was certain was a sound investment.

"And did you find someone to answer questions about

your tulips?"

"I did. The past two days were quite enjoyable. Baron Van Planate introduced me to Willem Ruigrok. The man was a fount of knowledge. I was even able to persuade him to sell me some of his specialty bulbs." A movement over his mother's shoulder caught his attention, and he arched his eyebrow quizzically at his mother. "I understand from Pendleton that you have a new secretary."

"I do, indeed. Phoebe, come meet my son."

Alva beamed as she turned slightly and stretched out her arm in a beckoning gesture. The woman quickly finished rearranging some papers on the top of a delicate secretaire, and the moment she turned toward them, Gideon grew rigid with tension. It had been almost five years to the day since that moment in Montjoy's gardens, but he'd never forgotten her or his anger when he'd learned who she was.

It had been a kick in the gut when he'd returned to the ballroom and learned his bewitching enchantress had crossed the ocean to land a title for herself. Lady Helstone was cut from the same cloth as another woman. Edith had been equally determined to marry money and a title.

When Edith had informed him of her betrothal to a duke almost twice her age, he'd wanted to throttle her. Several times before Edith had shown her true character to him, Gideon had considered offering for her. He hadn't been destitute at the time, but he'd had no expectation of inheriting great wealth or a title. In hindsight, he realized how fortunate he'd been not to propose marriage to Edith.

She would never have accepted his offer. If anything, she would have laughed at his audacity to even think she would accept his hand. That he'd ever thought himself in love with Edith was proof he'd been as wet behind the ears as a schoolboy. Money and social position were the only things women like Edith and Lady Helstone desired in life.

As the viscountess walked toward him, her movements

were as elegant and graceful as he remembered. The unwelcome memory of a lush thigh and silky skin made his jaw clench with anger. Despite his irritation, he could almost smell the musky scent of her desire and slick heat as he'd buried himself inside her. It was a visceral memory that hardened his muscles.

Lady Helstone's frown of confusion as she walked toward him intensified his fury. The woman belonged on the stage for looking at him as if they'd never met. As she drew closer, a polite smile tilted the corners of her mouth when she suddenly paled as if in shock. Her alarm obvious, she curtsied and hesitated for a fraction of a second before extending her hand to him. Before his mother could make the introductions, Gideon bent slightly to brush his mouth over soft fingers.

"Lady Helstone," he murmured in a cool tone.

"You know each other," Lady Wrotham exclaimed with delight, and Phoebe winced in dismay.

"I'm not—"

"Surely you've not forgotten our meeting at Lord Montjoy's home several years ago," he said mockingly quirked an eyebrow at her. The moment he spoke, she seemed to grow even paler, and her slender throat bobbed as she swallowed hard.

"For…forgive me, my lord," she stammered. "It was…that was a long time ago."

"I'm disappointed you would forget our meeting so easily."

His words sent a flush of color into her pale cheeks, and Gideon gritted his teeth. *Christ Jesus*, had he just made it sound as if he was irritated she'd forgotten him? Gideon stared into brown eyes that were wide with alarm. She should be afraid. The woman was going to regret using his mother to find a new husband and title.

"At last! It's finally happened," his mother exclaimed with a laugh as she eyed him with great delight.

"What has?" Gideon growled, certain he would not enjoy his mother's teasing.

"You've finally met a woman who found it as easy to forget you as easily as you forget all the women whose hearts you break." Gleefully, his mother teased him for having the tables reversed on him. Before he could protest his mother's assumption, Lady Helstone drew in an audible breath.

"Unless you have further need of me, my lady, I shall retire for the evening."

The soft words made Gideon's jaw clench. So the woman was living here as well. Lady Helstone would begin packing her things tonight when he was done with her.

"But of course, my dear. It's been a long day for both of us, but it was most productive."

"Good night, my lady. My lord."

Lady Helstone dipped her head slightly in Lady Wrotham's direction and then his. Not about to let her escape so easily, Gideon leaned forward to kiss his mother's cheek.

"I shall say goodnight, as well."

"But Gideon, you just arrived."

"Exactly," he said with an abrupt nod as he saw his quarry reach the door of his mother's suite. "I've been traveling since first light, and I need sleep. I simply wanted to say hello."

"You do look weary." Alva stared at him intently for a moment, then nodded. "We'll see you at breakfast?"

"Yes," he said as he kissed her cheek. "Goodnight, Mama."

Determined to catch his prey, Gideon closed the door to his mother's suite behind him as he stepped out into the hall. Phoebe was already halfway down the corridor, but he quickly ate up the distance between them with his long stride.

He was only three steps behind her as she darted into one of the rooms generally reserved for guests. As the door was closing, he slapped his palm against the wood to keep it open.

One hand pressed into the wood panel of the door, his other braced on the door jamb, Gideon stared at Phoebe standing only a few feet away.

"I seem to recall you ran away the last time, too," he bit out sharply.

She flinched at his harsh words and the moment Gideon took a step forward into her room, she fell back two. Grim satisfaction pounded its way through him. He'd wanted to put the fear of God in the woman, and from the way she was staring at him, he'd succeeded. Smiling coldly, he closed the door behind him, and she gasped.

"*Leave my room at once*," she exclaimed in horrified dismay.

Gideon studied her in silence for a moment. The soft glow of a nearby oil lamp highlighted gold flecks in her eyes. He'd not noticed them that night in Montjoy's gardens. It had been her vulnerability that had ensnared him then. That he'd even noticed it now or remembered her fragile state all those years ago irritated him all the more.

"I *said*, leave my room. *now*." Her command was fierce, and he saw golden highlights flare even brighter with anger.

"As this house belongs to *me*, I am entitled to venture into *whatever* room I please and to do whatever I *wish* in it, Lady Helstone." At his sardonic reply, her lips parted slightly in astonishment before anger sent color flushing up over her cheekbones.

"My singular moment of indiscretion does not entitle you to do as you please in this room," she spat out vehemently. "Although I confess, I am not surprised by your arrogant assumption. The depiction of you in the Currer Chronicles as a busy bee buzzing from one flower to the next in search of another conquest is quite accurate."

The mention of the serial made Gideon clench his jaw so hard it ached as if someone had hit him with a hard left jab in the ring. If she'd thought to anger him even more, the mention of those damned chronicles was precisely how to do it.

Gideon folded his arms across his chest for fear of unleashing the full force of his fury on her.

Fingers digging deep into hard muscles, he fought the urge to tug her into his arms and confirm her preconceived notions. Not that the idea wasn't a tempting one. The problem was, it was far too enticing a thought. In the shadows of Montjoy's garden, she'd been beautiful in a hauntingly fragile manner. Now, she exuded the fiery strength of a woman who would make bedroom sport exceptionally satisfying. Gideon arched his eyebrows.

"Perhaps I should show you how much more pleasurable it would be between us in a bed as opposed to being pressed up against a tree." Gideon surprised himself at his suggestion and was irritated at how the thought of bedding her again sent a rush of excitement surging through his body.

"I have *no intention* of sharing *any* bed with you, my lord."

Despite the adamant note in her voice, he saw the way her breasts rose and fell rapidly. Her lips were parted slightly, and the memory of silencing her cry of release five years ago sent pure lust hammering its way through him. Without thinking, he moved forward and stretched out his hand to rub his thumb across the side of her neck, where her pulse fluttered wildly beneath her skin. She trembled at his touch, and Gideon smiled at her reaction.

"Despite sounding like a termagant, your body betrays you, Phoebe. I think you're more than tempted to invite me into your bed," Gideon murmured.

He bent his head and brushed his mouth over her ear as he enjoyed the way another shudder wracked her body. The soft scent of roses wafted off her skin to fill his nostrils. Damn, but she smelled delicious. Gideon sucked in a deep breath of exasperation at his inability to control his attraction to her. He straightened and stared down at her.

"However, be forewarned that our mutual exchange of pleasure will not gain you the title of countess."

A look of astonishment and confusion made her protest with a slight shake of her head. The woman truly was an exceptional actress. If he hadn't known she'd bought herself a title by marrying Helstone, he'd almost think her appalled at the idea of marriage.

"I don't understand."

"Don't you?" Gideon snorted with disbelief. "You wouldn't be the first woman to ingratiate herself with my mother, all in the hope of becoming the next Countess of Chelmsford."

Phoebe stared at the man in shocked horror. Countess? Marriage? The equilibrium she'd only just regained disappeared again. She'd rather go cold and hungry than marry again, and she knew what those two companions were like. The man was mad to think she would even contemplate such an action.

As she'd crossed the floor of her employer's suite a few moments ago, it had taken her several seconds to recognize him. The shadows in Montjoy's garden had dimmed her memory of his handsome features, but any uncertainty as to his identity had disappeared the moment he spoke.

When Gideon had greeted her, the voice she'd never forgotten brushed across her senses with the same potency as the night she'd given herself to him in the shadows of Montjoy's garden. But it was his anger that had left her in a state of bewildered panic as she'd stared into his cold, silvery gaze. Whatever had aroused his fury, Phoebe had known it was directed at her.

At first, she'd thought he'd discovered she was the authoress of the Currer Chronicles. She'd immediately dismissed that possibility. The only person who knew she was

P. Currer was Lady Lyndham. The woman had promised to keep her secret, and despite their short friendship, Phoebe believed her.

The only other person who knew anything about her was her editor, Mr. Meade. But the newspaperman knew nothing about P. Currer other than she was a woman. The man would never recognize her if he saw her on the street as she wore a veil whenever she went visited the newspaper offices.

When she'd discarded that explanation, she'd considered the possibility that Gideon's anger was because he'd been denied the opportunity to select his mother's assistant. That seemed implausible as well knowing Lady Wrotham would have balked at giving up any say at all in the selection of a private secretary.

But to hear the man suggest she was at Chelmsford House hoping to land a marital prize—specifically *him*—was the height of conceit and arrogance. The man was even more pretentious than she'd realized when she'd created her caricature of him in the Chronicles.

A bleak disappointment rose from deep inside Phoebe. His accusation and ridiculous assumption was more than wrong. It was painful to know he would think such a thing of her. A voice in the back of her mind sneered at her for having thought more highly of him. For the past five years, she'd allowed herself to believe the man she'd met that night was different from others in the Marlborough Set. She'd been wrong—terribly wrong.

Angered by her dull-witted thinking, Phoebe allowed outrage to streak through her veins until the heat of it burned every inch of her. When Gideon arched an eyebrow, she dragged in a sharp breath of furious indignation and disgust.

"Of all the pompous, arrogant, *vain*, self-aggrandizing— you are *delusional* if you think I want *anything* to do with you at all, Lord Chelmsford."

"Then you won't object when I say that your services as

my mother's secretary are no longer needed."

Dread spiraled through Phoebe. It held her stiff and unmoving as she stared at him in horror. The hard set of his jaw and the contemptuous twist of his lips made her stomach lurch in a sickening manner. Dear God, he was serious.

Had Lady Wrotham expressed disappointment in her work and asked her son to release her. No, that wasn't possible. Phoebe knew the dowager marchioness was happy with her work, and Gideon had been too close on her heels to have had a serious discussion with his mother as to her dismissal.

While Phoebe had no desire to spend any more time in this man's presence than necessary, she had nowhere else to go. Without employment, her savings would quickly disappear, along with her hopes of a cottage in the country. She'd also grown quite fond of Lady Wrotham since her arrival at Chelmsford House almost a month ago. It would be difficult enough to say goodbye to the woman when Phoebe's savings were substantial enough to escape London for good.

But she'd not lived in obscure poverty for almost two years, saving every penny she earned to have Lord Chelmbee of the Currer Chronicles push her out into the streets as Jasper had done after Alfred's death. Phoebe tilted her chin upward and defiantly shook her head.

"*Your mother* offered me a position as her assistant, *not you*, and I will continue in her employ until she says otherwise."

"Do not test my patience, Phoebe," he snarled. "I'll not have you use my mother as a means of husband-hunting."

As he repeated and expanded on his accusation, an icy chill swept over her skin and sluiced through her veins until it froze every part of her body. His angry expression emphasized his belief she was using his mother in a way she found disgusting. The idea that she would do something to injure his mother caused a vicious antipathy to swell inside her. Incensed by his abhorrent suggestion, she eyed him with scorn.

"I would *never* do anything to hurt your mother," she spat with fiery anger. "And I am *not* husband hunting."

"Just like you weren't intent on securing a title for yourself in exchange for your American fortune when you married Helstone? A dowry too small to attract anything higher than a viscount."

Anger swept through her like a hot summer wind. The man knew nothing about her. It had been her father's ambition that had thrown her at the feet of her late husband. She'd paid a steep price for her father's ability to boast about having a viscountess for a daughter.

"Get out," she said, her words cold and sharp as ice.

The man had no idea how scathing her pen could be. If Gideon had been irate about her treatment of him in the Currer Chronicles the last time, he would be livid about the next installment. Lord Chelmbee would be ready to pulverize Mr. Meade simply to learn the identity of P. Currer. She would pour all her rage into every word and place he was mentioned in her next installment. It would be no less than he deserved. Exposing him for the man he truly was would be a cathartic exercise.

An odd expression crossed his features as she glared at him, which was almost identical to that moment in the dark when he'd offered her assistance. Phoebe immediately crushed the traitorous thought. The fact she still wanted to believe in him illustrated what a fool she really was.

Outrage made her movements stiff and jerky as she quickly skirted him to stride to the door and tugged it open with a furious jerk. She turned her head and glared at him with scornful disdain as she silently demanded he leave. A puzzled frown creased Gideon's forehead as he slowly moved toward her.

"You've changed. There's a fire in you now that you didn't have that night at Montjoy's," he said quietly as he stopped at her side to study her intently. It was a look of appraisal that alarmed her, and she shook her head.

"I said you were delusional, my lord, and you continue to confirm my conclusion."

"Then, you will think me even more so when I tell you I was too hasty in my desire to have you leave my house." A small smile tipped the corners of his mouth, and her heart skipped a beat. "I believe we will do quite well together, Phoebe."

"*What?*"

"Not marriage, of course, but as I said, a bed is much more preferable to a tree."

Horrified by his words, Phoebe stiffened as he bent his head toward her. The instant Gideon's teeth nipped at her ear with his teeth, she gasped. The warmth of his breath caressed her skin, and Phoebe shuddered at the delight the decadent caress aroused in her. How in God's name could this obnoxious man still devastate her senses as powerfully as he had five years ago? She didn't have an answer to the question. Another shiver of pleasure coursed through her, and she despised herself for revealing her susceptibility to him.

"You tremble, Phoebe. Are you afraid?"

He pulled back slightly and stared down at her. The desire blazing in his steely expression made her suck in a sharp breath. She refused to think it was a sound of anticipation, but a jeering laugh echoed in the back of her head. Terrified he might think the same thing, she smiled tightly.

"I have little to fear from you. I'm accustomed to the pity and scorn of others, my lord." At her fierce retort, he studied her in puzzlement before a slow smile curved his sensual lips.

"The only thing you need expect of me is pleasure, Phoebe."

"Your presumption I would want anything to do with a philandering wastrel is the height of arrogance, Lord Chelmbee." The moment she addressed him by the name she'd given him in the Chronicles, he stiffened. She smiled with triumph at having struck a blow to his pride. It was a small moment of victory. Gideon's anger vanished as he laughed softly.

"I like this change in you, Phoebe. This new, fiery spirit of yours is certain to make the pleasure of five years ago pale in comparison for what's to come."

"You are an arrogant bastard to think I would welcome you into my bed."

"Challenge accepted," he said with a quiet laugh that made her heart skip a beat. It was as sinful and wicked a sound as his voice. "And I shall enjoy every minute of it, Phoebe."

"I offered you *no* challenge," Phoebe snapped as she glowered at him with antipathy.

"Ah, but you did, my sweet. The moment you refused to leave my house, you threw down the gauntlet."

"Then I hope you are prepared for disappointment and the taste of defeat," she snapped fiercely as she fought to keep her breathing steady.

Gideon stretched out his hand to brush his fingers across her neck. Then, ever so slowly, he traced a path with his forefinger down across her breastbone to the valley between her breasts. Unable to control her reaction to his wicked caress, Phoebe gasped, and a tremor shook her body. Satisfaction settled on his features.

"We shall see, but I promise I shall be a benevolent conqueror. I will ensure your pleasure is equal to mine."

There was a silky note of seduction in his voice that sent Phoebe's heart skidding out of control. It reminded her of another moment when he had caressed her with a passion that had stirred her soul. Her mouth went dry as she saw his amused complacency.

If she'd thought him a force to be reckoned with that night in the gardens, it was nothing compared to what she saw now. Everything about him shouted raw, masculine power. It emphasized how close to the precipice she was where he was concerned. If she didn't take care, she would find herself surrendering to him without any resistance at all.

Once more, he dipped his head toward her, and this time his lips brushed lightly across hers. Fire streaked through her at the caress, and she barely managed to suppress her desire to kiss him back. He lifted his head and smiled down at her.

"I see we understand each other. This first skirmish is yours, Phoebe, but I shall win the war." Then, with one last touch of his fingers to her cheek, Gideon walked out of her room.

In a rush of movement, Phoebe closed and locked the door behind him. Drained from their battle of wills, Phoebe pressed her forehead against the wood. Dear God, what was she going to do? She should never have left Madame Sabine's, and it was unlikely the dressmaker would take her back, given Phoebe had already been replaced. Tomorrow morning she would begin searching advertisements in the London Times for a new position.

She didn't know what she would say to Lady Wrotham as to why she was leaving. Telling the woman the truth was out of the question. The marchioness loved her son dearly, and Phoebe refused to hurt the woman by denouncing her son for the reprobate he was. No, she would have to think of something else.

Although she was certain she was still short of funds to purchase anything suitable, she could at least consider lowering her standards to escape her current situation. Phoebe rubbed her fingertips across her forehead and moved to sit down in the chair facing the fireplace. Her mind jumped from one chaotic thought to the next as she tried to collect herself. It had been one thing to believe she could conceal her connection to the Chronicles while living in the house of a man she'd mocked in her writings. But nothing had prepared her for tonight's unexpected outcome.

If she'd known her lover of five years ago was the earl,

as well as Lady Wrotham's son, she would never have accepted the position as secretary to the marchioness. Phoebe would have known better than to tempt fate to put herself in Gideon's path again, even though she'd not known his name until tonight. Deep in her heart, she'd always known he had the potential to destroy her, and she'd not been wrong.

The Earl of Chelmsford was unrivaled when it came to breaking hearts. The absurdity of her situation was unlike anything she could have imagined, even when it came to writing the Currer Chronicles. Perhaps worst of all was Gideon's contempt when he'd accused her of using his mother to climb the social ladder.

Whatever he'd heard to make him believe she was a person of such low character, she didn't care. It wasn't true. Even if she had been what Gideon accused her of, his own behavior made him the last person in the world with any right to pass judgment. The disappointment she'd experienced earlier returned.

The stranger she'd given herself to in the shadows five years ago was nothing like the man who'd just left her room. The lover she remembered had been passionate, tender, gentle, and his offer to help her had been sincere. She'd been so tempted to tell him everything that night. Now she thanked the good Lord she had not.

The fire crackled and popped loudly, causing Phoebe to jump violently. Her heart racing, her fingers clutched at the ruffled trim that bordered the V-shaped neckline of her dress. She could still feel Gideon's finger sliding down across her skin. It had reminded her of how his hands had caressed her that night in the garden.

Another loud snap pierced the silence as the flames sizzled around sap leaking out of a burning log. Hypnotized by the fire, Phoebe's mind dragged her unwillingly into the past. For weeks and months, she had tried hard to forget what had happened between her and Gideon. She had failed miserably.

It had been impossible not to listen for the sound of his voice in the days and nights afterward wherever she'd gone. Even though she'd tried to pray she would never hear him speak again, it had been impossible not to pray that she would. After several months without hearing his voice, it had become apparent to her that they moved in different social circles.

Certain their paths would never cross again, Phoebe had resigned herself to the fact their meeting had been a single moment in time. It would never be repeated except in her dreams. Yet, as painful as the realization had been, she'd known it was for the best. If they had met again, she was positive what little self-respect she possessed would be lost entirely. Phoebe turned her head toward the bed, and she dragged in a deep breath.

Tonight they'd been adversaries, but it had not lessened her physical reaction to his presence. If anything, the sensations he'd aroused in her tonight had been even more potent than five years ago. Without even realizing it, Gideon had declared war on her senses the moment he'd greeted her in Lady Wrotham's suite.

His blatant declaration that he intended to seduce her wasn't anywhere near as alarming as the knowledge he would find it quite easy to do so. And there was one thing of which she had no doubt. If she succumbed to the fiery passion Gideon could arouse in her, it would eventually leave her heart burnt and scarred beyond recognition.

Chapter 6

The clatter of Xerxes's hooves on the stable yard's cobblestones brought Brown out of the stables as Gideon rode into the yard. He dismounted the stallion and patted the animal's neck as he handed the reins off to his stablemaster. A small, wiry-built man, Brown had once been a jockey, and Gideon was convinced the man could talk to horses.

"Xerxes did well for you today, my lord?" At the question, Gideon grinned and nodded in the older man's direction.

"He did. Please thank the new man for exercising this devil while I was away," he said as he rubbed the horse's jowl. "I'm certain he would have been much more fractious if he'd not been exercised so well while I was gone."

"I'll be certain to tell Myers, my lord."

Gideon bobbed his head in the stablemaster's direction before turning and heading toward the rear of the house. As he entered the back hall, he dropped his hat and riding gloves onto a small table at the door, then strode down the hallway to the breakfast room. As Gideon approached the small, intimate room used only for family meals, Phoebe's voice drifted through the air.

There was a sweetness to the sound that made him clenched his jaw as he released a soft grunt of irritation. He intended to have Phoebe in his bed, but he could not allow himself to be moved by her. The memory of his desperate search for her in Montjoy's ballroom that night was a stark reminder as to how he'd almost made a complete fool of himself that night. Even worse was his moment of weakness months afterward when he'd come close to calling on her at Helstone Place.

Gideon had almost reached the breakfast room doorway when the sound of his mother's laugh brought him to an abrupt halt. She'd been laughing just as merrily last night. A fact he'd overlooked with his attention being focused on Phoebe. Now he allowed himself to enjoy the sound of his mother's laughter.

It had been a long time since Gideon had heard her laugh so easily. It was similar to the sound he'd heard so often as a child. He'd thought never to hear his mother laugh again after his father had died. Although she'd never said it, Gideon was certain his father was the only man she'd ever really loved. The mother he'd known had been changed forever the day his father had died.

Gideon had been too young for his mother to lean on him for support when his father had died. Instead, Thomas Lancaster, the Earl of Chelmsford, had been the shoulder his mother had cried on during her moments of profound grief. The earl had been a distant cousin of his mother's, and the two of them had known each other since childhood. Thomas had once said that he had loved Gideon's mother since they were children.

The earl had adored his wife, and she had learned to love him and laugh again as well. Not as she once had, but her laughter had been a pleasant sound, nonetheless. When his half-sister was born, the doctor had said his mother could have no more children. The news had been a blow to Thomas as he'd wanted a son and heir.

Ironically, it had turned out that Gideon, as a distant relative of Thomas's great-great-grandfather, found himself next in line to the title. However, the earl had never tried to be a father to him. Instead, Thomas had become a friend and confidant as he invested his time and energy in training Gideon for his future role as the Earl of Chelmsford.

His step-father had often told Gideon he couldn't have asked for a more worthy heir, and when Thomas had died, Gideon had felt the loss of his step-father deeply. His mother had been heartbroken at the loss of her companion and friend. While her laughter hadn't died completely when Thomas died, it had taken on a softer, less hearty sound.

While the old earl had lived long enough to ease his wife's profound grief from the death of Gideon's father, that hadn't been true in the marquess's case. It had taken the man two years to convince Gideon's mother to marry again, and he had died less than a week after their wedding.

Both the earl and the marquess had been good men, but Gideon knew they could never replace the part of his mother's heart that had shriveled up and died along with his father. Now, as he heard his mother laugh again, he took pleasure in the sound. It was good to hear her laugh again, even if a social climber was responsible for his mother's amusement.

Another peal of laughter drifted out into the hallway again, and he resumed his course. At the door of the breakfast room, he paused on the threshold. Seated at his mother's left, Phoebe took notes while the marchioness examined several swatches of material lying on the table between the two women.

Phoebe murmured something, and his mother jerked her head up in surprise to look at her companion before she laughed again. A mischievous smile tilted Phoebe's mouth as she looked at his mother. The picture the two of them presented was one of companionship and harmony. It was a pleasing sight.

The thought made him release a barely audible growl of anger. *Christ Jesus*, it was bad enough the woman had haunted his dreams last night. Now he was viewing the scene in front of him like a maudlin fool. Begrudgingly, he was forced to admit that Phoebe hadn't been lying about never wanting to hurt his mother. It was apparent even to him that the two of them had become steadfast friends in a relatively short time.

It was an unforeseen complication that could make things difficult where his interest in Phoebe was concerned. His mother was forever matchmaking, and he had no intention of allowing her or Phoebe to trap him in the bonds of matrimony. In the back of his head, a voice cackled with mocking laughter. He ignored the sound as he walked toward the buffet to fix himself a plate of food.

"Good morning, my dear." At his mother's greeting, he glanced over his shoulder to see her beaming at him.

"Good morning, Mama," he paused for a moment before he turned back to the buffet and addressed Phoebe without looking at her. "Lady Helstone. I trust you slept well."

"Yes, my lord. *quite* soundly." There was the smallest hint of an acerbic note in her reply, but it was restrained enough to make her still sound polite.

Satisfied with the meal on his plate, he turned and walked across the floor to take the seat on his mother's right, directly across from Phoebe. She didn't look at him as he sat down, but he saw her stiffen in her chair. Gideon took a bite of beef and studied Phoebe for a moment. Out of the corner of his eye, he saw his mother watching him with amusement, and he shifted his attention to her.

"Something amuses you, Mama?"

"Did you enjoy your ride this morning, dear? I understand Xerxes was quite temperamental while you were gone."

The fact that she'd deliberately ignored his question indicated the marchioness had seen him watching Phoebe and had come to a conclusion. Clearly, he would have to be even more careful than he'd originally thought.

"Actually, the new man Brown hired exercised him quite a bit while I was gone." Gideon took a drink of the coffee his mother had poured for him. "The beast was bit cantankerous at first, but a good run in Hyde Park was enough to settle him down."

"You should take Phoebe with you tomorrow morning."

Gideon's cup stopped halfway to his mouth as he stared at his mother in amazement. Across from him, Phoebe coughed hard, and he was certain it was because she was trying not to choke on her food. With another cough, she shook her head, and her reaction to the suggestion was one of deep dismay.

"We've only just now caught up with the gala's planning details, my lady." At her protest, Lady Wrotham arched her eyebrow in curiosity. The shrewd look on the marchioness's face made Gideon switch his attention to Phoebe. Her expression illustrated how opposed to his mother's suggestion. Her panic evident, Phoebe quickly reinforced her protest. "And you cannot possibly expect his lordship to entertain the staff."

"I find the idea of entertaining you a pleasurable one, my lady." Gideon smiled pleasantly at Phoebe from across the table. His amusement increased at she scowled at him. If looks could kill, he would not have survived. He smiled pleasantly.

"Thank you, but I have no wish to——"

"You are most definitely *not* staff, Phoebe, and you need sunshine," Lady Wrotham said with a distinct note of motherly affection.

"Shall we say nine o'clock tomorrow?" Gideon said casually as he took another bite of his breakfast. Phoebe's scowled at him in obvious anger and shook her head.

"I don't——"

"It's settled then," Lady Wrotham said with a pleased smile on her still youthful features. "Gideon, I think Athena is the best choice for Phoebe, don't you? She's one of the sweetest horses we have in the stables, Phoebe. I know you'll enjoy riding her."

The satisfaction in his mother's voice made Phoebe blanch as she submitted to the marchioness's determination with great reluctance. As bowed her head and continued eating in silence, Phoebe appeared to wince as if she was humiliated, and he wondered what would cause her to feel embarrassed.

Gideon returned to eating his meal as well, but not before he saw his mother's sly smile, and he crushed his annoyance. It would only encourage her if he were to display any kind of resistance. If his mother knew what he did about Phoebe, he was certain she'd not be so eager to push the woman in his direction. He'd only taken a few bites of his meal when his mother dropped her napkin onto the table.

"Good heavens, I forgot to tell Mrs. Murray to make an orange layer cake. I know how much you love it, Gideon. It's the perfect dessert for the dinner party this evening."

"Dinner party?" Gideon frowned slightly. He'd been planning on spending the evening reading a horticulture book he'd bought before leaving for Amsterdam.

"Yes, I invited several people for dinner last week, thinking you would be home two days ago. I asked your friends, the Earl of Melton and his wife, as well as the Earl and Countess of Lyndham, and Lady Stewart."

"I was gone for three weeks, Mama." He cast an amused look in her direction, to which she shrugged with a laugh.

"Perhaps, but you know how much I love to entertain. I thought it a fitting occasion. It will be a pleasant evening with friends, and I know what good friends you are with Sebastian." As his mother quickly stood up. Gideon rose as well, but she waved her hand at him. "Do sit down and finish your breakfast, dearest."

Still smiling, Lady Wrotham left the breakfast room. The silence that fell in the wake of her departure was quickly broken as Phoebe laid her fork down on her plate with a soft clink. Although her outward appearance was one of serenity, but her chin tilted upward at a defiant angle while she glared at him with antipathy.

"I would like you to devise an excuse that will prevent me from riding with you tomorrow morning." Her lovely mouth thinned with anger as she eyed him coldly.

"Why would I want to do that?" He took another drink of coffee before setting it back in its saucer. Elbows resting on the table, he formed a steeple with his fingers, Gideon cocked his head slightly as he studied her reaction. A flush crested in her cheeks, and he frowned at her look of dismayed consternation.

"Because I do not wish to put your mother in the painful situation of feeling terrible when she learns I do not have a riding habit." Her confession made Gideon tipped his head to one side uncertain he'd heard her correctly.

"I beg your pardon?"

"I *said*, I do *not* own a riding habit." Her crisp response accentuated her humiliation as she bowed her head to stare down at her plate.

"I see."

"I don't think you do," she snapped fiercely as she jerked her head up to glare at him. "I refuse to cause your mother embarrassment, *or regret*, for insisting I ride with you, nor will I have her offer to procure any clothing for me. I have no intention of doing anything that might cause her distress."

Gideon slowly leaned back in his chair, draping one arm over the open, scrolled back of the Queen Anne chair. He studied her in silence, but she didn't flinch beneath his intense scrutiny. Instead, her chin tipped upward at a proud angle. Last night she'd been vehement that she would never hurt his mother.

He had attributed her protestation to that of a woman well-skilled in the art of deception, especially where men were concerned. Now he was no longer certain. Phoebe's refusal to mention her lack of a riding habit to his mother supported the assertion she'd made last night.

Equally confusing was her confession that her wardrobe was lacking, yet she'd neither asked nor implied he should consider buying her one. Instead, she'd simply asked him to devise a reason that would ensure his mother didn't discover she lacked a habit. Few women would be willing to admit such a thing, especially one intent on acquiring a new title.

The memory of Edith lamenting her inability to afford a new gown to wear to the annual Chesterfield affair pounded through his head. Edith had been so dejected, he'd actually loaned her a large sum to purchase a new dress. It had proven to be a mistake to give up such a large portion of his monthly allowance. Two weeks later, Edith had informed him that her engagement to the Duke of Stockdale would be posted the next day in the Times.

Gideon focused his attention on Phoebe again. She fiddled with the edges of her napkin with obvious embarrassment at having to explain herself. A riding habit was a standard article of clothing for women of the peerage. It made no sense for a woman intent on marrying up the ladder not to have one in her wardrobe.

For a brief moment, he considered the possibility he'd been too hasty in his judgment where Phoebe was concerned. Gideon suppressed a snort of disgust. Phoebe was one of the American Dollar Princesses who'd crossed the Atlantic in recent years. The heiresses had come to England for only one thing—a title.

Still, she clearly wished to save his mother embarrassment, something for which he was grateful. He could not fault her for that. If anything, he appreciated her thoughtful consideration where his mother was concerned. Her attention to her napkin shifted to him, and her demeanor was a silent plea for him to agree to her request. Gideon nodded.

"I shall devise an explanation of some sort."

"Thank you." Relief filled her voice as she looked down at her plate again.

"However, neither of us will be able to avoid the matter for any great length of time. I can easily remedy your lack of a riding habit." The moment he made his offer, Phoebe mouth parted slight as her head jerked up and she stared at him in horror. A brief second later, every trace of emotion disappeared from her lovely features, except for a scornful contempt.

"I would just as soon wear a feed sack than accept such an offer from you."

The antipathy in her voice made Gideon frown. He'd actually been prepared for her to tell him where she shopped. That she had refused him so vehemently surprised him.

"I think you should seriously reconsider the offer, " he said with a smile of confidence.

"I'm well aware of what you would expect in return, and I must reiterate what I said last night. You must prepare yourself for disappointment where I'm concerned."

"Even if I believed I would fail in my intentions to have you in my bed, it has no bearing on the fact as to how difficult it is to outmaneuver, my mother. Once she seizes upon an idea, she rarely abandons it."

"I have every confidence you shall find a way to dissuade Lady Wrotham, just as I'm confident you will fail in your attempt to seduce me," Phoebe said coldly before she pointed to the folded London Times near his plate. "If you have no use for it, would you please hand me the paper?"

"I presume you wish to read the latest gossip to find an unsuspecting victim to hoodwink." Irritated by her scorn, Gideon arched his eyebrow as he offered the paper.

Phoebe's lips thinned with anger at his sardonic amusement. Once more, he was the recipient of a glare that would have inflicted deadly harm if her look had been a weapon. Suddenly, her mouth curved into a beguiling smile.

"Actually, I was curious as to when the next Currer Chronicles edition will be on the street. I would love to read more of Lord Chelmbee's adventures as he buzzes to his next unsuspecting flower."

Anger sliced through Gideon at her sweetly spoken jibe. He wasn't sure if it was because he didn't enjoy being reminded of Currer's mockery or the complacent amusement that had replaced Phoebe's disdain. With deliberation, he slowly shifted his position in his chair before standing up. Although her deliciously plump lips were still curved upward with glee, he saw her smile falter the moment he began to circle the table. In a split second, her smile vanished and alarm swept across her beautiful face. This time Gideon was the one with the smug smile. As she moved to rise from her seat, he quickly closed the distance between them to stand behind her. His hands pressed into her shoulders to keep her in her seat and prevent her escape. The shudder that vibrated off of her and into his hands made him laugh softly. Gideon bent over her, breathing in the faint smell of roses wafting off her skin.

His gaze drifted down to where her breasts were rising and falling at a rapid pace. The dark, narrow space between them made his mouth go dry at the thought of tasting her there before he worked his way down to the heat of her. A vivid image filled his head as he imagined her response as he pleasured her with his mouth. He wanted to hear her cry out his name until the white-hot heat of her flowed fast and tangy over his tongue.

The erotic image made his cock stir in his trousers as he brushed his mouth across her cheek. Phoebe gasped softly, and another tremor pulsed through her into his body. It caused a knot to form in his throat as he struggled not to roughly pull her out of her chair and into his arms. His mouth brushed across her soft, scented skin at the side of her neck, where he circled his tongue around the spot where her pulse was beating fast and furious.

Another whisper of sound escaped her, and he reveled in the way her body relaxed beneath his hands. Even though she was a social climber, she would be one of the most delightful creatures ever to enter his bed. He was certain of it. Gideon drank in her scent as he pressed his lips to her ear.

"Lord Chelmbee is already cultivating his next flower, my sweet Phoebe. A flower he'll enjoy picking when it's in full bloom."

"Oh, dear, God."

Her whisper was so faint, Gideon wasn't sure if he'd actually heard her speak or if his mind imagined what she was thinking. Behind him, the sound of his mother's voice made him quickly step back from Phoebe and head toward the door leading to the hallway. Gideon paused in the breakfast room doorway to look back at Phoebe. She was sitting rigid in her chair, staring straight ahead as if she were a statue. He called out her name softly, and she jerked her head toward him.

"I told you I enjoy a challenge, Phoebe. I believe this round is mine." Satisfaction sailed through Gideon as he saw her grow pale and alarmed just before he turned away and left the room.

His stride filled with energy, Gideon experienced a rush of satisfaction flooding his limbs as he made his way upstairs. Phoebe had clearly been aroused by his touch. If they'd been in a locked room, he would have had her beneath him the moment he'd locked the door. The image of taking her on the floor in the most hedonistic manner possible was an arousing one.

By the time he was done with her, Phoebe would feel the same torment he'd endured in the months following the passion they'd shared five years ago. The memory of the sleepless nights that had followed those few short moments in a moonlit garden and how she'd haunted his dreams ever since wasn't something he enjoyed admitting.

Despite the reluctant confession, it didn't make him any

less determined to have her in his bed while denying her the title she obviously craved. The woman would regret ever having crossed the Atlantic in search of a title. A quiet voice in the back of his head protested his condemnation of Phoebe.

Seconds ago, her reaction had brought back the memory of her five years ago, fragile, frighten, and in need of protection. The moment the thought filled Gideon's head, he crushed it as he remembered the anger that had exploded inside him when he'd discovered Phoebe was one of the American Dollar Princesses. Even worse was the devastating disillusion and disappointment that had accompanied his anger.

It had prompted him to visit Whitechapel in search of a bare-knuckle street fight. Gideon had been fortunate the man running the fight had chosen to put him in a hack and send him home, albeit half-dead. In the days that followed, he had argued savagely with himself as to whether he should call on Phoebe at Helstone Place.

A part of him had wanted to coldly denounce her for the social climber she was, while another part had debated how best to bring her to her knees until she was in his bed. He'd done neither, although he'd come close to doing so several weeks after their meeting. Then his great-grandmother had died, and he'd spent almost an entire year in Lichtenberg managing the large sum of wealth his great-grandmother had bequeathed to him. When he'd returned from Lichtenberg, he'd been home only a month when he was left reeling from Thomas's death.

He'd thrown himself into comforting his grieving mother and filling his days with his new responsibilities. Thoughts of Phoebe had been regulated to the back of his mind during the daylight hours. But his nights had been hellish ones. Sleepless nights and dreams of their bodies entwined. When Helstone had been murdered, Gideon had considered going to her. Instead, he'd told himself that she could lie in a bed of her own making.

The real reason had been altogether different. Deep inside, Gideon had known it would have taken little effort on Phoebe's part to bring him to heel until he'd made her his countess. The idea of tying himself to a woman who'd married him solely for his wealth and title was the last thing he would ever do.

Gideon grimaced at the memory. Nothing had changed in that respect. He still had no intention of granting her the title, Countess of Chelmsford. She was unworthy of being his countess. However, the role of mistress would suit her quite well.

Phoebe pressed her hand to her stomach in an effort to quell the butterflies, frantically alerting her to the danger she was in. She stiffened as she heard Lady Wrotham return to the dining room. As the woman sat down, Phoebe forced a smile to her lips. Eyebrows arched in curiosity, Alva glanced at Gideon's empty seat, Phoebe immediately offered up an explanation.

"I believe Lord Chelmsford said something about going to his club." She didn't have any idea where Gideon had gone, but her reply seemed a logical one. As long as he wasn't near her, she was safe.

"I had hoped he would have stayed simply to chat for a little while," Lady Wrotham said as a sly look. "What did the two of you discuss while I was away?"

"We spoke very little, although I have discovered he loathes P. Currer." Phoebe allowed a small smile to touch her lips as she took a drink of tea. The dowager marchioness laughed heartily at Phoebe's comment and nodded.

"Yes, I learned that the first time I referenced his

prominence in the publication." Lady Wrotham laughed again. "Tell me, are you one of the flowers who escaped Lord Chelmbee's penchant for buzzing about."

"Until last night, his lordship and I had only met once before. It was a brief encounter several years ago at a ball Lord Montjoy hosted," Phoebe replied quietly as she picked up the London Times where she'd dropped it the moment Gideon had toyed with her while his mother was out of the room. "I'm surprised Lord Chelmsford even remembered me."

"Oh my dear, do you truly think yourself forgettable?" Her employer gently remonstrated Phoebe for her remark. "You are a lovely woman, Phoebe. Any man would be hard-pressed not to try and win your heart."

Lady Wrotham's words sent an icy chill rolling over Phoebe's skin. Marriage offered a woman nothing and a man everything. She shook her head and forced a laugh past the knot trying to close her throat.

"I have no heart to win," she said. "I am like Mr. Currer's character, Lady Waddlestone. I shall never marry again."

"You cannot possibly mean that, Phoebe," Lady Wrotham gasped in dismay.

"Well, perhaps comparing myself to Lady Waddlestone is unwise. I think the woman's dramatic protestation that she'll never marry again was simply designed to ensure Lord Nitwitherspoon pursues her. So, naturally, that was enough incentive for Lord Pluckward to announce that he will succeed in convincing the poor woman to marry him before Nitwitherspoon does," Phoebe paused to lean forward and speak in a loud, conspiratorially whisper. "I cannot think of anything more unpleasant than listening to the man drone on about how his prize cock won in a faceoff with Lord Nitwitherspoon."

Laughter broke past marchioness's lips at Phoebe's remark. Relief made Phoebe breathe easier as her effort to distract the woman succeeded. Alva wagged her finger at

Phoebe in an admonishing gesture, while still laughing.

"You are just as shockingly wicked as Mr. Currer, my dear. Prize fowl indeed." Lady Wrotham released an unladylike snort. "We both know Currer is poking fun at Pickward and Witherspoon strutting around like prized roosters as they fight each other for Lady Waddlestone's affections."

"Ah, but are we certain that's what Currer is referring to? It's quite possible the man might have meant something far more base and intimate."

Phoebe smiled mischievously at Lady Wrotham, who stared at her in horrified dismay for a moment before the woman began to laugh until she was gasping from the strength of her laugher. After several moments, Lady Wrotham finally caught her breath, one hand pressed against her chest.

"My dear, Phoebe. I'm so glad you came to work with me. I've laughed more in the past three weeks than I have in a very long time." The marchioness leaned forward and clasped Phoebe's hand in hers. "I look forward to watching you put Gideon in his place when he's being particularly pig-headed."

Phoebe's stomach lurched at the woman's comment. The proposition of putting Gideon in his place was only asking for more trouble than she needed. When it came to a battle of wills with Gideon, Phoebe was certain she would lose far more often than she would win. Lady Wrotham tipped her head to one side and frowned with concern.

"Are you feeling all right, my dear?" The woman's question jolted Phoebe out of her thoughts, and she smiled. Not every skirmish between her and Gideon had to be verbal or limited to the page.

"Yes, I was simply thinking about the buffet for the charity ball. We still need floral arrangements for the food table. I thought roses might be the best choice. They should be readily available."

"An excellent idea, my dear." Lady Wrotham nodded her head. "The roses at Lethbridge Farm will be in full bloom. Gideon has won several prizes for his roses at the county fair."

"We could also have the baker create a large cake for our dessert. It could be festooned with dozens of marzipan flowers of all kinds." Phoebe paused for a moment, uncertain how her employer would react to her next suggestion. "We could even have the baker hide one or two bumblebees in the foliage."

"What a clever idea. I think we should add one or two small frogs, a few caterpillars, although Gideon is certain to point out that caterpillars are not always good for plants. Perhaps even a small bunny nibbling on a leaf?"

"I'll discuss it with the baker when I meet with him tomorrow," Phoebe said with a smile of satisfaction as she imagined Gideon's reaction when he saw the cake. . The man would be livid because he would know she'd deliberately arranged for the insect to be added to the cake.

"Excellent. There was something else I needed to tell you. What was it?" Alva frowned in concentration before she smiled mischievously. "Ah yes, I forgot to mention I saw Constance at the milliner's yesterday. She asked as to how the two of us were faring in each other's company. I told her that she could ask you at dinner this evening."

"Tonight?" Phoebe dragged air into her lungs that had suddenly stopped working as she saw the woman's determined expression.

"Yes, tonight. I know Constance is looking forward to seeing you, and I invited Baron Tuttle and the Duke of Aveley to join us, so I have an even number of guests."

"It's hardly suitable—"

"Of course it is. I also do not wish to have an odd number at the table," Alva said as she waved her hand in dismissal of Phoebe's objections. "I plan on seating you next to the Duke of Aveley. He's a delightful man. He will make some lucky woman a good husband."

"I'm certain he is, my lady, but it's inappropriate." Phoebe's stomach lurched as she remembered Gideon accusing her of being a social climber. She had no doubt he would believe she'd convinced the marchioness to include her in the evening's events.

"Balderdash, my dear." Alva shook her head as she scolded Phoebe. "I wouldn't dream of leaving you out. Although we've only known each other for a short time, I have become quite fond of you, my dear."

"And I, you, my lady." Phoebe sighed softly, determined not to become any more attached to the woman than she already was. "While I am grateful for being treated as an equal, others will not view me in the same light."

"Why ever not?" Alva exclaimed in amazement. "You are a viscountess. If someone should treat you otherwise, they shall answer to me."

Phoebe's heart sank as she looked at the marchioness's indignant expression. It was impossible to tell her employer of Gideon's low opinion of her. Even if the woman believed her, Lady Wrotham loved her son dearly, and Phoebe could not imagine the disappointment the woman would feel. She bit down on her lip as she tried to think of something that would allow her to reject the invitation. Lady Wrotham reached out to touch Phoebe's hand.

"I can almost see your mind spinning trying to find a way to refuse me, but I won't let you," Alva said firmly. "I'll have your promise that you will join us for dinner this evening, Phoebe."

Phoebe had witnessed Lady Wrotham's tenacious trait several times as they'd worked together organizing the gala when it came to how she wanted to the event to be handled. But except for the day at Constance's home, the marchioness had never made it her mission to persuade Phoebe to do attend any social gathering.

Granted, Alva had not hosted a dinner party since she'd become the woman's secretary, but Phoebe had the distinct impression Lady Wrotham was playing matchmaker. The thought made her heart pound wildly in her chest at the idea of Alva throwing her in Gideon's path all the time.

When the marchioness arched her eyebrows expectantly, Phoebe realized it was pointless to argue. Alva was clearly not about to let the matter go until she had her own way. Phoebe released a soft sigh as reluctantly gave way to the woman's dogged demand. A voice whispered in her head that Gideon had inherited his mother's firm resolve when it came to having his own way as well. God help her if his tenaciousness matched or surpassed his mother's.

"Very well, I will come," she answered. Immediately, Alva smiled with delight.

"Thank you."

Satisfied with Phoebe's promise, the marchioness returned to the topic of the gala and began to review the guest list for the charity ball. Her employer's voice became a quiet murmur in Phoebe's ear as she became distracted with the question of which of her gowns would be suitable for the evening. She only had one or two dresses she could think of that were appropriate, but they were at least three years old and hopelessly outdated.

Phoebe's heart sank at the thought. She was going to look horribly out-of-place tonight, and no doubt Gideon would use the opportunity to mock her. She was beginning to bitterly regret allowing the marchioness to convince her to attend the evening's dinner party. While she could use her lack of a suitable dress as a reason to beg off making an appearance this evening, she knew better. The marchioness would stop everything and whisk her off to the dressmaker's.

As her looked down at the newspaper beside her plate, Phoebe's heart clenched tightly in her breast. She loved working with Lady Wrotham, but it had become painfully obvious she needed to leave Chelmsford House as soon as possible. Failure to do so would be disastrous.

Chapter 7

Phoebe froze at the bottom of the stairs as she heard the hum of conversation drifting out of the salon. One hand on the stairway balustrade, she wanted to turn around and hurry back up the stairs to her room. She could always send word that she had taken ill. A quiet tread on the stairs behind her made Phoebe spin around on her heel to see Gideon descending the stairs.

Her heart skipped a beat at the sight of him. The man was devastating, even when frowning. The dinner jacket and tie he wore was in the style made fashionable by the Prince of Wales several years earlier. Before he reached the foot of the stairs, she quickly stepped back, out of reach. She had yet to recover from this morning's encounter in the breakfast room.

Gideon's held her gaze as he descended the stairs and reached the foyer. In a lazy move, he rested his elbow on the flat curl of the bannister and folded his hands together. He looked completely relaxed as he leaned against the post. Despite the nonchalant pose, his stance was that of a predator contemplating how much he would enjoy his evening feast.

Phoebe's heart slammed into her chest as she knew exactly what kind of meal it would be. He would devour every inch of her with his mouth and hands—his entire body. The thought made every muscle in her body tighten. With just one look, the man could make her crave his touch.

The sensitive spot between her legs contracted in reaction to the erotic thoughts suddenly flowing through her head. Vivid images of her body entwined with his made her draw in a quick breath, which she quickly swallowed before drawing in another one. Dear God, she was mad to be imagining such things. Gideon's studied her intently as a small smile of derision touched his lips.

"So, you managed to secure an invitation to the table this evening." The condescension in his voice rankled, and Phoebe stiffened.

"I did *not* ask to be invited. I tried to refuse, but as you said this morning, Lady Wrotham can be quite determined when she's determine to have her own way."

"No doubt," he murmured satirically. Skepticism darkened his face, and Phoebe thought she saw a flash of disappointment there as well. "Although I find it difficult to believe you put up much of a protest as it's obvious you've dressed for battle this evening."

"Battle?" Startled, she blinked in confused surprise.

"If you thought to capture my attention, you have it. But I am surprised you decided to launch a counter-attack so quickly."

"Your—I *did not* dress to catch your eye, you arrogant beast," she hissed with disgust at his assumption. "This is the only gown—"

An eyebrow arched in surprise, Gideon eyed her with curiosity as she abruptly stopped speaking. Humiliation made her cheeks grow warm with embarrassment as Phoebe realized that for a second time today, she'd referred to her limited wardrobe. All too aware of his suspicious nature where she was concerned, the man most likely thought she hoped to secure a new dress from him. It was the last thing she would accept from any man, *especially* the Earl of Chelmsford.

He knew nothing about her. The man had judged her and found her wanting. She was tired of allowing others to make her feel small when they were no better or less than her. Worst of all, his poor opinion of her troubled her far more deeply than she wanted it to. The fact that he believed she was capable of marrying for money and position cut deep. It left her feeling as vulnerable and exposed as the night he'd made love to her.

"I'm disappointed," he said with a smile that made her heart skip a beat.

"I don't understand." She tipped her head to one side and scowled at him, and Gideon chuckled.

"I'm disappointed you didn't think of me while preparing for the evening." His smug comment angered Phoebe, and she eyed him with antipathy for a moment, then smiled.

"Oh, but I did, my lord," she said with cloying sweetness. "I thought about you a great deal."

"Ahh, and exactly *what* did you think about me, my sweet Phoebe? I hope your thoughts were pleasant ones."

"They were indeed. I plotted several different ways to bring about your demise, Lord Chelmbee."

Phoebe smiled cheerfully at the way he stiffened the moment she used the name she'd given him in the Currer Chronicles. With glee, she found herself warming to her success at verbally pricking his pride.

"And pray tell, what method did you settle on, Phoebe?" Something in his quiet question said she might pay a price if she continued to taunt him, but Phoebe was enjoying the fact that she'd managed to get under his skin.

"Well, Lord Chelmbee, I thought it would be amusing to tie you to a tree, drench you in honey, and wait for whatever animal arrived to feast on your limbs."

Irritation tightened his lips as she mocked him again with his nickname. Delighted with his reaction, she couldn't help the quiet laugh that blew past her lips. He truly loathed the nickname P. Currer had given him. The man would be livid by the time she was finished lampooning him in the next installment.

Phoebe had already begun the next chapter in the serial. She would have to come up with something even more disdainful than what was already on paper. In the back of her mind, a small voice warned her to take care. If he were ever to discover she was the author of the satirical chronicles, his reaction would be far from pleasant. Still, it was impossible not to enjoy his response to the volley of barbed words she'd inflicted on his pride.

The man deserved to be taken down a notch or two for arrogantly believing she'd dressed to please him. The mocking laughter echoing loudly in her head voice reminded her how she'd wished for something more fashionable to wear this evening. Phoebe quickly and blithely dismissed the thought. It was her vanity, nothing more, that had made her long for a new dress. She certainly hadn't wanted to impress her nemesis.

Gideon watched her closely, and the irritation on his handsome features made her choke back another laugh. Suddenly a wolfish smile curved his mouth. It instantly put her on her guard. The man was a formidable opponent when it came to verbal taunts. She had held her ground so far, but her ability to launch rapid salvos of scorn in his direction was limited when they were standing opposite one another. In a battle of wits, she was far better equipped to injure his pride with her pen than in a verbal exchange.

His movements were deceptively unhurried as he straightened to his full height and took a step toward her. Phoebe steeled herself not to take a step backward as he closed the small space between them. But, the instant mere inches separated them, she realized her mistake. Bergamot and pine flooded her senses, and she swallowed hard at how wonderful he smelled.

How was this man capable of overwhelming her faculties every time he came near her? He had managed to overpower her senses just as easily this morning in the breakfast room. Every inch of her was alive and craving something she knew better than to even consider satisfying.

Gideon lightly brushed his fingers across her mouth,

then traced a slow, barely discernible path down her throat and across her breastbone to the valley between her breasts. The feathery caress caused her heart to skid out of control. Her breathing had become unsteady, and his rakish smile became one of triumph.

"I like the way you respond to my touch, Phoebe," he whispered in a seductively wicked voice that threatened to bring her to her knees. If they'd been alone, she was certain she would be in his arms. His fingertips glided along the edge of her bodice. "I like the idea of dipping *you* in honey and listening to you whimper with need as I take my time sweeping my tongue over every inch of you. I can just imagine how honey would make that small bud between your legs even more succulent."

Decadent and fiery, his words created an image in her head that tightened her body and made her ache with longing for him to do precisely as he described. Her breathing hitched at her body's reaction to him, and she struggled not to give way to the white-hot heat of desire flowing through her blood. It was a need that was pushing her to the edge of a precipice she knew would cause her downfall.

"Shall I kiss you now, Phoebe, or should I wait until tonight when we're alone."

His soft question made her sway slightly on her feet, and Gideon's hands grasped her arms to steady her. A soft laugh sounded in her ear. It was the sound of a man who believed he was about to conquer new territory. The man was even more dangerous than she'd thought. With just a few words, he had brought her to the brink of surrender.

The thought made her gasp in horror. Dear God, she hadn't even uttered a single protest. The realization made her tug free of his light grasp and quickly darted past him. As much as she wanted to avoid the parlor, she wanted to escape Gideon even more. A strong hand caught her by the arm to pull her to an abrupt halt. Phoebe turned her head to glare at him.

"Unhand me," she snapped.

"I'll escort you into the parlor."

"*No, thank you.* The only thing I want from you, Lord Chelmsford, is for you to stay away from me."

"I don't think I can do that, Phoebe."

The husky note in his voice made her inhale a shallow breath. It became impossible to turn away from him, and her heart skipped a beat as she thought she saw his steely gaze soften. She blinked in surprise, before jeering laughter in her head made her flinch. To the Earl of Chelmsford, she was just another woman to seduce. With great difficulty she managed to swallow the knot closing off her throat.

"I fear you will be sadly disappointed trying to make sport of me, my lord."

As if she'd hit him, Gideon pulled away from her in a sharp movement. For a brief instant, she could have sworn she saw pained regret darken his eyes, but it disappeared so fast she dismissed. He didn't reply, but simply offered her a polite bow. Phoebe whirled away from him, she walked quickly toward the salon doorway. The moment she entered the room, Lady Wrotham saw her, and with a smile, the dowager moved quickly to Phoebe's side.

"There you are, my dear. I had begun to think you might renege on your promise."

"I'm sorry I'm late, my lady." Phoebe didn't explain why she'd been delayed, and the marchioness didn't ask. Instead, she pulled Phoebe over to where Constance was standing with two men.

"Constance, look who has finally arrived." At Lady Wrotham's exclamation, Lady Lyndham turned her head and smiled with delight.

"Phoebe, how wonderful to see you." The other woman said with a warm smile. Her new friend clasped Phoebe's hands in hers and leaned forward to kiss Phoebe on both cheeks. "You look wonderful."

"Thank you."

It was impossible not to smile at the countess's warm greeting, and it had a calming effect on Phoebe's nerves. For the first time, the qualms she'd had at having allowed the marchioness to persuade her to attend the small gathering began to ebb. Alva swiftly introduced Phoebe to Constance's brother and husband before she excused herself. Constance's brother, the Earl of Melton, and her friend's husband, Lord Lyndham, were as welcoming as her new friend.

Constance was teasing her brother about a recent incident with his youngest child when Alva returned with a gentleman at her side. As she stopped in front of Phoebe, the marchioness touched Phoebe's arm for a brief instant before turning her head toward the handsome man next to her.

"Duke, have you met Lady Helstone?" Alva asked as she made a small sweep of her hand in Phoebe's direction.

"I regret I've not had the pleasure," the duke shook his head at Lady Wrotham's question, and with a smile, he stepped forward to take Phoebe's hand. Alva smiled happily as she introduced Phoebe to the duke.

"Then I'm delighted to present Viscountess Helstone. Phoebe, this is His Grace, the Duke of Aveley."

"Good evening, Your Grace," Phoebe murmured a greeting as the duke bowed and brushed her fingers with his lips.

"The pleasure is all mine," the man said quietly as he smiled with open appreciation at Phoebe.

"I thought you might take Phoebe into dinner this evening, Duke." Alva's conspicuous satisfaction made Phoebe's heart slam into her chest. She'd been right to think Lady Wrotham was intent on playing matchmaker.

"I can think of nothing more delightful than having Lady Helstone on my arm at *any* time of the day or night." The man's quiet compliment sent heat rising in Phoebe's cheeks.

She returned his warm smile while Lady Wrotham set off to see to another guest.

"Her ladyship is obviously quite fond of you," the duke said as he studied Phoebe with curiosity. "I'm disappointed she's not introduced us until now. Are you long-time friends?"

"We met…several years ago. I've been…I've been helping the marchioness with plans for the gala benefiting St. Catherine's Home for the Poor." Phoebe stumbled over her words as she tried not to explain her role at Chelmsford House without making herself appear as though she were a charity cause the marchioness had taken on.

"Lady Wrotham says she's been of immense assistance in organizing the ball," Constance spoke up quickly as if instinctively knowing Phoebe was struggling for an explanation.

"Indeed, then I'm envious of the time her ladyship has spent in your company, my lady."

The duke's words sent another rush of heat into Phoebe's cheeks just as the back of her neck began to tingle. Without thinking, she glanced over her shoulder to see Gideon walk into the salon. Butterflies fluttered wildly in her stomach at the sight of him, and she quickly looked away before he realized she was watching him. Her reaction emphasized how dangerous the man was to her senses, not to mention her heart, if she did not take care.

A small shiver streaked through her as she remembered their exchange in the entryway. Beside her, Constance touched her arm in a silent query. With a small shake of her head, Phoebe gave her friend a smile of reassurance. Constance's brother and husband both smiled broadly at someone behind her, and Phoebe knew there was only one person it could be. The countess immediately turned to greet Gideon with a hug. As Constance released him, Gideon bowed in Phoebe's direction as if nothing had passed between them in the foyer.

"Lady Helstone," he murmured before shaking the

duke's hand. "Good evening, Your Grace."

"Happy to see you again, Chelmsford. I understand you just returned from Amsterdam."

"Yesterday evening, as a matter-of-fact."

"I take it your trip was successful in terms of your interest in horticulture?" the duke asked with a look of keen interest.

"Quite," Gideon said with a look of almost childish excitement. "I met with Willem Ruigrok, who gave me insight into how to improve the cultivation of my tulip beds at Lethbridge Hall."

"Good heavens," Constance said with a laugh. "While I'm certain Sebastian, and possibly even Lucien, is interested in the topic, Phoebe and I shall abstain from discussing the finer points of gardening,"

"As usual, you retreat when my favorite topic for discussion arises, Constance," Gideon chuckled as he smiled at the countess.

"I have listened to you wax poetic about gardening far too many times in the past to feel remorse at leaving you now, Gideon." Constance shook her head in amused disgust. "Come along, Phoebe. We will leave them to discuss plants to their heart's delight."

"Surely, you will allow Lady Helstone to have a say as to whether she goes or stays, Constance," Gideon said as his eyebrow arched upward. Gray eyes glittered with mockery as he silently challenged Phoebe to remain behind. His cynical amusement as he dared her to stay made Phoebe's spine stiffen with irritation. Before she could reply, the duke added his protest as well.

"I heartily agree with Chelmsford. While our topic is gardening, I am enjoying your company, Lady Helstone. There are some flowers one cannot find in a garden." At the duke's enthusiasm, Gideon's firm mouth thinned slightly with contempt as he eyed her with cold cynicism. All too aware of his opinion of her, Phoebe deliberately focused her attention on the duke and smiled warmly at him.

"Unfortunately, I've never been much of a gardener as I'm highly allergic to bees. So I'm afraid I would have little to offer to the conversation."

The moment Gideon's body stiffened, she smiled sweetly at him. The Earl of Chelmsford obviously didn't like being stung. Something indefinable darkened his expression as he bowed slightly in her direction.

"Duly noted, my lady. However, the duke is correct. Not all beautiful flowers are found in a garden."

There was a wicked note of sin in his voice that caressed her skin until she felt almost feverish. She pulled in a ragged breath as she remained transfixed beneath Gideon's mocking amusement. As if from a great distance, she heard someone speaking. Dismay spiraled through her at the ease with which Gideon had enthralled her. Phoebe jerked her attention away from him and turned back to the duke.

"Agreed, we are in the company of not just one, but two beautiful flowers," the duke said with a cheerful grin. Beside her, Constance laughed and nodded in the direction of her husband, who was listening attentively to the banter. Although the earl's appearance said he was amused, Lord Lyndham's voice indicated a possessiveness as he stared at his wife.

"You are flirting with a happily married woman, Duke." Constance laughed as the man grinned at her. "Come along, Phoebe. We shall leave the men to their discussion of plants."

"I believe I will join you, my love," the earl said as he stepped outside the small circle. "While I'm certain the conversation would be enlightening, there are some flowers one does not leave untended for too long."

Male laughter accompanied Lord Lyndham's comment, and Constance blushed as she shot her husband a look of exasperation. Her reaction did not go unnoticed, and the men laughed harder.

"Besides, Gideon's current flower obsession is tulips. I

doubt he has any new gardening techniques that would apply to the care of my rosebuds," Lord Lyndham said with a small smile. "You know I'm quite skilled when it comes to ensuring they are tended to with great care."

Constance's cheeks grew darker with color, and the earl smiled complacently. The men grinned as they watched the couple's verbal exchange, but there was a look of confusion on their faces. Certain the earl's remarks held an intimate meaning for Constance, who was clearly flustered, Phoebe took a quick step forward to slip her arm through the countess's.

"I believe we were going to leave the men to their gardening discussion, and I've yet to say hello to your aunt," Phoebe said with a smile. Constance nodded as she narrowed her gaze at her husband.

"If you intend to join us Lord Lyndham, I do not wish to hear anything else about rosebuds."

Her irritable tone made the earl chuckle, but the small bow he made in his wife's direction appeared to satisfy Lady Lyndham. With another glare of exasperation at her husband, the three of them crossed the room to join Lady Stewart and the marchioness. After several minutes, Constance leaned into Phoebe's side with a conspiratorial smile.

"I do believe you've captured the Duke's interest, Phoebe. Even Gideon seems enthralled with you."

"You exaggerate." Phoebe released a small sound of skepticism as she shook her head. Constance glanced toward the three men across the room and shook her head.

"No, I'm not. In fact, I'm not uncertain which one of them has been glancing in our direction the most since we left them to their conversation about gardening." The countess smiled with cheerful delight. "Gideon, in particular, seems unable to stop following your every move. Although the duke is equally intrigued."

"That, I sincerely doubt." Phoebe laughed with an

amusement she didn't feel, and Constance eyed her with curiosity.

"Why would you think otherwise?" At her friend's question, Phoebe rolled her shoulders in a small shrug.

"Lord Chelmsford thinks I am taking advantage of his mother's generosity."

"What?" Constance gasped softly as she pulled Phoebe out of hearing distance from her aunt and the marchioness. "What in heaven's name would make the man even think such a thing?"

"It's of no consequence," Phoebe murmured as she saw Constance's husband studying his wife intently, his mouth tight with irritation.

"Of course it is," Constance whispered. "I'm flabbergasted Gideon would think badly of you."

"I care little as to Lord Chelmsford's opinion of me. However, I intend to find other employment to avoid causing a rift between the marchioness and her son. I found several possibilities in the Times this afternoon and will post a response to them in the morning." Phoebe's words caused a look of distress to settle on Constance's features.

"Oh, but you mustn't leave, " the countess exclaimed beneath her breath. "I know Gideon can be stubborn, but he's a good man. I'm certain the two of you are perfect for each other."

At her friend's firm declaration, Phoebe stared at the woman in horror, then jumped at the sound of the earl, clearing his throat beside her. Phoebe darted a look in his direction, and his anger was plainly visible. Constance frowned then tipped her chin upward in a display of defiance.

As the couple glared at each other, Pendleton stepped into the room to announce dinner. Phoebe released a small breath of relief as she stepped away from the couple, who were dueling silently with each other. Lady Wrotham had already paired off her guests, and Phoebe smiled at the duke as he strode quickly in her direction. Gideon took a step toward her as well, but as if suddenly realizing the duke was headed for Phoebe, he stopped in mid-stride.

From across the distance separating them, her heart sank at the disparaging look on Gideon's face. As the duke halted in front of her and offered his arm to her, Phoebe forced a smile to her lips and allowed the man to lead her into dinner. As they walked out of the parlor, the back of her neck tingled, and she knew Gideon was watching her.

She was relatively certain what he was thinking at this very moment. His contempt for her was obvious. The man had convinced himself that she'd thrown herself at the duke. Of course, she'd done nothing of the sort, but if the Earl of Chelmsford thought she was a ne'er-do-well, so be it. Despite having resisted the idea of attending the dinner party, Phoebe decided to enjoy herself before she left Chelmsford House for good.

Chapter 8

The silence in the carriage was fraught with tension, and Constance stared out the window, her body stiff and unmoving. Beside her, Lucien had not spoken a word to her since overhearing her conversation with Phoebe. She should have known better than to say anything to her friend about Gideon with Lucien present, but she'd been so startled by Phoebe's decision to find another position, she'd spoken without thinking.

Now the question was how to deal with Lucien. It was apparent he was angry with her for meddling. While she knew how much he disliked her interfering in the lives of her friends. Phoebe was different. If Lucien knew the circumstances the woman had been in when Constance had found her in Madame Sabine's shop, she was confident she could make him see helping Phoebe had been the right decision.

The carriage rocked to a halt, and Lucien stepped out of the carriage, then offered his hand to assist her out of the vehicle. Almost immediately, he dropped her hand, and a vise tightened around her chest. He was angrier than she'd realized. The moment they entered the house, Lucien handed his hat and gloves to Carleton in several sharp movements, then disappeared into the library. Constance hesitated as she considered following him. Instead, she decided to let his anger subside before they spoke.

The memory of their argument two months ago made her wince. No, the best course of action was to leave Lucien be until his anger subsided. But, heaven help her if she were to confess in an argument that she'd deliberately invoked the *an dara sealladh* for the express purpose of learning more about Lady Helstone.

Constance sighed as she slowly climbed the stairs. For not the first time, she wished she'd held her tongue this evening. Although she didn't like to hide things from Lucien, there were times when she did so simply because it was the best thing for their marriage. Daisy, her lady's maid, was waiting for her when she entered her room. With a smile, the young woman helped Constance out of her evening gown.

"Did you have a nice time, my lady?"

"I did," she replied quietly, then sighed. "At least I did until I managed to upset Lord Lyndham."

"Oh, dear, my lady. Does this mean you've had a falling out?"

"I'm afraid so, but I'm certain he will forgive me eventually," Constance said quietly, but she heard the lack of conviction in her voice.

The door to the corridor between her and Lucien's room opened as Daisy was helping her slip on her robe. Anger made the scar on her husband's cheek stand out more prominently than usual. Constance quickly dismissed Daisy as she tightened the sash of her robe. She had expected Lucien to rain fire down on her head the moment they were alone, but he remained silent as he studied her.

Worried she might say something cruel as she had the last time they'd fought, Constance didn't say a word as she sank down onto the stool in front of her dressing table. Instead, she kept her eye on Lucien in the mirror, and when he still didn't speak, she became uneasy. Even though Lucien no longer believed in the Blakemore curse, she knew it was always in the back of his mind.

For years he'd believed his anger would be the catalyst for harming someone he loved. Logically, he might understand the curse didn't exist, but Constance knew it was always something he considered when he became angry. Had her actions where Phoebe was concerned aroused such deep anger in Lucien that he was afraid to speak to her?

Deciding it was best to wait until he spoke, Constance reached for a bottle of emollient. She would bite her tongue until he finished expressing his displeasure. Afterward, she would try to explain what she'd seen. Constance dropped her head for a moment as she opened the glass bottle and dipped her fingers into the cream. Surprised Lucien hadn't spoken yet, she glanced in the mirror as she rubbed the emollient into her hands. Instead of seeing her husband glowering at her, she saw the door to the corridor between their rooms, closing quietly behind him.

Stunned, she stared at the closed door. Lucien had shut himself off emotionally to her several times since they'd first met. But the only other time he'd ever walked away from her had been the day he'd discovered she was pregnant with Isabel. Inside her chest, her heart ached as if someone had tried to yank it out of her. How was she going to heal the breach between them this time? A soft knock on her bedroom door made her grant entry with a quietly spoken invitation.

She continued to stare at the door Lucien had just passed through until Constance heard her bedroom door closed. With a slight jerk, she turned toward the sound. Aurora Blakemore, Dowager Countess of Lyndham, stood just inside the room, studying Constance with the same piercing blue eyes her grandson possessed.

Powdery white hair piled atop her head in a soft-shaped bun that flattered her regal features, Lucien's grandmother was a tall woman. She was almost the same height as her grandson. Despite a difficult illness a month ago, her gaze was still bright with energy. Constance's deep love for the older woman had developed before she and Lucien were married.

As the long-time matriarch of the Lyndham family, the

woman had become as dear to Constance as the Rockwood family matriarch, Aunt Matilda. Opinionated, and as stubborn as her grandson, Lady Lyndham had been Constance's staunchest supporter from the first moment they'd met at Lyndham Keep. When the dowager had become sick several weeks ago, Constance had lovingly tended to the older woman for more than a week.

Not even when Lucien had demanded Constance rest had she left the dowager's side. It wasn't until the dowager had recovered enough to regally command Constance rest, that she'd agreed to leave the woman's side. Lucien had been as worried as Constance, and the two of them had taken turns watching over the woman through the night until Lady Lyndham's fever had abated.

Although it was apparent she'd still not regained all her strength, the dowager's ability to fill a room with her presence had not diminished. Blue-veined hands resting on the eagle's head that sat on top of her cane, Aurora studied Constance in silence for a moment. The dowager's brow furrowed with either worry or discomfort as she pointed to one of the chairs at the fireplace.

"May I, my dear?"

"Of course, Grandmama. I wasn't thinking," Constance exclaimed as she quickly sprang to her feet to go to the elderly lady's side. The dowager waved her away.

"I'm not a fragile piece of china, Constance. I'm simply old," Lucien's grandmother snapped. The sharp comment made Constance flinch, and the dowager reached out to squeeze her hand.

"Forgive me, dearest. I become frustrated when my body refuses to do what I wish it to do."

"Of course." Constance smiled as she kissed the papery skin on the dowager countess's cheek.

"I was in the library when you and Lucien returned from Lady Wrotham's affair. The boy barely greeted me, threw down two glasses of whiskey, then stalked out of the room with a brusque goodnight that was more of a snarl."

Disapproval gave the dowager's voice a hard edge, and Constance had the sensation of a being a butterfly a lepidopterist had pinned to board. The older woman sighed and shook her head.

"What happened between the two of you this evening?"

"He overheard something that angered him."

"Shall I guess? You used your gift to help someone who didn't ask for your assistance."

The pointed question made Constance feel as if she were a child again, standing in front of Sebastian, who was chastising her for something. She nodded her head slowly, and the dowager countess released another quiet sigh.

"Since you went to Chelmsford House, I assume Lady Helstone is the individual in question?"

"Yes." At her reply, Aurora nodded sagely while absently playing with the strand of pearls around her neck.

"As I recall, when the young woman was here for tea a few weeks ago, she became very upset when you recommended her as a personal secretary to Lady Wrotham."

"Phoebe was working for Madame Sabine, and I knew the marchioness needed someone." Constance shook her head as she remembered her friend's living quarters. "I knew Lucien would think me meddling again, but I had no choice."

"So your aunt *was* correct. Lucien *did* order you not to interfere in the affairs of others."

"It was wrong of him to do so," Constance exclaimed fiercely. "I am discreet when I do anything that Lucien refers to as meddling, but he won't listen to me. Whenever the *an dara sealladh* shows me something, it's impossible for me to simply ignore it as if nothing has happened."

"The two of you have been quarreling about your gift from the first day he found you at the keep cataloging those blasted antiquities of his."

"I'm not sure I would call it quarreling," Constance said in a bleak tone as she remembered Lucien walking out of the room just a short time ago.

"*Well*, what *do* you call it?" Aurora said in a no-nonsense tone that possessed a hint of laughter in her voice. "This isn't the first marital spat the two of you have had, nor will it be the last. William and I had many disagreements when he was alive, and we always mended the rift between us."

"This is different. While you were ill, we had a terrible row in front of the family." Constance sighed with regret. "I said some hurtful things I can never take back."

"We both know how stubborn the boy can be. *that* he inherited from his mother." Lady Lyndham frowned. Constance made a soft sound as she choked back a laugh. Aurora arched an eyebrow as she silently demanded Constance explain her amusement. Unable to help herself, she laughed.

"I think there are quite a few close relatives he inherited his stubborn nature from." Constance smiled at the woman.

"Harrumph," the dowager uttered softly.

Constance laughed again as she arched her eyebrows at the older woman. As a small smile tipped the corners of her mouth upward, the dowager countess's features relaxed slightly.

"We were discussing Lady Helstone, not my tenacious nature," Lady Lyndham said firmly, although there was a distinct trace of amusement in her voice. "The fact that you were willing to arouse Lucien's wrath to encourage the marchioness to hire Lady Helstone as an assistant tells me there is more to the story than my grandson knows."

"Exactly. I'm certain if Lucien would just listen, I could make him understand." Anger swept through Constance as she remembered what she'd seen in her vision. "Several weeks ago, we were at Madame Sabine's for Louisa to try on her wedding dress. That's when I discovered Lady Helstone was working as Sabine's bookkeeper."

"Bookkeeper?" Aurora frowned in surprise. "Surely, Helstone didn't leave the poor woman destitute."

"I can only assume that is the case given what the *an dara sealladh* showed me. Her living conditions were horrendous, Grandmama. I couldn't simply walk away and leave her to suffer." Constance flinched at the memory of Phoebe's terrible living conditions.

"Did you explain any of this to Lucien?"

"He hasn't given me the chance to. He's furious with me. I tried to broach the matter with him on the way home. He refused to discuss it and didn't say a word in the carriage on the way home, and he went straight to the library when we entered the house."

Constance fought off tears as she remembered the cold silence between them on the way home. Even more devastating was how he'd walked out of her room several moments ago without a single word. She shook her head as she saw the dowager's concerned look. The elderly woman shook her head in obvious frustration.

"I know the boy accepts the *an dara sealladh* is a part of who you are, but we both know it unsettles him, despite his support of you assisting those who *do* ask for your help."

"I know that," Constance rubbed her forehead in an attempt to ease the headache she'd suddenly developed. "And I know I meddle more than I should, but ever since that terrible business with Oliver…"

The dowager countess focused on her attention on her gnarled fingers that gripped the brass eagle head of her cane. Constance instinctively knew the elderly woman was remembering those terrible hours leading up to the moment when Jamie had been about to be sacrificed by a madman and Constance's own brush with death as she tried to save her son. Aurora lifted her head to look at Constance.

"It was a terrible time for you and Jamie—for all of us.

You've never said so, but I believe it also made you fear someone might come to harm if you didn't act on your visions."

The older woman's words made Constance start as she met the dowager countess's steady, blue-eyed gaze. There was understanding and deep affection on the dowager's face that warmed Constance's heart as she nodded her confirmation.

"I *do* feel obligated to use my gift in helping others. If I ignored my gift and what the *an dara sealladh* shows me, it would be reprehensible. It would be no less criminal than if I were to stand by and simply watch someone drown when I might have been able to save them." Constance paused for a second before a rueful smile tugged at her lips. "But we both know that is not always the case. After all, I am a reckless Rockwood."

"Reckless? No, my dear, impulsive is a far better word. Reckless implies you have little regard for others. You and your family *are not* thoughtless, uncaring people. On the contrary, you are quite the opposite."

"Perhaps," Constance shrugged slightly. "But reckless or impulsive, I cannot deny that my behavior is often frustrating for Lucien. I am certain I can be quite trying for him at times."

"And I know my grandson is far from being a saint," Aurora said with an ironic twist of her lip before she sighed. "He is a proud, stubborn man, but Lucien loves you deeply, Constance."

"I love him just as much, Grandmama. Sometimes it frightens me how much I love him." Constance drew in a deep breath, then released it. "We argue so seldom, and when we do, I'm miserable until we resolve our differences."

"Then we must make Lucien understand how the past changed you, changed all of us, and why you must act on your visions whether or not someone asks for your help. The boy needs to understand life is still a mystery no matter how illogical it may seem."

"What you suggest is easier said than done, Grandmama." Constance choked out a small sound of amusement.

"Perhaps, but we *will* find a way to make the boy understand he must be more accommodating in his expectations where your gift is concerned." The old woman made a small noise of exasperation.

The sound made Constance's lips twitch. Lucien would no doubt receive an earful from his grandmother at the next opportune moment. The dowager countess slowly rose from her seat. Despite her age, she was an indomitable woman when it came to setting things to right where her loved ones were concerned.

"Come along, my darling girl, kiss me good night. It is way past my bedtime." Despite the crisp, blunt manner, there a warm affection in Aurora's voice as Constance rose to kiss the woman's weathered cheek.

"Shall I walk you to your room, Grandmama?"

"There's no need, child, but you are thoughtful to ask." Aurora patted Constance's hand before making her way to the door. As the dowager countess opened the door, she looked over her shoulder at her. "Lucien will not stay angry with you for long, Constance. Go to him, and see if you can heal the divide between you before it widens."

As the old woman closed the bedroom door behind her, Constance turned around to stare at the door leading into the short corridor between her room and Lucien's. Her confidence wasn't as strong as her husband's grandmother when it came to Lucien's ability not to remain angry with her. In the past several months, he'd become increasingly irritated when she interfered in the lives of family friends. Ophelia and Mathias had been more Louisa's doing than hers, but Lucien knew she'd been involved.

In the past, she'd always been able to convince him that acting on her visions had been for the good of others. But that had become increasingly difficult to do. Things had come to a head two months ago when she'd advised Lady Reigate to reconsider accepting Lord Shively's proposal. Constance hadn't had a vision about the couple. She'd simply sensed the two belonged together.

A few days later, she and Lucien had hosted the family at Lyndham House for dinner. They were all to attend a play at the Lyceum later that evening. While the women waited on the men to finish their port before joining them in the salon, Constance had discussed Lady Reigate with Patience. She'd not heard the men coming from the dining room, and Lucien had overheard the tail end of her conversation with her sister about Lady Reigate's indecision about Lord Shively.

Lucien had immediately expressed his disapproval, and Constance remembered saying something cavalier in reply. Seconds later, they were arguing in front of everyone. It had been a terrible quarrel. Lucien had actually forbidden her to interfere in the lives of others again, unless specifically requested to do so. His autocratic manner was out of character for him where she was concerned, and she'd been too stunned for a moment to say anything.

It was the first time he'd ever tried to dictate her behavior, and the moment she recovered from her astonishment, anger had driven all reasonable thought from her head. Constance's heart twisted in her chest at the memory of her vicious words that night. Even her family had gasped as she'd accused Lucien of being just like her first husband, Graham. Perhaps worst of all, she'd questioned his love for her.

Lucien's stricken reaction had given her little pause before she'd stormed out of the salon, declaring she was no longer feeling up to attending the theater. Patience had followed her to her room in an effort to coax Constance into apologizing to Lucien, but she'd been adamant in her refusal to even speak with him.

It wasn't until hours later, when she'd woken up in a cold bed, that she thought her heart would break. It was the first time they'd gone to bed angry with one another, and she'd been miserable. It had taken her more than an hour to work up her courage to go to Lucien's room and apologize.

Her words had cut deep, and it had taken time to convince Lucien that she'd flung her accusations at him out of anger and nothing more. Not once since they'd married had Lucien ever made her feel as if he was ashamed of her for being different.

Although her husband might not like her ability to speak to the dead or see small glimpses of the past and future, Lucien had demonstrated on far too many occasions that he understood the *an dara sealladh* was part of who she was. It's why her accusation had been cruelly harsh and unjust. Even now, the memory of his pain and shock still haunted her.

Tonight, there had been no harsh words, only silence. Constance worked hard to squeeze back tears that threatened to roll down her cheeks. Interfering in Phoebe's life had been a calculated choice, but she'd done so with the best of intentions. It had been the right decision, even if Lucien was furious with her. All she needed to do was convince her husband that her choice had been the right one. She'd rescued Phoebe, whether the woman had asked to be rescued or not.

Without another thought, she quickly crossed the floor and entered the corridor leading to Lucien's room. Quietly, she turned the knob to open the door and froze as the brass handle didn't move. Locked. He'd locked her out.

Tears streamed down her cheeks as she released a soft cry of pain. Lucien could not have hurt her more than if he'd hit her. He hadn't simply shut her out. He'd banned her from his room, and the pain his action caused her was indescribable. With a sob, she fled back to her room and crawled into bed. Burying her face into her pillow, she cried herself to sleep.

The low burning fire in the hearth cast off a soft glow of light in the darkened room. A quiet sizzle and a pop pierced the air as a log protested the fire engulfing it. Lucien barely heard the sound as he stared up at the ceiling. The spot next to him was cold. It was rare for Constance not to be curled up next to him, and he missed her soft warmth as if he'd lost one of his limbs.

Lucien turned his head toward the door leading into Constance's room, which he'd locked earlier. He immediately looked away to block out the sight. Tonight, his anger had threatened to take complete control of him. A fury he'd almost managed to wrestle down to aggravation until he'd entered Constance's bedroom.

He'd been struggling to find the words to explain why he'd been so angry with her, but she'd ignored his presence with an aplomb that had left him stunned. Before he could gather his thoughts, she'd sat down at her dressing table as if he wasn't even in the room. Her actions had reignited his rage.

It had taken all the willpower he possessed not to jerk her up and shake her for dismissing him so casually. At least he'd still had enough sound judgment to leave Constance's room without laying a hand on her. Lucien's gut twisted painfully at the memory. It appalled him that the thought had even entered his mind.

The idea of his anger blinding him beyond reason to where he could hurt or frighten the woman he loved, horrified Lucien. By locking her out tonight he'd ensured her safety until his anger ebbed away. Not long after he'd turned the key to lock the door, he'd heard the quiet sound of the doorknob turning.

Seconds later, he'd heard Constance's choked sob of pain. He'd still been furious with her, but her soft cry had slammed into his chest like a sledgehammer. It was the first time since they'd been married that Lucien had closed himself off from her, both physically and emotionally. He winced as he remembered another time when he'd shut her out almost as cruelly.

The memory of his savage rejection that day at Lyndham Keep, just hours before she and Jamie had almost died, caused his chest to tighten as if a vise were wrapped around his chest. As always, Constance had forgiven him for his transgression, but he'd never been able to forgive himself.

Restless from the dark memories that had stolen his ability to sleep, Lucien climbed out of bed and pushed his arms through the sleeves of his robe. Like his anger, the fire had sputtered down until it was nothing more than embers with the occasional flame flaring to life. Lucien moved to the fireplace and reached for the poker leaning against the wall.

Lucien stirred what was left of the logs with fierce thrusts until flames sprang up to begin eating away at the remaining wood. One hand resting on the mantle, he stared down into the fire waiting for it to begin burning steadily without any more assistance. The anger he'd struggled with earlier had been replaced by a mood almost as dark and grim as the time before Constance had entered his life.

The memory of those bleak years knotted his gut in a sickening twist, and he dragged in a harsh breath. Ever since childhood, he'd believed his destiny was to go insane and kill those he loved. It was why he'd fought so hard not to fall in love with Constance. It had proven to be an impossible task.

His Isis had captured his heart from the first moment he'd seen her that night at the Black Widow's ball her full figure outlined by the fire. When he'd finally learned the truth about the Blakemore curse, he'd thought himself free to love Constance as she deserved to be loved. But of late, he had been questioning whether he was truly worthy of her.

Coming to grips with Constance's ability to speak with

the dead continued to be a challenge for him. But that battle had been outmatched by the lingering shadow of the Blakemore curse hanging over his head like Damocles's sword. For almost all of his life, he'd lived with the threat of madness. It was so deeply ingrained in him that there were times when he still believed he would succumb to the same madness his cousin had.

It had been almost three years since Oliver's death, but not even time had erased everything he'd believed for almost his entire life. From the moment he'd discovered the butchery of his parents, he'd lived with the dark threat of madness. It lurked in the back of his mind, constantly taunting him every time he became angry. His half-cousin, Oliver, had been insane, and Blakemore blood had flowed in the man's veins. The memory of how Oliver had almost succeeded in killing still had the ability to send a chill down Lucien's spine.

The snap of flames licking away at logs interrupted Lucien's thoughts. As the fire took on life again, Lucien returned the poker to its resting place, then sank down into the chair facing the fireplace. Arms resting on his thighs, he leaned forward and clasped his hands in front of him while he stared into the now steadily burning fire.

Constance had been the flame that had brought him back from the dead. The *an dara sealladh* was one of the many facets that made his wife who she was, but it had not been easy to learn how to live with her special talent. His wife's ability had always made him uncomfortable.

The first time she'd confessed she could speak with the dead, he'd been furious and called her a liar. Even when she'd told him the nickname he and his brother had used for their childhood professor, he'd not believed her. Lucien's mind drifted back to when she'd first revealed she had seen and talked to Nigel.

It had been the middle of the night, and he'd been in the keep's library trying to drink himself into oblivion with a decanter of brandy. His attempt to numb the pain of his hellish existence had been a vain one. When the soft strains of music had drifted into the library, he'd gone to investigate. As he'd entered the room, he'd heard Constance talking with someone, only to have her tell him she'd been speaking with his dead brother.

The following morning he'd ordered the salon torn apart as he looked for a hidden entrance into the keep's labyrinth. His grandmother had already known about Constance's gift and had taken him to task for not believing her. It was only when Constance had told him that Nigel's wife had been having an affair that he'd begun to understand the extent of her gift.

Then there had been his search for Jamie in the darkness of labyrinth corridors. The moment his brother's unseen hands had guided him to the small room in the north tower had been the point of no return for him. Nigel's spirit had enabled Lucien to reach Constance and Jamie before Oliver could sacrifice them to his Egyptian gods.

Even then, it had been difficult to believe Constance possessed the *an dara sealladh*. In the days that followed, he'd tried to dismiss what he'd experienced as part of his imagination. Constance had left Lyndham Keep shortly after she'd recovered from Oliver's attack, believing he would be ashamed of her and would never accept that the *an dara sealladh* was a part of who she was.

It couldn't have been further from the truth. Lucien loved Constance more than life itself, and he knew she wouldn't be the woman he loved without her unique talent. It was why on the night he'd proposed at Marlborough House, he'd given her a gold calling card case and the special cards inside. He had ordered the specialty cards printed that read.

> *The Right Honorable Countess of Lyndham*
> *Helping Others Communicate with Lost Loved Ones*
> *Lyndham House, Mayfair, Park Street*

It had been the only thing he could think of that would convince Constance that he loved and accepted her for the woman she was. The woman he wanted to spend the rest of his life with. He'd wanted to demonstrate in no uncertain terms that he would support her when she helped those who asked for her to reach out to a lost loved one. What he hadn't anticipated was Constance helping even those who *didn't* ask her for help.

Lucien leaned back and rested his elbow on the arm of his chair. His hand cupping his chin, he released a quiet sigh of frustration. That was the crux of the problem. Not everyone Constance felt compelled to help had asked her to do so. She continuously meddled in the lives of others whenever one of her visions gave her just enough information to interfere.

Constance had a loving, generous heart. It was one of the things he loved the most about her. She felt things deeply, and the last time they'd argued about her meddling, she'd told him that she wanted others to be as happy as they were. Lucien's mouth suddenly twisted in an ironic grimace. He wasn't happy at the moment, and he was certain Constance wasn't either.

Until now, Constance had managed not to misstep when using her gift to help those who didn't ask for her help. Her efforts had been successful on every occasion. What she didn't understand was that not everyone would appreciate her well-meant efforts. There were a great many people who either didn't believe or were afraid of people like Constance, who possessed the *an dara sealladh*. He understood how those people would react. He understood the reality of how unsettling her gift could be. God knows how hard he'd tried to take it all in stride.

It didn't matter that he loved Constance with all his heart. He loved everything about her, from her beautiful giving heart, her mischievous nature, the way she blushed like a schoolgirl when he teased her, the way her touch aroused him, and even the *an dara sealladh* that was a part of her. It gave her insight into people's souls.

Her special ability was the very thing that made her empathetic and understanding when someone was in pain. But not everyone would see what he saw in Constance. Worst of all, she didn't realize that one of these days, she would interfere once too often. The result would be hellish remorse on her part.

It was one of the reasons he'd begun to be more strident in his objections to her interfering in the lives of others. He didn't want to see her hurt or even ostracized simply for having such a warm and generous heart. The idea of seeing her vilified for trying to help someone was a day he prayed would never come. It was a prayer not just for her sake, but for his as well. Lucien had no doubt as to what his reaction would be if someone tried to hurt his wife. It wasn't a pleasant thought.

Chapter 9

Irritation made Gideon suppress a grunt of displeasure as he entered the breakfast room and saw his mother was the only occupant. Ever since the dinner party his mother had hosted a week ago, Phoebe had worked hard to vanish whenever he entered a room. It was becoming damned annoying.

The Duke of Aveley had been a regular visitor ever since that evening, but Gideon had failed to devise a reason for drawing his mother out as to what the duke wanted with Phoebe. He almost snorted out loud at his dull-witted thought. He knew exactly what the duke wanted from her, and he was damned if the man would succeed. Mocking laughter echoed in his head as a voice taunted him that such an action would be difficult to achieve if Phoebe continued to be so adept at avoiding him.

As he began to fix himself a plate of food from the dishes on the buffet, he was surprised his mother had not greeted him with her usual lighthearted manner. Gideon glanced over his shoulder and saw his mother eating in silence. Puzzled, he finished filling his plate and joined his mother at the table.

"Where is your Lady Helstone this morning?" he asked with as much disinterest in his voice as possible. He poured himself a cup of coffee and was lifting his cup off the saucer when the sound of silver violently hitting china made him jerk his head toward his mother. Lady Wrotham was glaring at him, and with a bewildered frown, he set his cup down on its saucer as he quirked an eyebrow in a questioning manner.

"What have you said to her, Gideon?"

"What do you mean?" He stared at his mother in amazement at the harsh note of anger in the marchioness's voice.

"Do not play the innocent with me, my lord. You've said something to upset Phoebe, and I wish to know what it is."

"I've not spoken to Lady Helstone since the dinner party a week ago." Gideon refrained from sharing how the woman had been avoiding him.

"Then why is she searching for a new position?" The ferocity in his mother's voice wasn't near as startling as her statement.

"I beg your pardon?" Gideon stared at his mother in astonishment.

"Yesterday afternoon, I needed to review the gala's guest list. When I couldn't find it, I went to Phoebe's room to ask if she'd seen it." The marchioness continued to glare at him, but he saw the worry behind her irritation. "She wasn't there, but yesterday's newspaper was on her dressing table with several advertisements for secretarial positions circled."

"Did you ask her about it?"

"No, I wanted to speak with you first." Lady Wrotham eyed him sternly. "I love you, Gideon, but I am not blind to your reputation with women."

"What the devil is that supposed to mean?" he growled at the implication Phoebe's apparent desire to flee was his fault. He wasn't the villain in the story. In the back of his head, a harsh voice called him a liar.

"It means Phoebe is not one of your usual flowers, Lord Chelmbee," his mother snapped. Gideon jerked at his mother's use of the insulting nickname P. Currer had given him before anger streaked through him.

"You're right. She isn't. Phoebe's efforts to ingratiate herself with the duke at dinner last week revealed her for what she is," he bit out between clenched teeth as he shook his head in disgust. "Your Lady Helstone is a social climber,"

"Social—" Anger and disapproval darkened Lady Wrotham's face. The marchioness directed a severe look at him. It was one he'd not seen since he was a boy when he'd been caught doing something he shouldn't have. "*Gideon Alexander*—Phoebe is *not* a social climber."

"I regret being the bearer of bad news, Mama, but Lady Helstone is precisely that."

"She's nothing of the sort. I had to practically order her to attend the dinner party." His mother's mouth thinned with anger. "*Now*, I understand what she meant when she said there were people who might find it inappropriate for her to join us."

"If by that, you mean I thought it was inappropriate to include her as one of the dinner guests, then yes, you would be correct." He returned his mother's scowl with one of his own. "And I was right. Like a spider spinning its web, your Lady Helstone set her sights on the duke the moment she entered the salon. Her efforts clearly proved worthwhile as Aveley has called on her almost every day since."

"Phoebe *did not* deliberately set out to entice the duke. I asked the duke to escort Phoebe into dinner. But I *am* surprised you've taken notice of the duke's visits when you have such a low opinion of Phoebe," his mother snapped. Gideon jerked slightly as he realized he'd allowed his mother to know he'd been paying attention to Aveley calling on Phoebe.

"It was hard *not* to notice when she's entertaining the man in the room across the hall from my study." He silenced the voice that mocked him for knowing exactly how many times the man had called and how long he'd stayed.

"And I think there is a very good reason the duke has been here daily since the dinner party. I believe Aveley has realized Phoebe would make a lovely duchess."

At his mother's suggestion that Phoebe might marry

Aveley, every muscle in Gideon's body knotted viciously. In his head, a voice shouted in protest at the thought of Phoebe marrying anyone, let alone the duke. The idea of her in another man's bed tightened his muscles even more as an image of Phoebe flashed through his head.

Large brown eyes that sparkled with gold fire whenever she glared at him. An oval-shaped face framed by silky, dark-brown hair with just a touch of golden red highlights and a mouth made for kissing. The memory of how sweet she'd tasted that night in Montjoy's garden incited another shout of protest in his head. The objection aroused something possessive inside him that was stronger than he cared to admit to, but could not deny.

The memory of what had followed their encounter in the garden that night five years ago jeered at him. The instant he'd discovered Phoebe had bought herself a title, it had been as though he'd been kicked in the stomach. Disappointment had sliced through him as neatly as a butcher's knife did a slab of meat. He had never understood why it had mattered so much to him then, or why he'd brooded about his deep disappointment for months afterward. At the moment, it was beginning to feel like the same thing was happening all over again

Gideon's jaw clenched as anger surged through him. What he was feeling wasn't disillusionment. It was merely his frustration that Phoebe was making him dance to her tune. She was proving to be far more elusive than he'd expected. He remembered his exhilaration after their verbal skirmish the morning after he arrived home. The prospect of him being the pursuer for a change had filled him with pleasurable anticipation.

He'd looked forward to the chase, even though he'd been certain of an easy conquest. It had been an arrogant misstep on his part. What he'd thought would be a relatively simple challenge was proving to be far more difficult than he'd expected. He was certain her efforts to avoid him were born out of the fact that she was far from indifferent to him.

Every time they were alone, Phoebe's body betrayed her. The way she trembled when there was little space between them, or the desire she tried to hide from him every time his fingers trailed across her skin in a light stroke. But her resistance had surprised him. For some reason, he'd thought she would succumb easily.

All the more surprising was the stinging regret he'd felt for treating her as if she were a toy for his amusement. When she'd accused him of doing so, her icy disdain had not been reflected in her eyes. Instead, he'd seen a bitter disappointment and pain that had made him jerk away from her as if she'd poured hot water over his hand.

Gideon uttered a soft oath beneath his breath. What the devil did it matter whose bed Phoebe slid into? The answer that whispered through his head deepened his anger. If Aveley was taken in by her, the man deserved to be hoodwinked. The sound of his mother releasing a disgusted sigh made Gideon look in the marchioness's direction.

"You disappoint me, Gideon. I thought you a better judge of character." His mother's statement made him stiffen as if that were possible, given the current state of his tight limbs already.

"I think Lady Helstone's considerable charm has blinded you to her other less than attractive qualities," he bit out between clenched teeth.

"You forget she was here for almost the entire month you were in Amsterdam," his mother snapped. "I might not know all her secrets, but I know her quite well. You, on the other hand, have judged and sentenced Phoebe on a mere hour or two of acquaintance."

"Since you profess to know several of her secrets, has she told you how Helstone was the best title she could secure with her father's money?" Gideon snarled as he frowned angrily at

Lady Wrotham. His mother's defense of Phoebe was proving to be well-crafted and quite exceptional. The realization only deepened his irritation.

"*Really*, Gideon, do you *honestly* believe a woman is free to reject a man her parents have selected for her?"

Gideon barely managed not to snarl that he'd considered that possibly thousands of times since that moment Phoebe had thrown herself into his arms in Montjoy's garden. Instead, he tightened his lips to avoid explaining what had happened between him and Phoebe that night five years ago or how deeply the experience had affected him. In the days, weeks, and months after those incredible moments in the dark, the voices in the back of his head had insisted he was wrong about Phoebe.

Those same voices had urged him to go to her and hear the truth from her lips. But every time the idea pressed its way into his thoughts, Gideon had ruthlessly crushed it for fear she would make a fool of him all over again. Even now, those same voices were insisting he believe in her innocence. Aggravated by his inner voices, he gritted his teeth.

"While I will concede that few women have a choice in whom they're to marry, Lady Helstone *is* one of the *American Dollar Princesses*." Gideon's jaw clenched hard as the memory of Phoebe standing next to Helstone at Montjoy's house. "It's no secret they came to London to exchange a title for their exceedingly large dowries."

As Gideon studied his mother's irate expression, his mouth twisted slightly in regret. The last time his mother had eyed him with such disappointment and dismay had been when he was a boy. Her condemnation now was no less pleasant today than it had been years ago.

"Phoebe is *not* one of those women. Like most American men, her father wanted the prestige of saying his daughter had married nobility. In fact, Helstone was the worst possible choice for *any* woman," the marchioness said with repugnance. "And God forgive me, but when the man's mistress killed him, my first thought was that the world was better off without a man like him in it. At least I believed that until I learned the new viscount had callously tossed Phoebe out on the street with no funds or friends to call upon."

Dumbfounded at the thought of Phoebe being thrown out of her home, Gideon stared at his mother in mute surprise. A moment later, his cynicism returned. He frowned with skepticism at the idea Phoebe had not had any income to live off of or a place to seek safe harbor. Instantly, his conscience lambasted him for failing to remember how contemptuous the Marlborough Set had been of the Americans whose doweries had saved the great families in England.

The marchioness was slowly knocking aside every wall he'd put into place where Phoebe was concerned. She was slowly forcing him to consider the idea that Phoebe might not be who he thought she was. A fact he didn't like because any change in his opinion had consequences where Phoebe was concerned. The thought made him resist the possibility that the woman had been completely without any options.

"Are you telling me the woman had nowhere to go? Why not return to America?" Gideon countered with growing frustration.

"Her father died almost five years ago, and she had no relatives to turn to," the marchioness snapped angrily. "To my knowledge, her only true friend was Lord Linshal. But he fled to the continent when he was accused of being a sodomite. Even if Linshal had still been in England, I doubt Phoebe would have asked for his help. I think she would have been too proud to have done so."

"Pride? She wasn't too proud to accept your generous offer of employment," Gideon scoffed. "No doubt she believed her social position would compel you to include her in any socials you hosted. An excellent opportunity to land another title."

"Do *not* insult me by suggesting I am a fool, my lord," Lady Wrotham said coldly as pain flashed across her features before her expression became stern and unforgiving. In less than a split second, a knot of regret formed in Gideon's throat. His mother was far from a fool, but she was a generous and giving person who people often took advantage of. He shook his head sharply.

"My apologies, Mama. I meant nothing of the sort. I simply know what a kind heart you have and how people take advantage of you."

"I am a grown woman, Gideon. I do not need your protection," the marchioness said quietly as his apology made her expression soften. "Phoebe did not ask to be my personal secretary. In fact, Constance recommended her, and it took a great deal of persuasion on my part to convince Phoebe to accept the position."

"No doubt a role she believed beneath her," he bit out as his cynicism returned.

"Beneath her?" Lady Wrotham's scathing look made Gideon flinch. The marchioness's anger spared him nothing. "Phoebe was Madame Sabine's bookkeeper at the time, and according to Constance, her living conditions were positively squalid."

Immediately, Gideon's muscles tightened with self-reproach as guilt crashed through him. He had no reason to doubt Constance or his mother, and he could only imagine what life must have been like for Phoebe before arriving at Chelmsford House. The pictures flooding his mind as he considered her state of existence were not pleasant ones. The images only bolstered the voices in the back of his head that declared loudly that Phoebe wasn't a social climber.

"That you would be so quick to judge her is something I would never have expected of you, Gideon." Quiet and firm, his mother's voice held a deep note of disappointment, which made him flinch again. "She *is not* what you think her to be,

Gideon. She is not Edith."

"Edith has *nothing* to do with my opinion of Phoebe," he lied.

Immediately, his mother uttered a small noise of disgust and anger before quickly rising from the table. He immediately rose to his feet as well and grimaced at the look of censure on his mother's face. "Think long and hard about what I've said here, my lord. If necessary, I shall make arrangements for new living quarters. I will not have Phoebe leaving my employ because of you."

Gideon remained silent in the shadow of his mother's anger and stood rigid as the marchioness swept out of the breakfast room.

Hours later, Gideon threw his newspaper down onto the side table in a violent gesture of disgust. For the past hour, he'd been trying to focus on an editorial espousing numerous reasons for the passage of a bill being deliberated in Parliament. The light was low in the library, and a glance out the window revealed twilight had set in.

Rising from his chair, Gideon crossed the floor to the gaslight hanging on the wall and turned the knob to increase the flame. As the room became brighter, Gideon rubbed his forehead to ease the headache he'd developed.

Irritable and restless, he began to prowl the library floor. No matter how hard he tried, he'd been unable to forget this morning's conversation with his mother or her obvious disappointment in him. Despite his best efforts to work, Gideon had spent the better part of his day recalling every word of his breakfast conversation with his mother. Her arguments in Phoebe's defense had been compelling. The marchioness's words had been further strengthened by his knowledge that he knew his mother to be an excellent judge of character.

The marchioness had an uncanny ability to read people and quickly see them for who they were. Phoebe had been in Lady Wrotham's employ for more than a month, and her defense of Phoebe had been all the more persuasive because of her ability to sift out the good from the bad. There was also the fact that Phoebe had never used her impoverishment to gain Gideon's or his mother's sympathy.

Edith, on the other hand, had slyly pointed out small things she'd wanted, which he'd always found a way to secure for her. The memory of a gown he'd paid for all those years ago only to see a betrothal announcement a short time later made Gideon's jaw clench in anger as his doubt returned. He'd been fooled once before.

Why should he believe Phoebe was different? Why should he be so eager to risk humiliation at the hands of another vain, deceitful woman no matter how enticing the thought of bedding her was? The moment the thought echoed in his head, a voice scornfully called him an ass. Phoebe was far from vain. That he'd seen for himself. And *how* had she deceived him?

The question drew him up short, and he stopped in front of the fireplace to stare into the flames as he considered the thought. Exactly how had Phoebe been dishonest with him? His mother had said he'd penalized Phoebe for Edith's betrayal. Was that true? Deep in the back of his mind, a voice sneered at Gideon for even asking the question. He already knew the answer. For the past five years, every time his thoughts centered on Phoebe, he'd reminded himself that she had chosen to exchange her body and dowry for a title.

Condemning Phoebe had been far easier than contemplating a different reason for his disillusion. The alternative explanation was far from rational, even though he knew his mother would disagree. Moreover, the implications of that rationale were far more disturbing than he cared to admit.

With a snort of scornful disbelief, Gideon pushed the illogical reason out of his head. He'd not been an impressionable youth the night he'd made love to Phoebe in shadows. But he *had* done what his mother had pointed out to him. He'd condemned Phoebe, and he owed her an apology for his contemptuous, ungentlemanly behavior. The thought of apologizing was not a pleasant one. It meant confronting his mistake, and there was the distinct possibility Phoebe wouldn't forgive him. The sound of a discrete cough broke through his thoughts, and he looked over his shoulder to see his Pendleton standing in the doorway of the study.

"Dinner is served, my lord." The butler's deep baritone voice echoed in the library like a sonorous church bell in a chapel. With a wave of his hand, Gideon nodded.

"Thank you, Pendleton. Has my mother come down yet?"

Before the butler could reply, a sharp cry pierced the air. Bolting forward, Gideon followed Pendleton out into the entryway. At the sight of his mother sitting on the stairs, he ran forward to climb the two steps below where she was sitting. Her hands had a death grip on the bannister, and as he reached her, he saw her fight back tears of pain.

A quiet gasp of concern above his head made Gideon look up to see Phoebe hurrying down the steps to where his mother was sitting. As she reached Lady Wrotham's side, Phoebe sat down on the stairs next to the older woman.

"Are you all right, my lady? Where do you hurt?" With obvious concern, Phoebe gently pulled the marchioness's hand off the railing to examine it and then the other.

"What happened?" Gideon asked soothingly.

"I'm not sure." Lady Wrotham's voice was husky with pain. "I must have caught my heel on the hem of my gown."

Gideon bent his head to examine the hem of his mother's

dress. He pushed the gown away from the back of her legs and found a section of the hem where the stitching had been torn away. In all likelihood, her shoe had been caught in the material and caused her fall. As Gideon quickly examined her left ankle, he was relieved to find nothing untoward about it. Gently, he pushed aside her gown to look at her right ankle and sucked in a sharp breath of concern.

"*Christ Jesus,*" he muttered. Her ankle was swollen to almost twice its size. Gideon took a quick look over his shoulder at Pendleton. "Send one of the footmen to fetch Doctor Compton at once."

"There's no need, Gideon," the marchioness protested as he carefully slipped her foot out of her evening slipper. "If you'll simply help me to into the dining room, I'll be fine. I'm just shaken, that's all."

"Mother, your ankle is badly swollen, and even without Compton here to confirm it, I would hazard a guess you will be unable to walk on this foot for several days."

"It was just a little fall. I'll be perfectly fine."

"You must listen to Gid…his lordship, my lady." The moment Phoebe stumbled over his name, he jerked his head up to look at her. She glanced in his direction and the moment she saw him watching her, pink color rose in her cheeks. Quickly turning her attention back to the marchioness, she touched the older woman's shoulder in an affectionate manner. "Even I can see it's a terrible sprain. I just hope it's not broken. Do you hurt anywhere else?"

"No, I'm fine. All I need is a little help into the dining room for dinner." At her reply, Gideon shook his head.

"You're not going anywhere except to your bed, which is where I'm going to carry you right now."

"But Gideon—"

"No arguments, Mama," he growled as Phoebe stepped out of the way, so he was able to lift his mother up off the steps and cradle her in his arms.

"All this fuss," Alva grumbled as Gideon scowled down at her. A remorseful look swept across her youthful face, and she reached up to touch his cheek as he carried her up the stairs. "You are a good man, Gideon, and I love you even when you can be stubborn as an old goat."

"I believe I come by it naturally," he said with a snort of laughter. "I cannot begin to compete with your obstinance."

A soft laugh escaped her, but she didn't reply as he strode down the hall toward his mother's suite. Phoebe suddenly brushed past him to hurry down the hall and open the door to the marchioness's rooms. As he crossed the threshold, Phoebe was already making his mother's bed ready for her. Gideon set his mother down on the mattress and stepped back.

"I'll go downstairs and wait on Doctor Compton." Gideon nodded toward Phoebe and Polly, who had just hurried into the room. "I'm leaving you in capable hands."

With a quick kiss to her cheek, Gideon walked toward the door. His hand on the doorknob, he paused as an idea popped into his head. His mother didn't want Phoebe to leave, and this accident would make it difficult to manage any last-minute problems with the gala. He was also willing to wager that Phoebe cared enough about his mother to agree to his request to stay.

Slowly turning around, he saw his mother remove the strand of pearls his father had given her years ago. Fear suddenly wrapped its way around his chest as he realized how his mother's injuries could have been much worse, even fatal. A memory of the emotions he'd experienced at the age of ten when his father had died rose up from the past. It had been a crushing blow to lose his father so young.

Alexander Lethbridge had always been a strong, towering figure, and to see him waste away from cancer had been a painfully hard thing to watch. He'd never considered the loss of his mother before, and the thought of losing her sent a wave of unpleasant emotion crashing through him.

As the marchioness handed her pearls to Phoebe, a wistful smile touched her lips. Almost as if she understood the bittersweet memory her employer was experiencing, Phoebe murmured something he couldn't quite catch. Whatever she'd said, it made his mother laugh, and for that, he was grateful.

"Phoebe." He liked the way her name rolled off his tongue. It was as sweet a sound as he remembered her mouth to be. She froze for a moment before she looked over her shoulder at him. "I would like a word with you in the library after the doctor is gone."

"A word?"

It was more than a question. It was a silent declaration that Phoebe doubted his intentions. She had every right too, and it didn't help the way his mother frowned at him in puzzlement. Gideon swallowed hard and nodded.

"Please." *Christ Jesus*, he sounded as if he was pleading with the woman.

Gideon shifted his attention to his mother, who was obviously trying to discern his reason for asking to speak with Phoebe. Indecision fluttered across Phoebe's features before she nodded her agreement, then turned back to his mother and effectively ended the brief exchange.

Gideon's muscles tightened at how easily she'd dismissed him. It wasn't a pleasant sensation. A glance at his mother revealed her amusement, and she smiled at him with more than a hint of mischief. Whatever she was thinking would most likely result in some form of teasing that he would not enjoy. Gideon suppressed a groan of foreboding as he tugged the door open and left the room.

Perhaps worst of all, Phoebe had just demonstrated to him just how wrong he'd been about her. She was clearly not the woman he'd allowed himself to believe. Worse, he knew he wouldn't just be pleading with Phoebe to stay for his mother's sake. He was about to endure a very painful moment of shame and humiliation when he apologized for having accused her of being something she was not.

Chapter 10

hoebe's heart was pounding in her chest like a drummer calling troops to battle as she entered Gideon's study. The doctor had come and gone some time ago, and she'd procrastinated as long as she could with Lady Wrotham. It wasn't until the woman had insisted she go see what Gideon wanted that Phoebe had been forced to come downstairs.

The room was softly lit by the gaslight on the wall and the fire in the hearth. Gideon stood in front of the fireplace with a brandy glass in his hand, staring into the flames. Without thinking, she automatically closed the study door behind her. The quiet thud made Gideon turn around.

Dear God, she'd shut herself in with a man whose voice could seduce her as easily as his touch. Flinching at the thought, instinct urged her to flee as if the hounds of hell were snapping at her ankles. Phoebe swallowed her trepidation as she rejected the notion to run. She wasn't a coward. Where would she go anyway? A voice in the back of her head whispered an answer. The answer was a mere sigh, and she refused to listen to it.

Gideon's features were unreadable as he gestured toward a couch sitting near the fireplace. When she didn't move, irritation slipped past his expressionless mask.

"It was a request, Phoebe, but if you wish, I can make it a command for you to sit."

Unwilling to see exactly how he might command her to be seated, Phoebe walked across the floor to the sofa. As

Phoebe sank down into the cushions, she frowned and tried to comprehend the exasperation she'd heard in his voice. Something was different about him. He wasn't as arrogant as she was accustomed to.

To her surprise, he'd turned away from her as she'd walked to the couch. When she was seated, she waited quietly for him to speak. He continued to stand with his back to her, and a rush of uncertainty streaked through her until her body was taut with apprehension.

She understood and could reasonably manage his arrogant behavior, but this was different. He seemed distracted almost. It was out of character for him, and his manner reminded her of the man who had made her feel alive for just a few short moments in a dark garden years ago. Phoebe's mouth went dry at the thought. It made him even more dangerous than ever before. She watched him finish off the last bit of brandy in his snifter, then set the crystal on the mantel.

"Thank you for caring for my mother this evening," he said quietly as he continued to stare into the fire. "I'm grateful."

"I…you're…welcome." Startled by his words, she tipped her head to one side to study his back. His entire body seemed frozen in place, and she frowned in confusion.

"My mother is under the impression that you are looking for a new position."

His quiet statement made her inhale a sharp breath. How had Lady Wrotham discovered her plan to leave? Her mind raced along in several different directions until she remembered the dowager saying she'd come looking for her about the extra wait staff they needed for the gala's buffet. If the dowager marchioness had entered Phoebe's room, it would have been difficult to miss the newspaper on her secretaire. She'd left it folded on her desk with the potential advertisements circled.

When she didn't respond, he slowly turned to study her in silence. His profile could have been carved out of stone, and it was impossible to know what he was thinking. A tremor raced through her as the silence stretched out between them. She was completely at a loss as to how to deal with the change in him. Phoebe looked at him and thought she saw the indecision in his gray eyes, but it was gone as quickly as it came.

As if aware that he'd thrown her off-balance, he arched his eyebrows as his mouth twisted slightly in a smile of mockery she recognized. It was exactly what she needed to regain her footing when it came to dealing with the man. In the back of her mind, she made a mental note to include his smile in her description of him in the chronicles. Annoyance sped through her, and she eyed him with antipathy and answered his question.

"I am." At her abrupt response, he frowned. It was almost as if he'd expected her to deny it.

"I would never have mistaken you for a coward, Phoebe." The sound of her name flying past his lips did something pleasurable to her inside, and she barely managed to keep from gasping at the effect it had on her. A second later, the word coward registered in her head. Angered by his accusation, she stiffened with indignation.

"I am *not* a coward. I simply know when to fight and when to retreat."

"Then, you're admitting to the fact that I'm winning the war." There was an odd note of surprise in his voice, despite the wolfish smile curving his lips. She shook her head in denial.

"No, but I have no intention of being outflanked and maneuvered into a corner."

At her crisp retort, his smile disappeared, and he bowed his head as if he were studying the floor in front of him. Once more, she was thrown off-kilter by his odd behavior.

"It appears I've done you a disservice, and I regret having done so."

His words were so astonishing she could only stare at him in mute amazement. Gideon lifted his head to look at her, then turned away to stare into the fire again. Again the silence stretched out between them as she struggled to understand what he was trying to say. Was he apologizing for believing she was using his mother, or was it for something else?

"I don't understand," she said quietly. There was a tension in Gideon that filled the small area of space between them. Then, almost as if he'd reached a decision, he straightened his shoulders, clasped his hands behind his back, and turned back to her once more.

"I accused you of marrying Helstone for his title. It was an ill-informed assumption, and it was wrong of me to suggest such a thing. I regret the accusation." This time she gaped at him, unable to believe what she was hearing. Annoyance made him furrowed his brow when she didn't reply. "Am I to assume you are trying to decide which insult suits the occasion best?"

The sharp words held a trace of humiliation, which made Phoebe bite back a smile. It was obvious the man was unaccustomed to apologizing. When she remained silent, his features suddenly became shuttered, and it was no longer possible to tell what he was thinking. With a small shake of her head, she met accepted his apology.

"I am not one to bear grievances." At her reply, his body became less rigid, and something told her it was the result of relief. His reaction made her frown. Why would he have been worried she wouldn't accept his apology? More importantly, why would he care.

"Thank you."

"Then, if that is all," she murmured as she rose from her seat. "I would—"

"No. I have a request."

Phoebe eyed him with suspicion. From the moment she'd entered the study, the man had knocked her off-balance. Now he had a favor to ask, and she had the distinct feeling it had to do with his mother. Phoebe bit down on her bottom lip, and a flash of something dangerous and exciting flare in his eyes. It set her blood racing through her veins. She swallowed hard to dislodge the knot in her throat.

"You would like me to stay until your mother is well."

"Yes," he said with an abrupt jerk of his head. Clearly, the man found asking for favors as difficult as apologies.

"Very well." At her softly spoken agreement, Gideon jerked slightly. At his reaction, she studied him carefully. His features revealed nothing, but Phoebe could tell she'd surprised him. Anger spiraled through her as she realized he had expected her to say no. She eyed him with disgust. "You thought I would decline."

"I thought it possible, given our contentious relationship."

"You think far too highly of yourself, Lord Chelmbee," she snapped.

First the man had apologized and in the next breath indicated he thought her callous enough to leave the marchioness in a position that would have caused her employer considerable distress.

"One day, you will call me that once too often, Phoebe." There was a dangerous note in his quiet words of anger. She ignored the warning in his voice as she quickly stood up to stand rigid with fury in front of him.

"And one day, I will no longer have to be in the presence of a man I find arrogant, ignoble, and far too enamored with himself to comprehend that not every woman finds him irresistible."

Anger hardened Gideon's features as if the planes of his face had been carved out of a piece of marble. It was clear her insult had struck deep at his pride. In the back of her mind, a voice chided her for her scathing accusation. The man might be arrogant to the point of exasperation but he was far from dishonorable.

As to being enamored with himself, she thought he might be more of a homebody than the reputation he had in society. In fact, she'd observed Gideon with his head in a book several nights a week. It was why she was now regretting losing her temper. Suddenly, a small smile tipped the corners of his mouth, and she sensed danger.

"As reluctant as you are to admit it, Phoebe, we both know I excite you." He stepped forward until he was inches away. Instantly, her body hummed with a familiar tingling tension. "We both know how your body responds to me every time I touch you."

He reached out to catch her chin in his fingers and ran his thumb over her bottom lip. Unable to help herself, a tremor shook its way through her. A wicked smile tilted his lips upward at her response. Aware of the precarious position she was in, Phoebe tried to take a step back, only for her calves to bump into the edge of the couch. The movement threw her off balance, and she lurched to one side before she fell forward into his chest.

"See," he murmured seductively as his hands wrapped firmly around her upper arms and tugged her closer. "Your body betrays you."

Her heart skipped a beat then began to race at a frantic pace. Something sinful and mesmerizing wove its way through his voice. It sent a shiver of fear and excitement down her spine. Senses heightened to a high pitch of awareness, she sucked in a sharp breath at the fire she saw in his gaze. All he had to do was look at her like this to drag her to the edge of the abyss. If she didn't end this madness now, she would regret it tomorrow.

"Let me go," she gasped. The softness of her exclamation made her realize it wasn't a protest at all. Her heartbeat thundered in her ears as Gideon smiled.

"I seem to recall you saying the same thing five years ago, and we know how that turned out."

"That…that was diff….different," she stammered as her pulse quickened to twice its normal pace.

"Was it?" he asked in a husky voice that caused a tingling sensation to race across her skin. "I have a feeling your mouth will taste just as sweet as it did before. Should I find out, Phoebe?"

As he bent his head, another gasp escaped Phoebe. It was silenced the instant Gideon's mouth captured hers. Exhilaration rushed through her body as her heartbeat pounded wildly in her chest. Just as he had once before, he didn't conquer with force. Instead, he cajoled her surrender with the heat of his mouth, teasing and tempting hers.

Hard, muscular arms pulled her snug against him, and she drew in a quick breath as he molded her into the hardness of his body. The moment her lips parted, his tongue delved into her mouth. Brandy still lingered on his tongue, and the flavor of it danced across hers. He tasted like a tangy bite of toffee and caramel.

With an eagerness she knew she shouldn't feel, she allowed her tongue to swirl around his in a fervent response to the almost hedonistic caress. Her response elicited a low growl of pleasure from him. The sound skated across her senses, igniting a stark need inside her that left her craving a pleasure she knew only he could satisfy. Her arms wrapped around his neck, she slid one hand through his silky, golden-brown hair. As his hand slid up over her waist to press into the side of her breast, she arched her body upward into his caress. The instant his mouth left hers to explore her throat, she moaned softly.

Dear God, how she wanted him. Had the sensations he was arousing in her now been this intense the last time. No, this was different. She wasn't afraid now. She was free to feel and experience and give. Every inch of her was alive with sensation, and she didn't want it to end. As his mouth skimmed lower to brush across the top of her breasts, she sighed with delight.

The moment he reached the small valley between her breasts, his tongue probed the small cavern of flesh in a slow, sensual stroke. It sent an electric current racing through her limbs until it hit the spot between her legs. Instantly, her sex throbbed and silently cried out for more.

"Do you like that, sweetheart?"

The words whispered across her skin as his tongue delved into the small valley again in two hot strokes before his mouth continued to explore the tops of her breasts. Lost in a whirlpool of sensation, she tried to speak, but the only thing to escape her lips was a moan. He probed the spot between her breasts once more before his mouth caressed its way upward and his teeth nipped at the swells of her breasts.

"Tell me. Do you?" It was a command that insisted she respond.

"Ye…yes." At her reply, his mouth continued upward to her throat, where his mouth nipped, sucked, and teased her skin with his tongue. Her head rolled to one side to expose more of her throat, and he took advantage of the silent invitation.

"But it's not enough, is it?" he rasped.

"I…No…I…want more."

The moment the words escaped her lips, his body gently guided her down onto the couch. His mouth captured hers again, and a delicious shiver rippled through her as a hard, firm hand gently grasped her ankle. His fingers burned through her stocking as his hand slowly worked its way up her leg to her thigh. As he caressed her leg, his mouth teased and tempted hers until her body was crying out for his.

The moment his fingers caressed the bare flesh above the top of her stocking, it made her sex ache with a raw intensity that she wanted—needed—him to satisfy. Her hand slid downward to find his hard length, and the instant her fingers traced the outline of him beneath his trousers, a growl vibrated out of him to pulse its way into her body.

He shifted his position so he was cradled against her palm, and another sound of his pleasure echoed against her lips. The sensual touch made her breath hitch in her throat as his hand brushed past the soft linen of her undergarment, and he slid two fingers into her. Even though she'd anticipated the intimate touch, it still made her suck in a sharp breath of delight. Every stroke of his fingers inside her set her blood on fire.

Hot. Probing. Sultry.

The caress heated her from the inside out until she was dragging in small, frantic breaths of air. The moment his thumb rubbed across the sensitive piece of flesh on the rim of her sex, her body jerked hard against his hand. With each fiery touch, he carried her upward to a heightened state of pleasure where everything was rich, vibrant, and filled with raw, primitive sensations that left her whimpering for more.

Her body was filled with a growing pressure she'd not felt since the last time he'd touched her. It was an undeniable force that pushed its way past her belly into the heart of her. Blinded by the sudden, wild need streaking through, her breaths became soft pants as her hips rocked against each stroke of his fingers. The sensations built up inside her, the power of it like the swift current of a river. It dragged her along with a promise of an intense physical and emotional ecstasy.

A small shudder rippled through her, and she arched up from the couch cushions. Her lips parted to release a cry of pleasure, but he quickly silenced the sound with a hard kiss. Strong fingers continued to stroke, press, and create a wave of sultry heat that left her ready to weep as the sensations inside her spread outward, taking her to a precipice she wanted to fall off of into the delicious fires of satisfaction.

Another moan whispered out of her as he deepened the intensity of their kiss. Pleasure grasped her more firmly in its hold, tightening her body until she was silently begged for him to send her plummeting over the edge of a cliff into a blazing inferno. The fire that was just about to consume her suddenly vanished as he pulled his hand away from her. Frustrated at being denied satisfaction, she released a small cry of protest. Her eyelids fluttered open, and she stared up into gray eyes glittering with desire.

"It still isn't enough, is it?"

"You know…it's not," she whispered with a sob that revealed how much she craved his touch.

"I agree." The growl of need in his hoarse reply sent a thrill of excitement rushing across her skin.

He wanted her as much as she wanted him. A second later, their gazes locked as he pushed the skirt of her gown up and the tip of him pressed against her sex. Eager to feel him inside her, she slid her hand over the taut muscles of his back, down to his hard hips.

She pulled hard on him as she silently urged him to fill her with his hard length. In one swift stroke, he buried himself inside her. The dark groan that rumbled out of him made her nerve endings tingle. Sheer delight scraped its way along her senses, and she sucked in a deep breath of pleasurable gratification. Her eyes fluttered open to see him watching her with a look of untamed desire.

The intensity of it made her drag in another deep breath of excitement. A small smile tipped the corners of his mouth at the sound as his weight pressed her deeper into the cushions. Unexpected and fierce, she experienced the need to taste him again, and she tugged his head down to kiss him.

Boldly, she thrust her tongue into his mouth to dance with his. The soft groan that rumbled up out of his chest reverberated into her body. Hunger and need pulsed their way through her as she pushed her hips upward to meet him stroke for stroke. Fingers splayed against his chest, another low rumble of sound vibrated out of him and into her hands. It was a delicious sound of passion, and she loved the way it echoed in her ears.

There wasn't any part of her that wasn't alive with the fiery heat his touch had aroused in her. The moment his mouth left hers to work its way along her neck, she trembled with a need for a fulfillment that was still outside her reach. His lips nipped and tugged at her skin, followed by the tip of his tongue teasing the spot he'd made sensitive with his mouth.

Pressure began to build inside her again, pushing its way down to her sex. It heightened her senses, and she whimpered her frustration at the slow pace of his body melding with hers. The need growing inside her was quickly reaching a feverish pitch. It was growing harder with each passing minute not to beg and plead with him to assuage her thirst for that ultimate crescendo of pleasure.

Need and desire pulsated their way through her. With every stroke of his body, he teased and taunted hers. Small shock waves of delight spiraled through her with each breath she drew in. They gave her just enough taste of the release she craved while whetting her appetite and making her crave something more.

The intensity of it was quickly building inside her, and she shuddered against him. Never in her life had she ever felt so out of control. He'd unleashed something wild in her that threatened to overtake her senses until she was sobbing and begging him to quench her need for him. As she pleaded for completion, his only reply was to claim her lips in another kiss that threatened to be her undoing.

Chapter 11

Gideon uttered a harsh groan of pleasure as her body flexed around his. Christ Jesus, she felt good around his cock. This was even better than that night so long ago. He lifted his head to watch her as he filled the hot, creamy center of her before he retreated slowly then sank into her again. Long, dark lashes brushed her cheeks, and her mouth parted in a soft gasp of delight as his mouth nibbled at her shoulder.

She pulled in a quick breath, then moaned with pleasure as he pressed his body into hers again with another slow stroke. Her hands clutched at his hips in a clear sign she wanted him to increase his pace. He complied with her silent request and increased his pace slightly. The way she responded to his touch made him even harder, although he hadn't thought it possible. Watching her reaction to his physical possession was as exciting as the way her body continued to flex and tighten around him.

Muscles taut with tension, he couldn't remember a time when he'd ever felt this complete with a woman. No, he had. This was exactly what he'd experience that night in Montjoy's garden. He lowered his head to nip at the side of her neck, which pulled another sob of delight out of her. She smelled of honey and citrus. It was a sweet, tart aroma that was as tantalizing as everything else about her. With an unexpected strength, she pulled his head down and lifted hers to kiss him.

The slight pinch of her teeth against his lower lip made him grant her access to his mouth. Eagerly, her tongue slipped past his lips to tease and tantalize him until a deep groan rose from deep within his chest. Desire surged through his veins with a force that startled him. The power of it swiftly dragged him down into a blood-red mist of passion. Everything fell away until the only thing he breathed, tasted, saw, or heard was her. There was a frantic edge to her kiss as her mouth nipped and teased his.

With every retreat and surge of his body into hers, her hips moved against his with unrestrained passion. A small pulse tightened around his cock as her body gripped him and resisted his retreat. Suddenly she jerked hard beneath him, then arched upward to cling to him, her fingers digging deep, almost painfully, into his shoulders. Her rapturous look of ecstasy made him pound his body into hers more rapidly as she bucked against him once more.

In the next instant, her lips parted, and he quickly silenced her cry of release with his mouth as he absorbed the shock waves of her body contracting around his cock. The strength of her climax tugged at him hard. It pulled him along as he pumped his body into hers even faster. Hot velvet clenched around him like a vise as one contraction after another issued her body's silent demand for his surrender.

With one last hard thrust, his body tightened with anticipation, then shuddered as he spilled his seed. His breathing ragged, he buried his face in her neck for a long moment. Small tremors still rippled through her, and the pulse on the side of her neck fluttered wildly against his mouth.

Gideon nibbled at her neck, then slowly lifted his head to stare down at her. Eyes closed, her shallow breathing had begun to ease. There was an afterglow about her that made him ache for her all over again. Her cheeks were a dusky pink while her red mouth glistened in the light of the oil lamp from his kisses. Phoebe's eyes fluttered open, to meet his.

"I think the next time we should consider a bed-chamber," he murmured huskily as his fingers brushed a strand of hair away from her cheek. When she didn't say anything, he realized she'd grown still and frozen beneath him. Gideon frowned in puzzlement. Gently, he brushed his mouth across hers. "What is it, Phoebe?"

"It appears you've successfully picked your most recent flower." The soft words were devoid of emotion, and he stiffened.

"What the hell does that mean?" he bit out between clenched teeth.

"It means you won the war, Lord Chelmbee," she said quietly and turned her head away from him. Gideon went rigid as she called him by the detestable name he'd been given in the Currer Chronicles. He'd barely opened his mouth to speak when there was a knock on the library door. Before he could order the individual to wait, the door swung wide open.

"Excuse me, my lord, her ladyship was—"

Gideon quickly shifted his body to shield Phoebe as she sucked in a sharp breath of horror. As he looked over his shoulder, he saw his mother's lady's maid staring at them in horrified dismay. The woman's mouth was working as if she were trying to speak, while her cheeks was a brilliant shade of red.

"*Get out,*" he ordered in a viciously harsh tone.

The woman didn't need to be told twice, and she bolted from the room, pulling the door closed behind her. Gideon turned his head back to Phoebe and saw she was white as a sheet. Concern swept through him as she began to tremble.

"It will be—"

"Let me go," she rasped in an almost inaudible voice.

Her hands pushed at his chest, and Gideon quickly lifted himself off of her and rose to his feet while adjusting his trousers. The moment she was free, Phoebe scrambled off the couch. She had barely shaken out her skirts when she ran toward the door. He charged after her and caught her by the arm to drag her to a halt.

"Phoebe, I'll fix this."

"Fix what?" she said bitterly. "My reputation? Do you seriously believe Polly won't tell anyone that she saw you rutting with me like a common whore?"

"She won't unless she wishes to be discharged without a character," he said grimly as he was forced to admit that the scenario Phoebe had just described was a distinct possibility. Suddenly, horrified dismay made the color drain from Phoebe's cheeks.

"Oh, dear God. She'll tell your mother," she choked out. She'd become so pale, he feared she might faint. It was obvious how appalled and afraid she was of further degradation.

"*Damnit, Phoebe*, I will not let the woman say anything to anyone."

"I can't stay here. I need to go."

Every emotion flitting across her face indicated she was in a state of shock. With a savage twist of her body, she raised her arm and broke free of his grasp. The moment she was no longer restrained, she headed toward the door again.

"Phoebe. *Listen* to me."

Gideon quickly followed her and pulled her to a halt once more. Hands grasping her upper arms, he forced her to look at him. She was still mumbling to herself, and he shook her slightly to grab her full attention. The sight of her panic and fear twisted his gut.

It was her stark vulnerability that shook him the most. It was the same look he'd seen on five years ago in Montjoy's garden. The same fragility that had made him want to pull her close and keep her safe. Every tenuous emotion he'd seen in her that night had returned to replace the strong, spirited woman he'd verbally sparred with since his return home. The same passionate woman he'd just made love to.

That woman had been replaced by the stranger he'd met long ago. The change in her struck a blow to his body. This time *he* was the reason for her pain, mortification, and fear, not someone else. Almost as if she could read his mind, her expression became unreadable. She'd closed herself off to him, and it was impossible to deduce what she was thinking.

"Let me go, Gideon. There's nothing you can do," she said in a dispassionate voice.

"Yes, there is. You're going to marry me." The moment the words left his mouth, Gideon clenched his jaw. He wasn't sure what had prompted him to propose marriage, but he knew it was the only viable option that would protect her.

"*What?*" Phoebe recoiled from him with in appalled disbelief.

"I *said* I want to marry you."

As he repeated the solution to their dilemma, he heard a quiet voice inside him urging her to say yes. The strength of the silent plea held him rigid as he watched her confused reaction to his declaration. Just as he had that night in Montjoy's dark garden, Gideon frantically tried to think of a reason that would convince her to accept his offer.

Brown eyes wide with shock, Phoebe's mouth moved as if trying to speak. For the briefest of moments, Gideon thought she would say yes to his proposal. Bitter disappointment assailed him a split-second later as he saw anger erase her bewilderment. With unrestrained vehemence she shook her head.

"*No, my lord.* I will *never* marry again. I have no intention of enduring the hell of my first marriage a second time."

"I'd advise you not to compare me to Helstone, Phoebe," he said with quiet anger. The inference that he was no different than her late husband was an insult even worse than being labeled Lord Chelmbee.

"*Or what?*" she snapped with a defiance that increased his ire. "You'll destroy my reputation? I think I managed to do *that* all by myself a few moments ago."

There was a note of self-disgust in her voice that doused

his anger in an instant. Stunned by her statement, he stared at her in disbelief. Did she really think she was to blame for what had just happened? Gideon shook her gently again and scowled with exasperation.

"What in God's name makes—"

She didn't let him finish as the palms of her hands suddenly hit his chest in a savage blow, and she shoved him away from her to break free of his grasp. Blindsided by the strength and ferocity of her hands slamming into his chest, Gideon stumbled back a few steps. Before he could stop her, Phoebe raced toward the door once more. His slow recovery gave her just enough time to reach the study door, tug it open, and make her escape. Gideon raced after her, but she was already halfway up the stairs by the time he reached the main hall.

"*Fuck.*"

The harsh word echoed softly in the entryway, and he viciously shoved his hand through his hair. *Christ Almighty*, what the hell had he been thinking to make love to Phoebe in his study. At least in her room or his, the door could have been locked to prevent discovery. With a violent snort of rage, he lambasted himself for being such a fool.

The memory of Phoebe's response immediately after they'd both been satiated slammed into him. That she'd believed he'd intentionally seduced her angered him. Not with Phoebe, but with himself. Making love to Phoebe hadn't even entered his mind when he'd asked her to meet with him. The only thing he'd intended to do was apologize for his accusation and ask her to stay, at least until his mother was on her feet again.

As he stared at the couch, he grimly recalled the look on Polly's face the moment the maid had seen him and Phoebe in a compromising position. Compromising? It had been a hell of a lot more than that. The maid had been shocked and embarrassed, but Phoebe had experienced something far more devastating.

His actions had caused her to be stripped of her dignity. Gideon could only imagine the agony she was certain to feel the next time she came face-to-face with Polly. Even if the maid acted as if nothing had ever happened, Phoebe would continue to relive her humiliation every time she encountered the maid.

"*Christ Jesus*, you're a *sorry* fuck, Chelmsford," he muttered as he began to pace the study floor.

Despite his self-castigation, he knew he needed to formulate a plan quickly and clean up the mess he'd made of things. He couldn't risk Polly being indiscreet. The maid had been with his mother for years, and was the soul of discretion according to the marchioness. But he intended to do everything in his power to persuade Phoebe to marry him, which meant the maid couldn't remain at Chelmsford House.

He could always find the woman another position, but the risk of her speaking out of turn with a new employer was too great. Even an accidental slip of the tongue by Polly would ensure a scandal, which would further humiliate Phoebe. That he refused to let happen. No, he would set the maid up in a home of her own along with an annual stipend, provided she never told another soul what she'd witnessed tonight.

One problem solved, he began to strategize how to convince Phoebe to marry him. Marriage was encumbrance he'd resisted for a long time. Edith's betrayal had played a role in his avoidance of the marital state, but he'd also seen the institution as an impediment to how he lived his life. It was why he'd always walked in the opposite direction the instant one of his lovers even hinted at the word. However, Phoebe was a different matter altogether.

Gideon could easily see a marriage between them as one that would be infinitely satisfying. Phoebe was intelligent, caring, had no difficulty putting him in his place, and they were good together in bed. He grimaced at the last point. They'd yet to enjoy each other in a bed, but he was certain it would be as pleasurable, if not more so, than their previous experiences.

The only real question was how to convince her to accept his proposal. The vehement manner in which she'd rejected the idea of being his wife made it clear her marriage to the viscount had been a terrible existence. While a marriage between the two of them wouldn't even remotely resemble her union with Helstone, Gideon didn't know how to convince her of that.

Phoebe would have the freedom to do as she wished as his wife. He paused his thinking for a brief second before resuming his thoughts. Naturally, the freedom she enjoyed would need to have certain boundaries. The last thing he wanted was to be cuckold by his wife, any more than he would allow himself to humiliate Phoebe by taking a mistress. She'd endured enough degradation and pain at Helstone's hands. From this point forward, he would take care never to cause her any further humiliation.

While a servant finding them in a compromising situation had been a somewhat uncomfortable sensation for him, the incident had been a withering experience for Phoebe. The look of humiliation that drained her cheeks of color the moment they were discovered was an image that would remain with him for the rest of his life.

The memory of pale features frozen in shock and horror, made him utter another violent curse. Her reaction to Polly finding them in a compromising situation had been bad enough. But it had been nothing compared to when she'd realized the maid might inform his mother of their indiscretion.

Phoebe's mortification the instant she realized his mother might learn of the incident had been so acute it still made his gut twist painfully. He knew Phoebe was fond of his mother, and the possibility of Phoebe falling out of grace with the marchioness would be as painful for Phoebe as what she'd just suffered moments ago.

He knew his mother well enough to know it was unlikely she would condemn Phoebe. The dowager would blame him, and rightfully so. She'd already warned him—Gideon stiffened in the middle of his thought. *Christ Jesus*, what if he'd made Phoebe with child? What if she were to give him a son? His son. A boy who would carry on the family name. He'd never considered having a son before. When his half-sister, Alice, had given birth to Thomas last year, he'd simply believed his nephew would inherit the title. The thought created a sense of satisfaction through him.

Another grandchild would make his mother happy. The pleasure he experienced at the thought vanished in an instant. Even if she became pregnant, Gideon was certain it would be difficult for him to convince Phoebe a union between them would be a good one. He needed help.

Gideon grimaced. There was only one person he knew who was up to the task of persuading Phoebe to marry him. His mother. She loved Phoebe, and the dowager marchioness would welcome Phoebe as a daughter-in-law with open arms. In fact, he was certain she would use every bit of sway she had over Phoebe to convince her to marry him.

Unwilling to wait to resolve the situation, he left the study and took the stairs two steps at a time. As he headed down the hallway, he grimaced as he saw Polly leaving his mother's suite of rooms. The maid glanced in his direction, then quickly turned to head in the opposite direction. In a low voice, he ordered her to stop. She hesitated, then slowly turned to watch him approach. Gideon shook his head the moment he saw how fearful the maid was and gestured he had no intention of berating her.

"Is her ladyship still awake?" he asked quietly.

"Yes, my lord, her ankle was bothering her a bit. She refused to take any laudanum, so the doctor left some willow bark for me to brew in the kettle for her. She just finished it a moment ago." The maid bobbed her head toward the empty teacup on the salver she carried.

"Thank you for taking care of her ladyship," he said with a nod before he cleared his throat. Before he could speak, Polly shook her head quickly, her fear making pale.

"I won't say a thing, my lord."

"Thank you, Polly. I was certain you wouldn't," Gideon said soothingly. "But there's the matter of Lady Helstone. What happened was humiliating for her, and I'm afraid that every time the two of you pass each other, her ladyship will relive that moment in my study."

"Oh my lord, I would never hurt, Lady Helstone." Teary-eyed, the woman shook her head. "She's so kind to me and the rest of the servants."

"That doesn't surprise—"

"Please, my lord, I don't want to lose my position. I won't say a word, I promise."

"I don't doubt you, Polly, but Lady Helstone and I are to be married, so you can see what a problem that creates as to her happiness." Gideon raised his hand as the maid started to protest, tears sliding down her cheeks. "But I have no intention of allowing you to be harmed by this unfortunate incident. Tomorrow we'll discuss finding a small home for you wherever you like. I'll handle all the financial arrangements for turning the property over to you as well as providing you with an annual stipend."

"I don't know what to say, my lord," the maid gasped. Eyes wide with shock, Polly shook her head in disbelief.

"You're not to worry about any of this. We'll devise a story about a relative leaving you a small inheritance to explain your leaving. The only thing I require of you is to forget whatever it was you thought you saw."

"Oh yes, my lord," she said with a vigorous bob of her head. "I won't tell a soul."

"Thank you," Gideon said quietly. "I'll send for you sometime tomorrow to go over the details."

"Yes, my lord, thank you, my lord. Thank you very much."

Eyes shimmering with more tears, Polly's relief brightened her face as she expressed her gratitude in a breathless voice. Gideon acknowledged her thanks and indicated she could continue on her way as he turned toward his mother's door. He stood staring at wood paneling for a moment. If his mother was in pain, it wasn't necessarily the best time to ask for her help. Still, he couldn't afford to give Phoebe the chance to leave Chelmsford House before she agreed to marry him.

Quietly knocking on the door of his mother's room, he waited a moment before his hand twisted the doorknob. A sudden memory of Polly stumbling into the study without waiting for permission to enter made him jerk his hand away from the doorknob. Instead, he knocked again and waited. When he heard his mother's voice inviting him in, Gideon slowly opened the door of the marchioness's suite.

As he stepped into the room, he saw Lady Wrotham reclined against the headboard of her bed with a book in her hand. Startled by the fact she appeared to be feeling hale and hearty, he stared at her in surprise.

"Hello dearest, Polly said you might not come to see me until tomorrow as you were with Phoebe."

She arched her eyebrows with without any attempt to hide her curiosity. It was a look that said she knew something had happened, and she intended to find out exactly what. Gideon crossed the room to her bed and sank down onto the mattress as gently as he could to avoid jarring her ankle and causing her distress. Gideon ignored the question in her voice and took her hand in his.

"How are you feeling?"

"Surprisingly, I feel quite well. I'm in only a small amount of pain. Doctor Compton said I was quite fortunate I didn't break a bone."

"I agree."

"Are you going to tell me what happened between you and Phoebe?" It was a direct question that shouldn't have startled him, but it did nonetheless. When he didn't answer her immediately, Lady Wrotham's studied him like a hawk eyeing its prey. "So help me, Gideon, if you've hurt her, I'll…I'll…I'm not sure what I'll do, but I will certainly make sure you never forget it."

Gideon grimaced as he suddenly realized he wasn't sure how to go about asking his mother for her assistance. He'd simply charged upstairs to ask for help. Gideon's throat tightened as a knot formed there. How was to explain his sudden change of heart from this morning, let alone the urgent and imperative need for him to marry Phoebe? The minute he asked her to persuade Phoebe to marry him, she would demand to know why. When he remained silent, Lady Wrotham frowned.

"If you are attempting to fabricate a lie, my lord, I suggest you do not. I will know if you're lying to me."

"I'm not about to lie to you. I simply wish to spare your feelings…and Phoebe's," he muttered. The moment she froze and looked at him in surprise, Gideon shook his head and looked away. " I would not lie to you."

"Then simply say whatever it is you wish to say." The dowager marchioness arched her eyebrow in exasperation.

"I have a problem I need your help with," he said, suddenly feeling like he was a boy again about to confess to a transgression for which his mother would express her deep disappointment. But, this time, it wouldn't just be her disappointment he'd see. It would be far worse than that as he knew her disappointment would only be one reaction. She would be shocked, shamed, and furious too.

"Go on." The dowager's frown darkened.

"It involves Phoebe, I—"

"Of *that*, I had little doubt. I *knew* something was wrong when Polly came back all in a flutter and refused to tell me what had upset her so badly," his mother snapped with an outrage that caused him to tighten his lips. "I thought you understood me this morning when I told you I wouldn't tolerate you hurting Phoebe. What did you say to her, Gideon?"

"I asked her to marry me," he growled. Despite knowing it was pointless to do so, Gideon experienced a flicker of hope that his mother would be so surprised she wouldn't probe deeper.

"*You did what?*" His mother's expression would have been laughable at any other time, but at the moment, he didn't find any humor in the way her jaw had sagged in astonishment.

"I *said* I asked Phoebe to marry me."

"I *heard* what you said, Gideon, but I do *not* understand why you would propose to her," his mother said as she studied him with suspicion. "You've made it quite clear you don't like her."

"No, I said I thought her intentions were less than noble. Your words this morning made me change my mind."

"Do you mean to tell me that in a matter of *hours*, you've changed your mind about Phoebe simply based on my opinion?" the dowager marchioness scoffed.

"Yes…no."

"Which is it, Gideon? It's a simple yes or no answer."

"I would think you would be happy that I've finally decided to marry," he growled, deliberately ignoring her question. "You've hounded me long enough to find a wife and start a family. Now you seem to object to my marrying at all."

"Then explain to me why you chose Phoebe?"

"Are you saying you disapprove?"

"*Of course not,*" his mother exclaimed sharply. "I love Phoebe. She's become very dear to me."

"Then what is it you object to?" he bit out through clenched teeth.

"I'm not objecting at all. I'm simply flabbergasted that you would ask someone you don't like to be your wife."

"I never said I didn't like her," he bit out between clenched teeth.

"Well, considering your attitude this morning, I would have wagered a large sum to the contrary," his mother said with skepticism. "Why do I think there's more to this sudden change of heart where Phoebe's concerned?"

Desperately, Gideon struggled to offer an explanation that would appease his mother and end her interrogation. Phoebe had been terrified his mother would learn what had happened from Polly. If he could spare her any further humiliation, he would. Still struggling to come up with a rational explanation for his decision, Gideon's heart sank as his mother's expression darkened with suspicion and anger.

"What have you done, Gideon?"

The sharp question grated on him as if someone had sliced him open. As he struggled to find the right words to explain things, his brain ran into a wall in every direction. For the first time in his life, Gideon was afraid of his mother's reaction. He'd seen her disappointment in him this morning, and he was certain it would be even greater now.

"Tell me now, Gideon. What have you done?" she snapped in a voice that demanded he answer her with the truth and nothing else. He drew in a deep breath. God help him. He could only pray Phoebe would forgive him for this betrayal. Gideon drew in a deep breath, then released it as he forced himself to face his mother's wrath.

"I compromised her," he said quietly. The dowager paled as she stared at him in shock.

"*You did what?*" she whispered.

The note of disbelief in her voice was all the more painful for the condemnation he heard there as well. If she had shouted at him, it would have been less excoriating. At the moment, it was as if someone had doused him in acid. He didn't know which was the most painful, that he'd disappointed his mother or the injury he'd done to Phoebe for a second time within an hour.

"I believe you heard me correctly," he snarled as he stood up and began to pace the floor, no longer able to bear the contempt he saw on his mother's face.

Her judgment of him only increased the heavy weight of his guilty conscience. He fully deserved his mother's condemnation, but admitting it did little to ease the pain he was suffering for giving her, and Phoebe, the opportunity to judge him and finding him lacking.

"I know I did. I am simply trying to comprehend how *my son* could do such a thing." Icicles could not have been as cold as the dowager's voice.

The anger, shocked dismay, and deep disappointment in the marchioness's voice made her every word as vicious a blow as the ones he'd taken in the ring the night he and Phoebe had first met. Gideon's flinched beneath her scorn.

"It was not intentional," he said quietly as he struggled not to sound defensive.

As he prowled the floor, he remembered Phoebe's willingness to surrender to his touch, but he was the one who should have shown restraint. He should have had more respect for her tonight and five years ago. He'd failed on both occasions, and he had no excuse to fall back on. Nothing except he'd allowed his body to control his actions and not his head.

It was why he bore the lion's share of blame and responsibility for what had happened this evening. Gideon doubted he would ever be able to forgive himself for being the cause of Phoebe's humiliation. As difficult as it was to admit, he truly deserved the name P. Currer had given him in the author's satirical work.

Never in his life had his actions been so dishonorable. There was no excuse he could offer that would absolve him of his actions. The realization made his mother's obvious contempt for him all the more painful. That his mother would be ashamed of him was something he would never have thought possible until tonight. Unable to bear the contempt the marchioness made no effort to hide, he continued to pace the floor.

"She's refused to marry me," Gideon bit out with self-loathing. In the back of his mind, a voice reminded him that he hadn't really asked. He'd simply come up with a solution that would protect her reputation.

"Can you blame her?" Lady Wrotham sneered.

Gideon's muscles grew taut as he came to a halt and forced himself to turn back to his mother. The scorn and outrage in the dowager marchioness's voice was reflected in her expression. He flinched, then shook his head as he remembered Phoebe's horrified look when he'd said they would marry.

It had further emphasized the horrible life she'd lived as Helstone's wife. He'd recognized her vulnerability that night in Montjoy's garden, but he'd allowed her to leave him, only to condemn her a short while later for something that had been out of her hands.

"No. Phoebe's marriage to Helstone was hellish enough. I can understand her reluctance to marry me, which is why I'm asking for your help."

It had been painful enough to confess his sin to his mother, and the humiliation of being forced to plead for her help was doubly so, but it was the only option he had at this point. Lady Wrotham's withering glare skimmed over him as she looked him up and down. It was a look meant to eviscerate him with scorn, and it cut deep because he deserved every bit of anger she heaped on him.

"If I agreed to your request, what makes you believe I

can be any more persuasive than you in making Phoebe agree to marry you?" She huffed a sound of disdainful skepticism.

"I don't, but my offer is sincere." Gideon stiffened as he suddenly realized the full ramifications of what had happened. "I have no desire to see Phoebe bear the brunt of any potential scandal. But, God help her if P. Currer catches wind of this. It could very well destroy her."

"Not, God help you?" The dowager arched an eyebrow in a derogatory manner.

"No, I'll take Currer's scathing assault on my character without protest. I deserve it. Phoebe doesn't," he said quietly. The dowager uttered a soft sound of derisive agreement before she nodded sharply.

"Very well, I'll send for her in the morning."

"Thank you, my lady." Gideon bowed slightly in her direction. "I've one other favor to ask."

"Another one?" His mother eyed him with disdain. "What is it?"

"I know you are always considerate of the feelings of others, which is why my request may seem insulting. However, it's not intended as such." Gideon released a harsh breath. "I only wish to spare Phoebe any further pain or humiliation. Please do not send Polly to fetch her."

"I had *no intention* of doing so." The dowager sniffed her displeasure, indicating his request had been an insult despite his reassurance to the contrary. "Whether Phoebe agrees to marry you or not, we will need to handle the problem of Polly."

"I have already dealt with that. I informed Polly that a dead relative has left her the deed to a small property as well as an annual income. In exchange, she will forget whatever she thinks she saw this evening."

"Very well," his mother huffed her approval. Gideon bowed again and moved toward the door. His hand had just wrapped around the crystalline doorknob when his mother called out his name. He paused and turned slightly in her direction. It was impossible to know what she was thinking as she tipped her head to one side and eyed him with puzzlement and curiosity.

"Why?" Her single-word question caught him by surprise as he stared at her in confusion.

"I don't understand."

"Why are you suddenly so concerned about Phoebe's welfare? This morning you were convinced she was a social climber."

"I realized I'd been wrong for the past five years. I'm the reason Phoebe was in the study to begin with. I wanted to apologize for insulting her."

"And did she forgive you?"

"Yes, although I will be surprised if she forgives what I've done tonight. God knows I never shall. Goodnight, my lady."

Without another word, Gideon walked out of his mother's room feeling as if he was in the lowest level of hell itself.

Chapter 12

Phoebe sank down onto the bed and stared at the small purse in her hand that held one pound, six shillings. Other than the money she had deposited in the bank, it was all she had. Phoebe glanced at the small trunk and satchel she had begun to fill before dawn this morning. Leaving Chelmsford House as soon as possible was the only plan she had at the moment.

Yesterday she'd seen an advertisement for a small cottage in Staplefield that was available for purchase. She had planned on inquiring about it today, never expecting to be in dire need of it immediately. She could only pray the price would be within her means and still give her enough to live on until she found some form of employment. The memory of why she needed to find a home so quickly made her flinch.

It was impossible for her to stay. It didn't matter what Gideon said. She couldn't expect tongues not to wag. They always did. Phoebe had considered simply leaving Chelmsford House without saying goodbye to Lady Wrotham, but she owed the woman too much to run away like a coward. Facing the marchioness was quite likely to be even more humiliatingly painful than when the dowager's maid had entered the library. She had no explanation for her sudden departure that the marchioness would accept. The only thing her employer would accept was the truth, which was something Phoebe could not share. Although Lady Wrotham was caring and generous, the woman might see her actions as a means of trapping her son into marriage.

Phoebe's stomach lurched as she considered what would have happened if the maid had entered the library only a moment or two earlier. The woman would have witnessed Phoebe coming apart in Gideon's arms. The memory of their passionate lovemaking made her draw in a sharp breath. Even now, she could still feel his mouth on hers. It was a tangible sensation that made her fingers trace the plumpness of her bottom lip. She'd surrendered to him so quickly, so easily.

As she recalled his wicked voice whispering her bedchamber would be a better place to experience each other again, her mouth went dry. It was at that moment that she'd been forced to accept she would continue to surrender to him until he'd finished with her and moved on to his next conquest. Seconds later, everything had erupted in a sickening degradation that had left her ill. In those few short moments after Lady Wrotham's maid ran from the library, she'd been overwhelmed with shame and humiliation.

When he'd asked her to marry him—no, in typical Gideon fashion, he'd not asked. He'd simply stated they would marry. As much as she abhorred the thought of marriage, the word yes had been on the tip of her tongue when he'd proposed. She was horrified that without hesitation or clarity of thought, she'd actually been about to accept his offer.

It was a warning she was even more vulnerable to him than she thought. If he had known how close she'd come to saying yes in those first few seconds, he would not have accepted any other answer to his proposal. After she'd fled the study last night, she'd been terrified Gideon would follow her. It wasn't until long after she'd reached her room that her fear of him following her had ebbed away.

Deep in the back of her mind, a voice chided her for not admitting a small part of her had longed for him to seek her out. Phoebe's heart skipped a beat. It was madness to think such a thing, and she quickly reminded herself that she was simply one more flower Lord Chelmbee had picked.

With her next breath, the voice in her head reminded her of Gideon's apology and then his proposal. They were not the actions of a man whose sole intention was to seduce her. He'd offered his name and protection to her without hesitation, reluctance, or resignation. It had been the act of an honorable man.

Phoebe's mind flitted back to that moment and Gideon's expression when she'd refused to marry him. He'd looked as if she'd struck him a blow before warning her not to compare him to Alfred. The sudden sound of a quiet knock made her jump as she jerked her head toward the door. For a moment, she considered not answering, but if Gideon was on the opposite side, she knew he wouldn't go away. Slowly, she stood up and began to walk to the door.

"Who is it?"

"Mr. Pendleton, my lady," the butler's deep baritone voice made her breathe a sigh of relief. "Her ladyship is requesting that you join her in her suite."

Tension locked every one of her muscles at the man's words. Dear God, she wasn't ready to leave yet. Phoebe glanced over her shoulder at the half-filled trunk. She needed more time.

"I'm sorry, Mr. Pendleton, but I'm feeling unwell at the moment. Would you please let her ladyship know I shall come to her as soon as I am able?"

"Very good, my lady."

One hand on her hip and her fingers pressed into her forehead, Phoebe realized how important it was for her to move quickly. She needed to be able to walk out of the house immediately after speaking with Lady Wrotham. If not, there was the chance Gideon would try once more to convince her to stay. At the moment, she wasn't sure she had the strength to reject him again. It was a risk she couldn't afford to take.

Phoebe moved quickly to resume her packing. She'd just finished clearing the top of her dresser when she heard another knock on her door. Startled, Phoebe whirled around to stare at the door. Dear Lord, if it was Gideon and he saw she was packing…she didn't continue the thought. Hands pressed into her stomach in a vain effort to ease the sudden nausea she was feeling, she swallowed hard.

"Yes?"

"Phoebe, may I come in?" The dowager's voice echoed through the closed door, and Phoebe swayed on her feet.

Dear God, Lady Wrotham had limped her way down to Phoebe's room. Dismayed the woman had walked down the hall despite the doctor's orders to remain in bed, Phoebe ran forward. As she threw the door open, she gasped at the sight of Gideon holding his mother in his arms. Without a word, he carried Lady Wrotham into Phoebe's room.

"Set me down in that chair, Gideon."

Lady Wrotham pointed to the chair closest to Phoebe's half-filled trunk. In silence, Gideon followed his mother's directions and crossed the floor to set the dowager down in the high-back chair she'd selected. With his mother situated, Gideon stared down at Phoebe's open trunk for a moment as his mouth thinned with frustration. Stiffening her back, she tilted her chin upward, refusing to look away from him as he frowned at her.

"You may go now, Gideon. I wish to speak with Phoebe alone. When we're done, I'll send for you."

At Lady Wrotham's command, Gideon hesitated, then bowed slightly in the dowager's direction. There was an odd formality to his behavior, and Phoebe was puzzled by his marchioness's irritation she dismissed him in a sharp voice. When Phoebe glanced in Gideon's direction, his features had become an unreadable mask. A moment later, he left the room, closing the door behind him.

Left alone with her employer, Phoebe trembled slightly. The woman acted as if it were perfectly natural for Gideon to carry her to Phoebe's room simply to have a chat. There was nothing about the dowager's expression that indicated disapproval or contempt. The woman had not even batted an eyelash when she'd seen Phoebe's open trunk and satchel. In fact, she didn't appear shocked to see Phoebe packing at all. That could mean only one thing. Either Polly had told Lady Wrotham what had happened, or the maid had been so flustered, the dowager had come in search of answers.

Although they'd only known each other for a short time, her employer wouldn't be here if she wasn't worried about Phoebe. Like all the other times the woman had treated her with the kindness a mother might, now was no different. Phoebe had never known her own mother, who had died when she was two. It was why she'd always found the marchioness's caring manner heart-warming, but now, it meant she would have to hurt a woman she'd become quite fond of. Phoebe jumped slightly as the dowager nodded toward the open trunk.

"You're leaving?"

Sadness, and perhaps even disappointment, settled on Lady Wrotham's face as she studied Phoebe in silence. Her mouth dry, Phoebe didn't know how to answer the woman and could only stare helplessly at the dowager. The older woman nodded toward Phoebe's dresser, and a small smile tilted the marchioness's lips.

"We'll address your luggage later. Bring that stool from your dresser over here and sit beside me. I wish to speak with you and would prefer not to earn a crick in my neck looking up at you."

Uncertainty flooded Phoebe's limbs as she stared at the dowager in confusion. When the woman quirked her eyebrow slightly and nodded toward the stool a second time, and Phoebe did as the dowager instructed. When she was seated next to Lady Wrotham, shame, followed by humiliation, rolled over her.

Even if her employer didn't know exactly what had

happened between her and Gideon last night, she was certain the marchioness knew it had been momentous. It would explain the tension between mother and son, and it had been obvious the two were at odds with one another. Phoebe jumped as Lady Wrotham leaned forward and squeezed her hand as if understanding her discomfort.

"Gideon tells me he proposed to you last night."

At Lady Wrotham's pragmatic statement, Phoebe felt the blood draining from her cheeks. Did the marchioness know why Gideon had proposed? Humiliation encased her body in ice, and it sank into her pores and then into her bones. Hands clasped in her lap, Phoebe's fingers tightened in a painful grip. Dear Lord, if only she could run from here. She didn't know where, but anyplace would do as long as she could escape the weight of having disappointed Lady Wrotham. Phoebe replied to the marchioness's question with a sharp nod and turning her head away.

"He said you refused him?"

"I cannot marry again." Phoebe choked out the words as a voice in her head called her a fool.

"Gideon is not the viscount, Phoebe. My son has his faults, that I will admit, but he is a good man. He will be kind and generous to you, and nothing would make me happier than if you were to marry my son." There was a heartfelt plea in Lady Wrotham's voice that made Phoebe shudder. When she remained silent, the dowager smiled gently.

"Dearest, we have become fast friends in a short time, have we not?" At the woman's question, Phoebe nodded, and Lady Wrotham leaned forward to touch her tightly clasped hands. "I've not said it, but I have come to care for you a great deal."

"I think you know…I have a deep affection for you as well, my lady."

"Not only have I come to care deeply about your happiness, Phoebe, but I've also come to know you quite well, perhaps better than you realize." Lady Wrotham paused and brushed her fingers across Phoebe's cheeks in a motherly gesture. "I know you are not the kind of woman who dallies in frivolous flirtations or seeks to trap a man into marriage."

Another icy chill swept across Phoebe's skin. Did Lady Wrotham know the complete truth about her and Gideon? She wasn't sure she could bear it if the woman knew what had happened the night she and Gideon had first met. Helplessly, she stared at Lady Wrotham, unable to respond.

"So, if you would *not* do either of those things, there can be only one answer. You're in love with my son."

The marchioness's pragmatic tone had returned, and her astute look sucked the air out of Phoebe's lungs. A cornered mouse could not have been more still as Phoebe stared at Lady Wrotham in shocked dismay. A voice in her head mocked her as she denied what her employer was implying with a shake of her head. She barely knew Gideon.

"What you're suggesting…we barely know each other," she stammered. Inside her, a voice reminded her that they knew each other quite well.

"It only takes a moment, " Lady Wrotham replied as she eyed Phoebe carefully. "As I recall, you and Gideon met each other at Lord Montjoy's five years ago."

"Yes, but it was a…it was such a brief meeting."

Once more, Phoebe shook her head in objection. A voice in her head taunted her with the memory of how Gideon's touch had rendered her helpless to do anything but respond to him that night. Her heart twisted viciously in her chest at the reminder of what those short, blissful moments had meant to her. For the past five years, her heart had been telling her the one truth she'd refused to admit where Gideon was concerned.

"And yet, I *know* how deep a mark your first meeting left on my son," Lady Wrotham replied quietly. "The night Gideon came home from Amsterdam, I saw the sparks flying between the two of you. At first, I simply put it down to Gideon having met a woman who wouldn't dance to his tune. But later, I remembered him mentioning the two of you had met at Montjoy's, and suddenly it all fell into place."

"I don't understand." Phoebe's reply made the marchioness wince and shake her head as if she'd suddenly discovered a puzzle piece that had been in front of her all along.

"The night you and Gideon met at Montjoy's, he came home from an unholy brawl in the lower East End. He was barely conscious when a hack delivered him to the front door. Jeremy and Pendleton had to carry him to his rooms. My son enjoys the boxing ring, but he'd always boxed under the Marquess of Queensbury rules until that night. It was obvious from his injuries that he'd been in a ring where those rules had not been observed. In those first few hours, I thought he might actually die."

Lady Wrotham's expression reflected how serious Gideon's injuries had been. The fear reflected on the marchioness's face as she remembered the event made Phoebe's stomach lurch sickeningly. The thought of Gideon being in pain or possibly dying sent fear streaking through her. Inside her, a voice asked her why it troubled her so deeply. The answer assaulted her senses in a way that made her tremble.

"Gideon's recklessness cost him two broken ribs and bruised kidneys. The doctor ordered him never to fight in the ring again unless he wished to die an untimely death." Lady Wrotham flinched, then released a pained sigh. "When I pressed Gideon about his actions, his surly manner erupted into the harshest, coldest words he's ever spoken to me. He made it clear I was never to speak of the matter again."

"But there was…there was no ill-will between us when we went our separate ways."

It was the truth. Gideon's anger had been frustration at

her refusal to see him again or accept his help. But he had appeared reconciled to her decision. He'd demonstrated none of the seething rage the marchioness described. If anything, their parting had been a moment of deep pain and sorrow for her. Gideon had appeared equally tormented.

It had been his obvious desire to keep him with her that had sustained her for the last five years. Why she had dreamt of him almost every night, hoping he would find her after Alfred's death. Lady Wrotham nodded her head as if she could read Phoebe's thoughts.

"I've no doubt of that, dearest. I believe Gideon became angry when he learned you were an American heiress who had married Helstone. Gideon has a low opinion of women who marry for a title."

"But Father was the one who insisted I have a title," she exclaimed. As Phoebe stared at the marchioness in dismay, the older woman soothingly patted her hand.

"I know, dear, but men can be quite obtuse about such things. I think Gideon recognized immediately how special you were. The moment he learned you were married to Helstone, I imagine he saw it as having made a fool of himself even though you'd done nothing wrong."

Phoebe sucked in a quick breath at the marchioness's description of Gideon's emotional state the night of Montjoy's party. Was it possible those passionate moments they'd shared in the shadows had left Gideon as moved and shaken as they had her? He'd obviously discovered who she was, which meant he knew where to find her. He'd given her his word that he wouldn't seek her out. If those moments in the garden had meant anything at all to him, he would have moved heaven and earth to come to her when Alfred had been shot. But he hadn't.

No, Lady Wrotham was wrong. Whatever had provoked Gideon's anger that night five years ago had nothing to do with her. To Gideon, she was just one more flower to plant in his garden of conquests. The man who'd haunted her dreams every night for the past five years had been a figment of her imagination. Phoebe had allowed herself to hope that one day they would meet again. But when her wish had come true, his disdain and arrogance had made her realize she'd fallen in love with a man who didn't exist.

Instantly, Phoebe stiffened in horrified disbelief. Lady Wrotham was right. She was in love with Gideon, or at least, the man she'd believed Gideon to be. The realization was an invisible blow to her body that forced her to choke back a cry of pain. Desperate to hide her revelation, Phoebe swallowed the knot in her throat, threatening her ability to breathe. Schooling her features into an unreadable expression, she shook her head.

"I'm sorry, my lady, but I seriously doubt I was the cause of Lord Chelmsford's fighting in the East End."

"So nothing I've said here has made you change your mind about accepting Gideon's offer of marriage?"

"No, my lady."

The marchioness leaned back into her chair and studied Phoebe in silence for a long moment. Lady Wrotham's assessment made the knot in Phoebe's throat grow larger. She recognized that expression. It said the marchioness was not ready to admit defeat and was strategizing her next move. Phoebe tried not to shiver from the chill embracing her. If the marchioness realized Phoebe was in love with her son, the woman would not rest until Phoebe agreed to marry Gideon. Desperate to escape, she swallowed the knot in her throat.

"Shall I ask Lord Chelmsford to come take you back to your suite?" Phoebe's question made Lady Wrotham frowned before she smiled as if she'd suddenly discovered a new weapon at her disposal.

"Not just yet, Phoebe. I want to tell you a story."

"A story, my lady?" Thoroughly confused by the woman's sudden change in direction, Phoebe shook her head in confusion as Lady Wrotham smiled slightly.

"Yes. What I'm about to tell you has the possibility of creating a scandal, and I have no wish to cause Gideon any discomfort. Although at the moment, I wouldn't mind seeing him suffer a little, but he is my son, so I must ask that you not speak of this matter to anyone."

"Of course, I would never intentionally do anything that would injure…or disappoint you," Phoebe said with a catch in her voice. Lady Wrotham nodded her acknowledgment.

"I know you wouldn't, my darling girl." The dowager marchioness reached out to pat her hand before she began. "You already know how Gideon's father and I met. Matilda and Robert had taken me in, and one of Robert's friends invited us to dinner. It was there that I was introduced to Alexander's grandmother, the Grand Dowager Duchess of Lichtenberg. We took to each other quickly, and before I knew what was happening, I was her companion."

"I remember," Phoebe said softly as Lady Wrotham smiled at her and nodded.

"I'd been with her two days when she insisted I accompany her to the grand duke's birthday celebration. I didn't know until later that she had been playing matchmaker from the moment she and I met. How she knew Alexander and I were meant for each other, I don't know, but she did. When she was certain Alexander had seen me from a distance, she'd claimed fatigue, and we left the party. The next morning Alexander called to be introduced to me. For Alexander and me, it was love at first sight.

"I knew instantly there would never be another man to possess my whole heart. I loved Thomas and Cornelius, but not with every fiber of my being as I did Alexander. He was a part of me—a part of my soul. The moment I walked into his grandmother's salon that morning, it was as if no one else was with us. Even when we couldn't see each other, we knew the moment the other entered the room. It was like that until the day he died, and a part of me died with him."

The dowager's face took on a distant look, and Phoebe contemplated the woman's description of how she'd met Gideon's father. Instantly, her heart slammed into her chest. Like the marchioness, she knew when Gideon was close, even if she couldn't see him. The realization made her stomach lurch with dread. The marchioness's first marriage had been one of love. If she were to accept Gideon's proposal, she would be married to a man who would never love her as deeply as she loved him. With a sense of despair, Phoebe swallowed the tears rising in her throat. Lady Wrotham suddenly emerged from her memories of the past and smiled at Phoebe as she continued with her story.

"The grand dowager duchess had her own residence several miles away from the palace. The day after Alexander and I met, his grandmother insisted I was to begin riding every afternoon. She said it was good for my constitution, and she sent Alexander a note as to when I would be out riding. The dowager grand duchess knew Alexander wouldn't hesitate to seek me out. The woman could be quite wily when she wanted something to happen." Lady Wrotham laughed, and it was a happy sound that said she was enjoying her chance to share the account of a happier time in her life.

"She knew Alexander's father would frown on our romance, so our notes to each other were enclosed with the correspondence she sent to Alexander almost daily. My afternoons quickly became the highlight of my day. Alexander would ride out to meet me, and we'd spend our time together talking about everything.

"Alexander was brilliant. He could speak seven different languages, and he excelled at diplomacy. As third in line to the title, he did various legislative and diplomatic work for the duchy. When his two older brothers died of influenza after we were married, I blamed myself for depriving the duchy of his leadership. He became extremely angry with me and punished me to make it quite clear he had no regrets."

A small smile touched the dowager's lips as she stared down at a sapphire ring on her finger. Phoebe knew her first husband had given it to the other woman, and the dowager never took it off, even when she retired for the night. Lady Wrotham directed a mischievous look at her, and instantly, Phoebe knew the punishment her husband had administered had been anything but punitive. The thought made her cheeks grow warm. Lady Wrotham laughed and reached out to pat her hand.

"My dearest Phoebe, for a woman who has, on numerous occasions, pointed out the quite bawdy double entendre of P. Currer's writings, you're blushing like a schoolgirl."

"It simply that the room is warm, my lady."

At her small lie, the dowager blew out a puff of air that emphasized her disbelief and laughed. Phoebe's cheeks burned hotter, and the dowager laughed again as she wagged her finger at Phoebe in a teasing manner.

"Where was I? Oh yes, while out riding one summer afternoon, Alexander and I were caught in a rainstorm. It was a torrential downpour, and the closest shelter was a hunting lodge. By the time we reached it, we were both drenched. The rain lasted for some time, but it was one of the most wonderful days of my life. Alexander asked me to marry him that day."

The dowager paused again, her mouth tilted in a whimsical smile that illustrated she was caught up in the happiness she'd known in the distant past. Lady Wrotham drew in a deep breath, then released it as if she'd decided something momentous. The dowager met Phoebe's gaze steadily.

"I always found it difficult to say no to Alexander. He was always decisive about things. When he made up his mind about something, it was a rare instance when someone could change his mind. He was also extremely persuasive. *those* two traits I *know* Alexander inherited from his grandmother. Gideon is exactly the same way. That day in the hunting lodge was one of those moments when it was impossible for me to say no to Alexander.

"We were married two months later on a lovely September day. Gideon was born the following March. Everyone was amazed at how big and strong he was for having been born so early. The dowager duchess declared to all and sundry that Lethbridge blood flowed in Gideon's veins, which explained why he was such a healthy baby for having been born so early."

As Lady Wrotham fell silent, Phoebe stared at the dowager in confusion. What had made the woman share her story? There was a soft flush of color on Lady Wrotham's cheeks, and Phoebe was almost certain she saw a devil-may-care gleam in the woman's eyes. A small smile played on the marchioness's lips as she arched her eyebrows in the same way Gideon often did. Phoebe shook her head as she tried to comprehend the point of Lady Wrotham sharing her memory.

"I'm not sure I under—"

Phoebe gasped as her brain suddenly calculated the months between Gideon's parents' marriage and his birth. Gideon had been conceived before his parents had exchanged their vows. Wide-eyed, Phoebe stared at the marchioness and her heart sank. Something in the woman's expression made her draw in a quick breath of horrified dismay.

Dear God, did the marchioness know what had happened between her and Gideon? She had too. What other reason would the woman have for sharing her story about an indiscretion that had led to Gideon's conception? Ice coated her skin as Lady Wrotham's confirmed Phoebe's suspicions with a nod.

"Other than Alexander, his grandmother, and Gideon, you are the only other person who knows the truth. It wouldn't jeopardize Gideon's title as he acquired that from my side of the family in a confusing line of succession, but it *would* create a small scandal and embarrass Gideon. Do you understand now why I asked you to keep my confidence?"

"Yes, my lady."

"I think you know I don't care what the Marlborough Set thinks of me, but heaven forbid if P. Currer were to discover my secret. The author would find a mortal enemy in Gideon, and I fear that divulging the story would be seen as an unforgiveable act and betrayal."

Phoebe saw something in the woman's demeanor that revealed the dowager either knew or suspected Phoebe was associated with the Chronicles. Instantly, as if she were standing in the middle of a snowstorm, an icy cold layer swept over her skin, and her lungs constricted until she could barely breathe.

"I would…I would never betray you…or Gideon in such a way, my lady."

"Nor would I reveal any secret of yours, dearest." The marchioness's reply made Phoebe's stomach lurch. Dear God, her employer didn't just suspect. She knew. The marchioness knew the truth as to who P. Currer was. Lady Wrotham leaned forward and squeezed her hand. "I knew you would keep my secret as well as understand why I told you."

Humiliation flooded its way through Phoebe as she bowed her head, unable to bear seeing the marchioness's disappointment and disapproval. She jumped as Lady Wrotham reached out to gently take one of Phoebe's hands in her and squeezed it in a consoling gesture.

"Even though you wish to deny me a second daughter, would you deny me a grandchild?" Lady Wrotham said softly. "You need to consider the welfare of any child that may have been conceived, Phoebe."

Shock swept through her to mix with her humiliation. The marchioness hadn't told her about Gideon's birth just to ease Phoebe's conscience and embarrassment. In sharing her story, the dowager had been conveying another message as well. Lady Wrotham was telling her that a child might have been conceived last night. A child.

Gideon's child.

A wave of happiness and joy swept through her at the thought she might be carrying Gideon's child. Quick on the heels of her euphoria was the memory of her last two pregnancies that ended far too soon to give her a child to love. Phoebe pressed her fingertips against her forehead and bowed her head.

"I see you understand how refusing Gideon's offer of marriage puts you in a precarious position, Phoebe."

"Yes," she whispered hoarsely.

Panic swept through her as she sagged beneath the marchioness's steady, compassionate look. Lady Wrotham's argument was a logical one *if* she were carrying Gideon's child, but what if she wasn't pregnant? Even if she was carrying Gideon's child, the likelihood of her carrying the child to full-term was unlikely. Her miscarriages while married to Helstone were evidence of that probability. A voice in the back of her mind asked her what she would do if she was wrong.

What would she do if she left Chelmsford House, and despite her history of miscarriages, what if she gave birth to Gideon's child? How would she manage on her own with a child along the way? And if she wasn't with child? Phoebe's entire body grew stiff, and she shivered from the cold enveloping her.

If she wasn't with child, it meant she would be married to a man who had offered his hand simply as a matter of honor. Not only would she be trapped, but Gideon would be as well. Even worse was the knowledge that being married to Gideon without his love meant she would endure a level of hell she'd never experienced before—not even with Alfred.

She would be forced to hide her love from Gideon

simply to save herself from his pity if he discovered the truth. How could she marry him, not knowing if she was actually carrying his child? Immediately on the heels of that thought was the memory of the past two years.

Since Alfred's death, she'd learned the meaning of what it was to be cold and hungry. It had been difficult enough for her to survive the poverty she'd lived in before coming to Chelmsford House. How could she possibly provide for a child in such conditions? At least with Gideon's offer, if she were pregnant, the child would be well-cared for. Could she really risk leaving Chelmsford House only to learn a short time later that she was carrying his child?

Phoebe released a half-cry, half-sob. For the sake of any child that might have been conceived last night, there was really only one choice she could make. She would have to learn to live with the pain of being married to Gideon without his love. But if she was carrying Gideon's child, her sacrifice would ensure the baby's well-being. Lady Wrotham touched Phoebe's cheek in a tender gesture.

"He will be good to you, Phoebe. I have no doubt as to that fact."

Despite the dowager's reassurance, Phoebe knew it didn't matter whether Gideon was kind to her or not. She would exist between heaven and hell for the rest of her life. How could it be anything but that when she was in love with a man who didn't love her?

Chapter 13

Gideon stabbed viciously at the soil he was preparing to spread out on top of several beds of flowers. Earlier, before he'd begun to assault the dirt, he'd verified the tulip bulbs he'd brought home from Amsterdam were still dry and safe in their storage bin. He would have to monitor them until it was time to plant them in the fall. More importantly, the fact they weren't ready for planting had saved them from destruction.

Scooping up a spade full of compost, he shoved it into the loam in the box of soil on his workbench. If the soil had been the tulip bulbs, they would have been destroyed by his aggressive attack on the dirt. A dark growl of self-disgust and anger rumbled in his chest and was released as a harsh oath. What the hell had he been thinking to make love to Phoebe in the library without locking the door?

That was the problem. He hadn't been thinking. He never seemed capable of thinking straight when she was near. In the back of his head, a cackling laugh taunted him. No, it was the fact he'd not been able to *stop* thinking about her for the past five years. A fact he'd refused to admit until last night.

Not a day had passed when a memory of that night at Montjoy's didn't slip its way into his thoughts. Several months after he'd watched Phoebe flee down that moonlit garden path, he had decided it was time he confronted his demons and proved his torment was nothing more than anger at having been hoodwinked by the woman.

Fortunately, he'd managed to avoid making a fool of

himself just before his carriage had rolled to a stop in front of Helstone Place. Gideon remembered how he'd been ready to storm into her salon and condemn her for being one of the 'American Dollar Princesses.'

Denouncing her for having sold herself to Helstone hadn't been the only reason Gideon had wanted to see her again. He had wanted to make Phoebe pay for the torment he'd endured since that night in Montjoy's garden. Not even the beating he'd taken a few hours after making love to Phoebe had been brutal enough to drive her from his thoughts.

As his carriage had rolled up to Helstone Place, Gideon had suddenly realized the folly of his actions, and he'd directed the driver to continue to another destination. He hadn't been willing to play the fool again. But it was his inability to forget her that frustrated him because it defied logic.

When he'd heard the news that Helstone had been shot and killed by his mistress, he'd been ready to charge out the door and rush to Phoebe's side. With each new article the Times printed about the sordid affair, he'd struggled not to go to her. It had become an excruciating daily argument with himself as to what he should do.

The answer was taken out of his hands when his great-grandmother had died and left him her entire fortune. The dowager grand duchess's holdings were extensive, and he'd used the duchess's passing and his subsequent time in Lichtenberg as an excuse not to seek Phoebe out. Even though she continued to haunt his dreams, he'd begun to think he was close to pushing her out of his daily thoughts.

The night he'd returned home from Amsterdam, and he'd seen Phoebe walking toward him, it was as if he'd been hit by lightning. It had enraged him that despite his best efforts to forget her, in seconds, she'd reignited the vivid memories of their passionate moment in the dark. When he'd confronted her in her bedroom, he'd not known whether to throttle her or make love to her, preferably both. But having her walk back into his life again emphasized that she'd never been far from his thoughts for the past five years.

Last night it had been painfully difficult to tell her that he'd been wrong to accuse her of marrying Helstone for his title. Gideon wasn't sure if it had been a fear of appearing like a complete ass or the distinct possibility that she might not forgive him. It had startled him how much he'd wanted her forgiveness. Even more surprising was the relief that had crashed through him when she'd quietly accepted his apology.

He'd thought he'd had everything well in hand until Phoebe had stunned him by agreeing to stay. His obvious surprise had made her prickly as a Scots thistle. The moment she'd call him Lord Chelmbee, his extreme dislike for the offensive nickname had made him lose control of his anger.

No, that wasn't what had pushed him over the boundary he should never have crossed. Insulting him with that loathsome name Currer had given him had been irritating, but it hadn't stirred his anger to a boiling point. Instead, it had been Phoebe's scathing denial that he had any effect on her at all that had infuriated him.

It wasn't true, and they both knew it. Every time he was within a few feet of Phoebe, an electrical charge crackled in the space between them. Gideon had only meant to kiss her until she'd admitted their attraction to one another was an almost tangible thread linking them together. It was an invisible connection that had existed from the very first time Gideon had kissed her in that dark garden.

He should have known to anticipate his reaction to her, but he hadn't. He'd lost his head and not released her when he should have. The moment his mouth touched hers, the only thought crashing through his brain was how sweet she tasted and smelled. Her response to him had been just as eager as it had that night at Montjoy's, although last night, it had been different.

Unlike those stolen moments in that dark garden, Phoebe had responded to him without fear, hesitation, or guilt. The way she'd pressed her body into his, silently begging for his touch, had been a demonstration of unrestrained desire. Even her kiss had been passionate and completely uninhibited. She'd been hot and fiery in his arms.

With every heartbeat, his need for her had grown into something insatiable. It had taken hold of him until the only thing he was aware of was Phoebe. Then, when she'd come apart in his arms, he'd realized his need to experience her over and over again was perhaps even stronger than before.

The memory of what had happened afterward made Gideon stab harder at the soil he was working with. The short-lived moment of release, satisfaction, and the unexpected sensation of contentment had been brutally snatched away from him by Phoebe's belief she was simply another conquest.

He'd not even had a chance to correct her impression before his mother's maid had stumbled upon their intimate moment. Gideon muttered an oath as he angrily dumped more soil into the flat wood tray. The small spade in his hand savagely turned over one clump of loam after another in the box.

When Polly had entered the library, it had been as if the world had slapped him hard. As if it would alleviate his guilt, Gideon's small spade sliced through the soil like a hoe viciously hacking away at weeds. The fury of his motions did nothing to ease his remorse. He wasn't sure anything ever would. Not only had he been the cause of Phoebe's humiliation. She'd actually believed she was just one more flower for him to pluck.

Phoebe wasn't a conquest by any definition of the word. He wasn't sure what that meant. He just knew she was unlike any other woman he'd been with. The opportunity to convince her of that fact had been lost the moment Polly had stumbled upon them. Phoebe believed last night was entirely her fault. She was wrong. The blame for her humiliation rested solely on his shoulders.

It didn't matter how passionately she'd responded to his touch. He was the reason for her humiliation and pain. And she *had* been in pain. That much had been vividly apparent to Gideon. Her vulnerability had been gut-wrenchingly painful to see, especially because he knew he was the cause of it.

When he'd proposed they marry, Gideon had been stunned by his impulsive offer. Not because he'd made the offer, but because he'd not thought twice about doing so. Other than proposing marriage in name only to his friend, Ophelia, Gideon had never asked another woman to be his wife. Although he'd come close to asking Edith, he'd been saved from making a fool of himself by her betrothal announcement to Stockdale.

Ophelia had been a different matter altogether. Gideon had considered all the pros and cons of a platonic marriage. He knew neither of them had been in love with each other, but he also knew companionship as one grew older was preferable to growing old alone.

Deep down, he'd known Ophelia would refuse him, which had made it easy to make his offer. Gideon had instinctively known Ophelia would never marry anyone unless it was Mathias. If he'd thought differently, he was certain he would never have suggested the idea to his friend. It had been a wise decision on his friend's part to reject him, given Ophelia and Mathias had reconciled and were now happily married.

Gideon's troubled thoughts returned to the moment he'd proposed to Phoebe for a second time. Frowning, he recalled her hesitation for a few seconds as she'd stared at him in confusion. For a moment, he'd been certain Phoebe was on the verge of saying yes, and he'd silently urged her to accept. Then, in the next instant, she'd gasped and recoiled from him in obvious horror.

Not only had she vehemently refused his proposal, but

she'd also assumed all responsibility for what had happened. When she'd darted from the room, it was as if he were standing on the garden path at Montjoy's again, watching her vanish into the night. Last night, just as he had five years ago, he'd felt powerless and frustrated.

More than an hour ago, Pendleton had informed him of his mother's wish to return to her room. Phoebe had been nowhere in sight when he'd walked into her room, but her open, half-filled trunk was still where it had been the first time he'd entered her room this morning. The sight of it had sent relief crashing through Gideon with an intensity he still found surprising.

He'd dismissed his reaction as a part of the guilt he'd been feeling since the moment Phoebe had fled the library last night. As Gideon had carried his mother back to her room, neither of them had said anything. He'd wanted to ask if she'd been able to convince Phoebe to consider his proposal, but he'd remained silent. Gideon knew his mother was still angry with him, but less so than he was with himself.

With a twist of his lips, he returned his attention to mixing the soil for the flower beds that had gone untended while he was in Holland. He'd added the small orangery to the house several years ago, and it was one of his favorite places in the house. Normally working in the arboretum relaxed him. Today it had done little to ease his dark mood. Determined to focus on what he was doing, Gideon turned his attention back to the soil he'd placed in a shallow wood box.

More than an hour later, Gideon was kneeling in front of one of the flower beds with the flat box of soil on the walkway beside him. Still angry at his behavior, Gideon struggled to take care as he spread out the soil around the base of several small rose bushes he was cultivating for transfer to Lethbridge Farms.

Suddenly aware of shadows drifting across his hand. Gideon frowned. Lifting his head, he looked out the arboretum's tall glass windows and saw the sunshine had vanished behind dark clouds. A scattering of several raindrops splattered the orangery's glass roof, then stopped. The plants were in need of water, and if he opened the windows on the glass roof, the rain would water the plants. It would save him and Jimmy, the cook's son, from watering everything by hand. It was also close to lunch, and he was hungry.

Quickly spreading the last of the soil in the flower bed, he was patting the dirt down when quiet footsteps echoed behind him. Gideon didn't bother to look over his shoulder as he was accustomed to Pendleton coming to remind him when lunch or dinner would be served.

"I'll be along shortly, Pendleton. I just need to open the roof windows."

"I'm not Pendleton."

Phoebe's quiet words whispered across his back and into his ears. Gideon went rigid for a moment before he looked over his shoulder. She appeared serenely composed, but was pale compared to her normal color. Slowly rising to his feet, he turned toward her. As flush of color filled her cheeks until her wan appearance vanished. The fire she'd exhibited last night in his arms was gone, and he gritted his teeth at how his actions had extinguished her spirit.

"Your mother asked that I bring her some flowers."

"Did she ask for any specific kind?" Gideon asked.

She answered his question with a simple shake of her head. With a nod of understanding, Gideon resisted the urge to ask her forgiveness. He didn't deserve her charity after what he'd done. Deliberately, he also refrained from asking her if she'd changed her mind about his proposal. Gideon wasn't ready to hear her answer yet.

The thought of her refusing him made him realize how afraid he was that Phoebe might have come to reject his offer again. A knot formed in Gideon's stomach at the possibility, and he didn't want to contemplate why the thought of her refusing to marry him troubled him so much. Suddenly aware he'd been staring at her like a dimwitted fool, he cleared his throat.

"Her favorites are hyacinths," he said gruffly.

Gideon turned and picked up a nearby flower basket he kept in the orangery, along with a pair of clippers. As he handed Phoebe the basket, he tipped his head in a silent gesture for her to follow him. The bed of hyacinths and lilies he maintained for his mother was just around the bend of the pathway that wandered through the solarium. Although the extension had reduced the gardens' size, the path winding its way through the arboretum was a pleasant walk that allowed one to enter the gardens or circle back to the doorway that led into the house.

In the wintertime, it allowed one to enjoy the outdoors despite the cold temperatures and snow-covered grounds outside. It was larger than most solariums in the city, and not even the Duke of Aveley's was as large. The thought of the duke made Gideon clench his jaw. The man had called on Phoebe daily since the night after the dinner party his mother had hosted.

Although Phoebe hadn't attended any social events with the man, Aveley's persistent visits had become quite lengthy. So much so that on more than one occasion, Gideon had thought of interrupting their tête-à-tête with some excuse, but he hadn't. Worse, the gossip Gideon had overheard yesterday morning at his club had been disheartening. Tongues had been set wagging as Aveley had apparently hinted he was seriously considering marriage.

The gossip had put Gideon in a foul mood at the thought of another man taking Phoebe as a wife. It had aroused an unfamiliar, possessive emotion inside Gideon. The knot in his stomach twisted painfully at the possibility Aveley might have gained Phoebe's affections. Gideon scowled with displeasure as he came to a halt in front of the flower bed he used for growing his mother's favorite flowers. With decisive movements, he quickly cut the stems of several flowers he knew would last several days.

As he placed a handful of the blooms in the basket Phoebe held, he glanced at her for a brief moment. It was impossible to tell what she was thinking, and his lips tightened with frustration at the havoc his loss of self-control had created. With a grimace of self-disgust, Gideon returned his attention to cutting flowers. When he'd cut a sufficient number of blooms for a vase arrangement, he straightened and dropped the last of the flowers into Phoebe's basket. In silence, he stepped around her and headed back toward his workbench.

Gideon tossed the clippers into the box of tools he used regularly. Still angered by his behavior the night before, he pulled viciously at the strings of the work apron he wore to protect his clothing. In a savage gesture, he tugged it off and flung it to one side. He pulled his gardening gloves off his hands with equal brutality and threw them onto the flat workspace. For some reason, he'd expected Phoebe to leave the arboretum, but she had remained.

Even with his back to her, Gideon knew exactly where she stood. She was only a few feet away, but just out of reach. The tension in the air between them was heavy and thick as the silence continued. It made him damned uncomfortable. He wasn't used to being in the wrong, and it didn't speak well of his character that he needed to apologize for the second time in less than a day.

Palms pressing into the surface of the workbench, Gideon steeled himself to apologize for the second time in twenty-four hours. Slowly turning around, his jaw tightened as he watched her quickly step backward. From the moment he'd found her living in Chelmsford House, she'd displayed a fiery spirit he'd come to enjoy. It was unlike her to retreat. Gideon's gut suddenly twisted with a savage jerk.

Christ Jesus, she was afraid of him. Never before had he ever given a woman reason to fear him, and he didn't like the sensation. Worst of all, he didn't like that it was Phoebe. He didn't want her to be frightened of him. He wanted something much different. The thought tightened every muscle in his body, and he quickly slammed the door closed on a slowly awakening revelation. Gideon cleared his throat as he studied her for a moment and struggled to find the right words with which to apologize.

"My conduct last night was that of a disreputable rogue, Phoebe," he said quietly.

Some of the color drained from her cheeks, and Gideon's body became rigid at her fleeting look of embarrassment. She bowed her head to stare at the brick walkway. Just as she had last night, she looked as vulnerable as she had five years ago. It made him want to pull her into his arms and simply hold her, but he held himself in check. The strained silence between them seemed to intensify, and Gideon fought to find the right words to apologize to her.

"You blamed yourself for what happened, Phoebe, but that burden is mine to carry. My lack of judgement and restraint caused you pain. I deeply regret that." As he apologized, Phoebe raised her head. She shook her head in protest as her cheeks flushed a bright pink.

"I disagree. You are not solely responsible for my humil…my discomfort. I was…I didn't object. If anything, I…encouraged you." The color in her cheeks deepened, and she turned her head away from him. "I know you would have released me if I'd protested."

"If I were as honorable as you suggest, I would not have taken things beyond the point of no return. If I'd been thinking clearly, the outcome of last night would not have placed you in such a difficult position."

Gideon clasped his hands behind his back as he leaned slightly to the right to force her to look at him. As their gazes met, she straightened to look directly at him, and he did the same. Phoebe's expression was unreadable as she studied him for a long moment.

"You mean your proposal of marriage?"

The words were barely a whisper, but each one of them hammered their way into his chest. He'd unintentionally backed her into a corner from which there was only one logical escape. The thought made him want to visit the boxing ring with one hand tied behind his back. He deserved to have someone spar with him until he fell senseless to the floor of the ring for what he'd done to her.

"Yes. It's the most logical solution to the situation. If a child was conceived last night, things would be difficult for you," Gideon said grimly. "While I would not shirk my duty to you or our child, I believe you would refuse any assistance from me, even though I'm certain your financial state would be, and currently is, less than desirable."

The color flushing over her cheeks again made her look as lovely as the first time he'd seen the moonlight casting its glow on her. The memory of how she'd responded to his caresses flooded Gideon's head, and he failed to stop the small rush of desire stirring inside him. Disgusted with himself, he folded his arms across his chest to prevent himself from acting impulsively. What was it about this woman that left him without any grasp on reason where she was concerned? Gideon saw her throat bob as she nodded.

"I will not deny my finances are limited."

"Then accept my offer of marriage, Phoebe. I promise you will never go without. I shall never harm you intentionally or force you to do anything against your will, and I will protect you from anyone who tries to hurt you. I will ensure you are provided for in the event I precede you in death, and you will have the freedom to do as you please with one exception."

Phoebe gasped softly as he finished detailing the list of items he'd thought of while lying sleepless in his bed last night.

They were conditions he believed would convince her a marriage between them would be a satisfying and fulfilling one. She stared at him in astonishment for several seconds, then as if she'd just absorbed his last statement, she scrutinized him with suspicion.

"And this one exception?" Phoebe's mouth thinned slightly as a small spark of her spirit echoed in her voice. It was as if she was preparing to fight a predator hovering nearby and ready to strike. Gideon's jaw clenched as he saw her distrust. He cleared his throat.

"The only caveat to the freedom you will have is that you will not make a fool of me by taking a lover. I promise to do the same.

"Are you saying you intend to grant me *all* of these conditions if I marry you?" she asked softly in obvious surprise as she studied him carefully.

"Yes. I will have a nuptial agreement drawn up with all the details for us to sign before we are wed."

Gideon's muscles hardened as a voice in the back of his head pleaded with her to say yes. He quickly crushed the thought. What the hell was wrong with him? He was negotiating a marriage contract and nothing more. In his head he heard jeering laughter at . Phoebe stared at him for a moment with misgiving.

"And will you…do you…expect me to…"

Her cheeks grew red with embarrassment, and she turned away from him once more. Gideon's mouth tightened as he suddenly considered the possibility she wouldn't allow him into her bed. It was the one condition he'd contemplated making a required stipulation before quickly tossing it aside.

When he'd told her last night that he wanted to make love to her again, it had been true. He wanted her, and he knew she wanted him. Now, confronted by her question, he wasn't quite sure how to answer her. Gideon cleared his throat choosing his words carefully as he answered her question.

"I've already said I will never force you to do something against your will. Our marriage will be nothing like the one you endured with Helstone. An appropriate name for a man who clearly made your life miserable."

"But you expect to share my bed."

The breathless note in her voice was either one of anticipation or trepidation. Gideon couldn't determine which. Every muscle in his body tightened into knots of tension as he considered the possibility this might be the one condition that would override the others when it came to her final decision whether or not to marry him.

"I do not see it as being an unreasonable expectation. We are good together, Phoebe." Gideon saw conflicting emotions furrow her brow, and he stepped forward to lightly touch her cheek. "I know I excite you, and I've not hidden my desire for you. Would you deny both of us the pleasure of experiencing each other again?"

"No, I…I cannot deny any of what you said." She inhaled a deep breath, then met his gaze steadily. "Very well, I agree to your conditions. I will marry you."

The moment she agreed to his proposal, exhilaration barreled through him. Startled by the emotion, he pushed it aside. He was marrying Phoebe to protect her from any potential scandal if she were with child and take responsibility for the babe. The last thing he would allow himself to do was fall in love with his countess. He knew affection between them would grow, but love was for fools, and Phoebe wasn't a fool.

Gently cupping her cheeks and kissed her lightly. To his surprise, her lips clung to his as he started to pull away. Unwilling to let her go just yet, he deepened the kiss. She tasted sweet with just a hint of the tart apple pastry Cook had made for breakfast. His mind began to shut down as she released a soft sigh against his lips. The memory of last night's disastrous outcome filled his consciousness, and he immediately knew he was too close to the edge of the cliff.

Gideon quickly broke the kiss and lifted his head to stare down at her. The gold flecks in her eyes sparkled brightly with desire, and his heart slammed violently into his chest. The image of the small bench in the rear of the garden crashed through his thoughts, and Gideon stifled a groan. Determined to avoid a repeat of last night, he cleared his throat.

"At least Currer will no longer be able to address me as Lord Chelmbee."

Phoebe stiffened at his mention of the satirist, and her eyes widened with an emotion that quickly disappeared as her expression became shuttered. Gideon frowned in puzzlement. If he didn't know better, he would have thought she'd been horrified and afraid at his mention of Currer. He dismissed the thought and smiled at her. Pink tinged her cheeks as she looked away.

"You blush like a schoolgirl."

His fingertips brushed over a high cheekbone, and her cheek warmed the pads of his fingers as the color in her cheeks darken. Gideon dragged in a harsh breath. Just looking at her like this made him want to drag her upstairs to his bedroom, where he could quench his thirst for her. God help him, the things he wanted to do to her, the things he wanted her to feel as he pleasured her with his mouth and body.

Gideon swallowed hard as his cock stirred in his trousers at the thought. How was it possible she could drive every thought out of his head so easily until she was holding his mind and body hostage? Gideon reluctantly stepped back from her as he shut out the erotic images threatening his self-control. Phoebe's studied him for a long moment before a hesitant look of resignation cast a shadow over her face.

"Gideon…there's something I need…something you should know about me before we are married." The quiet words sent his eyebrows upward as he saw guilt darken her face before she turned her head away. "If I truly am with child, it is quite possible, almost a certainty, that I will lose the babe."

"Why would you think such a thing?" he exclaimed softly in puzzlement.

"I have been with child twice before and miscarried both times. It's unlikely I shall give you a son and heir. I wanted you to know the truth and allow you to withdraw your offer of marriage."

"I did not propose a union between us because I wanted a son, Phoebe."

"No, I think guilt was your motivation." Startled by her belief that he'd proposed out of remorse, Gideon shook his head in disagreement and eyed her sternly.

"Guilt had nothing to do with my decision, Phoebe. If you *are* carrying my child, which is quite possible, I do not wish the child to be born out of wedlock."

Gideon heard a voice in the back of his mind suggest he had another reason for marrying her. Before it grew louder, he slammed it back into the box it had emerged from. Phoebe studied him for a moment as if to assure herself that he was being honest with her, then nodded. Satisfied that she was clear on his intentions, Gideon smiled.

"I'll visit my solicitor after lunch with instructions as to the nuptial agreement. I'll also visit the Vicar-General's office and secure a license so we can be wed the day after tomorrow." Gideon paused and cleared his throat as her readied himself for his next question. "Would you like for me to make arrangements for a wedding trip? Paris perhaps? It's a beautiful city, and I think you would find it enjoyable."

Phoebe grew still as she bit down on her lower lip with what he recognized as indecision. Gideon's jaw tightened at her hesitation. Why would she possibly want to go on a nuptial tour with him, given the circumstances under which they were marrying? He was about to dismiss the idea when she drew in a shallow breath.

"Would it be possible to travel to Rome instead?" Her question startled him as he'd been prepared for her to reject his suggestion. Pleased that she was willing to agree to a wedding trip, he smiled.

"Certainly, if that's what you wish."

"I doubt I would enjoy Paris." When she didn't elaborate, he arched his eyebrows in a silent demand for her to expand on her statement. Phoebe stiffened slightly before she looked away from him. "Alfred took me to Paris after our wedding. I did not…it wasn't a pleasant experience."

The anger that surged through his veins at lightning speed made him wish Helstone was still alive so he could beat the man senseless. Helstone had been an even worse bastard than he'd originally thought. Eager to reassure her that being married to him would be different, Gideon caught Phoebe's hand in his and carried it to his lips.

"I promise you, Phoebe, neither our wedding trip nor our marriage will *ever* bear any resemblance to what you endured with Helstone." The manner in which he stressed his words seemed to ease her tension. "If Rome is where you wish to go, then that's where we shall go."

"Thank you, Gideon. I would like that," she murmured as he heard a note of relief whisper through her voice. Pleased that he'd alleviated some of her fears with his promise, he released her hand and took a small step back from her.

"We will need witnesses at the wedding ceremony. Is there someone you wish to ask?"

Phoebe frowned for a moment as she considered his question. Then her expression lightened as she nodded.

"I would like to ask Lady Lyndham to stand with me."

"Constance?" He stared at her in surprise, and her cheeks became bright pink.

"Yes, unless you think it inappropriate." She winced slightly with embarrassment. "I have no one else to ask."

"Not at all. I had simply assumed there would be someone of long acquaintance you would like to have stand with you. However, I'm certain Constance would be delighted to act as a witness. I intend to ask Sebastian to stand with me."

"And could we be married here, in Chelmsford House?" Despite her quiet question, there was a strength in her voice that eased some of his concerns about her vulnerability. "I know your mother would like to be present, and it will be easier for her that way."

"Are you certain you would not prefer to be married in a church?"

"No, a civil ceremony will be fine. A church wedding would simply ensure news of our marriage reached the Set much more quickly than a ceremony here." Her mouth twisted slightly in a wry smile. "Even then, it won't take long for the Set to discover the Earl of Chelmsford has married. Once word of it reaches their ears, there will be a massive influx of callers arriving on your doorstep. They will want to know if there is any truth to the rumor that Lord Chelmsford married *that woman*."

Phoebe's words were self-deprecating, but he heard the soft note of pain in her voice. With a frown, he caught her chin with his fingers and forced her to look at him.

"You are to tell me the minute anyone treats you unkindly or with disrespect. I'll not tolerate anyone causing the Countess of Chelmsford pain or embarrassment." At the inflexible note in his voice, Phoebe laughed. The sound lightened his heart. Amusement made her shake her head at him as she arched her eyebrows.

"If you ever thought to become Prime Minister one day, your ambition is apt to go unfulfilled. Your autocratic tendencies, not to mention your complete lack of diplomatic skills, will ensure that any such aspirations will fail to reach fruition."

"I'm quite serious about this, Phoebe. I'll not have anyone treating you badly." Gideon's emphatic statement vibrated in the air before he clenched his teeth. "God help Currer if he even comes close to mentioning your name."

At his fierce words, Phoebe jumped slightly as if he'd frightened her. Her trepidation made him look at her with puzzlement. It was the second time she'd reacted oddly at the mention of Currer. He studied her for a long moment, and his bewilderment deepened as he tried to determine why she might be apprehensive. Whatever he'd seen had vanished, and all he saw was gratitude.

"Thank you," she said quietly as she stepped forward and kissed his cheek. "Currer has done you an injustice. No woman could ask for a more gallant champion."

Gideon stiffened at her mention of the satirist, and he frowned as he saw something akin to remorse fly across face before it disappeared. He started to ask what was wrong, but Phoebe didn't give him the chance to question her, as she quickly turned around and left the conservatory.

As he watched her walk away, Gideon wondered if she would actually do as he'd ordered. If there was one thing he had already learned about Phoebe, it was that she was independent. Moreover, she didn't enjoy taking orders from him. Worst of all, he was certain she still didn't trust him.

Not that he could blame her. He'd done his best to seduce her, and when he'd finally succeeded, he'd brought her nothing but humiliation. It would take a great deal of work to convince her that she could trust him, but he intended to do his damnedest to persuade her. It would never undo what had happened in the library, but he could at least prove that his efforts were sincere.

Pulling his pocket watch out of his vest pocket, Gideon calculated the amount of time he would need to secure a marriage license, call on Sebastian, and visit Chesterton, his solicitor. He could make all the arrangements this afternoon and ensure he and Phoebe were married the day after tomorrow. Satisfied he'd settled on a plan of action, Gideon moved quickly through the conservatory to open the roof windows so the now steady rainfall would water the plants.

When he'd finished, he headed toward the door of the orangery, all too aware of the way his life was about to change forever.

Chapter 14

Phoebe closed the door to her room and pressed her back into the wooden barrier. Eyes closed, she fought back the panic, making her heart race and thunder in her ears as if a train were flying past her. Oh God, what had she done? Until Gideon had mentioned Currer a few moments ago, she'd completely forgotten about the Chronicles.

Tears pushed against Phoebe's eyelids as she remembered the installment she'd handed to Mr. Meade's assistant the day before yesterday. Not once since she'd begun writing the Chronicles had she ever eviscerated anyone as she had Gideon in the chapter she'd submitted the other day. It would have been a terrible thing to do to anyone, but she'd done it to the man she loved.

Now it had all gone wrong.

Terribly wrong.

She'd allowed her anger to flow from her pen to the page. From the moment he'd arrived home, Gideon had done little to endear himself to her. His condescending manner and arrogant assumption that she would welcome him into his bed had infuriated her.

It hadn't mattered that he'd been right about her desire for him. And Phoebe did crave his touch. She did so with an intensity that had alarmed her. But it was his low opinion of her that had cut deep. In retaliation, she'd lashed out in the only way she knew how. She'd brutally insulted him in the latest chapter of the Chronicles she'd turned in. Phoebe had even used Lord Nitwitherspoon as the foil and competitor to Gideon's flower garden, knowing full well how dull and obsequious the man was. It was designed to stab at Gideon's pride, and Phoebe was fairly certain how he would react.

Nausea threatening to make her retch, Phoebe pressed one hand against her stomach in an effort to control the churning. How clever she'd thought she was in mocking Gideon. The truth was, in wielding her sword of ink, she'd not been clever at all. Her words were unworthy of her, and Gideon didn't deserve them. Even though they'd been at odds since his return home, she'd seen his goodness in the way he treated his mother, the staff, and even her to some degree.

Gideon's words might have cut deep or threatened her senses, but he'd never demonstrated any propensity for violence or base cruelty where others were concerned. She'd misjudged him based on his reaction to her own foibles. That he'd assumed she'd married Alfred to become a viscountess wasn't unreasonable. The entire Marlborough Set believed it. He had nothing else to judge her by except those passionate moments in the dark with a woman he'd never met.

Ever since that terrible moment when Polly had entered the library, Gideon had displayed the character and goodness she'd instinctively recognized in him that night at Montjoy's. The memory of the marchioness stating that if Currer were to learn of Lady Wrotham's secret, Gideon would become her mortal enemy. Although she'd not revealed any dark secret, Phoebe *had* wronged him. Worse, she knew reading what she'd handed to her editor would hurt and disappoint a woman she was deeply fond of. She needed to fix it before it was too late.

Brushing aside her tears of regret and pain, Phoebe hurried toward the secretaire. She would write a new chapter and deliver it to Mr. Mead today. The marchioness had been in a small amount of pain, and Phoebe had insisted that her employer rest. Their plans for the charity ball were almost complete, and hopefully, the marchioness wouldn't send for her until late in the afternoon.

As Phoebe sank down into her chair, she forced everything out of her head and began to write a new installment for the Chronicles. A chapter that mentioned Gideon only twice. It was difficult to restructure the plotline stored in her head, but she laid her pen down more than three hours later. Staring down at the words she'd written, she experienced a rush of release that she'd managed to poke fun of Gideon with a lighter note than her original ridicule or even her subtle barbs in past chapters.

Phoebe glanced at the mantel clock, then winced and bit down on her lip. For a moment, she debated whether or not to change her dress, but the idea of wasting valuable minutes made Phoebe dismiss the idea. She barely had enough time to reach Mr. Meade's office and exchange the chapters before the editor sent the installment to the printer. Once she'd dealt with changing out the chapter, she would go to Lyndham House to ask Constance to stand with her.

Terrified she might miss the print deadline, Phoebe quickly collected all the chapter pages and slid them into the envelope her editor had given her. Frantically rushing toward her dresser, she put on her hat with its netted veil and jabbed a hatpin through the hat's material and into her hair to hold it in place.

The pin went deeper than it should have, and she winced as the pin bit into her scalp. Ignoring the sting, Phoebe rolled the net veil down until it curled under her chin, picked up her gloves, and scurried out of her room. As she raced down the stairs, she feared Gideon would suddenly appear and offer to escort her to Lyndham House.

Terrified of such a thing happening, she hurried across the marble floor toward the front door and quickly exited the house. Still frightened of running into Gideon, Phoebe quickly walked a short block before waving for a hack to stop. It wasn't until she was seated in the hansom cab that she was able to relax slightly.

Until she replaced her old chapter with the fresh one she held in her hands, she would not rest easy. As Phoebe leaned back into the squabs of the hack, she stared blindly out at the passing scenery as her thoughts drifted back to how the Chronicles had started.

From the moment Jasper had thrown her out of Helstone House, and she'd been forced to find employment, Phoebe had vowed to find a way to escape London. Her father had died two years before she met Gideon, and she had no other family to call upon for assistance. She had considered writing to Lawrence, but she wasn't about to jeopardize her friend's safety for her.

With no one to turn to, Phoebe had remembered hearing Madame Sabine needed a new bookkeeper, and she offered the dressmaker her services. The woman had been skeptical at first, but when Phoebe explained she had nowhere to go, Sabine had taken pity on her.

The dressmaker paid well, but Phoebe had to live, which left little for savings every month. The Chronicles had changed that. Writing the Currer Chronicles had been her chance to escape London sooner than she'd ever dared hope. Every pound of her extra income went straight into the bank.

Determined to purchase a small cottage in the country, she'd vowed not to touch her savings, no matter how cold or hungry she was. And there had been times when she'd gone without heat or coin to buy a loaf of bread and some cheese. Phoebe had been very close to her goal when Lady Wrotham had convinced her to come to Chelmsford House.

The Currer Chronicles was meant to poke fun at the ridiculous, obnoxious, and often superficial behavior of the Marlborough Set. She'd not even allowed the Prince of Wales to escape her pen, but she'd dealt kindly with Bertie. She'd even heard the future king had enjoyed a good laugh at her gentle satire of him.

But not once had she ever singled out a member of the Set as she had Gideon in the installment she'd turned in the other day. Her anger had gotten the best of her, and she'd done more than just poked fun of Gideon. She'd specifically made him the focus of the chapter. Phoebe could only pray that Mr. Meade had not sent the latest installment to press.

As the cab came to a halt in front of the London Times building, Phoebe ensured her veil was secure to ensure no one would recognize her if they were to pass on the street. She'd done everything possible to keep her identity as P. Currer a secret. Not even Mr. Meade had seen her without a veil obscuring her identity. Quickly paying the driver, Phoebe hurried into the newspaper's business offices and through the corridors to the editor's office.

Normally, Meade's door was closed, and she had to wait to be admitted to the man's office. Today it was open, and as she stepped through the doorway, Phoebe was relieved to see the short, stout man behind his desk. The afternoon sun shining through the window made his bald scalp shine.

"Good afternoon, Mr. Meade." At her quiet greeting, the editor lifted his head, and a broad smile curved his mouth.

"Miss Currer, what a delightful pleasure. What brings you to the office today?" Beaming at her, the man gestured at the chair in front of his desk. Eager to do what was needed, Phoebe shook her head slightly as she rejected the man's invitation.

"No, thank you, I'm only here for a brief moment," she said breathlessly as she remembered her mission. "I have a new chapter that I have written to replace the one I delivered the other day."

"A new chapter?" Meade arched his eyebrows in surprise. "Whatever for? The one you submitted is the best installment to date."

"It is a matter of utmost importance. It was imperative

that I rewrite the installment to avoid injuring an innocent party. I *must* have the chapter switched out." At her fervent plea, the editor shook his head with regret.

"I'm sorry to say this, Miss Currer, but the chapter has already gone to the typesetter. It will go into tomorrow morning's edition."

A wave of nausea rolled over her. Dear God, Gideon would never forgive her if he learned she was P. Currer. Suddenly weak, Phoebe stumbled forward to sink down into the chair the editor had encouraged her to sit in previously. Mr. Meade quickly circled his desk and bent over her with concern.

"My dear Miss Currer, are you all right? Is there something I can get you?"

"No, thank you. The only thing that could help me now is a miracle," Phoebe choked out as she fought back tears of horror and regret.

"Are you certain this innocent party you mention would be so offended by the chapter?" Mr. Meade asked in a puzzled tone. "While the installment took particular aim at Lord Chelmbee, the other characters in the story were mocked as well. I cannot imagine anyone finding it insulting, and it was exceedingly amusing."

The curiosity in the man's voice made Phoebe tremble. She knew the editor had always wondered who she really was. Phoebe had refused to identify herself, stating it was the best for all concerned. Now she was grateful that she had been so adamant in refusing to tell the editor who she was.

It was more than possible the editor would realize who she was when it became known she had married Gideon. Her mouth dry with fear at the hell she was certain to descend into, Phoebe shook her head in a quick, sharp movement as her nausea intensified.

"I cannot begin to explain how terrible it would be if this individual discovered who P. Currer is," she whispered as she struggled to fight back her tears of pain and remorse. "The damage…it would be…I cannot begin to describe how terrible it would be for all concerned."

She bent her head as she struggled with the reality of what her anger and pen had done. There's was only one thing that would prevent a catastrophe. The poisonous chapter would never be printed. Over the top of her head, Mr. Meade uttered a noise of concern, and he squeezed her shoulder in a reassuring manner.

"You're obviously deeply distressed by this matter, and as it's of such great importance to you, let me see if I can prevent the chapter's publication. I assume you have a different installment for me?"

Hope swept through Phoebe as she nodded and pulled the second chapter she'd written from her purse. The editor gently patted her on the shoulder in a reassuring manner.

"I'll return as soon as I can."

The man hurried from the room, and Phoebe shuddered as she contemplated what she would do if Mr. Meade failed to stop the publication of the damaging chapter. She would never forgive herself. Not only that, but how could she still marry Gideon? The thought of confessing she was P. Currer was almost as terrifying as him discovering the truth on his own.

This morning he'd given her reassurances that their marriage would give her a great deal of freedom. But he'd also stated his wishes when it came to sharing her bed. Hiding her identity from him had taken its toll on her already. Now it would be almost impossible to continue writing the serial without Gideon discovering the truth.

Gideon would have access to her rooms whenever he liked, which made writing future installments of the Chronicles even more dangerous for her. Phoebe prayed fervently that the editor would return with news that he'd been able to change out the chapter. Although she wanted desperately to pace the floor to try and calm her fears, Phoebe remained where she was, terrified she would faint if she stood up. Finally, after what seemed like an eternity, the editor walked back into his office. He still carried the papers she'd given him, and Phoebe's heart sank as the man moved toward her.

"Success, my dear Miss Currer. I was able to change out the chapters. The new installment will run in tomorrow morning's edition, not this one," he said with satisfaction as he waved the offensive chapter in the air.

The man's triumphant words sent relief washing over Phoebe with the strength of a tidal wave. With a sob, she buried her face in her palms, and tears of relief streamed down her cheeks. Immediately, the editor was at her side.

"Did you not understand me, Miss Currer? Your new chapter has replaced the original installment."

The man sounded uncomfortable at the manner in which Phoebe was sobbing, and he tentatively patted her shoulder. The action emphasized his uncertainty as to how to address her crying.

"There's no need to cry, Miss Currer. The new chapter has been exchanged for the old one. Lord Chelmsford will be portrayed far more gently now than in the original."

Phoebe grew still at the man's reference to Gideon. She lifted her veil slightly to slide her fingertips beneath the netting to wipe off her damp cheeks.

"Why would you think Lord Chelmbee is the earl or that he is the reason for my concern?" she asked as calmly as she could.

"A great number of your characters are easily recognizable if not by their name, then by their actions," the editor replied in a quiet, matter-of-fact tone. "Your distress told me the innocent party you referenced had to be someone of prominence in the chapter. Therefore, it was not difficult to assume his lordship was the innocent party since the focus of the piece was him."

Phoebe's breathing hitched at the man's words, and she frantically tried to devise an explanation as to why she'd made Gideon the focus of the chapter.

"Then you would be correct in assuming that Lord Chelmsford was the character involved in the matter, but I did not do this to spare the earl any discomfort," Phoebe lied. "A dear friend of mine would have been deeply hurt if this piece had been made public. I did not wish to cause her any pain."

"Then, I'm happy we were able to switch out the chapter." The editor patted her on the shoulder again. As he circled his desk, Phoebe made a quick decision and leaned forward in her chair.

"Mr. Meade, I will be leaving London sometime in the next two weeks. I'm uncertain when I shall return, and regrettably, P. Currer must meet an untimely death. Naturally, this means the Currer Chronicles will also cease to exist. I shall have the last chapter for you within the next week. "

Thunderstruck, the editor haphazardly plopped his short, stubby body into the wooden swivel chair. Dismay furrowed his brow as he straightened in his seat and leaned forward to rest his forearms on the desk, his hands clasped in front of him.

"*No,*" the man objected with strong disappointment. "You cannot possibly do this, Miss Currer. Think of your audience. Every time we run one of your serial installments, our sales almost double. Your readers have been clamoring for more. I'm certain we could work around your schedule."

"Unfortunately, gossip is fodder for my storyline, and if I'm not here, it's impossible to continue with the serial. It cannot be helped," Phoebe said as she shook her head.

The editor slid his hands across the top of his bald head before they settled on the back of his neck, and he stared at her with a look of helplessness. Frustration made him rub his bald head.

"I should have made you sign a contract for a specific

number of installments."

"But you didn't," she murmured with relief. "As I recall, you didn't even think the serial would be popular."

"I was wrong," Meade sighed. With a shake of his head, he peered at her as if he could see through her veil. "If you insist on ending the Chronicles, I must ask that you provide me with three more chapters so we may prepare our readers for the end of the Chronicles."

"Oh, but—"

"I must insist, Miss Currer," the editor interrupted with a firm shake of his head. "It is the courteous thing to do. I took a chance on you, and I must now ask that you give me time to prepare our readers."

Phoebe shook her head in objection as she tried to refuse the man, but she knew he was right. The editor *had* taken a chance on her serial, and the extra income had meant she could buy a small home in the country. While Phoebe had no need for a cottage now, it was impossible to forget how grateful she'd been for the Chronicles' success. With a slow nod, she released a sigh.

"Very well, I shall have the last three chapters to you by next week, if not sooner."

"Thank you," the man said quietly. "I appreciate you agreeing to my request."

"I have enjoyed working with you, Mr. Meade, and I regret I cannot continue the Chronicles." To her surprise, Phoebe realized it was true. She had enjoyed writing the serial, but it would be foolish and dangerous to continue.

"I regret it as well, the editor said as he stood up when Phoebe rose from her chair.

"You have been very kind, Mr. Meade," she said quietly. "I am grateful for your enthusiasm for the Chronicles."

"Of course." The editor quickly moved around the desk to shake her hand. "Thank you again, Miss Currer. Your work will be missed by many people, including me."

With a nod, Phoebe walked out of the editorial office with the offensive chapter she'd written and made her way through the building to the street. As she stepped out onto the sidewalk, she stared around her. Her relief at having managed to avert disaster had been replaced by a new worry.

She needed to write three chapters without Gideon discovering her identity as the author of the Chronicles. The charity ball was in just a few days, and she had no idea how quickly Gideon would wish to leave for the wedding trip he'd proposed. How had life suddenly become so complicated, all because of an indiscretion? The thought made her wish that Mr. Currer was already dead.

The sight of a hansom cab drawing near made her lift her hand and waved to the driver. She had one more task today, and she was certain Constance's curiosity would need to be satisfied before she could return home.

"Married," Constance exclaimed with a stunned amazement.

"Yes," Phoebe said quietly. "I was hoping you would do me the kindness of being my witness."

"But you *barely* know each other."

"Actually, we met five years ago." Phoebe winced at her friend's astonishment before she shook her head.

"Five years ago," Constance exclaimed. "You never said anything. I simply assumed you'd only just met.

"I was still married to Alfred at the time, so nothing came of it. When Gideon returned from Amsterdam, things simply progressed from there." Phoebe choked out the half-truth as she remembered the incident that had led her to this point in time.

"Do you love him?" The small note of censure in her

friend's voice made Phoebe's entire body jerk as her heart twisted painfully in her breast.

"Yes," she whispered. At her reply, Constance sank down in a chair next to her.

"That was not a very confident yes."

"I do love him, Constance. I love him more than I thought it possible to love someone," Phoebe said fervently as she stared at her friend for a moment before dropping her head to stare at the purse in her lap.

"But?"

At the single-word question, Phoebe looked up at the other woman, who was studying her with concern. How could she possibly explain that she was about to marry a man who didn't love her? Dragging in a deep breath, she released it as she saw her friend's uncertainty and tried to find a way to answer Constance's question.

"It's the Chronicles you're worried about."

"Yes." Phoebe gratefully accepted the lifeline her friend had unknowingly thrown her. "Mr. Currer will meet an untimely death after the next few installments are published. The problem is how to write my chapters without Gideon discovering the truth."

Constance nodded her head at Phoebe's problem. Her friend remained still for a moment before she rose to her feet to pace the floor. While walking back and forth in front of Phoebe, the countess raised her hand to nibble on the tip of her thumb. Suddenly, she came to an abrupt halt to look at Phoebe.

"How are you paid for your articles?"

"In pound notes. I have always delivered my next installment to my editor in person and received payment then. Mr. Meade wasn't happy about the arrangement, but I refused to budge on the matter."

"Does the man know your real name?

"No, and he would not recognize me as I have always

worn a veil to hide my identity." Phoebe shook her head. "I was worried someone from the Set might see me going into the newspaper's offices and connect me with the Chronicles."

"Then it's unlikely Gideon will learn you're P. Currer if you can keep the chapters a secret."

"Actually..." Phoebe sighed as she remembered her conversation with the marchioness early this morning. Constance frowned with concern.

"Actually, *what?*"

"I am fairly certain Lady Wrotham knows I'm P. Currer."

"Good lord," Constance exclaimed. "Are you certain?"

"I think she deduced it from things I've pointed out in the Chronicles that have amused her," Phoebe replied as she shook her head in confusion. "She did not openly say she believed I was Currer, but she gave me her word that she would never reveal my secret, and I believe her."

"Lady Wrotham is a woman I trust implicitly." With a nod, Constance indicated her strong belief in the marchioness's word. "And like the marchioness, I will never reveal your secret. Even if your Mr. Meade were to disclose anything, what more could he say other than that P. Currer is a woman."

"The real problem is finding a specific time when Gideon isn't at home, so I'm able to write without being discovered," Phoebe said softly as she tried to remember Gideon's daily schedule.

Even if he had a standard routine, their marriage could easily change that. Phoebe had no idea when she would have any private time to write. With the gala this coming Saturday, and no date set for when they would leave on their wedding trip, her time was even more limited.

"I have a solution for that as well," Constance said with a smile. "You will write your chapters here."

The satisfaction in her friend's voice made Phoebe's heart skip a beat. Was it possible she could do that?

"Are you certain, Constance? I do not—"

"It will not be a problem at all. You will simply be spending time with me," Constance said with a small laugh. "Now, when and where do I need to be for this wedding?"

Phoebe sprang to her feet and hurried toward her friend. She clasped the other woman's hands in hers and kissed the countess's cheek.

"I don't know the time yet, but the ceremony will be at Chelmsford House the day after tomorrow. I cannot tell you how grateful I am, Constance. I have no words."

"There is no need to say thank you. I'm happy to help," Constance said with a smile before she stiffened and stared at something over Phoebe's shoulder.

She followed the direction of the countess's gaze and saw the Earl of Lyndham standing in the salon doorway. Clearly furious, the earl's outrage was emphasized by the way his vicious scar was pulled tight over cheek muscles taut with tension. The man appeared almost menacing, and the air in the room had become dark with underlying emotions that stretched between the couple. Lord Lyndham's stark, visible fury made Phoebe suddenly feel as if she'd instigated the discord between the couple.

"Lord Lyndham, it's a pleasure to see you again."

"And you, my lady. I take it you were leaving?" The earl's abrupt reply bordered on the edge of rude and Phoebe flinched. The sound of Constance drawing in a sharp breath, made Phoebe cast a glance at her friend. The countess stood rigid as a statue beside her, while her eyes glittered with what could only be interpreted as a warning. The silent communication between the two was indecipherable, Phoebe only knew her friend was livid at her husband's borderline boorishness. As if remembering Phoebe was still in the room, Constance's turned to smile at Phoebe, but it was more of a grimace than a smile.

"Let me show you to the door."

The earl stepped aside so Phoebe could walk out into the main entryway. In seconds, she was at the front door. She gave Constance a quick hug and smiled at her.

"I truly am grateful, Constance."

The countess smiled at her, but Phoebe could tell it was a façade. Something was wrong between her and the earl. She hesitated, and Constance shook her head.

"It's quite all right. Lucien is simply in one of his moods. It will pass," she murmured. Phoebe nodded, but was certain her friend was making light of the earl's anger. As she walked out of Lyndham House, she smiled at Constance over her shoulder. Constance smiled in return, but it was a bleak one that made Phoebe wish she could do something to help her friend.

Chapter 15

Constance closed the door behind Phoebe, but didn't move. It was obvious Lucien had heard enough of her conversation to believe she was meddling again, but not enough to realize she wasn't.

At the moment, she wasn't mentally prepared for an argument. The last few nights had not been easy ones. She was exhausted. Whether it was from feeding Isabel or simply tossing and turning because Lucien wasn't beside her, she'd barely slept in several days.

Slowly turning away from the door, Constance saw the salon doorway was empty. Eager to avoid a battle of words, she hurried toward the stairs. It wasn't until she was halfway up the staircase that she realized Lucien hadn't even bothered to stop her. The fact that he'd not even questioned her said he believed her guilty and judged her. The knowledge sliced through her like a knife, and she ran the rest of the way up the stairs and along the hall to her room.

Shutting the door behind her, Constance fought back the tears threatening to stream down her cheeks. Instead, she allowed her anger to prevent her from crying. She didn't know whether to be angry that Lucien didn't trust himself to argue with her, or that he still questioned how her gift was to be used for good.

Constance walked across the room to stare down at the garden. Jamie and Imogene were sitting on the grass, their heads together as if they were plotting something. She smiled slightly. Whatever it was, she had no doubt it was her son's idea.

Behind her, the door opened with a loud crack as it slammed into the chifforobe positioned next to the doorway. Startled, Constance whirled around to see Lucien cross over the threshold into her room. Lucien sent the door crashing back into the door frame with a vicious swing of his arm, where it shuddered for a second from the force of his action.

Like a panther stalking its prey, Lucien slowly walked forward to stand in the middle of the room. His fury made the jagged scar on his cheek stand out more prominently than usual. In the back of her mind, she remembered the first time she'd ever seen Lucien. Just like the night of the Black Widows ball, he was as dangerous-looking now as he had been the moment he'd touched her.

There had been a dark edge about him that night that had excited her. Aroused her. Nothing had changed that. Even when she was furious with him, the darkness just below his surface was as thrilling and potent as it always had been. It generated a tension between them that had always set her heart racing because she knew she was the only one capable of helping him tame his demons. She wanted to help him do so once more.

Irritated at how easily she was ready to forgive him and fall into his arms, Constance tightened her lips in anger. He'd locked her out of his room, been unwilling to talk, and now he'd stormed into her room, believing the worst of her. Not about to be intimidated by him, Constance eyed him with angry indignation.

"What do you want, Lucien?"

"I want my wife to stop meddling in the affairs of others."

"What makes you think I'm meddling," she snapped.

"I have eyes and ears, Constance."

"Do you really?" Her gaze skimmed down his hard, muscular body, then back up to stare at him scornfully. "I think *your* eyes and ears allow you to see and hear what you want."

"What the hell does that mean?"

"It means Lady Helstone came to the house to ask me to stand as her witness when she marries Gideon." At her statement, Lucien jerked with surprise, and Constance gave him a bitter look. "Get out, Lucien. I'm tired, and I'm in no mood for this conversation."

"Perhaps not, but for a change, you *will* talk to me, my lady."

"And I *said* I'm in no mood for this today. So if you refuse to leave, then I will," she bit out fiercely.

With an abrupt movement, Constance headed toward the bedroom door. As she tried to sweep past Lucien, his hand snaked out and grasped her arm to restrain her. Instantly, she tried to tug free of his hold.

"Damn you, Lucien. Let me go."

"Not until we have this matter settled between us."

"There's nothing *to* settle. You condemned, tried, and judged me before speaking to me."

"I'm speaking with you, now," Lucien growled fiercely as he pulled her into his chest.

"No, you're not. You haven't spoken to me since the night you walked out of here without saying a word."

"I *did not* simply walk out of here. You ignored me. You didn't even acknowledge my presence."

"I ignored—" Constance sputtered in outrage as she stared up at her husband and gritted her teeth at how he was blaming her for their discord. "For *once* in our marriage, I was willing to wait for *you* to speak. I was waiting patiently for you to bring down the wrath of God on my head."

"God knows I wanted to, my lady," he snarled. "I left before I found myself wrapping my fingers around this pretty throat of yours."

"Are you telling me you're not just as angry now?"

Constance lifted her chin defiantly. "Then have at it. End your frustration, Lucien. You've judged me. Now carry out your sentence."

Lucien's face drained of color at her fierce words, and Constance's heart slammed into her chest. Dear God, what was she thinking? She knew better than to feed his fears that Oliver's madness might be something he had inherited as well. Perhaps that was what it would take to make Lucien see he could be angry without fearing he was on the brink of madness.

Before she could say a word, Lucien's fingers brushed across her throat. Startled, by his touch a knot formed in her throat then immediately vanished. This was Lucien, her husband, and he was the most ridiculously stubborn man she'd ever met.

"Well, my lord. What are you waiting for?" she sneered. "I stand ready to accept your punishment, whatever it may be."

Fury darkened her husband's stony features, and for a brief instant, Constance wondered if she'd pushed him too far. She was being deliberately provocative, and she knew it. But Constance was no longer willing to let Lucien use the excuse of possible madness as a reason to avoid an argument with her.

She was tired of walking on eggshells whenever he was angry. Their love for each other wasn't enough to ensure their relationship remained strong. They had to trust each other, too. Constance trusted him not to hurt her, but she was all too aware that Lucien didn't trust himself.

Suddenly, his hand slipped around her throat to cup the back of her neck. In a sharp movement, he tugged her even closer and captured her lips in a bruising kiss. It was a harsh caress, filled with anger and frustration. Constance didn't protest. She simply pressed herself deeper into his body and willingly gave herself up to his fierce embrace.

Determined to demonstrate how certain she was that he would never hurt her, she bit down on his lower lip much harder than she normally would. It was a quick action that caused him to utter a sound of surprised discomfort, and she quickly thrust her tongue into his mouth, where it tangled with his.

Beneath the palm of her hand, Lucien's heart pounded a wild rhythm. It was as strong as her own frantic heartbeat. Her fingers spiked through his dark, silky hair as his mouth left hers and made its way down the side of her neck, where his teeth lightly abraded the dip in her shoulder. With her hips pressed tight against his, the hard length of his erection pressed into her inner thigh, and she shuddered as need spiraled its way through her blood.

God, she'd missed him these past few nights. Missed falling to sleep in his arms and waking to a gentle kiss in the morning or simply watching him as he slept. A raw sound rumbled out of his chest as his fingers began to undo the buttons of her dress in the back. She reached behind to help, but as their fingers tangled, he uttered a soft oath, and with a vicious tug, pulled the bodice apart.

The rough handling of her dress indicated the strength of his desire, and she released a soft gasp of delight. Eagerly, she slipped out of her gown as he swiftly discarded his jacket and vest. As they undressed, his mouth sought hers again. The passionate kiss made her weak at the knees until she was forced to brace herself with one hand on his shoulder.

Fumbling with the strings of her corset, she was startled when the boned stays were roughly tugged downward. The garment grazed against her hard nipples, and shock of electricity streaked across her skin. It sent pleasure spinning through her body as she utter a soft cry of delight. A moment later, the tip of one breast was lightly clenched between his teeth, and she gasped at the hedonistic sensation.

Desire flared inside her with a strength that took her

breath away as she quickly unhooked the corset in the front, and it fell to the floor. She moved to pull the chemise over her head, but it was suddenly ripped off her body as his hands tore the fine lawn material away from her. An instant later, he was singeing her bare flesh as his mouth kissed and nipped at her breasts.

Her fingers moved as quickly as they could to undo her skirt and undergarments and let them fall to the floor. Need throbbed its way through her, and she pushed aside his half-opened shirt to touch the hard muscle of his chest. A dark growl whispered its way across her senses as her feet suddenly left the floor, and he carried her to the bed.

From where he'd placed her on the mattress, she watched him finish undressing. There wasn't an inch of him that wasn't hard muscle and linear lines of raw, male power. She drew in a breath at the passion blazing in his cerulean eyes. She stretched out her hand to him and smiled as his hard fingers slipped around hers.

"If this is your punishment for my insolence and willful disobedience, my lord, I am eager for you to administer it."

A muscle in his cheek twitched violently, and he jerked away from her as a fleeting look of pain made his scar become a taut jagged line. She flinched at his reaction to her playful invitation. Her heart ached for him at his obvious fear he might hurt her. How could she make him see he could never hurt her?

Lucien has always believed his darkness was a side of him that would frighten her. It never had. Her only fear had been the thought of the darkness driving him away from her. Quickly sitting up, her face was a hairbreadth away from his as she caressed his cheek, her finger trailing down the long scar that made him look so dangerous.

"I don't fear you, my love. I know you could never hurt me."

"Do you?" he snarled softly as he jerked back from her

again. "Can you honestly say you've never feared me? Think long and hard before you answer my question, *yâ sabāha.*"

"You once asked me if I trusted you, Lucien." Her touch gentle, Constance brushed her fingertips across his brow. The memory of the night he'd branded her with his touch and made it impossible for her to be with any other man made her heart pound. "I told you then, as I'm telling you now, I know you could never hurt me. Will you not trust me now as I trusted you then, Lucien? Will you not trust yourself—trust your love for me?"

As if a dam had broken inside him, a dark noise rumbled out of him, then vibrated against her mouth as he kissed her hard and pressed her into the bed. His hand warmed her skin as it slid up her leg to pause at the apex of her thighs. Eager for his touch, she raised her hips up off the mattress in a silent demand he continue. When his hand moved up over her rounded belly instead, she murmured a protest. Unwilling to be teased by him without some form of retribution, she traced a path with her forefinger down his chest to the flat plane of his stomach, pausing just above his erection. The sound of his sharp inhalation made her smile.

"Isis doesn't like it when a mortal man keeps her waiting," she whispered. A faint smile touched his firm lips as his gaze burned its way into her soul.

"And who am I to disobey the command of a goddess."

In a split second, he buried himself inside her, and she uttered a small cry of pleasure. Her hands caressed his back as she opened herself up to him completely. Reveling in his possession, her heart raced at a frantic pace as his body worshiped hers.

Every inch of her was hot and feverish as she clung to him. The exquisite rise of pleasure inside her drew a small moan from her. It was a soft cry, and he stifled it with his lips. Desire threaded its way through her like a finely woven cord. It teased her senses and tugged her upward as her body moved with his at a frenetic pace. Suddenly, a familiar sensation swirled through her blood to race downward into the heart of her.

The intensity of it made her jerk her hips upward and shudder hard against him. At almost the same instant, a deep groan of pleasure echoed out of him, and together they tumbled into the abyss of blissful sensation their lovemaking always sent them to.

Slowly, the pleasurable tension between them eased, and as Lucien's body relaxed, he pressed her deeper into the mattress. The labored breaths whispering out of him drifted pleasantly against her shoulder as he pressed his face into the side of her neck. They laid like that for a few moments before Lucien rolled away from her to lie on his back, but he caught her hand in his in a gesture that displayed his reluctance to part with her completely. There was a warmth to the silence between them, but there was tension, too.

Rolling onto her side, Constance gently traced the zigzag scar on his cheek. Eyes closed, he smiled slightly.

"You have always been fascinated by my scar,."

"It makes you look dangerous and exciting, and you know how much I enjoy doing dangerous things," she teased. He turned his head toward her to study her solemnly.

"Be careful what you wish for *yâ sabāha.* I think you underestimate the danger I present."

"You are the most incredibly stubborn, hard-headed man I've ever met, Lucien Blakemore," she sighed with exasperation.

"Why? Because I recognize the truth?" There was a bleak resignation in his voice that tore at her heart.

"The truth," she snapped as she sat up and leaned over him, eyeing him with frustration. "The truth, Lord Lyndham, is that I'm beginning to wonder if you regret marrying me."

Lucien pushed her away from him with a restrained strength, but not before she saw his stark desolation.

Constance gasped with horror as he sat up in bed and made to leave her. She was losing him, and she didn't know how to save him—save them both. Furious that he refused to see how ridiculous his fears were, Constance scrambled out of bed to search for her underdrawers.

"Then it appears I was wrong, my lord," she said bitterly over her shoulder as she found what she was looking for. "Your love for me isn't as strong as you led me to believe."

Out of the corner of her eye, she saw a flash of movement. Before she could dart away, Lucien was across the width of the mattress and tugging her down onto the bed. Pinning her body under his, Lucien glared down at her.

"Do not *ever* say that to me again, Constance." Beneath his fury, she saw despair. "My love for you is far greater than you could ever imagine."

"If that's true, then why do you persist in believing you're like Oliver? Why do you believe you'll hurt me in a fit of rage? Oliver was insane as a child. Have you ever exhibited any such tendencies?" Constance paused slightly as she saw his confusion. Frustrated, she scowled. "No, you have not. However, what you have displayed is an irritating penchant for being a bullheaded man who still refuses to see he can argue with his wife without harming her."

"Damn it, Constance. Are you deliberately trying to provoke me?" he snarled like an angry animal someone had poked with a stick. Angry as well, Constance smiled up at him with condescension.

"Yes," she hissed fiercely. "If that's what it takes to prove I'm right. You're angry now, aren't you? Furious. My guess is that just like earlier, you're imagining how satisfying it would be to wring my neck."

"I'm warning you, *yâ sabāha*, you're treading dangerous waters."

The words were a dark growl of rage that indicated how angry he was at the moment. Perhaps even angrier than he'd been the other night when he'd walked out of her bedroom and locked her out of his room. Yet, he still hadn't exhibited the first indication that he would harm her.

"I'll always be in dangerous waters with you because if something happens to you, life will no longer hold any meaning for me. So if you think I'm provocative now, prepare yourself for a fight, Lord Lyndham," she spat out viciously. "I'm tired of seeing you retreat from me every time we exchange a sharp word. I'm tired of trying to be the wife you want me to be. I'm a Rock—"

"What the hell is that supposed to mean," Lucien's voice was cold with anger, but there was a distinct look of bewilderment about him too that made her frown in confusion.

"I don't under—"

"You understood it well enough to say it," he said with restrained violence she'd seen him exhibit in the past. "Exactly what kind of wife do you think I expect you to be, Constance?"

"The kind that walks on eggshells to avoid angering you not because she's afraid of you, but because she knows that if she doesn't, you'll retreat from her and go off to brood by yourself. The kind of wife who only uses her gift when someone asks her for help because her husband is worried he can't protect her from the vicious words of the Marlborough Set."

Constance eyed him with a look of deep outrage, and the ferocity of her words made Lucien stiffen against her. He'd only seen her this furious once or twice since they'd known each other. At the moment, she looked as if she could easily step into the ring with him and knock him on his ass with one blow.

But it was the pain threading its way through her voice that pierced his own anger like a hammer against glass. The shards sliced into him as he took in Constance's words. In his efforts to protect her, he'd only managed to drive a wedge between them.

"Christ Jesus," he said hoarsely as he lowered his head to press his brow against hers. "Why haven't you said anything before now."

"Because I knew it would only anger you, and then you would shut me out as you always do."

The anger in her voice had evaporated, and the sigh that escaped her was soft with resignation. Lucien kissed her brow gently, then pulling her with him, he rolled onto his side to study her intently. As he watched her face, he saw something bleak darken her countenance, and his gut twisted so hard he almost cried out from the pain.

"I have never meant to shut you out, *yâ sabāha.*" Lucien stroked her cheek tenderly. "I only meant to protect you— keep you safe."

"From what? Who? Yourself?"

Defeat darkened her face, and his heart slam into his chest with an almost paralyzing force. How could he have been so blind not to see what he had been doing to her? Constance had given him his life back, and yet in his efforts to protect her, he'd continued to keep her at a distance. When he didn't answer her, Constance pulled away from him to lie on her back and stare up at the ceiling.

"Lucien, I love you," she whispered. She continued to focus her attention at some spot on the ceiling. "But trust and love are at the heart of a marriage. Without those two things, we'll become like every other unhappy couple we know who envies our happiness."

"What you ask of me, *yâ sabāha,* is difficult." Lucien inhaled a deep breath.

"But not impossible," she said quietly without turning her attention from the ceiling.

Lucien tightened his mouth in a grimace. How could he make her understand the extent to which the curse of madness in his family had dominated everything in his life since childhood?

"The Blakemore curse might be nothing more than a myth, Constance, but Oliver's madness was very real. I cannot ignore that fact."

"Have you ever raised a hand to Grandmama? Imogene? Jamie?" Constance snapped with renewed anger as she turned her head toward him. He jerked in surprise before irritation crashed through him.

"No," he growled.

"Have you ever hit me?"

"If this is your way of baiting—"

"Not once, Lucien. Not once in all the time you've known me have you ever raised a hand to me. Even when you believed you were under the family curse, you only touched me in acts of passion or tenderness." Her mouth thinned with determination as she scowled at him. "I've made you furious twice in the past hour, and yet you still haven't raised a hand to me. What stopped you from striking out?"

Hesitation and indecision warred inside him as Constance's look of love and acceptance sucked the air out of his lungs. Lucien couldn't deny what she'd said was true. From the moment they'd met, she'd aroused his anger on numerous occasions, but Lucien had never raised a hand to her. They'd been married for more than two years, and in that time, he'd lived between heaven and hell.

And he *had* been angry earlier. No, rage was a better word for how angry Constance had made him. When she'd ordered him to carry out a punishment that would take her from him, his anger had blinded him. But instead of hurting her, he'd kissed her. Lucien knew it had been a harsh, punishing kiss, but she'd responded with the same passion she always demonstrated where he was concerned.

From the first moment he found her in the library at Lyndham Keep, cataloging his antiquities, until now, he'd lived with the fear she might come to harm at his hand. Yet, in all that time, no matter how angry he was, he'd never hit her, even though there had been times when he'd thought it might have been possible, but something had always held him back. A warm, soft hand pressed into his chest as Constance rolled onto her side.

"Even people who are as happy as we are, Lucien, still have the occasional disagreement. If there was a monster inside of you, it would have shown itself by now."

Constance's soft words wrapped a vice around his chest. It sought to squeeze the air out of his lungs as his mind warred with itself, and he fought his fear. Her fingers brushed hair off his forehead before she brushed her lips across his in a gentle kiss.

"Can't you see you have nothing to fear, my love?"

"Of all the Rockwoods, *yâ sabāha,* I think you would be the last to admit to defeat in any battle." Lucien smiled as a look of annoyance darkened her beautiful face. "I shall grant your request, and I will no longer walk away from you when we have a disagreement. But God help me if my anger becomes a blinding rage."

Constance's face brightened with relief as she pushed him onto his back and kissed him. It was a sweet caress of tenderness, love, and a hint of passion. She lifted her head, and with a mischievous smile, eyed him provocatively.

"I think I shall make you angry more often if you intend to punish me in the same way you did moments ago." Her smile became sultry and seductive as she straddled him in a quick movement. "What can Isis say to anger you now, my lord?"

Lucien smiled up at her with a shake of his head as the core of her brushed against his cock that was growing harder by the second.

"You do not have to anger me, *yâ sabāha,* because all I can think about is how to please my beloved Isis until she cries out my name."

His wife's smile became even more seductive as she lowered her head to kiss him again, and her body began to pleasure his with the same passion she had the first night they'd met.

# Chapter 16

hoebe quietly closed the front door behind her and removed her hat as she walked toward the stairs. Despite the relief she'd experienced at Mr. Meade's success in changing out the chapter that eviscerated Gideon for the new one, she was drained of energy. Her visit with Constance had added to her listless state.

While her friend's understanding and assistance were appreciated, the idea of writing three more chapters under the pretense of visiting Constance made her uneasy. Phoebe was uncertain whether it was because she didn't want to write the chapters at all or the possibility someone other than Constance would discover the truth about P. Currer.

Phoebe was on the second step of the staircase when Gideon emerged from his library and called her name. She turned her head and watched him stride across the entryway floor toward her. The smile curving his beautiful mouth made her heart skip a beat, and butterflies fluttered like mad in her stomach. Dear God, if he looked at her like this on a daily basis, she wasn't sure she could hide how much she loved him.

And hiding her feelings was the only way to prevent the pain she would endure if he knew the truth. The last thing Phoebe wanted was Gideon's pity for loving him when he didn't reciprocate her love. It was understandable why he'd broken so many hearts. Everything about him was splendid.

The moment the smile on his lips vanished, and his expression became one of deep concern, she stiffened. Was it possible he cared for her? The thought sparked a small flame of hope in her breast that she quickly extinguished. Gideon wasn't marrying her for love. He was marrying her out of a sense of honor and duty.

Gideon came to a halt in front of her, with only the stairway bannister separating them. His hand covered hers where it rested on the railing. The instant he touched her, an electric current streaked up her arm. Phoebe jumped slightly at the touch, and Gideon eyebrows rose at her reaction.

"You're unwell." It was an emphatic statement, but behind it was a concern that made her heart skip a beat. She forced a smile to her lips and shook her head.

"No, I'm simply tired. I did not sleep…well last night."

Phoebe tripped over her words to avoid saying she'd not slept at all. He studied her for a moment, as if questioning her explanation, then he nodded. Gideon's smile returned, and she fought hard to extinguish the hope that tried to flare to life as he offered his hand to her.

"Come, I'd like you to review the nuptial agreement Chesterton has drawn up for us."

"I'm sure everything is in order," she said as she hesitated to take the hand he'd offered her. Gideon gave her a stern look.

"I believe that to be the case, but nonetheless, I wish you to review the document. It also requires your signature, and Chesterton is here to witness the signing."

Gideon's fingers flicked slightly in a silent demand that she accept his hand. As her palm slid against his, a small tremor rippled through her. Instantly, his fingers tightened around hers as she descended the two stairs to the entryway's tiled floor. The air in her lungs vanished as the indecipherable emotion in his gaze became a smoldering look of passion. The sight of it caused her heartbeat to become a thunderous roar in her ears.

Desperate to keep as much emotional and physical distance between them as possible, Phoebe tried to pull her hand from his. The moment she did so, Gideon's grip tightened again. Glancing down at their joined hands, her stomach lurched the instant his thumb began to trace small circles over the back of her hand.

Phoebe inhaled a sharp breath, and as she saw the unspoken promise of something wild and potent in him. It called to her as if he were a mesmerist, controlling her simply with his silence. Almost as if she was in a dream, she watched Gideon slowly turned her hand over and bend his head to kiss the inside of her wrist. The instant she shuddered, he straightened upright to study her for a long moment.

Gideon's appeared as though he were about to ask her something, but he didn't. Instead, he pulled her gently toward the library doorway. A tall, plainly dressed man immediately rose from a chair in front of Gideon's desk as they entered the room.

"Chesterton, this is Lady Helstone, my fiancée. Phoebe, this is Wilbur Chesterton, my solicitor."

"Mr. Chesterton," she murmured with a nod.

"A pleasure, my lady," the man said with a pleasant smile that softened the solicitor's plain features. "My best wishes for your forthcoming marriage to Lord Chelmsford."

Phoebe murmured a thank you as Gideon, with his hand at her elbow, guided her around the desk to his chair and tapped on the papers lying on the leather desk blotter.

"It's a simple, straightforward agreement, which lists everything we discussed. If you see something you don't like, we can make adjustments."

"This really isn't necessary, Gideon."

"I think it is," he said quietly as he lowered his head to brush his mouth against her ear. "I want you to trust me never to hurt you again."

His words were a scourge on her heart. Gideon might not want to hurt her again, but he would. Phoebe had no doubt about that fact. Even now, despite knowing the heartache she would endure in the future, she wanted to be in his arms again. Phoebe's body hummed with tiny vibrations at his nearness. She wanted him touching her—bringing her to life again.

The thought tightened the muscles at the apex of her thighs. She was mad to be doing this. She should run away as fast and as far away as she could this very minute. Gideon didn't give her the option. The instant he raised her hand to his mouth and brushed his lips across her fingertips, she was lost. Fire streaked across her skin with the strength of a raging inferno, and she sank down into his desk chair to review the marriage contract Gideon had asked the solicitor to draw up.

When she came to the section as to the annual stipend she would receive, she gasped in shock. Two thousand pounds a year until her death was exorbitant. With a vehement shake of her head, she jerked her head up to look at him.

"This is too much, Gideon. Half of this, even a quarter, would be more than sufficient for my means.

"It is the sum I've decided on, Phoebe. It will not be changed. How you wish to spend or invest the allowance is entirely up to you." Despite the emphatic note in his voice, she protested.

"I cannot agree to this." Her reply caused his jawline to harden. It indicated he had no intention of being swayed on the matter.

"Just as there are conditions you would never agree to alter, this is one I refuse to change. The annual sum will stand as is." Suddenly a small smile tipped the corners of Gideon's mouth when she objected once more with a shake of her head. "At least I am reassured you are not marrying me for my money."

Phoebe flinched at his comment, and he immediately covered her hand where it rested on the desktop. The warmth and reassurance in his touch as he looked at her said he'd been teasing her, but it did little to assuage the pain in Phoebe's heart. His generosity was more than she deserved, given her treatment of him in the Currer Chronicles. When Gideon arched his eyebrow at her in an autocratic fashion, Phoebe was forced to accept his decision.

It didn't take long for her to finish reviewing the document, and Gideon had been true to his word as to the freedom he intended to give her. The only objection she had was the stipend Gideon refused to change. A knot formed in Phoebe's throat as she reread the stipulation they would both remain faithful to their vows.

Should either of them failed to comply with the condition, an immediate petition for divorce would be filed by the injured party. It was a pointless item to include as Gideon was the only man she would ever want until she drew her last breath. Phoebe raised her head and looked at the solicitor seated across from her.

"Where am I to sign, Mr. Chesterton?"

At her question, the man pulled out two additional copies of the agreement from a portfolio he held and moved around the desk to point out all the places she was to initial or add her signature to each copy. When she'd finished, Phoebe rose from her seat and stepped aside to give Gideon room to sign the papers as well. Long, strong fingers took up the pen while his other hand held the paperwork in place. The memory of those powerful hands caressing her made Phoebe draw in a sharp breath.

Gideon immediately paused and turn his head to look at her. Phoebe swallowed the knot blocking her throat and forced a smile to her lips, which appeared to satisfy him enough to continue signing the marriage contract. Several seconds later, she watched him sign his full name in hard, firm strokes, with the final letter of his title ending in a small flourish.

Phoebe wasn't surprised by the fact his middle name was Alexander. The silent pronunciation of his name in her head made her want to whisper it out loud. Just like everything else about him, it was as powerful as the man. His name possessed a strength that signaled he would do as he said. He would protect her, even from himself.

But he was the last person she wanted protection from. What she wanted—needed from him was his love. It was something she knew she would never have, but it didn't stop her from wishing for it. As Gideon straightened upright, he eyed her with amused curiosity. His expression made her cheeks grow hot, and he trailed his forefinger across her cheek with a smile before he nodded at his solicitor.

"Thank you, Chesterton. If you'll keep one of these copies in your office safe, Lady Helstone and I will ensure the safety of our individual copies of the contract."

"Of course, my lord," the man said with a polite nod of his head. With efficient speed, the solicitor collected his paperwork, stored them away in his leather satchel. When he was finished, he offered them a small bow. "If you have questions or wish to make any changes, please let me know, my lord, my lady. I have one last stop to make on my way home, so if you will excuse me, I shall see myself out."

"Thank you for drawing up the document so quickly. I am appreciative, although I imagine I will pay dearly for it." Gideon's cheerful reply made the solicitor smile.

"It was a pleasure to accommodate one of my most valuable clients." With another bow, the man hurried out of the library.

When they were alone, Phoebe's heart began to race. She wasn't sure whether it was excitement or trepidation at being alone with him in the same room where the change in their relationship began. Gideon became somber as the solicitor left.

"Unless you've objections, I made arrangements for us to be married the day after tomorrow at eleven o'clock. I was able to convince the registrar to come to Chelmsford House to perform the ceremony."

"Convince?" Phoebe's tension eased slightly as she smiled with amusement. She was certain Gideon's method of convincing was more of a demand than persuasion.

"Perhaps persuaded would be a better word."

"Of that, I have no doubt." She laughed.

A second later, the grin on Gideon's handsome features took Phoebe's breath away. With every passing minute in his company, she was beginning to fully understand the man she'd dreamed about for the past five years was real. She'd not been wrong about him. Gideon wasn't the debauched rogue she'd depicted in the Chronicles.

He was pleasant, thoughtful, generous, and kind. They were only a few of the reasons was a trail of broken hearts followed in his wake. With that realization came the reminder that her life was about to become an existence of joy and pain. No, it already was.

Just being in his presence had Phoebe teetering between happiness and sadness. She should have left Chelmsford House when she'd had the chance, even if it had meant living in a cottage that was smaller than she'd planned. Oblivious to her inner turmoil, Gideon smiled.

"I did allow him to select the time, although I would have preferred to give Sebastian and Constance more notice. But when I spoke with Sebastian, he indicated his mornings were free for the remainder of the week."

"I'll send a note to Constance this evening. She didn't express any conflict that might prevent her from being present."

Phoebe glanced down at the copies of the marriage contract the solicitor had left for them. If she'd been able to resist Gideon last night, she wouldn't be standing here discussing their wedding. Sensing he was studying her, Phoebe looked up at him. The puzzlement on his face made her body tense.

Without thinking, her gaze flitted to the couch where they'd made love, then back to him. Regret crossed his chiseled, aristocratic features, and Phoebe wanted to sob from the pain it caused her. It was obvious Gideon was regretting the actions that had forced him into this situation.

She drew in a breath and released it as she swallowed hard. Phoebe knew better than to suggest they wait until they were certain she was with child. Gideon had fought hard to convince her to marry him and had refused to wait. He'd made up his mind to do the honorable thing, and her stubborn nature was no match for his in the matter. This morning she'd been too tired and drained of emotion to say no to him. That hadn't changed.

"If you'll excuse me, I need to see if your mother requires anything of me." Unwilling to let him see how much his remorse pained her, she turned to leave him, but his hand caught her arm to hold her back.

"Before you go, I have something for you."

There was a strange note in his voice, and his gaze darkened with an emotion she didn't recognize. He reached into the pocket of his trousers to pull out a small box. Certain she knew what he held in his hand, she took a quick step back. It was one more thing tying her to him that illustrated the deep water she was treading. Not even a fairy dancing on the fine strings of a cobweb was an adequate description as to the state of her emotions right now.

"I don't think—"

"*Damnit, Phoebe*, you can't keep jumping away from me every time I say something or, God forbid, touch you." Frustration filled his voice as he slapped the small box down on the desktop and viciously shoved it toward her. "Every Countess of Chelmsford has worn this for the past two hundred years. It's yours now."

Uncertain how to respond, Phoebe looked at him for a moment. Frustration had tightened his mouth to a thin line, and she flinched before reaching for the box and slowly opening it. The late afternoon light shining through the windows danced off the brilliant emerald ring nestled inside a bed of midnight-blue velvet. Set inside a circle of diamonds, the gemstone sparkled like a small light in the room's shadows. It was exquisite, and it was impossible for her not to draw in a sharp breath of pleasure.

"It's beautiful," she said quietly with awe as her fingertips brushed over the gem.

In an unexpected movement, Gideon took her hand in his and pulled the ring from the box. Gently, he slid it onto her finger. When the ring was in place, he held onto her hand.

"It's not half as lovely as you are, Phoebe."

His words made her cheeks grow hot, but it was the sincerity in his voice that alarmed Phoebe. If the man decided to use his renowned charm on her, it would be impossible to hide her feelings. The barrier that shielded her heart from him was far too weak to protect her if she didn't take care.

"While I think you might need glasses, I thank you for the compliment." She forced a smile to her lips as she pulled her hand free of his and stepped back. "I must go see Lady Wrotham. There are still a few final arrangements to make for the ball Saturday night."

"I'll see you at dinner then."

It was more an edict than a question, and Phoebe simply nodded. The thought of dining alone with Gideon was more than she was capable of at the moment. The emotional strain of the day had depleted what little energy Phoebe had after a sleepless night. The past few moments were enough for her to know she had nothing in reserve to withstand any intimate time in his company. She would look in on the dowager marchioness and then retire for the night.

Phoebe winced as Madame Sabine accidentally stabbed her with a straight pin. Immediately, the modiste apologized, but Phoebe reassured her it was nothing. From her seat in a comfortable chair near the window, Lady Wrotham pointed to a bolt of material that Sabine's assistant showed her. The assistant made a note on a small notepad she carried while the marchioness looked at Phoebe with a smile of satisfaction.

"On Sunday morning, the Set will be talking about the new Countess of Chelmsford and vying for her attention with their invitations and calling cards." At the woman's elation, Phoebe shook her head.

"Invitations I have no wish to accept."

"There are some you will need to accept, dearest," the dowager marchioness chided gently. "As Gideon's wife, there are some people you cannot ignore."

Phoebe glanced down at Madame Sabine who was almost finished pinning the gown the woman had thrown over Phoebe's head a few moments ago. For the past four hours, the seamstress had taken measurements for day dresses, evening gowns, and accessories as part of the trousseau the marchioness had insisted Phoebe needed.

After leaving Gideon in the study yesterday evening, Phoebe had gone to look in on the dowager marchioness. The older woman had greeted her enthusiastically and declared that Sabine was coming to fit Phoebe for a trousseau and wedding dress. Phoebe had protested that a full wardrobe was unnecessary, but the marchioness had pleaded that she wanted the trousseau to be a special wedding gift just for Phoebe.

Phoebe had reluctantly agreed, which was why she'd been standing in front of the dressmaker for longer than she wanted. Her attention swung to Lady Wrotham. The marchioness was examining a pair of gloves Sabine's assistant had provided for inspection. The excitement and happiness radiating off her future mother-in-law were almost tangible sensations. For the last several hours, the woman had directed the small scene in front of her from a nearby chair. Every time Phoebe tried to override the older woman's demand for another gown, Lady Wrotham dismissed her protests with a wave of her hand.

"Sabine, you are certain the dress for tomorrow morning will be ready in time?" Lady Wrotham's voice echoed with concern, and the dressmaker nodded her head without stopping her work.

"It will be delivered first thing in the morning, my lady," the dressmaker said with deference. "The evening gown you order for Lady Helstone will be ready tomorrow as well."

"What gown?" Phoebe asked in surprise as she looked at the dressmaker, who quickly bowed her head. Phoebe immediately turned her head toward the marchioness. The woman felt the texture of the material on a bolt of cloth the dressmaker's assistant had undone for her. Either the woman hadn't heard her or was ignoring her, and Phoebe believed it was the latter. She repeated her question. "*What* gown?"

"For the charity ball, Saturday night." Lady Wrotham looked at her as if Phoebe knew all about the gown.

"I didn't order a gown."

"I did," the dowager said with a happy smile as Sabine's assistant offered up another bolt of material for the marchioness's examination. "I placed the order two weeks ago. I wanted to surprise you with a new gown for the gala."

"Two weeks—"

"Oh, and Sabine, she'll need at least three traveling dresses."

"*Three*," Phoebe exclaimed with a shake of her head. "My la—"

"*Phoebe*," the dowager interrupted her in a chastising manner as she directed a stern look in her direction. Phoebe sighed quietly.

"Mama, I *do not* need three traveling dresses."

"Why must you insist on refusing me a small amount of

fun, dearest?" The marchioness shook her head and eyed Phoebe with affectionate exasperation. "I've not enjoyed myself so much since Alice was to be married."

"Very well." Phoebe drew in a deep breath and exhaled it in defeat.

"Really, Phoebe, I am having fun. If Alice were here, she would tell you it's true." Lady Wrotham released a sigh of disappointment. "I do wish she and Duncan could be here tomorrow, but they will meet you this fall when they come to visit."

As Sabine continued to pin different parts of Phoebe's dress, the door to the marchioness's room opened. She glanced over her shoulder and breathed a sigh of relief that it wasn't Polly. It was one of the other maids who hurried to the dowager's side. The young girl handed Lady Wrotham a note, then stepped back to wait. The marchioness quickly read the note before her head jerked up to eye Phoebe in dismay as she waved the paper in the air.

"Gideon says you didn't eat dinner last night, and he suspects you didn't eat this morning either. Is this true?"

"I was exhausted last night and wasn't hungry."

"And breakfast?"

"I had tea and toast."

"That is hardly enough to feed a mouse, Phoebe." The marchioness's mouth was a thin line of disapproval as she studied Phoebe with a stern expression. Lady Wrotham shook her head to further emphasize her dismay. The marchioness turned her attention to the maid waiting patiently near the foot of the bed. "Mabel, tell his lordship, Lady Helstone, and I will be down for lunch shortly."

"But your ankle, my la…Mama, you should not be walking on it yet," Phoebe said in dismay as Lady Wrotham nodded for the maid to leave and convey her message.

"My ankle is fine, and I am tired of being a prisoner in this room." The marchioness brushed Phoebe's protest aside with a wave of her hand, then turned her attention to the dressmaker. "Sabine, I think we can continue with the rest of the fittings the first of next week in your shop. However, the wedding gown must be here no later than nine o'clock tomorrow morning."

Sabine murmured her understanding of the marchioness's instructions and stood up to make one last pin adjustment before she stepped back to study the gown on Phoebe. As if satisfied with her work, the dressmaker nodded. With Sabine's help, Phoebe removed the gown the dressmaker had been pinning for alterations.

While the seamstress carefully packed the gown she'd been pinning, Phoebe began to dress in what she'd been wearing when she'd first entered Lady Wrotham's rooms. The dressmaker helped her do up the buttons at the back of her day dress while Sabine's assistant collected the bolts of materials that the modiste had brought with her.

In a flurry of movement, the dressmaker was walking out the door a few moments later. As the modiste and her assistant disappeared, Lady Wrotham rose to her feet, and Phoebe quickly went to the woman's side.

"You really shouldn't be out of bed, let alone going downstairs," Phoebe scolded gently. Lady Wrotham shook her head in dismissal.

"Simply give me your arm, Phoebe. I shall be fine." Phoebe released a sound of exasperation at her reply, and the marchioness laughed. "My son isn't the only one with a stubborn streak. Besides, I have an important reason for going downstairs to eat with my son."

"Oh?"

"The latest chapter in the Currer Chronicles is in the Times this morning. I've not read it yet because I wanted to do so with Gideon present. I want to see his reaction."

There was laughter in Lady Wrotham's voice, and a ripple of guilt sped through Phoebe. She hadn't seen Gideon this morning, but it wasn't difficult for her to imagine what his reaction had been when he'd read the latest installment of the serial. Thank God she'd been able to stop the original chapter from running. Phoebe remained silent as she assisted the marchioness out of her room, and the two of them slowly made their way downstairs.

Dumbfounded, Gideon stared at the maid in silence for several seconds as he took in the fact that his mother intended to come downstairs for lunch. As his gaze focused on the maid's uneasy expression, he waved his hand at her.

"Thank you, Mabel."

As the young woman left the study, Gideon signed one of the documents his estate manager had sent him, then pushed his chair away from the desk. His mother clearly wasn't in her right mind to be thinking of coming downstairs with an injured ankle. The thought had barely penetrated his brain before he saw the morning edition of the London Times out of the corner of his eye.

He had tossed it aside earlier after having read Currer's column. Lips twisting in a harsh grimace, he suddenly knew his mother's motivation in coming downstairs to lunch. She intended to tease him mercilessly. It was her way of reminding him that he was no better than anyone else. A tenet she'd fostered in him since he was a child.

Normally, he didn't mind her poking fun at him, but there was something about Currer's depiction of him that always set him on edge. Gideon knew how ridiculous it was to allow Currer's satirical jabs to anger him. In the back of his head, he heard mocking laughter. He knew exactly why Currer's characterization irritated him. He'd just not been willing to acknowledge it until this moment.

The satirist's words struck deep because, in some ways, he was what the author described. In the Chronicles, Lord Chelmbee was a ne'er-do-well focused only on cultivating his garden of flowers. Flowers that included not just those of the botanical variety but the fairer sex as well. It was understandable why Currer would focus on the superficial aspects of his caricature of Gideon. But it was the author's delivery that stung.

It was as if the man knew him and was disappointed in Gideon's failure to meet some unspoken potential. He'd confirmed Currer's characterization of himself by egregiously compromising Phoebe. Gideon's gaze drifted to the couch near the fireplace. If Currer were here now, no doubt, the man would ask Gideon if he had regrets about making love to Phoebe the other night.

Regrets? Not for the passion they'd share. Those few short moments when he'd experienced Phoebe again had been exhilarating. But being the catalyst and cause of her humiliation was something he regretted deeply. The memory of Phoebe's pale features and her anguish made his gut twist viciously. It was impossible to go back and do things differently, but he intended to do everything in his power to make amends for his behavior from this point forward.

Gideon picked up the business card Luke Ashford had left with him at the end of their meeting late yesterday morning. God only knew what Currer would think to write when the author learned Gideon and Phoebe had married. But he had no intention of giving the man the chance to think about it.

When he'd said he would protect Phoebe, he'd meant every word. It was why he'd asked Ashford to meet with him. He knew of the man's reputation from when Percy Rockwood had worked with the man last year.

Quiet and unassuming, Ashford had indicated he believed he would be able to discover the identity and whereabouts of P. Currer. Once the investigator found the man, Gideon would make it worthwhile for Currer not to ever mention Phoebe in any form or fashion. The soft murmur of female voices interrupted his thoughts, and with a growl of exasperation, he pushed himself up out of his chair.

His stride quick, Gideon strode out of his study into the entryway to see his mother and Phoebe halfway down the stairs. Quickly crossing the floor, Gideon came to a halt at the foot of the stairs to watch the two women descending the steps. The marchioness didn't seem to be in any pain, but that didn't mean she should be on her feet. He narrowed his eyes at Phoebe, and then at his mother.

"When Mabel said you intended to come downstairs, I was certain she was mistaken, yet here you are, mama."

"Stop scowling, Gideon. My ankle is fine." Lady Wrotham simply laughed and stretched out her hand to him as she reached the last few steps of the staircase.

"I highly doubt that." Gideon took her hand in his and assisted her down the last step. "If need be, I'll strap you down Saturday night to keep you off the dance floor."

"You are being over-protective, Lord Chelmbee." The marchioness's reference to the Chronicles made him glare at her.

"I find your humor far from amusing, my lady."

"Does this mean the Chronicles were not pleasant reading for you this morning?"

At the laughter in his mother's voice, Gideon scowled darkly at her, but didn't reply. Instead, he released the marchioness's hand to greet Phoebe. As if it were something he'd done dozens of times before, Gideon leaned forward to brush his lips across the silky softness of Phoebe's cheek. The scent of orange blossoms filled his nostrils as he lifted his head.

"I was disappointed not to see you at dinner last night," he murmured. It was a true statement. In fact, he'd been far unhappier at her absence than he cared to admit.

"I was tired and decided to retire early."

It was a reasonable explanation, but Gideon was certain it was more than exhaustion that had prompted Phoebe to avoid dining alone with him. Yesterday, when he'd presented her with the Chelmsford's emerald, she'd been as skittish as a young filly. It filled him with frustration. Had he made a mistake insisting they marry quickly? Gideon pushed the thought aside and accepted Phoebe's explanation with a nod.

Offering the marchioness his arm, Gideon escorted her to the dining room with Phoebe following them. As he helped his mother take her seat at the table, Phoebe moved to sit next to her, but the marchioness waved her hand in objection.

"Please sit across from me, Phoebe," Lady Wrotham said with a mischievous smile. "I have no desire to feel as if I'm at Wimbledon with my head turning back and forth during a conversation between the three of us."

As his mother sat down at the table, Gideon turned to Phoebe, whose expression was unreadable. She offered him a half-smile, as she did as his mother decreed, and allowed Gideon to help her take the seat on his left.

Once he was seated at the head of the table, Gideon gestured for Pendleton to serve lunch. Their meal was brought out in less than a minute, and the footmen made their way around the table with dishes of veal cutlets, asparagus, and braised carrots. The footman serving the veal bent his head as Lady Wrotham murmured something to him. With a nod, the man waited on the marchioness to finish selecting her cutlet before returning to the pantry.

Gideon had just taken a bite of veal when the footman reappeared with the morning's edition of the London Times. The dowager accepted the paper with a word of thanks and a cheerful smile. Gideon's mouth tightened with annoyance as his mother opened the paper, and he cleared his throat.

"I thought you would have read the morning's paper by

now, mama."

"I didn't have time to read Currer's Chronicles."

"And you simply couldn't wait until later to read the damned thing," he grumbled as he scowled at his mother.

"And *clearly*, Currer's latest column managed to put you in a foul mood." Lady Wrotham released a sound of amused exasperation.

"I am *not* in a foul mood," Gideon said coolly.

"*Really?*" the dowager said with an arched look of motherly dissent.

Gideon muttered an oath beneath his breath and focused on his meal. As the marchioness opened the newspaper, Gideon looked at Phoebe. Fear and pain shadowed her features as she darted a look in his direction. Puzzled, he quirked his eyebrow upward in a questioning manner. The moment he did so, alarm swept across Phoebe's face, and she quickly turned her head away.

Perplexed, Gideon was about to ask what was troubling her when the newspaper rustled slightly. A second later, Lady Wrotham gasped, then laughed. The sound made Phoebe jerk her head up to look at him. It was impossible to tell if she was studying him in dismay or sympathy. Almost as if she wanted to reassure him, she stretched out her hand and gently touched his arm.

Instantly, the heat of her touch drove its way through the material of his jacket and shirt, then pierced his skin like a hot iron to fire his blood. Her touch emphasized how easily she could stir his emotions. There was a quiet intimacy about the way her hand rested on his arm. Desire always hovered in the background whenever he was close to her, but this was altogether different.

If someone had asked him to describe the sensation he was experiencing, he would be unable to do so. It was a strange yet familiar sensation in the silent communication that passed between them. As he met Phoebe's eyes, an emotion flickered in their depths that made his heart slam into his chest.

In the next moment, his mother made a soft sound from behind the newspaper, and his connection with Phoebe was lost as she pulled her hand away. Irritated that his link with Phoebe had been broken, Gideon scowled at the newspaper his mother was hiding behind. He looked back at Phoebe, but she was cutting her meat into bite-size portions.

The newspaper rustled again as the marchioness folded it and laid it beside her plate. A serene expression on her timeless features, Lady Wrotham picked up her fork and began to eat her lunch. Gideon laid down his silverware and leaned back in his chair when she didn't say anything to provoke him.

"It appears Currer's latest chapter amused you immensely, my lady," he said with annoyance as he studied his mother. Lady Wrotham smiled at him.

"I think Mr. Currer was quite kind to you in his latest chapter, Gideon." The dowager's voice held a distinct note of amusement. "Although I confess, I didn't know you gave names to your plants."

"I do *not* name my flowers in the solarium," he coolly. "Nor have I ever lost a boxing match with the Duke of Aveley."

"The Duke?" The marchioness eyed him in confusion before laughing. "*Of course*, strand instead of avenue. So that's who Sir Strandley is. Currer was clever to use 'sir' as one would after being introduced to the Duke."

"The man might be clever, but his work has the potential to damage innocent people, which is why I hired a private investigator to discover the man's identity."

"*What?*" his mother looked at him in horrified amazement, and beside him, Phoebe made a gurgling sound. He looked at his bride-to-be and frowned at how pale she'd become.

"Are you feeling unwell?" Gideon reached out to touch her hand. His frown deepened as she jumped at his touch and quickly pulled away from him.

"I'm fine," she said with a shake of her head as her lips thinned with obvious anger. "I'm simply appalled that you would wish to bring harm to Mr. Currer."

"I quite agree, Phoebe," the marchioness snapped. "Whatever would possess you to seek retribution where Mr. Currer is concerned, Gideon."

"I am not seeking vengeance," he snarled.

Furious they thought him so vain as to extract punishment from Currer, Gideon glared at both women. In the back of his head, a voice reminded him that on more than one occasion, the man's words had made Gideon want to thrash the author until he never wrote another word. He brushed the censuring voice aside. If he'd wanted vengeance, he would have done it long before now. This was about protecting Phoebe.

"Then, if you're not out for retribution, what do you hope to gain by learning the man's identity?" his mother demanded.

"I intend to ensure he never mentions Phoebe in his work. *Ever.*" Next to him, he heard Phoebe draw in a quick breath.

"Mama is right. You are far too over-protective. Unlike some people, I am perfectly capable of ignoring anything Mr. Currer might say about me." The glare she directed at him caught him off-guard, and he shook his head in disagreement.

"I told you I would protect you, Phoebe," he said with quiet resolution. "And I intend to keep that promise. The moment Currer learns we're married, it is almost certain the man will mention us in his next chapter."

"Then let him," she snapped. Her color had returned, and he frowned at how angry she was. "There are far worse things in the world than being a target of Currer's pen. If I need your protection, Gideon, then I shall tell you. You agreed that I would have the freedom to do as I please, yet already you are seeking to control me."

Phoebe with a vicious shove of her hands on the table, pushed her chair backward then sprang to her feet and stalked out of the room. Gideon quickly rose to his feet to follow her before his mother grabbed his wrist.

"*Sit down*, Gideon." The harsh command startled him, and when he didn't obey, his mother released a sigh of irritation. "Going after her will only make matters worse, now *sit down*."

Lady Wrotham sternly gestured for him to sit down, and he slowly did as she ordered. The marchioness turned her head and ordered the servants in the room to leave. When they were alone, his mother eyed him with exasperation, and Gideon shook his head in protest.

"She misunderstands—"

"Of that, I have no doubt, but for all your experience with women, you have yet to learn how we think. And you *clearly* have no understanding of Phoebe."

"What the hell is that supposed to mean?" His mother arched her eyebrow in disapproval at his language, but he glared back at her refusing to apologize as if he were a child.

"Phoebe's had one of two choices before she agreed to marry you. Leave or stay. She chose to stay in the event a child was conceived the other night." Lady Wrotham shook her head in angry condemnation and disappointment. A bolt of guilt sliced through him.

"Are you saying I did the wrong thing offering to marry her," he growled as he remembered the disgust and disappointment his mother had shown him the other night when he'd sought her help with Phoebe.

"No, you did the right thing in offering your hand in marriage. But your failure to consult her when you decided to discover Mr. Currer's identity simply demonstrated how much control you will have as her husband."

"I've given my word she will have the freedom to do as she wishes," he said with quiet restraint. "I even documented it in a legal document we both signed."

"Phoebe also knows what the law says about a married woman's rights. Even with a contract, she knows it would be difficult to challenge you in the courts," the marchioness said in an accusatory tone.

"And you know my honor would never allow me to go back on anything I ever agreed to."

"Yes, I know that, but Phoebe doesn't. She doesn't know you well enough to trust you, let alone believe you will keep your word,"

"*Christ Jesus,*" Gideon muttered as he leaned back in his chair.

"Give her time, Gideon. Show her the man I know you are." Lady Wrotham's quiet words made Gideon stare at his mother for a moment before he shook his head.

"The man I am?" Gideon roughly shoved his chair away from the table and sprang to his feet. "As you pointed out, Mama, I've given her no choice except to enter a gilded cage. That's hardly a man to be admired."

Without giving her a chance to reply, Gideon walked out of the dining room. As he stepped out into the hall, he made his way to his study. The door slammed closed behind him, and Gideon strode toward his desk. As he reached his chair, he saw the nuptial agreement lying on a stack of papers that needed to be placed in the safe he'd had installed in his bedroom.

Ever since he'd returned from Amsterdam, he'd made misstep after misstep where Phoebe was concerned. He'd misjudged her, seduced her, and had then put her in a position that had left her with only two options. Was it any wonder she didn't trust him? Gideon reached out to touch the document. His fingers brushed across Phoebe's signature. There were no flourishes or large curves to her feminine writing. But there was strength in the simplicity of it. She would be a credit to him as a wife. They could be comfortable in dealings with each other. But convincing her to believe he would never betray her would be the most challenging task he'd ever faced. But it was a challenge he was determined to win.

Chapter 17

Phoebe stared at her image in the beveled mirror. In the reflection, she could see the door leading into Gideon's bedroom. They'd been married earlier in the day with Constance and her brother, the Earl of Melton, acting as witnesses. It had been a simple ceremony, and afterward, the brother and sister had stayed for a special wedding luncheon Gideon's mother had arranged to celebrate the occasion.

When she'd come upstairs to change out of her wedding gown after their friends had left, she'd found her things had been moved to the room next to Gideon's. It had emphasized how drastically her life had changed in less than a week. The remainder of the day, she'd spent reading in the salon with Lady Wrotham.

Gideon had left the house shortly after she'd changed, saying he had an appointment. He'd kissed her cheek as he'd said goodbye, and it was as if they'd been married for months, not hours. Although he'd said he wouldn't be gone long, he'd still not returned by the time she'd come upstairs to change for dinner.

Phoebe sighed and glanced down at the Chelmsford emerald on her finger. If someone had asked her to describe how she was feeling at the moment, Phoebe would have been forced to say she felt numb. She was married. It was a state Phoebe had vowed never to enter into ever again. While Gideon had given his word not to control her, it was impossible not to feel uneasy about what the future held.

Yesterday, when he'd announced his intentions to find P. Currer, she'd been in a state of panic. She knew her fierce reaction to Gideon's news had startled him, and she'd fled the dining room without any thought as to how suspicious her behavior might look. Later in the afternoon, he'd apologized for not consulting her about it.

When he had tried to convince Phoebe to allow him to continue with his efforts to find Currer, she'd adamantly rejected the idea. He had been far from happy with her decision, and a part of her wondered if he still might try to find Currer without her knowledge.

The thought made her realize she couldn't risk visiting the newspaper more than once. Phoebe would need to submit all three of the chapters she'd promised Mr. Meade at the same time. It meant she would need to visit Constance almost daily if she wanted to rid herself of P. Currer quickly. Worse, she would be unable to avoid mentioning Gideon and their marriage. Not mentioning their wedding would arouse suspicion.

Eyes closed, she massaged her forehead as she contemplated how to finish the Chronicles without Gideon discovering the truth. Behind her, a quiet knock on the door between her room and Gideon's made her body grow taut. Steeling herself for whatever might come, she called out a quiet invitation to enter her room.

As the door between the two chambers slowly opened, she stood up as Gideon entered her bedroom. The sight of him made her heart skip a beat. He was dressed for dinner, and as always, he looked splendid. Phoebe's mouth became dry as he crossed the floor toward her.

"The color blue suits you. It always has."

The quiet appreciation in his voice made her heart flutter. She glanced down at the dark blue gown. The color was similar to that of the dress she'd worn the first time they'd met. The memory of that night caused her cheeks to grow hot.

As if he could read her thoughts, a small yet wicked smile tilted his mouth.

"Sometimes the male sex *does* pay attention to what a beautiful woman wears." His words made her cheeks grow hotter, and he laughed softly. "And you blush as sweetly now as you did five years ago."

"It was dark. How could you tell?" she said with a sniff of irritated disbelief. This time his laugh was rich and full-bodied.

"Because I could feel the heat of your skin beneath my hand."

"Oh," she uttered, unable to think of a suitable reply. Gideon, his mouth still curled slightly with amusement, reached into his pocket.

"I had thought this would be ready by this morning, but it wasn't. It's why I was gone so long this afternoon."

He closed the distance between them and offered her a slim jeweler's box. Uncertainty swept through her, and Gideon bobbed his head, silently urging her to take it. Phoebe accepted the box and slowly opened it. Nestled in the blue velvet was a necklace of small emeralds that sparkled in the soft glow of the gaslights on the wall. She drew in a sharp breath and looked up at Gideon.

"It's beautiful. Thank you," Phoebe said before looking down at the necklace again and lightly running her fingertips across the jewels.

"Here, let me put it on you."

Before she could speak, Gideon stepped forward and took the necklace from its box while gently turning her away from him. As he placed his gift around her neck, the masculine smell of him drifted beneath her nose. The scent of pine, leather, and something spicy made her breath hitch. As she drank him into her senses, the words 'if only' kept spinning through her head.

A second later, his lips seared her flesh as he kissed the

hollow between her neck and shoulder. Phoebe drew in a quick breath as she looked at him in the mirror. Something in his gray eyes stirred a fire in her belly, and she didn't protest as he turned her around. Silence hovered between them, and Phoebe trembled as Gideon stroked her cheek lightly before he took a step back and glanced around the room.

"It's been some time since this room was last renovated. If there's something you'd like to change, simply mention it to Mrs. Albright. Between her and Pendleton, they can find an architect to meet with you about any changes you'd like to see made."

"I see no need to change anything," Phoebe said as she looked around the room.

It was true. There was nothing that displeased her about the room. At her reply, Gideon released a heavy sigh. Confused by his reaction, she turned her head to look up at him. Frustration furrowed his brow as he gestured toward the door.

"We should go downstairs. I'm sure Mama is waiting in the salon." At his somewhat brusque statement, Phoebe laughed.

"You know, as well as I do, that she is *never* early."

"Perhaps, but there is always a first time," he said with a small smile curving his lips. Phoebe laughed again as she walked toward the door.

"There are many things about the marchioness that are unpredictable, but timeliness will never be one of them."

As they stepped out into the hall, Gideon offered his arm. Without thinking, she curled her hand around a hard, muscular arm. The instant she touched him, heat streaked up her arm to spread its way through her body. A small tremor rippled through her, but if Gideon noticed it, he didn't comment on it. Phoebe darted a quick look up at Gideon's profile as they made their way toward the stairs. Although his expression was unreadable, there was quiet strength to his profile that gave her an unexpected sense of calm. When they reached the salon, Phoebe turned her head to eye Gideon with amusement.

"As I said, Mama is not known for her timeliness." Before Gideon could reply, Pendleton appeared in the salon doorway.

"My lord, her ladyship has sent word that she will not be joining you this evening." The butler's words made Phoebe inhale a small gasp of alarm.

"Is she feeling unwell?" Gideon asked with a note of concern in his voice.

"No, my lord, Lady Wrotham indicated you and Lady Chelmsford had no need of company tonight."

Phoebe looked at Gideon, who was studying the butler with a small frown. Gideon glanced at Phoebe, then nodded his understanding.

"I take it dinner is ready?"

"It is, my lord," Pendleton said with a slight bow. Gideon turned to Phoebe and offered his arm. "Shall we?"

Trepidation swept through Phoebe as she met her new husband's gaze. Dear God, what could the two of them possibly discuss during their meal without the marchioness on hand to stimulate conversation? When she didn't move, Gideon arched his eyebrow with sardonic amusement, but something about the way he looked at her made her body tighten.

Not even the fierce pace of a butterfly's wings could have matched the way her heartbeat fluttered as Phoebe accepted his arm and allowed him to lead her into the dining room. As she released her hand from his arm, she moved to take her seat opposite him at the end of the table. Gideon's strong hand held her back.

"Come sit next to me. I prefer not to shout down the length of the table."

It was a request, but there was no mistaking the

command underlying the quiet words that Phoebe instinctively knew better than to protest. With a nod, she allowed Gideon to guide her to the chair at his left. Without even a hint of surprise, one of the footmen hurried forward to move Phoebe's place setting to the seat Gideon had led her to. When their glasses were filled with wine, Gideon lifted his goblet toward her.

"To the beautiful new Countess of Chelmsford."

The quiet words rang with a sincerity that made Phoebe's cheek grow hot as she murmured a word of gratitude and took a sip of her own wine. Silence drifted between them as they began their meal. The consommé was a warm beef broth, which was followed by Vol au vents. The savory pastries were filled with mincemeat and served warm. As Phoebe took a small bite of her pastry, Gideon cleared his throat.

"Plans for our wedding trip are almost complete, and I thought we might leave at the end of next week."

Phoebe barely managed to suppress her gasp of horror. That left her only three days, four at the most, to write the Chronicles' last three chapters. She would need to visit Constance tomorrow afternoon, write at least one chapter, and start on the second. Friday and Saturday would be filled with last-minute things to do for the gala on Saturday night.

Sunday, it would be impossible to visit Constance, and Monday was her scheduled visit to Madame Sabine's. Phoebe was certain the marchioness would undoubtedly keep her there most of the day, particularly when she learned Phoebe and Gideon would be leaving at the end of the week. As she tried to determine how to finish the Chronicles, Gideon frowned, and his mouth thinned with obvious irritation.

"If you prefer, I can do away with all the plans for the trip." Startled by his abrupt words, Phoebe jerked her head toward him.

"I'm sorry, I was simply calculating all the things I needed to do before we leave. There's the gala on Saturday, and Mama has arranged for the two of us to visit Madame Sabine on Monday for fittings."

"I see," Gideon's expression swiftly changed from annoyance to amusement. "I would not wish to prevent you from having enough dresses before we leave."

"Mama is insisting on far too many." At her sigh of disgust, Gideon laughed.

"I believe my sister expressed a similar exasperation at all the fittings when she and Mama were acquiring Alice's wedding trousseau."

"She's unrelenting." Phoebe smiled and arched her eyebrows in amused disgust. "But her enthusiasm shows exactly how much pleasure she's deriving from selecting the fabrics, patterns, and all the accessories."

"Mama has always enjoyed her visits to the dressmaker's."

"At the rate with which she's insisting I need this or that gown, I will have a wardrobe filled with far too many dresses. I'll not be able to pull one from the chifforobe without six more falling out behind it."

"I think you are the first woman I have ever met who has shown a tendency *not* to be preoccupied with fashion." Gideon laughed. "However, I hope you're planning on acquiring one or two riding habits."

"If I recall correctly, Mama insisted on two. I was appalled when she insisted I have *three* travel gowns."

"Then I'll arrange for us to go riding while we are in Tuscany."

"You might regret that. My skills at horseback riding are sadly lacking, and you're quite apt to find me lagging or even forced to chase after me when the animal I'm riding runs wild."

"Something tells me you're far more proficient than you give yourself credit for."

"No," Phoebe said with a laugh. "I truly am a poor

horsewoman."

"Then I'll help you improve your skills."

"And I thought I was the optimist," Phoebe said wryly. "However, if you insist, I will be an attentive pupil. Although, I have given you fair warning as to my hopelessness."

Gideon chuckled softly as one of the footmen held a platter of roast beef and potatoes in front of him. Using the serving spoon and fork, he placed the meat and vegetables on his plate.

"Even if you're correct in the assessment of your riding skills, you clearly have a head for figures. Mama has mentioned several times that you've made life much easier to bear when it comes to the gala."

"I've always had a talent for bookkeeping. I used to maintain the household accounts long before father became so obsessed...so obsessed with things."

Phoebe winced slightly as she reached for her glass to take a sip of wine. A glance in Gideon's direction made her heart sink as she saw his expression. Dear God, he pitied her. A voice in her head gleefully pointed out the humiliation and pain she was feeling now would pale in comparison to what she would suffer if Gideon were to discover she loved him.

"Exactly what type of business was your father in?"

"He was a tailor and haberdasher of men's clothing. At least he was until he discovered the gold mine. Everything changed from that point forward."

From the moment her father had discovered the small gold mine on a piece of property he owned, he'd become fixated on having only the best for himself and for her. In truth, her father hadn't even bought the property. He'd accepted the deed for the small parcel of land from one of his customers in exchange for payment of their debt. There had been numerous times when she'd hated that unsuspecting customer for giving her father that land deed.

"Changed how?"

"My father became obsessed with the idea of being a leader in society. He'd always admired the financiers who'd made their fortunes from the sum of their labors. Father had wanted to be one of them."

"And you became a part of that change?"

"Yes." Phoebe nodded as sadness filtered its way through her. "No matter what he achieved, he needed to surpass it. When I was fourteen, he sent me to finishing school in Switzerland. While I was away at school, my father met Leonard Jerome, Lady Randolph Churchill's father. I think it was then my father decided his daughter was going to marry a peer of the realm."

Phoebe looked down at her plate, remembering the hellish existence she'd lived with Alfred. The price she'd paid had been far greater than the title of viscountess had been worth. Despite the savory appearance of her dinner, she realized she'd suddenly lost her appetite. The warm touch of Gideon's strong hand capturing hers made her jump slightly.

As their gazes locked, something undefinable darkened his features as he carried her hand to his mouth and kissed her fingertips. Flustered by the heat brushing across her skin, Phoebe didn't move for a moment, relishing the caress. It was as if he was saying he was sorry for everything she'd endured in the past.

It was a silent commitment that said he would make good on his promise to protect her. Gently pulling her hand free, she forced herself to take a bite of her meal. As if understanding she didn't want to speak at the moment, Gideon remained silent and resumed eating.

The roast beef tasted like sawdust, and Phoebe released an inaudible sigh. Conversation seemed to be the only option open to her if she wanted to prevent Gideon from noticing she wasn't eating. She'd learned that he was quick to notice the small things.

"Since you insist I must be exaggerating my ineptitude

when it comes to horsemanship, what talent do *you* believe you lack finesse?"

"Hunting." The immediate response took her aback as she eyed him with amused disbelief. With a wry twist of his mouth, Gideon shrugged. "My inability to shoot straight is a source of great amusement with my friends."

"Surely your aim cannot be that terrible."

"Unfortunately, it is. Sebastian finds it comical how bad my aim is, considering my exceptional ability to hit my mark when boxing. Percy always earns quite a tidy sum when making a wager with an unsuspecting gentleman as to what I might hit instead of the bird."

"That's unkind of him," Phoebe said as she fought not to laugh at the idea of Percy Rockwood winning money from Gideon's lack of skill using a rifle. Gideon arched an eyebrow in reproof.

"You find that funny." There was a distinct note of pique in his voice, and Phoebe laughed as she leaned forward to touch his arm.

"I will not lie. I do find it amusing." She smiled teasingly at him. "But only because Lord Melton is right. I find it very humorous that your aim would be less than accurate with a rifle when I know your reputation as a pugilist borders on legendary."

"I would not go that far," he said with a self-deprecating chuckle, but Phoebe could tell her compliment had pleased him.

"Still, you excel at the sport, albeit quite brutal from what I've heard." The memory of Lady Wrotham's description of Gideon's boxing injuries the night they first met sent a shiver down her spine.

"It's not for the faint of heart. I couldn't hold my own against Gentleman Jim or John L. Sullivan in the ring even under the Marquess of Queensbury rules." He grimaced with a trace of humiliation, and she wondered if he was remembering his near-fatal fight in the East End. He shrugged as a wry smile twisted his firm lips. "But I am far superior in the ring than I am in a shooting party."

"Then I take it house parties are not something you enjoy." Phoebe laughed at his pained expression

"I cannot abide them. I enjoy riding to the hounds, but when my host organizes a shooting party, I do everything I can to avoid being included."

"I would think the nightly entertainment would compensate you for whatever humiliation you might suffer in the field," Phoebe said with amusement. As she glanced at Gideon, the anger darkening his face made her flinch. With a shake of her head, she reached out to touch his hand. "I was merely teasing you, Gideon. You cannot deny your reputation for charming the ladies."

"I would be a hypocrite to deny that I'm worthy of the nickname Currer has given me in his satire." Gideon grimaced before he began slicing into his beef and shook his head slightly." But it is one thing to admit one's fallacies to one's self and another matter altogether for someone else to point out I am not the most honorable of men."

There was a note of pained regret in his voice that made Phoebe's heart sink. Was he thinking about the reason for their marrying earlier today? She stared down at her plate for a moment before she raised her head to eye him steadily.

"You are the most honorable man I know, Gideon. This morning your actions proved that fact. You married me, believing it was the right thing to do. I only hope you do not live to regret it." Her statement made him jerk his head up to study her intently.

"I have many regrets, Phoebe, but making you the Countess of Chelmsford is not one of them."

The emphatic note in his voice matched his intensity as he stared at her unflinchingly. Uncertain how to respond, Phoebe nodded and picked up her fork to prod the meat on her plate. She took another small bite of the entrée and swallowed as quickly as she could.

Moments later, she breathed a sigh of relief as the footman removed her plate, then replaced it with a dish on which rested a small cheese pastry. The cooked cheese savory smelled delicious, and she eagerly took a bite of the Talmouse. It was as heavenly as it smelled. A chuckle from Gideon made her look at him, and he grinned.

"I'm glad to see something on the menu pleases you."

"Everything has been excellent."

"Except for the beef." A soft snort of amusement escaped him as he arched his eyebrows at her in a clear challenge for her to deny the observation.

"The beef was excellent. I simply wasn't hungry."

"And now your appetite has been renewed."

"Yes," she sniffed with exasperation. "I believe it's a prerogative, as well as an expectation by men, that a woman should always demonstrate a tendency to change her opinion whenever the mood strikes."

"A fact you have illustrated quite well tonight."

"Are you mocking me?" Phoebe scowled at him, and Gideon laughed.

"Yes, I think I am. I enjoy seeing you glare at me. Your eyes sparkle when you're irritated, and you blush quite prettily."

For a moment, Phoebe continued to frown with displeasure before she shook her head in disgruntled disgust.

"I cannot compete with you in a verbal battle. I am far better with my pen."

The moment she spoke, Phoebe froze in her seat and her mouth went dry with fear. Dear God, what in heaven's name had possessed her to say such a thing.

"Your pen? Are you telling me you're a fledgling writer?" Gideon's smile was disarming and free of any suspicion. Grasping at the lifeline he'd given her, Phoebe rolled her shoulders in a small, dismissive shrug.

"A terrible one, I'm afraid," she lied. "But I do enjoy putting my thoughts on paper."

"Perhaps you should engage Currer in a duel of pens and write your own column."

"Good Lord, no," she gasped. Phoebe's panic escalated as she tried to think of a way to escape the corner she'd managed to back herself in. Her only available option was to lie again. "My writing is nowhere as scintillating as Currer's."

"Why not let me be the judge of that?" Gideon's mischievous expression made her heart stop beating before it resumed and crashed into her chest.

"Absolutely not," she exclaimed in horror.

"I am baiting you, my sweet." Laughing, Gideon captured her hand in his and kissed the inside of her wrist. "I enjoy seeing you flustered. It makes you all the more beautiful to look at."

Gideon's words made her draw in a sharp breath. If only his endearment had been heartfelt. His lips pressed into her wrist again, and a second later, his tongue flicked out to swirl across her skin. A gasp escaped Phoebe at the sensual caress, as Gideon's intense gaze made her breathing erratic. Her heartbeat racing out of control, she trembled at his touch. Suddenly aware of her vulnerable state, she quickly pulled her hand free of his grasp.

"You are a rogue, Gideon Alexander," she said breathlessly. His pleased reaction to her husky reprimand made him look even more devastating than usual.

"If you chastise me so sweetly, I shall need to act the rogue more often."

Gideon grinned with satisfaction as he leaned back slightly to allow the footman space to set a pastry tart in front of him. The smoldering fire in the look he sent her made Phoebe's body tense as an electric pulse streaked through her. She barely managed to suppress a soft gasp as she drank in the masculine beauty of him.

Although he was completely relaxed, there was a latent animalistic magnetism about him that declared how easily he could bring a woman to her knees. Phoebe's heart crashed into her breast at the thought. If the man had not owned her heart already, she would be in danger of losing it now. She looked down at the pastry the footman had set in front of her and drew in a quick breath. The pastry was in the shape of a heart, and on either side of the heart were the letters G and P.

"I see Mama and her romantic nature has been conspiring with Mrs. Murray."

"Yes, I can see that." Phoebe fought to keep her voice from sounding breathless, but clearly failed as Gideon leaned forward to clasp her hand in his once more.

"I didn't lie the other day when I said things would be good between us, Phoebe. I am quite sincere in that belief." A glint of emotion flickered in his gray eyes, and it ignited a small flame of hope in her heart. Unable to think of a suitable reply, she nodded her understanding, then looked down at the pastry again.

"Shall I start on the G while you devour the P?"

Phoebe had meant it to be a light-hearted remark, but realized it was anything but that. He had already stolen her heart, and she had no doubt he would soon possess her body and soul. It was inevitable. She glanced at Gideon and saw him staring down at the tart as if he was uncertain about something. She frowned in puzzlement as she studied him.

When he realized she was watching him, Gideon looked at her with an emotion that almost appeared to be one of affection as his beautiful mouth curled upward. His smile was a glimpse of heaven, and she knew that no matter how careful she was in hiding her love, she would eventually fail.

One day soon, he would realize how much she loved him. It would be a devastating moment, but until then, she would take every moment of happiness she could and keep each of those precious minutes locked inside her heart. They would sustain her in the years to come when Gideon would look at her and only feel pity. "Why don't we start with the heart and work our way outward."

It was a simple suggestion, but something in his voice made her think there might be hope for the future. Phoebe returned his smile and immediately pressed her fork into the dessert and prayed for a miracle.

"Are you certain hunting is the thing you are the least skilled in?" Phoebe laughed as she pulled the rubber and game's last trick over to her stack of cards won.

"I am playing with a card-sharp," Gideon muttered with obvious frustration.

"I am not a card-sharp." Phoebe sniffed as she eyed him in amused self-disgust. "Either you're worse at cards than shooting, or you're having extremely bad luck with the hands you've been dealt."

"Or it could be that my beautiful wife has proven to be the worst distraction a man could have while playing All Fours." There was a mischievous, almost boyish look on his face as Gideon teased her, and she shook her head as she rejected his comment.

"Your compliments are falling on deaf ears if you think I shall take pity on you and add up the points wrong."

Laughing, she picked up the small pencil next to the narrow notepad. Before she could sum up the final score, a strong hand wrapped around her wrist. Startled, Phoebe jerked her head up to see Gideon staring at her. The desire smoldering in his eyes mesmerized her, and it was impossible to look away from him. His thumb began to rub small circles over the spot where her heartbeat pulsed.

"It is not just a compliment. It's a fact. The Countess of Chelmsford is enough to drive her husband to distraction."

The soft words wrapped around Phoebe's senses, and her cheeks began to burn as if she were standing too close to a flame. In truth, she was. Gideon was the flame, and she was simply the moth flirting with danger. A voice inside her urged her to embrace the danger. It told her to fly into the flame and let it singe every inch of her until his touch consumed her.

"Are you trying to seduce me, Lord Chelmsford?"

"At least you did not refer to me as Lord Chelmbee," he murmured with a self-deprecating smile as he avoided answering her question.

"Was I wrong in failing to do so?" she asked breathlessly as a wave of excitement washed over her. It signaled she was more than ready to embrace the danger. Gideon looked down at his thumb, which was stroking the inside of her wrist.

"No, the only honey I shall ever seek again is that which you possess, my sweet Phoebe."

The soft words were like a feather drifting across her skin, and his endearment made her pulse flutter wildly. The moment her heartbeat accelerated, Gideon stopped circling his thumb over the inside of her wrist. He lifted his head, and the hunger she saw on his face made her draw in a quick breath. A split second later, he released her and began to gather up the cards to replace them in the wood box they belonged in.

Disappointment spiraled through Phoebe as she silently helped him collect the cards off the braise-covered tabletop. Even though he was still shuffling the cards together and storing them in the box, she could see how hard his muscles were beneath his jacket. The tension in the air seemed to expand as he stood up and carried the card box to the cabinet where it was kept.

"Gideon…"

"Yes?" He didn't look at her, but she saw the muscles of

his back flex as he rearranged items in the cabinet. All too aware of the fire she was walking into, a desperate need to be in his arms made Phoebe's entire body tightened with a familiar hunger. Damn the future. She wanted to live in the present.

"I think I will go to bed now."

His reply was a sharp jerk of his head as he closed the cabinet door in front of him and kept his back to her. Disappointment washed over her again. Was it possible he didn't want her? No, she didn't believe that. He'd already expressed how much he desired her.

Gideon's silence left her with only one other possibility. He'd said he would not force her to do anything she didn't want to do. It was the only explanation she could think of as to why he had not turned to face her or suggest he join her. He wanted her to come to him of her own accord. Taking that final leap, she drew in a deep breath, then released it.

"Would you…would you wish to join me?"

At her hesitant question, Gideon stiffened, then slowly turned around. The tension radiating off him was almost palpable, and his handsome profile was sharply defined in the room's soft glow of the gaslight sconces on the wall. Gideon studied her with a penetrating look as he clasped his hands behind his back. He could have been a statue as the only sign that said he wasn't made of stone was a small tic in his cheek.

"Is that what you want, or are you asking because you feel obligated to do so?"

The strained note in Gideon's voice emphasized he was struggling to hold himself in check. Phoebe stiffened as the enormity of Gideon's question swept over her. He'd promised she would have the right to do as she wished, and his words said he intended to honor his vow.

Gideon was making it clear that entering his bed was a choice for her, not an obligation. If only he loved her. She would not have even asked the question. She would simply run to him and tell him how much she loved him, needed him—needed his touch to make her feel truly alive.

"I do not feel obligated. I would like…very much…for you to join me."

Chapter 18

Gideon's body was as taut as a bowstring as he waited for Phoebe's reply to his question. The fact that she'd invited him into her bed was something he'd not expected tonight. It had been his intention to make her feel at ease with him. She was still somewhat skittish in his presence. Yesterday's misstep when it came to his intention to find Currer had been a regrettable decision.

His mother had been right. Phoebe didn't know him well. In fact, neither one of them knew much about the other. Although tonight had been an excellent start to convincing her that their marriage would be one she didn't have to fear. The evening had also emphasized how deeply he'd wronged her by believing she was like Edith.

If her father had been present when she'd shared how the man had used her to gain his own personal goals, Gideon would have found it impossible not to leave the man lying on the ground, bloodied and battered. The small amount she'd shared with him had made him ashamed to have believed ill of her.

Gideon knew of only a few women who possessed the inner strength in surviving the worst life had thrown at them. Phoebe was one of them. It had made him even more determined to ensure she was happy from this day forward. She had been a delightful companion throughout the evening.

Phoebe's reaction to his teasing and compliments had only strengthened his belief that they would be comfortable with each other in the years to come. He also believed he'd succeeded in making her see he wanted more from their marriage than simply bedding her. But he would have been lying if he'd allowed himself to believe his efforts not to seduce her this evening had been easy.

It had been exceedingly difficult not to seduce her. Everything about her had fired Gideon's imagination. The way his compliments made her cheeks become a bright pink had filled him with pleasure. Gideon had complimented dozens of women over the years, but Phoebe was the first woman who hadn't simpered in response to his flattery.

Even more satisfying was his certainty that she had known he was being sincere in his comments. It had surprised him how much pleasure he'd derived from her reactions to his words. His enjoyment of the evening had exploded into a desire that had caught him off guard moments ago when her pulse had quickened beneath his thumb. It had been the hardest thing he'd ever done not to act on her obvious reaction to him.

Instead, Gideon had occupied himself with the mundane task of putting the cards back where they belonged, but the moment she'd asked him to join her, his body had shouted with jubilation. He'd wanted to act immediately on her request, but he'd held back, albeit with great difficulty.

It was one thing to act out of desire, but Gideon suddenly realized he wanted more when it came to their marriage. What that was, he couldn't define or even understand. But he was certain of one thing. Gideon needed her to come to him not out of obligation, but because she desired him. Now, as he studied her in silence, the strain of not having accepted her invitation immediately was becoming more difficult by the second.

"I do not feel obligated. I would like…very much…for you to join me."

The moment her whisper drifted through the air, shouts of triumph echoed in his head. Slowly, Gideon closed the distance between them to reach out and caress her cheek with his fingers. Phoebe trembled at his touch, and he drew in a sharp breath at her reaction. Before he could move, she took a step forward and pulled his head down and kissed him while her soft body pressed deeply into his.

Instantly, he wrapped his arms around her and pulled her even closer. Her mouth was soft beneath his, and he struggled to contain the raging desire surging through him. As her lips parted to give him access to the inner warmth of her mouth, a groan rumbled in his chest. The gooseberry tart they'd had for dinner echoed faintly on her tongue as she tentatively swirled her tongue around his.

Hard inside his trousers, he sucked in a harsh breath as her hand glided over his erection. Christ Jesus, he wanted her now more than he had the other night if that were possible. Everything about her was drawing him into a blinding mist of craving to take her now, right here on the card table.

No, he was tired of not having complete access to her beautiful body. He wanted to taste every inch of her. With a harsh oath, he thrust her from him. Embarrassment made her pale and flinch as he took a small step back. He shook his head.

"I'm not rejecting you, my sweet. I simply want to spend our wedding night in a bed, not against a tree or on a couch," he growled as he bent slightly and lifted her up into her arms. At her gasp of surprise, he bent his head to nibble at her neck. "I want complete access to every inch of you, Phoebe. I intend to feast on you until you cry out my name in ecstasy, and then I want to do it again."

Pink color flooded her cheeks, and his body hardened with desire at the slumberous look she gave him. It stirred his blood and made his heart crash into his chest. My God, but she was lovely. Almost as if she were embarrassed by his open display of need, she pressed her face into his shoulder as he strode quickly out of the salon and made his way up the steps.

She murmured a small protest when he was halfway up the stairs.

"I can walk of my own accord, Gideon."

"Of that, I have no doubt," he said in a husky voice as he breathed in the fragrance of roses in her golden brown hair. "I simply don't want to let you go."

"Oh."

The soft exclamation made him smile with satisfaction as he walked down the hallway to his bedroom. His bedroom door was opened, and as he carried Phoebe over the threshold, he used his foot to close the door behind them. The moment he set her on her feet, Phoebe began undoing her gown.

"Stop," he commanded softly. "I want to do that. Tonight, I want to discover you slowly."

"I'm not sure I…I don't think I can wait that long." Her breathless response made him smile as anticipation barreled through him.

"Good," he murmured as he turned her around and began to undo the buttons of her dress. Gideon's fingers quickly worked their way downward as he bent his head to kiss the silky soft curve of her neck. "I want you to feel needy. I want you to sob—no, plead with me to satisfy you completely."

"Oh God, I'm ready to beg now."

Phoebe's voice vibrated with desire, and he wondered if he was going to have the wherewithal to restrain himself from sinking into her hot core until they were both completely disrobed. As Gideon slid her gown downward, he allowed her to push it past her full hips while he made short work of her corset.

Piece by piece, he removed her clothing until she was naked in front of him. The sight of her made his body cry out for her, unlike any other woman he'd ever been with. Obviously flustered by his intense scrutiny, her cheeks were flooded with color, and he smiled.

"Do you have any idea how beautiful you are?" he rasped as he studied her with a need that was threatening his control.

Phoebe flushed again, her cheeks a bright pink in the soft gaslight. Indecision flashed in her gaze before she appeared to reach a decision. With an expression that easily passed for shyness, she stepped forward to push his jacket off his shoulders. As he shrugged out of the coat, he tossed it to one side and fought to control his harsh breaths as she dropped his vest to the floor and then his shirt.

She drew in a soft breath as she reached out to press her hand into his chest. The warmth of her fingers on his skin made him shudder, and a small, womanly smile tipped her lips upward. Her smile didn't vanish as she reached for the buttons of his trousers, and in seconds he pulled them off, followed by his underdrawers. Appreciation lightened her features as her gaze roamed across his body and downward.

"I think you're beautiful too," she whispered as she tentatively reached out to stroke his hard length. His body immediately reacted, and grabbing her hand, he pulled her to the bed.

Sinking down onto the mattress, he tugged gently on her hand and pulled her down into his lap. He trailed his fingers down between her breasts with his free hand, then over the round swell of the one closest to his mouth. His thumb rubbed across her nipple as he bent his head to kiss his way across her skin until he could take the stiff peak into his mouth.

The scent of roses mixed with the musky scent of desire. His teeth abraded the hard tip of her breast, and he was rewarded with a muted cry of pleasure. The soft sound was followed by her hand sliding between them to touch him. He drew in a harsh breath, and he quickly released his mouth from her lush breast.

"Not yet, sweetheart." Gently guiding her to stretch out

on the bed, he lifted one exquisite foot and kissed the top of it. Taking his time, he nibbled his way up along her calf to her knee and then her inner thigh as he continued upward. The scent of her need was heady, and as his mouth reached the apex of her thigh, she drew in a sharp breath.

"Oh, you mustn't."

"I told you I wanted to explore every inch of you, and I meant it," he murmured as he parted her velvety smooth folds and dipped his tongue into the hot, spicy, creamy center of her core.

Over the top of his head, she released a cry of pleasure. When his mouth found the small bud between her succulent folds, he swirled his tongue around the nub, then bit down gently at the fleshy heart of her. Instantly she jerked against his mouth, and the moment he sucked hard on the bud of flesh, a keening cry escaped her. The sound tightened his cock as his tongue swirled and stroked the delicate heat of her. Christ Jesus, he wanted to bury himself inside her.

Instead of listening to his body's demands, he focused his mind on pleasing her. A second later, she bucked against his mouth. It encouraged him to nip harder at the small bud. The action elicited another passionate cry from her as he continued exploring her sweet, tangy heat. Fingers spiked through his hair as her moans of pleasure echoed above his head.

The shouts of need inside his mind were growing, but he suppressed them as he continued to pleasure her with his mouth. His reward was a small rush of buttery heat flowing across his tongue. The soft moans escaping her became sharp pants as she writhed beneath him. The sounds encouraged him to increase the speed of his tongue as it flicked and swirled around the heart of her.

A moment later, she called out his name, and another strong gush of tangy cream swept across his tongue. Pleasure rolled through him at her reaction to his attentions, and taking his time, he kissed his way upward over her stomach to her breasts, where he sucked on first one hard nipple and then the other.

His mouth continued to explore her fragrant scented skin across the base of her throat to her cheek and then her ear, which he nipped before capturing her mouth with his. The passion with which she welcomed his kiss made his body cry out sharply with hunger for her. As if she understood his craving, she shifted her body beneath him until his cock was poised on the edge of her sex. Her hands slid down his back to cup his buttocks, and she urged him to take her.

"Oh, God, please. I need…I need you now."

The soft plea made him lift his head to stare down at her. She was the most beautiful creature he'd ever seen. Her eyes fluttered open, and she arched upward into his body.

"I like the way you look and sound when you plead with me," he whispered as he buried himself inside her with one hard thrust.

In the next breath, he breathed her scent and the musk of passion into his nostrils and didn't move. Hot velvet. She was hot velvet wrapped around his cock. Each one of his senses was being hammered by the beautiful essence of her. It was as if her body had been made for him. A small shudder rippled through her, and her body tightened around him. Instantly, every muscle in his entire body became taut with anticipation.

It was a sensation he'd only ever experienced with her. As her body contracted around him again, he slowly retreated, and a groan escaped him at the pleasure it gave him. Tight and hot, her body clutched at his in a way that came close to undoing him. One silky leg wrapped around his as she tried to keep him locked inside her.

Her strength was no match for his, and when he stopped his retreat at the edge of her sex, she protested with the whisper of a sob. Lowering his head, he nibbled at her lips, loving the sweet, hot taste of her. In response, she arched her body up into his.

"Don't stop," she gasped as her fingers dug into his flesh and tried to pull his body deeper into hers.

Her soft plea excited him, and with a hard, fast thrust, he pressed his body deeper into hers. Another keening cry of pleasure filled the air, and he was lost. It was as if a dam inside him broke, and he began to move at an increasingly rapid pace as he claimed her as his. With each stroke of his body against hers, the world fell away until there was only her and this moment.

Chapter 19

Every inch of her was on fire, and she reveled in the sensation. Moments ago, when Gideon had used his mouth to send her careening into a state of bliss, the ecstasy blinded her to everything. Even after she'd shattered into a million pieces, he'd continued to tease her body with his. Never had she dreamed a man's mouth could take her to the brink over and over again.

Now, as the tip of him hovered at the heart of her, a moan of need whispered past her lips as her body cried out for him to complete her and drive her over the edge into a glorious state of mind-numbing bliss. A white-hot heat spiraled through her veins as she writhed beneath him in a silent plea for fulfillment. She stared up at him, and her heart slammed into her chest at the blazing passion darkening his features.

In the next breath, he filled her with a speed that pulled a cry of intense pleasure from her. The heady scent of bergamot and pine swept across her senses as he lowered his head to kiss the length of her shoulder up to her mouth. The faint essence of her lingered on his lips and tongue as he captured her mouth in a hard kiss of possession.

Eagerly, she met fire with fire as her tongue tangled with his in an imitation of the carnal act he was already tempting and teasing her with. As he slowly retreated from her, she whimpered her protest. Desperate for the intense pleasure and satisfaction she knew only he could give her, her body tightened in a futile effort to hold him in place. A second later, he filled her again in a blinding flash of movement, and she cried out his name as fire rushed through her veins and spread its way across her skin.

Wild and turbulent emotions coursed through her blood as her heart raced out of control. Everything around her faded until she was aware of only his touch, and she willingly gave herself up to his possession. A familiar sensation began to build inside her as she wantonly met his thrusts with unrestrained fervor. Harsh breaths rolled out of him, matching her own frantic gasps of pleasure.

With a suddenness that stole her breath away, her body jerked hard against his. Teetering on the edge of a place she knew only he could carry her, she cried out his name and the sound mixed with the dark, primal growl rolling out of him at the same time. As their bodies shuddered violently against each other, she fell over a precipice with him and into a climax that left her quivering against him.

Slowly, he sank down into her, and she welcomed the warm weight of him as he covered her body with his. A joy she'd never known intensified the slowly receding pleasure she'd just experienced. The rapid beating of his heart reverberated against her breast while his heavy breathing tingled her skin as he nuzzled her neck. A wave of happiness washed over her as she closed her eyes and sighed softly with contentment.

Gideon's mouth brushed across the curve where her neck met her shoulder, then lifted his head. Phoebe could sense him studying her, but she didn't look at him. She wanted to pretend, if only for a brief moment, that what they'd just shared had been a mutual exchange of passion born of love. Although she hadn't admitted it until two days ago, she'd given her heart to him that night in a dark garden.

Tonight she'd not only opened up her heart to him completely, but her body as well. With each breath she'd drawn into her lungs, she'd offered herself in a silent declaration of love. In doing so, he'd claimed her soul as well. The gentle caress of his fingers brushing across Phoebe's cheek made her look at him.

Gideon's forehead wrinkled slightly in a slight frown of confusion as he studied her. For a moment, she thought it might be the beginning awareness of affection, even love, but she quickly dismissed the thought. Life had taught her to be a realist. Reaching up, she cupped the side of his cheek, and he turned his head to kiss her palm.

"That was infinitely more comfortable and pleasurable than against a tree," Gideon murmured as he kissed her gently.

Although he didn't mention the couch in the library, she knew it had to have crossed his mind. When she didn't reply to his comment, Gideon kissed her again, then moved to lie beside her. Entwining his fingers with hers, he carried her hand to his lips and kissed the back of her hand.

Phoebe shut her eyes again, fearful she might begin to cry at the tender gesture. Tonight had pushed her love for him even deeper into her heart. It created emotions she'd never experienced before. Had he treated his other lovers with such gentle affection as well after bedding them? Had he teased them with the same tender words and caresses? Jealousy twisted its way through her body until her heart ached so badly it became a physical pain in her chest.

Gideon stirred beside her and rolled onto his side. He brushed a lock of hair off her brow before lightly kissing her temple. Tension tightened her muscles at the caress. Despite her attempt not to react, she flinched. Immediately, strong fingers caught her by the chin and forced her to turn her head toward him.

"Look at me, Phoebe." The command in his voice warned her that he'd sensed her distress. She forced herself to smile brightly as she met his gaze that only moments ago had been blazing with passion.

"Yes?"

"Tell me what you're thinking." The demand twisted her insides with fear. Oh, how easily he could discover her true feelings if she didn't take care. She breathed a small laugh in an effort to hide her deepest thoughts.

"I'm simply thinking that I agree with you. A bed is far more preferable than a tree." Satisfied with her reply, Gideon relaxed, and a complacent smile twisted his firm mouth.

"I think I shall enjoy having a wife that is so agreeable."

"Are you forgetting our agreement?" Phoebe frowned with irritation and a hint of apprehension. "I have no intention of letting you dictate to me, my lord."

"I'm teasing you, Phoebe," he murmured. There was a note of indignation and anger in his voice as he chastised her for doubting him. "I thought I made myself clear earlier that I would never force you to do something you didn't want to do."

Phoebe met his fierce gaze for a moment, then released a sigh and nodded before staring up at the ceiling. Tension radiated off of Gideon, and she winced with regret. Once again, fear had caused her to misjudge him. As she pondered how to heal the small breach between them, a small voice in the back of her mind noted the Chelmsford coronet detailed in the plaster. Swallowing the knot that had formed in her throat, she released a breath of relief she'd not realized she'd been holding in.

"I'm sorry. I am…I know you will keep your word. If you had any intention of doing otherwise, you would not have given me a choice as to entering your bed."

Silence reigned between them for several moments longer until Gideon's fingers stroked her brow in a caress that left her floating on the edge of joy and the brink of despair. God, how she wanted his caress to be one of love, not simply the gentle touch of a lover.

"Helstone made your life a living hell." It was an observation that didn't demand an answer, but she felt a need to make him understand why she'd given herself to him that night in Montjoy's gardens.

"Yes. It was why…those few moments in the dark with you…" Phoebe paused as she came perilously close to revealing how often the thought of him had bolstered her spirits for the past five years.

"I've always wondered why you were in the garden that night."

"I was trying to help a friend."

"By meeting them in a place where only lovers met for clandestine purposes?" There was almost a judgmental note in his question, and she stiffened.

"My friend had been accused of something that would injure him, and I came up with a plan that I was certain would convince others we were in a liaison."

"And that plan was for the two of you to meet and hope someone found you in each other's arms."

"Yes." Phoebe chose her next words carefully for fear she would reveal Lawrence's identity. Even if Gideon had heard the rumors as to how different her friend was, she would never betray Lawrence's confidence.

"I made sure to drop hints to one or two people as to my assignation with someone in the garden that night. I was certain someone would try to discover who I was meeting. I also knew the gossip would spread quickly among the Set."

"Which is why you thought I was your friend." At Gideon's statement, she simply nodded.

"I'd heard voices just before you appeared on the path, so I simply rushed forward without thinking. I thought you were…that you were my friend." She stumbled over her words as she saved herself from mentioning Lawrence by name. "I had hoped someone would be curious enough to investigate when I greeted you."

Gideon's fingers slowly traced a path along the length of his arm. It was a light, innocent touch, but it created a small rush of desire inside her. Dear God, she was like molding clay in his hands.

"But you didn't leave me when you had the chance. Why?" Gideon's voice was soft as his hand turned hers over to rub his thumb across the spot where her pulse beat. While his question was understandable, it still sent an icy finger scraping along Phoebe's spine.

"I'm not sure." It wasn't a lie. Initially, she had been confused as to why she'd allowed him to continue kissing her. "At first, I was simply shocked that I hadn't struggled to be free of you. But after…when we…I'd never been touched like that before. Alfred had always treated me as if…you were not completely incorrect when you said it was as if I'd never been kissed before."

"*Christ Jesus,*" he snarled softly.

"I was starved for even the smallest amount of affection. The way you…the way you touched me made me feel alive, and I couldn't walk away. Even if it was only for a few brief moments, I wanted to feel again. I wanted to know desire and the gentle touch of a lover."

Gideon drew in a sharp breath as her voice died away, and in an abrupt movement, he gathered her into his embrace and held her close. It was such an unexpected gesture of solace that Phoebe struggled to hold back the hot tears pressing at her eyelids. It was one thing to find solace in his arms, but she had no wish to be the recipient of his pity.

Even though he didn't love her, Gideon's generous display of comfort made her love for him deepen even more. She'd been right all these years to believe he was a good man. The warmth of his mouth on her brow made her tremble slightly, and Gideon pulled her closer.

"I swear to you, sweetheart. No one will ever treat you so badly again. *No one.*"

She didn't acknowledge his reply. Instead, she simply accepted his warm embrace as a moment to treasure in the future. A moment to sustain her when he discovered the truth about her feelings for him and looked upon her with pity.

Phoebe didn't know how long she'd been tucked in his embrace, but the sound of Gideon's heartbeat in her ear slowed to a small murmur. Above her head, she could hear his gentle breathing with the occasional breath that was almost a snore. Even in his sleep, he hadn't released her. As she gently twisted her body away from him, Gideon's arms tightened around her. Startled, she threw her head back slightly to look up to see him studying her intently.

"Are you so eager to leave my bed, Lady Chelmsford?" There was a possessive note underlying the question that made her heart skip a beat. She shook her head.

"No. I thought you were asleep and that you might be more comfortable without me clinging to you."

"I like it when you cling to me," he said with a smile that made her drawn in a sharp breath of pleasure.

In a swift move, he rolled her onto her back and slid his hand along her body until he reached her hip. A second later, Phoebe gasped as his fingers parted her folds, and he pressed two fingers into her. Gideon's smile broadened.

"Shall I make you cling to me again, my sweet?" The question was emphasized with a stroke of his fingers, and all she was capable of was a small moan of pleasure. "I'll take that as a yes."

With his fingers still teasing her body, Gideon lowered his head and kissed her. Without hesitation, Phoebe responded to his caresses by sliding one hand down across his chest to his thick, hard erection. The moment he sucked in a sharp breath, she murmured her own question against his mouth. His only answer was to deepen his kiss.

Phoebe woke to a soft sound of metal against stone. She reached behind her for the warm body that had been pressed into her back when she'd fallen asleep, but she was alone. Sitting up in bed, Phoebe saw Gideon poking at the fire. A robe covered his body, but his legs were clearly visible, and she remembered how those strong legs had tangled with hers as they'd made love several more times in the past few hours. Amusement spread through her as Gideon muttered an oath as he continued to poke at the fire. She laughed softly, and he looked over her shoulder at her.

"It appears you are also not very good at stoking fires."

At her light-hearted teasing, Gideon scowled at her, and she laughed harder. With obvious disgust, he muttered another oath and shoved the poker into its stand. Striding back toward the bed, he threw off his robe, and she drew in a silent breath at how beautifully male he was. Gideon slipped beneath the covers and pulled her into his arms.

"You were shivering, and I was trying to warm up the room. So it appears I'll have to hold you to keep you from freezing," Gideon said as he sank back into the pillows and nestled her into his side before dragging the covers up over them.

"It's the beginning of May," she teased. "I can hardly believe I was shivering *that* badly."

"The weather is still chilly at night, and stop protesting when I'm trying to care for you." The disgruntled note in Gideon's voice made her smile as she looked up at him.

"Are you always so irascible when you are having a restless night?"

"As I recall, *you* are the reason for my inability to sleep well, my lady."

"*Me?* Don't you *dare* blame me." She laughed as he scowled at her again. "I'm the one who's been awakened at least twice in order for you too—"

"Indulge myself in the delicious sweet charms of my

wife?" He finished her statement with a satisfied grin.

"Aha, so you *admit* that you have no one to blame but yourself for your lack of sleep." Phoebe laughed again as she watched his satisfaction became one of annoyance, but she saw the laughter gleaming his eyes. His aggravation vanished to be replaced with a wide grin of self-satisfaction.

"I admit only that my wife is beautiful, and that I cannot be blamed for finding pleasure in her arms."

Although his words were playful, there was something in his voice that said he was sincere in his statement. Phoebe's heart skipped a beat as her cheeks grew warm beneath his gaze. She quickly dropped her head and pressed her cheek into his chest. Content to lie quietly in his arms, Phoebe watched the fire that had suddenly sprung to life in the fireplace. The rumble of exasperation drifting out of him made her smile. It said he'd seen the fire beginning to burn brightly in the hearth. The silence between them had a calming effect on Phoebe, and her eyes were drooping slightly when Gideon shifted his position.

"Phoebe?"

The serious note in his voice made her look up at him. In the firelight, his sober expression gave his strong features a severe look. Instantly, her nerve endings fired off warnings as dread sailed through her. Uncertain as to what was to come, she slid away from him slightly into the pillows and waited for him to continue.

"Mama told me that you were working at Sabine's before she persuaded you to come work for her." The question in his voice made her flinch, and she looked away from him.

"Yes."

"I'd like a bit more explanation than a simple yes, Phoebe." Despite the gentleness in his voice, she heard the demand as well.

"There is little to explain," she shrugged as she continued to avoid looking at him. "Alfred's heir arrived a few months after Alfred was dead, and as I had no claim to Helstone Place, I was shown the door."

"Did your father not make accommodations for you in the event of Helstone's death?" Disapproval and anger filled his voice, and it warmed her heart that he cared enough to be outraged on her behalf.

"No. My father wasn't the best businessman, despite his desire to be one."

"Was there no one you could turn to?" His voice sounded strained, but she put it down to his being angry at her misfortune.

"My father died two years before you and I met in Montjoy's garden. I had very few friends, and certainly none I felt comfortable calling upon for help. I remembered from my last dress fitting that Madame Sabine had mentioned she was in need of a bookkeeper. The rest you know."

As her voice died away, Gideon remained silent, but his body had become rigid with tension as she'd shared her past with him. Phoebe turned her head to look at him. Eyes closed, his stony expression reminded her of a statue. As if sensing her watching him, Gideon's turned his head toward her. Something flickered in the gray depths, but she couldn't determine what he was thinking.

"Do you have any idea what a remarkable woman you are, Phoebe?" Gideon brushed the back of his hand across her cheek as he studied her. "You have more strength and courage than anyone I've ever known."

"You make me sound like a saint, and I am far from it," she protested fiercely.

Guilt curled through Phoebe as she quickly rolled onto her back to avoid his look of admiration. If he knew she was the author of the Chronicles, he would call her the devil incarnate. She wished to God she'd never submitted the serial to the Times. As if aware of her heightened emotions, Gideon caught her hand and carried it to his lips.

"No. You're a survivor, and I admire that about you."

The sincerity in his voice made Phoebe accept his compliment with a small bob of her head. Silence fell between them, but it was a comfortable one, and Gideon still held her hand. After a moment, his quiet laugh was a gentle breeze across the top of her head as he leaned into her.

"As for sainthood, need I remind you that you're married to the Earl of Chelmsford? A man who's not yet finished indulging himself in his countess's delectable charms. Indulgences that will be far too wicked for his wife to ever have any hope of attaining such a lofty title. "

"Far be it from me to dispute an earl, who happens to be a rogue." Phoebe laughed as her arm curled around Gideon's neck to pull him down into her. "And I prefer wicked rogues to sainthood any day of the week."

A sinful chuckle fell past Gideon's lips as he nipped at Phoebe's mouth before he kissed her. Sighing softly at the caress, Phoebe pushed aside all her fears and dark secrets. There would be plenty of time tomorrow to be afraid. Tonight she only wanted to feel alive in the arms of the man she adored.

Chapter 20

Gideon swirled the brandy in his snifter with a gentle movement of his hand. A small smile twisted his lips as he studied the liquor in the glass. It was an excellent brandy, but it possessed none of the fire that his countess did. He took a sip of the cognac as he contemplated the recent changes in his life.

For the past three days, he'd awoken to the sweet scent of roses. Waking up to see Phoebe's lovely head on the pillow next to his every morning was proving to be an unexpected pleasure. He'd taken to watching his wife while she slept. She had a delightful way of nibbling on her bottom lip while sleeping. It always created the urge for Gideon to soothe the bruised flesh.

Yesterday afternoon, he'd seen Sebastian at the Club, and his friend had cheerfully commented on the fact that it appeared married life suited him. As he reflected on his friend's comment, Gideon had to agree with him. He was happier now than he'd ever been in his life. If this was what loving a woman was like, he could highly recommend it. Instantly, Gideon froze. He was in love with Phoebe.

Stunned, Gideon stared down at his brandy as he tried to fully comprehend the fact that he was in love with his wife. When had he fallen in love with her? Although the past three days had given them time to learn more about each other, they still didn't know each other as well as most married couples. A voice in the back of Gideon's head snorted with mocking laughter. He'd been in love with Phoebe for the past five years.

The night they'd met in Montjoy's garden, Gideon had known something significant had passed between them. While his head hadn't understood it, his heart had. But when he'd discovered who Phoebe was, his head had overruled his instincts. He'd judged her unfairly and ignored the truth. Deep down, he'd always known the reason why he'd been willing to have someone nearly beat him to death that same night.

Worse, he'd not gone to her when she'd needed him the most. Gideon's muscles tightened as he remembered Phoebe telling him how she'd been tossed out onto the street after Helstone had been killed. Never in his entire life had he ever experienced such a pang of deep guilt. The memory of her reluctance to speak of the past emphasized how terrible things must have been for her. A polite cough behind him made Gideon turn around. Pendleton stood in the doorway of the parlor with a look of discomfort on his face. It was rare that the butler ever look rattled, and Gideon eyed the man with puzzlement. His expression troubled, the man walked toward him.

"Forgive me, my lord. This note just arrived. It is addressed to Lady Chelmsford, but …the staff is quite fond of her ladyship and would not like to see her hurt in any way. I recognized the seal straight away, and as I am familiar with the letter writer in question, I thought it best to give it to you."

Gideon frowned as the butler extended his hand to offer Gideon a small notecard. As he took the card from Pendleton, the heavy smell of an exotic perfume drifted up to his nostrils. The moment he turned the card over, Gideon went rigid as he saw the Duchess of Stockdale's waxed seal. Edith.

"Thank you, Pendleton. You did the right thing bringing this to me," Gideon said as he met the man's troubled gaze. "Give me a moment."

The servant nodded as Gideon turned away and broke the seal of the missive. God help him if Phoebe ever discovered he'd intercepted and opened a note addressed to her. However, a note from Edith was a different matter altogether. A few months after she married the duke, the woman had audaciously proposed they become lovers. Gideon had coldly rejected her offering, and in doing so, he'd made an enemy. Over the years, Edith had proven spiteful when it came to his liaisons, and he was certain the woman was attempting to drive a wedge between him and Phoebe.

My dear Lady Chelmsford,

Allow me to offer you best wishes on the occasion of your recent marriage. Gideon and I are old friends, and our intimate relationship prompted me to write to you.

If you are available, I would like to call on you Monday morning. then again, perhaps we will meet this evening at the gala for St. Catherine's home for the poor.

Yours respectfully,
Edith Bailor, Duchess of Stockdale

"God damn the woman. I'll see her in hell first," he muttered as he spun around on his heel. "Pendleton, come with me."

Quickly striding out of the salon, he crossed the foyer into his study. At his desk, he pulled out a piece of stationary and picked up a pen. The writing instrument hovered over the parchment for a moment before he began to write.

Edith,

While your title will still provide you access to society, I can easily make you a pariah in a substantially large segment of the Marlborough Set. I will not allow you to distress Lady Chelmsford with your vindictive, malicious games. I also believe your husband might be unhappy to hear you have been enjoying bedroom sport with his good friend, Lord Marberry.

I know such a betrayal would deeply anger his grace. as we both know how much you loathe the countryside, I'm *certain you will be quite unhappy when the duke decides to spend the majority of time in the country taking you with him. I highly recommend that you keep your distance from my wife. Failing to heed this advice will be to your detriment.*

Chelmsford

Gideon folded the note in short, choppy movements before handing it to the butler.

"Have this sent to the Duchess of Stockdale. Immediately."

"Yes, my lord," Pendleton said firmly as he accepted the note and left the study.

Still furious at Edith's maliciousness, Gideon paced the floor in front of his desk. God help the woman if she hurt Phoebe. He'd see Edith destroyed, even if it meant calling in every marker he was owed or selling his soul.

The sound of female laughter made him suppress his anger, and he walked out into the entryway to see his mother coming down the steps with Phoebe behind her. At the sight of his wife, Gideon's heart slammed into his chest as the air was sucked out of his lungs. Tonight she wasn't simply beautiful. She was radiant. The gown she wore was the vibrant pink of the inner petals of a Comte De Chambord Portland Rose. The hue complimented her warm, peach-colored complexion, and Phoebe's cheeks flushed with color as he stared at her. Lady Wrotham reached his side, and he absently offered his cheek for her to kiss. Laughter bubbling out of her, the marchioness patted him on the shoulder in almost a sympathetic gesture.

"You see, Phoebe. I told you he'd be speechless."

At his mother's cheerful observation, the flush of color in his wife's face deepened. Still unable to stop staring at his wife, he closed the distance between them and took her hand in his. As he brushed his mouth across Phoebe's fingers,

Gideon smiled.

"You'll be the most beautiful woman at the gala, my lady."

"Thank you." She blushed again, and Gideon chuckled as he leaned forward to kiss her. At the last second, she turned her head slightly so his mouth caressed her cheek instead. Gideon was uncertain what to make of her movement, and as Phoebe's gaze met his, she darted a glance toward his mother.

"Are you suddenly afraid to kiss your husband, Lady Chelmsford?" he asked softly.

"No," she whispered in dismay. "But we are *not* alone."

"Mama, would you mind terribly if I kissed my wife properly?" Gideon tossed the question over his shoulder while his gaze remained locked with Phoebe's.

"*Gideon.*" Phoebe's soft gasp was drowned out by Lady Wrotham's laughter.

"Not at all, dearest."

He arched an eyebrow at her, and Phoebe uttered a noise of amused exasperation. Satisfied that he would have his way, Gideon grinned as he bent his head and kissed her soundly. As he broke the kiss, he was pleased to see her eyelids fall slightly until she had a sultry, slumberous look about her.

"Consider that a taste of what's to come later this evening, my lady," Gideon murmured.

"I was right to call you a rogue, Lord Chelmsford." The breathless note in her voice pleased him.

"As I recall, you find rogues quite exciting. And later tonight, the Countess of Chelmsford will find out just how much of a rogue her husband is."

"You're impossible," she whispered, but her eyes shimmered with laughter and an emotion that took his breath away. Was it possible she was in love with him? The thought was an exhilarating one, and he had the sudden urge to drag her upstairs and declare his feelings for her.

"Gideon, if you've finished teasing your wife, do you

think we might leave? I told Lady Gresham we would arrive early to ensure everything is in order. I do wish I'd not agreed to the woman holding the gala at Gresham Place. Our ballroom isn't that much smaller than hers, and it would have made things so much easier."

"As I recall," Gideon said with amusement. "I did tell you *not* to let the countess convince you to do all the work while she takes all the glory."

"Must you keep reminding me?" Lady Wrotham said with a note of pique in her voice before she arched her eyebrow and smiled with triumph. "But, if I had refused, Phoebe would not be with us now."

"A point well taken." Gideon smiled as he turned to look at his wife. A haunted look flitted across her face before she met his gaze. The warmth in her brown eyes and her happy smile made him dismiss her troubled expression as one of his imagination.

"Well, we shouldn't delay any further. I have a distinct feeling Lady Gresham is in a state of panic as we speak."

"Of course, Mama," he said as he gave her a small bow and followed his mother and wife to the front door.

A short time later, the three of them were standing in the entryway of Gresham Place. They were met by the Countess of Gresham, who was clearly frantic as she greeted them.

"Oh my dear, Lady Wrotham," the woman exclaimed in an overwrought voice. "Thank heavens you are here. I've been beside myself as I don't have an answer for any of the servants' questions." Suddenly Lady Gresham gasped loudly, and the countess brushed past his mother to grab Phoebe's hands in hers.

"My dear, Lady Hel—Chelmsford, welcome. I just heard the joyous news this morning at Madame Sabine's. My dress needed a last-minute alteration, and I saw Lady Mary Pepperell in the shop. She told me that Lord Chelmsford had married and that I would never guess who his new bride was. Of course, I had no idea, but when Lady Mary said it was you, well, naturally, I was astonished. Not that you could be blamed—"

"Lady Chelmsford and I thank you for your best wishes, Lady Gresham. However, I believe you were in need of the marchioness's assistance?" Gideon's icy voice made the woman flinched as Phoebe pulled her hand from the countess's.

"Yes, thank you for your best wishes, my lady." Phoebe's reply was soft, and it wasn't difficult to see the woman's words had made his wife deeply uncomfortable.

Angered by Lady Gresham's behavior, Gideon eyed the woman with open disdain. Clearly disconcerted by his abrupt manner, Lady Gresham's lips moved, but she said nothing. Although Phoebe's mouth was curved in a small smile, her distress was almost palpable.

Gideon gently pulled Phoebe's hand into the crook of his arm. Her fingers immediately clutched at his arm fiercely, and her slight trembling pulsated into him. Another jolt of anger barreled through him at Lady Gresham's insensitive greeting. Arrogantly arching his eyebrow, Gideon eyed the woman coldly and gestured toward the ballroom.

"But...but...of course. How...silly of me. The first guests...they will be arriving...in a few minutes," the woman stammered. "Forgive me. If you'll come with me."

With a frown, the marchioness took a quick step toward Phoebe and kissed her cheek. His mother whispered something to Phoebe before squeezing her hand and turning back to Lady Gresham. The umbrage on Lady Wrotham's face as she frowned angrily at the countess made the other woman suddenly looked uneasy as her gaze flitted between the three of them.

Aware she'd made a grievous error in the way she'd greeted Phoebe, the woman quickly turned and led the way into the ballroom. Lady Wrotham's posture as she followed

Lady Gresham indicated his mother was as furious as he was. Their hostess's behavior had been the kind of petty indiscretion Gideon had always found objectionable. As the two women moved away from him, he bent his head to kiss his wife's cheek.

"The woman's an infernal gossip, and you're to ignore her."

"I did warn you that people would talk if you married me," Phoebe said quietly as she watched his mother disappear into the ballroom.

"I don't give a damn what others say or think," he said with a ferocity that made her jerk her head up to look at him in surprise. "And I'm ordering you to do the same."

"A command?" Her smile was genuine, but the pain he saw in her eyes wrenched at his gut.

"A request then," he said firmly. "I'll not tolerate anyone treating you with anything less than respect. Anyone who dares to treat you with condescension will find me unforgiving when it comes to my family."

"Oh Gideon, if only—I don't deserve you as a defender."

"If only, what?"

"It's…it's simply that the circumstances under which you married me were less than desirable," she said softly. "I know it wasn't something you wanted."

"As I told you at our first dinner as husband and wife, I have no regrets. In fact, I find being married to you even more pleasurable than I expected." Gideon smiled as he lowered his voice. "And while our conjugal exchanges are as exciting as they are intoxicating, I find your company equally enjoyable."

Phoebe's cheeks grew pink, and she scowled at him in feigned anger. She didn't reply to his playful comments, but it was the light shining in her eyes that stole his breath away. Gideon bent his head and kissed her brow. Inhaling the sweet scent of roses off her hair, desire stirred inside him, and he wished they were in his bedroom where he could worship her as she deserved to be.

With a smile, he guided her into the ballroom. Froom where they stood, Gideon saw his mother walk through the doorway to a room next to the ballroom. Laughing, the marchioness waved to them to join her. As they entered the room serving as a buffet, Gideon saw a dessert table with a large cake as its centerpiece. It was decorated with an array of different flowers and smaller cakes disguised as small animals and birds. Beside him, Phoebe inhaled a sharp breath and came to an abrupt halt.

"Gideon…I'm afraid you're going to be furious with me," she said in a soft, apologetic tone.

"It would take a great deal for me to be angry with you."

"Oh, I think this will meet that challenge." There was a look of deep regret and dismay shadowing her features, and Gideon eyed her with puzzlement. As if realizing he wanted an answer. Phoebe rolled her shoulders. "When you first returned home from Amsterdam, you made me so angry, and I…well, I…"

"What are you trying to say, Phoebe?" He frowned at her growing distraught manner.

"I…truly am sorry, Gideon…I shouldn't…but I was furious…I wanted—"

"Phoebe. Gideon." The marchioness called out with a wave of her hand. "Come look at the artistry of this cake. It's marvelous."

Frowning with puzzlement, Gideon took a step forward and hesitated as Phoebe pulled away from him. She met his gaze before quickly bowing her head. She had paled slightly, and he caught her hand as concern sped through him.

"Are you feeling unwell, sweetheart?"

"Yes…no… it's the bumblebees," Phoebe whispered.

"Bumblebees?"

"On the cake," she said hesitantly before rushing into an explanation. "I didn't know then what I do now. It was wrong of me to instruct the baker to do it, but I thought you were so beastly that morning at breakfast, I wanted…"

"Phoebe, you're not making any sense. Show me what you're so upset about." Gideon tried to pull her toward the dessert table, but she wouldn't budge.

"No, I can't. It was petty of me. You aren't anything at all like Lord Chelmbee, and I'm so sorry—so terribly sorry."

Gideon frowned as he stared down at Phoebe's remorseful expression. He turned his head toward his mother to see she'd moved on to another section of the food-laden tables. With one more glance at Phoebe, he crossed the floor to the dessert table. As Gideon came to a halt in front of the cake, he studied its ornate decorations. His mother was right. The artistry of the cake was extraordinary.

As he examined the cake, he saw several flowers with a single bumblebee hovering over them. The baker had attached the bee to a large fern hanging over the flowers. Gideon continued to survey the confection in silence. There were one or two small frogs, a rabbit hiding under another large fern. There were even two songbirds attached to the side of the cake, as well as several other instances of bumblebees poised near other flowers. It truly was a masterpiece, and he was having a difficult time understanding why Phoebe was so distraught.

Suddenly Gideon stiffened as he remembered her saying he was nothing like Lord Chelmbee, and his gaze settled on the bee closest to him. The insect appeared ready to dive into the flowers below it. What Phoebe had been trying to explain was that the bumblebee represented him and the flowers his liaisons.

It was such a subtle message that it was unlikely he would have made the connection if not for Phoebe's remorse. When combined with the rest of the display, the bees seemed a natural addition to the cleverly created confection.

For a long moment, he stood staring down at the

decorated cake with growing amusement. Over the past few days, Gideon had quickly learned that Phoebe possessed a dry humor that required a moment or two for him to realize she was poking fun at him. The bumblebees on the cake were an example of just how subtle her humor could be.

Although anger had made her request the bees be added to the confection, she'd clearly used discretion. The bumblebees were positioned in such a way that no one would even consider the possibility they had been placed there intentionally. Even if he and Phoebe were still at odds, it was doubtful someone would think Phoebe responsible for the bumblebees being added to the extravagant dessert.

If one of the Marlborough Set actually recognized the subtle irony of the multiple bees that had been added to the the cake, the worst that might happen would be laughter. The Set would simply say Lord Chelmbee's pollination days were over, at least until he grew tired of his marriage. But they would be wrong about him straying from his wife. That he might grow weary of Phoebe was beyond the realm of possibility. He would love his countess until he drew his last breath.

Mentally shrugging his shoulders, he told himself the Set could whisper all they wanted. Gideon had always dismissed their gossip, innuendo, and blatant insults. Currer was the only exception. The man's depiction of him in the Chronicles was different. Gideon's abhorrence of the serial hadn't been that Currer had made him a figure of fun. It had been the fact that the author's words held a ring of truth. It had infuriated him that someone else had seen what he'd been blind to.

Now the author's fascination with Gideon might easily extend to Phoebe. The thought made him frown. If the author were to focus his attention on Phoebe, it would only acerbate the distress he'd witnessed earlier. Phoebe's reaction to Lady Gresham's greeting had been one of humiliation and pain. While the woman's words hadn't been malevolent, they'd been insensitive.

Others, however, would not hesitate to be unkind. Edith was a perfect example of that. The woman wouldn't hesitate to make life difficult for Phoebe. The scandal around Helstone's death would be bad enough when it came to tongue wagging. Even worse, the gossip would rage like an out-of-control fire when people learned Phoebe had worked for Madame Sabine. And he had no doubt that someone would discover that fact. It was only a matter of time.

Gideon wasn't sure how he would shield Phoebe from the gossip and insults, but he'd find a way. Reaching out, he gently pulled the closest bumblebee off its resting place. He turned and walked back to where Phoebe stood, watching him with a helpless look of guilt, remorse, and trepidation. She flinched as he halted in front of her.

"I found one of the bumblebees you mentioned on the cake," he murmured with a smile. "I thought you might like to see how they look."

"What?" Phoebe stared at him in utter bewilderment.

"It's made of some sort of hardened sugar."

Gideon broke off a wing off the bumblebee's back and popped it into his mouth, then offered the sugary confection to her on the palm of his hand. Smiling, he silently encouraged her to try the sweet. Warily eyeing him with confusion, Phoebe broke off a piece of the cleverly designed treat only to stare at it in confusion.

"I don't…I expected you to be outraged."

"Did you? Then am I correct in thinking the bees are a reference to Currer's insulting name for me?" As he murmured the question, Phoebe winced with obvious regret.

"Yes. I thought once you saw them that you would be furious with me."

"Do I look furious?" Gideon's mouth twitched with amusement.

"I don't understand. You're not angry with me?"

"Should I be?" His mouth twitched slightly as he arched an eyebrow at her.

"I'm…yes…I don't…you're *deliberately* seeking to confuse me, aren't you?" The frustration in her voice made him smile.

"I believe I am."

"But why aren't you angry? Currer provokes you into a state of rage every time he references you as Lord Chelmbee. When I instructed the baker to have them hover over the flowers, I was certain you would go on a tirade. I simply don't understand why you aren't furious with me."

"First, I've never gone into a rage over Currer's serial. Two, I'm not angry because I've learned to appreciate your dry wit and humor. You have never hesitated to put me in my place when need be, and the bees would have done exactly that if we were still at odds with one another. Three, your remorse and apology are clearly genuine."

"I am sorry, Gideon. I truly am. If I had been thinking better, I would have arranged for the bees to be removed."

"At least you're not Currer, who would most likely have covered the entire cake in bumblebees," he chuckled. Phoebe paled as anguish swept across her features. Frowning in puzzlement, Gideon cocked his head slightly to the left to study her more intently. "Are you all right, sweetheart?"

"Yes, of course." Phoebe nodded as she averted her gaze. "It was simply the idea of Currer doing such a thing."

"Well, I'm not blind to the fact that if we were still at odds, you would have gleefully pointed these out to me." He chuckled and bobbed his head toward the confection fragments in his hand. "In fact, I imagine you would have put my head on a silver platter and included one of these on the side."

"While I'll not deny I would have been gleeful in pointing out the bees, I know I would have been remorseful shortly thereafter," she said.

"Of that, I'm certain, as I would have eventually found an opportunity to administer a suitable punishment." Gideon smiled before he bowed his head to study her intently. "In fact, I think I will extract a penalty from you tonight simply to remind you that there are consequences to teasing me."

"I think I will most likely sanction your…punishment as something quite pleasurable." The sultry look of passion flaring in Phoebe's eyes made Gideon draw in a sharp breath as his body knotted with need. Christ Jesus, the woman had him well and fully at her mercy, and she didn't even know it.

Laughter echoed through the air behind him, and Gideon turned his head to see a small cohort of the Rockwood family walking toward them. Louisa was the first to reach them, and she greeted Phoebe warmly.

"Oh, Phoebe, you look beautiful. That dress is the perfect color for you." Louisa lightly kissed his wife's cheek and then the other. "And now you're the Countess of Chelmsford. How *wonderfully* romantic."

The youngest of the Rockwood family turned to a tall man behind her wearing a black eye patch. Dressed in the traditional Scottish formalwear, the man cut a striking figure. Terrible scars extended past the man's leather eye covering, and Gideon's gaze fell on the black glove covering one of the Scotsman's hands. Apparently, the man had lost more than just an eye.

Gideon noted the Black Watch pin on the Scotsman's kilt. The Scottish regiment was known for their fearlessness and bravery on the field of battle. In all likelihood, the Scotsman had earned his battle scars somewhere in the Sudan.

"I don't believe either of you has met my betrothed, the Earl of Argaty." Love made Louisa glow as she touched the man's arm and gestured toward Gideon and Phoebe. "Ewan, this is the Earl and Countess of Chelmsford. Gideon is a dear friend of the family. He and Sebastian attended Cambridge together."

"A pleasure, my lady." Argaty bowed over Phoebe's hand, then turned and used his left hand to shake Gideon's in an awkward move. "Lord Chelmsford."

The earl stepped aside to allow Percy and Rhea to cheerfully greet the two of them with their best wishes. As Rhea joined Louisa and Argaty to converse with Phoebe, Percy clapped him on the shoulder.

"I was delighted when Sebastian said he'd stood with you at your wedding, Gideon. Although I'll be honest, I thought you were hell-bent on avoiding marriage." Percy shook his head as he grinned. "But I have to agree with my brother. It appears marriage suits you."

"It does," Gideon said with a smile as he turned to look at Phoebe. Almost as if she could sense him watching her, she turned her head slightly. Their eyes met, and her smile made his heart crashed into his chest. Reluctantly, he turned away from his wife to look at Percy. "I can't remember a time when I've ever been happier."

"Well, all marriages have the occasional rough spots, but I cannot recommend the institution enough."

"I think I'll collect my bride for a dance." Gideon nodded toward the doorway as the orchestra began to play a waltz.

"An excellent idea," Percy exclaimed as he moved toward Rhea.

Moments later, Gideon guided Phoebe out onto the dance floor. As he pulled her into his arms, she smiled up at him. The sweetness of her smile made his heart swell in his chest. Gideon had no idea what he'd done to deserve the happiness he was feeling at the moment, and he didn't want to know. All that mattered was that Phoebe was his, and he would do whatever it took to make her happy.

"You're looking pleased with yourself," Phoebe said with a laugh. "What are you thinking?"

"That I'm happy."

"Oh," she gasped softly and averted her gaze. Gideon's

gut twisted into a painful knot.

"Am I to assume you're not?" he asked. Phoebe jerked her head as surprise illuminate her sweet features.

"No. Not at all. I mean…I am quite content."

"Just content?" Gideon's lips twisted in a small, ironic smile. He had his work cut out for him when it came to capturing her heart. "You cut me to the quick, Lady Chelmsford."

"I regret having done so." Phoebe laughed, and he drew in a sharp breath at the intoxicating sensation her smile had on his body. "If it pleases you for me to say I'm happy, then I shall."

"Thus it begins." Gideon arched his eyebrows as he stared down at her. "A wife agreeing with her husband simply to silence his protests."

"I am doing no such thing."

Phoebe laughed and wrinkled her nose at him in the most adorable fashion, and frustration swept through him that they were here instead of at home. A small voice in his head reminded him they were leaving for their wedding trip in a few days. He would have plenty of time to woo his wife then. And he had *every* intention of sweeping Phoebe off her feet.

The waltz was over far too quickly, and Gideon guided Phoebe to the edge of the dance floor, where Constance and her husband, the Earl of Lyndham, greeted them. Phoebe was laughing at a witty remark Constance had made when Gideon saw Edith out of the corner of his eye. The woman was obviously making her way toward them, but her progress was hindered by people continually greeting her and forcing her to stop every few feet. Determined to protect Phoebe, Gideon leaned over to brush his lips across her ear.

"I just saw someone I know, and I need to have a word with them. I won't be gone long. Will you be all right until I return?"

"Of course," she said with a ready smile. "Constance will

keep me occupied until you return."

"Oh, Gideon, don't tell me you're off to find a card game already." The Countess of Lyndham laughed as she shook her head at him.

"I take it someone's mentioned there's one to be had this evening?" Gideon pretended to be enthused by the possibility, and Constance shook her head as, with a flip of her wrist, she closed her fan to point it at him.

"No, they haven't, but I know how bored men can be when it comes to dancing, and it would not surprise me to hear of one in the works."

"Then you'll be glad to know I have no intention of leaving my bride alone for more than a few minutes. I simply need to have a word with an old friend." Gideon caught Phoebe's hand to brush h. "I promise I will return momentarily and will not leave your side for the remainder of the evening."

The brilliant smile curving his wife's lips made Gideon wish once again that they'd not come to this infernal event. Turning away, his gaze scanned the now crowded ballroom. In seconds, he caught sight of Edith, and he made his way toward her. Although several people tried to stop him, he easily extricated himself from any lengthy conversation. Edith was speaking with Baroness Nevey as Gideon reached her side.

"Gideon, how lovely to see you this evening."

To those who didn't know her well, her smile would appear beguiling. He knew better. There was a calculating aspect to Edith that was visible to anyone who looked closely enough to see the hardness beneath the façade. How in the hell had he ever thought himself in love with her? Gideon bowed and accepted the hand she offered. Politely, he carried her hand to his mouth, but his lips simply brushed the air over her fingertips.

"Your Grace," he murmured as he released Edith's hand

to greet the baroness. "Lady Nevey, you're looking lovely as always."

Gideon didn't have to look at Edith to know his compliment to the baroness had angered her, especially when he'd made no such observation where she was concerned. As Lady Nevey blushed, Gideon glanced at Edith for a moment before he smiled at the baroness.

"If you will pardon my interruption, my lady, I'm afraid the duke is suffering from a sudden attack of gout. I told his grace that I would find and take his duchess to him."

"Oh dear, I do hope his grace is not in too much pain," the baroness said with a gasp of dismay.

Edith eyed him with suspicion as he waited patiently. As if suddenly realizing she'd not displayed any concern for her husband, a worried frown furrowed the duchess's brow.

"It was kind of you to come find me on the duke's behalf, my lord. The dear man was actually looking forward to dancing with me this evening." The duchess's voice was filled with dismay and concern, but Gideon knew the woman couldn't care less if her husband was in pain or not.

"Shall we?" Gideon offered his arm to Edith, and she linked her arm through his and pressed herself into his side in a manner that suggested intimacy.

Gideon released a low sound of irritation at her behavior, but forced a polite smile to his lips as he pulled Edith away from the woman. As he guided Edith to the outer edges of the growing crowd, he remembered the small salon that adjoined the ballroom. It wasn't suitable for the conversation he intended to have with Edith, but if memory served him well, there was a door leading out into the garden.

In silence, he guided Edith around the crowd and to the salon. As they stepped into the room, Gideon was relieved to see it was empty. It made it all the easier to pull Edith out onto the darkened terrace and out into the gardens without someone seeing them. He'd visited the gardens more than a year ago when Lord Gresham had asked for advice on several plants the man was cultivating.

As they walked through the doorway out into the garden, Edith looked up at him and laughed. The sound was meant to be charming, but it was merely brittle and scraped on the nerves.

"Obviously, my husband isn't having a gout attack."

Gideon didn't answer the duchess. He simply ushered her into the darkness and down the steps lined with torches. Intent on finding a secluded spot where they could talk uninterrupted, he pulled Edith along with him until she protested.

"Gideon, please, you're walking too fast."

He ignored her protest and continued to make his way along the walkway and past a small fountain. The musical sound of the splashing water brought to mind an image of Phoebe the night they met in Montjoy's gardens. His mouth tightened with resentful anger. The last place he wanted to be was in the garden with Edith, but he intended to make it clear that the woman wasn't to go anywhere near his wife.

As they reached the small alcove he remembered, Gideon came to an abrupt halt. Before he could say a word, Edith threw her arms around his neck and tugged his head down to press her lips against his. Immediately, he recoiled from her and tugged her arms off of his neck, then pushed her away from him. A flirtatious pout on her lips, she shook her head.

"Surely, you didn't bring me out here to talk, darling. It's obvious you still care for me," she exclaimed as she threw herself into his arms again. "All these years, you've been so cruel in refusing to come to me. Now I understand why. You've simply been waiting to find a way to strike back at me. Oh my darling, if you intended to make me jealous, you've succeeded—"

"I did *not* marry Phoebe to make you jealous." Gideon's

jaw tightened with repressed anger.

"Now, you're simply being cruel. Please don't, Gideon. I want you to take me in your arms and kiss me the way you used to. Make love to me."

"You are under the misguided notion I want anything to do with you at all, your grace." Gideon's studied the duchess with contempt. What in God's name had he ever seen in this woman?

"Then why *did* you bring me out here?" she eyed him with a petulant look as if suddenly realizing this was not the intimate rendezvous she'd expected.

"I brought you out here to emphasize what I said in the note I sent you. You are not to do or say anything that will hurt my wife."

"What note? I received no note," Edith snapped.

"The note you sent Phoebe this evening never reached her. I burned it and replied for her."

"*Burned it.* Why on earth would you do such a thing?" Edith snapped as she glared up at him. "I was merely being thoughtful and wished to call on your wife and offer my best wishes on the occasion of your marriage."

"You've never done a kind or thoughtful thing in your life, Edith."

"How *dare* you talk to me that way."

"I'm stating facts, Edith. You are cold, calculating, and shallow." At his sharp, pointed words, Edith blanched, and she took a quick step backward. In the next instant, anger flashed across the duchess's face.

"You seem to have forgotten that I can easily make your little mouse of a wife unwelcome in all the best houses," Edith sneered with disdain, her features ugly with scorn. "It won't be difficult. After all, she's an American who whored her way into not just one, but two titles."

At her insult to Phoebe, Gideon went rigid with a raw fury, and he struggled to keep from wrapping his hands around the woman's throat. His jaw locked with tension, he glared at the duchess.

"I strongly suggest you think twice about saying that again to anyone."

"I will say what—"

"And if you do, I'm certain you will sorely regret doing so, your grace. While I would hate to involve the duke in the matter, I will if I believe it's necessary," Gideon said with an icy look of disgust. Edith blanched at his cold words as she straightened her shoulders.

"Your threats are pointless where the duke is concerned. He adores me."

"Does he adore you enough to look away when he hears about your bed sport with Marberry?"

"I don't know what you're talking about," Edith sniffed dismissively, but Gideon heard the trepidation in her voice.

"I think you do, and if I catch you within arm's length of Phoebe, his grace will know every sordid detail of your liaison with Marberry."

"You wouldn't," she gasped in obvious fear.

"Try me," Gideon said in an icy, detached voice. "If you do anything, Edith, even the slightest hint of gossip about Phoebe, you will wish to God you had paid heed to my words here."

Satisfied that Edith understood the consequences of doing anything to injure Phoebe in any way, Gideon spun about on his heel and stalked away. The raw fury still pounding its way through him made Gideon's stride fast, and he forced himself to slow his pace. He needed to give himself a moment to let his anger subside. But it was more than anger.

It was fear.

Although Gideon had made it clear to Edith that her life would be a living hell if she harmed Phoebe, the woman might still be a threat. Edith was a viper. She wouldn't hesitate to make trouble if she could, if simply for the pleasure of making someone else as miserable as she was. The thought of the woman upsetting the delicate balance of his marriage made Gideon's muscles tighten.

Aside from Lady Gresham's insensitive greeting, Phoebe seemed to be enjoying herself. But when he'd said he was happy, her response had been less than he'd hoped for. The word content meant different things to different people. Perhaps for Phoebe, contentment *was* happiness. From everything she'd shared with him, it was clear she'd not had a very happy life.

Phoebe had numerous reasons to be wary of him and any potential happiness she might find as the Countess of Chelmsford. It was easy to understand why she might choose her words carefully when it came to admitting she was happy. The light from the ballroom brightened the path in front of him, and a surge of determination swept through him.

As he entered the small salon and strode out into the ballroom, the memory of how his wife had smiled at him a short time ago made his heart lighter. Gideon grinned. Lady Chelmsford had told him she was content being married to him. But his wife was about to learn how much better happiness was than contentment.

Chapter 21

hoebe smiled up at Gideon as he promised to return quickly. The warmth in his gray eyes caused butterflies to flutter wildly in her stomach. He hesitated for a brief second as if reluctant to leave her before he turned and walked away. As Phoebe watched his walk away, the sound of Constance's soft laughter echoed in her ears.

"The man is well and truly besotted with you." Her friend's observation made Phoebe wince slightly as she rejected the countess's suggestion with a shake of her head.

"I would like to believe that, but I have no desire to have my hopes crushed if you are wrong. There is also the other matter that has yet to be resolved. Until it is settled, hope is something I can't afford."

"I've known Gideon for years, Phoebe. If he is not already in love with you, he is well on his way." Constance caught her hand in hers and squeezed it reassuringly. "As for a certain gentleman, you worked well into the afternoon in our library yesterday. I have no idea how you finished so quickly, but you did, and the package was successfully delivered."

Phoebe nodded as she tried to stifle the hope Constance's words ignited in her heart. A confident smile on her lips, Constance laid a reassuring hand on Phoebe's arm before a woman Phoebe didn't recognize caught her friend's attention. After greeting the woman, Constance immediately introduced Lady Frances Woodburn to Phoebe. Still distracted, Phoebe took a half-hearted interest in the conversation as she looked around the room in the hope she would see Gideon.

Disappointment threaded through her when she didn't see him. Phoebe was just about to turn her full attention to the conversation between Constance and Lady Frances when she saw Gideon's tall, handsome figure across the room. Happiness sped through her at the sight of him, but a split second later, the emotion was dealt a crushing blow as a small group of guests shifted their positions to reveal a woman clinging to Gideon's arm.

In horrified dismay, she watched as he escorted the woman into one of the small salon rooms situated off the ballroom. Several days ago, she and Lady Wrotham had visited Gresham Place to determine the best place to set up the buffet. The room Gideon and the woman on his arm had entered was one Phoebe remembered vividly. It was a small salon with a door that opened into the garden.

Frozen in place, Phoebe felt as if someone had reached into her chest and squeezed her heart to stop it from beating. For a long moment, she stared at the room's empty doorway. Unable to think straight, she blindly accepted a glass of champagne a footman offered her from the tray he carried.

She took a deep drink of the bubbly beverage, only to cough as the champagne went down wrong. Jumbled thoughts crashed against each other in her head as she tried to accept the reality of what she'd just seen. Constance had been wrong. Gideon didn't love her. The man wasn't even besotted with her. If he had been, he would not have disappeared from the ballroom with another woman.

Phoebe took another sip of champagne as her gaze flitted toward the doorway Gideon and the woman had disappeared through. The thought that he might have used the adjoining room as a discrete way to usher the woman into the gardens made her stomach churn. A voice in the back of her head screamed out a sharp rejection of the searingly painful thoughts hovering on the edge of her senses.

No. Gideon's behavior toward her this evening had hardly been that of a man intent on humiliating his wife. He'd kissed her soundly before leaving the house. He'd coldly condemned Lady Gresham for the way the woman had greeted Phoebe. He'd teased her about the bumblebees on the cake. How could she possibly judge him without knowing more? She simply had to find the courage to ask him who the woman was when he returned.

A voice in her head sneered at her. Had she forgotten he was Lord Chelmbee? A man, who like a bumblebee, moved quickly from flower to flower. The voice reminded her of what had happened between the two of them in Montjoy's garden. Desperately, Phoebe tried to push the image of the woman clinging to Gideon's arm out of her mind.

Shouts of horror and pain created a cacophony in her head as Phoebe tried to suppress her growing fear. She was being irrational. Phoebe knew there had to be some reasonable explanation for what she'd seen. All she had to do was ask him to explain things. Gideon was an honorable man. He would tell her the truth. Perhaps the woman had fallen ill, and Gideon was simply being solicitous by escorting her away from the heat and noise.

Instantly, a wild cackling erupted in the back of her head, followed by a voice that mocked her for thinking Gideon's behavior this evening meant more than it did. The voice laughed at her for even daring to think Gideon might be coming to care for her. Phoebe vehemently argued with the voice.

Why would he have said he was happy if he didn't care? He had nothing to gain by saying such a thing. He'd even been disappointed when she would only admit to being content. It made no sense to judge his behavior without hearing what he had to say. Another voice in her head sneered at her for ignoring the fact that Gideon had said he wished to speak with a friend.

"Phoebe? Are you all right, dearest?"

The sound of Lady Wrotham's voice made her start violently as her mother-in-law touched her arm. With a strength she pulled from deep within, Phoebe hid her fear as she forced a smile to her lips and turned her head toward the marchioness.

"What?"

"I asked if you were all right."

"Of course, why wouldn't I be," Phoebe replied with a quiet laugh that sounded hollow to her ears. Lady Wrotham nodded as she eyed Phoebe carefully.

"I was worried someone might have upset you as Lady Gresham did earlier." The marchioness's look of concern eased slightly but didn't fade away completely. Phoebe turned her attention back to the crowded room, searching for a glimpse of Gideon.

"No, Constance has proven to be quite skillful in diverting attention away from me," she said absently

"Where did Gideon run off to?" the marchioness asked quietly.

"He said he had to speak with…with a friend."

Phoebe winced as she stumbled over her words. Just as she was about to turn her head toward the marchioness, Gideon walked out of the room he'd entered a short time earlier, only now he was alone. The woman who'd been with him was nowhere in sight. She must have been feeling ill, and Gideon had acted the gentleman he was by seeing to the lady's comfort.

Relief made Phoebe release a deep breath. He turned his head to look around the room, and a brief moment later, their gazes locked across the dance floor and the crowd separating the two of them. The smile he sent her made her heart sing as she watched him begin to make his way around the crowded room to where she stood.

"Ah, there he is," Lady Wrotham said with what Phoebe

thought might have been relief. "Some political discussion, no doubt. Why men feel the need to conduct business during a social event is of constant amazement to me."

Phoebe laughed at her mother-in-law's statement, feeling light-hearted and relieved. Almost giddy with relief, Phoebe lost sight of Gideon, and as she turned toward Lady Wrotham, she saw someone entering the ballroom from the gardens. The moment her gaze settled on the woman Gideon had been with a short time ago, the air left Phoebe's lungs.

The woman looked disheveled and appeared as if she had just come from a tête-à-tête with someone. A cold numbness slid its way over Phoebe's skin as she watched the woman adjust her gown and hair. Phoebe's stomach lurched with a painful, sickening sensation.

Gideon *had* gone into the garden with the woman.

As if sensing she was the object of someone's attention, the woman turned her head and looked directly at Phoebe. The moment their gazes met, a slow smile of satisfaction and triumph curved the woman's lips.

Instantly, Phoebe was plunged into the depths of hell as she was forced to accept the cold reality that Gideon and the woman had been in the garden together. She swayed on her feet and flinched as Lady Wrotham gasped with concern and cupped Phoebe's elbow to steady her.

"Something *is* wrong." Lady Wrotham exclaimed softly.

"It's nothing," Phoebe shook her head and pressed her fingertips to her forehead. "It's a headache. I thought it would go away, but…but it's becoming worse. Do you think it would cause a stir if I were to go home?"

"What people think is of no concern. You're ill, and we will go home at once."

"But you cannot leave until the ball is over," she said to the marchioness.

"Then Gideon will see you home and take care of you."

Despite her senses being assaulted from every direction,

Phoebe's nerve endings tingled with awareness, and she instinctively knew Gideon was close. Unable to help herself, she looked for him. The moment she saw him, it was as if her heart became a solid chunk of ice. Gideon's smile vanished as he quickly closed the distance between them to take her hands in his. How she managed not to recoil from his touch was beyond her comprehension.

"You're unwell." It wasn't a question, and Phoebe swallowed the bile rising in her throat.

"I have a headache, and I would like to go home, but I don't want to cause a scene or draw attention. Perhaps Constance could walk me out as if we are going to refresh ourselves."

Phoebe had no idea how she managed to sound coherent with every muscle in her body screaming as if someone was beating her with a stick. With an abrupt nod, Gideon circled her and Lady Wrotham to speak with Constance. Her friend was at her side in an instant, and she locked arms with Phoebe. Without a word, she began to lead Phoebe toward the exit, her head bent in a conspiratorial manner.

"I sent Lucien to call for your carriage. No one will think anything is amiss if Gideon lingers behind for a moment."

Phoebe nodded and remained silent. She wanted to crawl into a hole somewhere to either die or simply find a way to end her pain. It took only a minute to reach the main entryway, and Constance walked Phoebe out into the warm late spring air. They waited in silence for several moments, and when her senses began to hum, she knew Gideon was close once more.

Dear God, the thought of being alone with him in the carriage was almost too much to bear. As his hand cupped her elbow, Phoebe flinched, but she didn't pull away. It would indicate something other than a headache was troubling her. The carriage rolled up in front of Gresham Place, and in less than a minute, Phoebe was huddled in the corner of the carriage. Gideon slid toward her on the seat to brush a stray tendril of hair off her cheek.

"We'll be home soon, my darling."

The endearment he uttered was an invisible weapon, hitting her viciously. Unable to speak for fear of crying, Phoebe simply answered with a brief nod.

It seemed to take an eternity for them to reach Chelmsford House, and with each passing second, she fought to ignore the warmth of his body sitting so close to her. When they finally arrived home, Phoebe automatically accepted Gideon's hand to exit the carriage. However, his solicitous manner was even more difficult to endure than the carriage ride home. She tried to object to his assisting her up the stairs, but she had no strength to do so. As they stopped in front of Gideon's bedroom door, she drew in a sharp breath.

"I think I shall sleep in my own room tonight." Although he stiffened beside her, Gideon simply nodded and steadied her as they walked to her room.

"I'll have Mrs. Murray send up some tea to help you sleep."

"Thank you, but that won't be necessary. Goodnight," she murmured as she entered her room and closed it behind her without another word.

Phoebe stirred under the covers as she heard a whisper of a sound. Groggily, her hand reached out to touch Gideon, but her fingertips only felt the cool sheets where his warm body should be. Eyes fluttering open, she stared at the spot next to her. Had he risen early? Her next breath brought back the pain of the night before.

She'd cried herself to sleep last night as she tried to forget the woman Gideon had led out into the garden. The woman who'd returned to the ballroom with a rumpled gown and hair out of place. Phoebe was miserable, and the only way out of her situation was to use the marital agreement she and Gideon had signed.

Fingers sliding through her hair to push it off of her face, Phoebe stared up at the ceiling, trying to decide what she should do. A sane person would have told her to leave and hold Gideon to the agreement they'd signed before they were married. But how could she leave? She loved him. Was she willing to live in misery for the rest of her life here in Chelmsford House, or did she want to live in misery elsewhere? Someplace where she would never see Gideon again?

Tears blurred her vision, and she quickly wiped them away. She'd cried enough into her pillow last night. If she continued to weep, her eyes would be red and puffy, which meant Gideon would question her. It was a conversation she wasn't ready to have just yet, but she would be unable to hold off for long.

A quiet knock on her bedroom door made her jerk upright in bed. Gideon? No, he would have come through the corridor that connected their rooms. Lady Wrotham? Quickly brushing away any sign of tears, she invited her visitor to enter. The sight of Mabel's sweet countenance made her release a quiet sigh of relief.

"My lady, I brought you breakfast," the maid said quietly as she entered the room carrying a large tray. The maid smiled at Phoebe as she walked toward the bed. Phoebe had no real appetite, and she gestured for Mabel to set the tray down on the small table in front of the window overlooking Gideon's arboretum.

"His lordship told Mrs. Murray that you'd come home with a headache last night. He asked her to send up some chamomile tea in case you might still be feeling unwell."

"Thank you. Is his lordship still here?"

"No, my lady. He left a short while ago, but there is a note from him on your breakfast tray. There is another letter as well that was delivered after Lord Chelmsford left."

"Is Lady Wrotham up yet?"

"No, my lady, she asked not to be disturbed until eleven."

"Thank you, Mabel. That will be all."

Sliding out of bed, Phoebe pulled on her robe as the young maid bobbed a small curtsey, then quietly left the room. Her gaze fell on the tray and the two letters that were placed on top of the morning's newspaper. Slowly, she walked over to the table and stared down at the two letters. The one on top displayed her name, written in Gideon's strong hand. Unprepared to read his words just yet, she pushed it aside and pick up the letter beneath it. As Phoebe turned over the note, she gasped at the crest on the wax seal. Sinking down into a chair, she quickly tore open the letter.

My dearest, Phoebe,

I am quite angry with you, my pet, which we will discuss shortly. Meet me at ten-thirty in Victoria Gardens at the Buxton Memorial Fountain. I am incognito for obvious reasons. I've grown a rather refined beard, which compliments my dark brown hair.

If you cannot come now, send me word of time and place where you can meet. Send the note to the clarendon hotel care of M. Louis Bisset Of Villiers-Le-Mahieu. Hurry now. I am eager to see you, my darling, darling, Phoebe.

Lawrence

Stunned, Phoebe stared down at the letter. Lawrence had returned to London. But why? She'd not heard anything about his father's passing. It didn't matter why he was here, and she was eager to see her friend. She'd missed him dearly. The mantel clock chimed the quarter-hour. It was almost ten. She would need to hurry.

Springing to her feet, Phoebe ran to the chifforobe and pulled out the first-day dress she touched. It was almost a quarter after the hour as she hurried down the steps and out the front door. She quickly hailed a nearby hack and provided the driver with her destination. The hack seemed to proceed at a snail's pace, and Phoebe breathed a sigh of relief when the vehicle finally reached Victoria Gardens.

Phoebe quickly paid the driver, then hurried along the garden pathways toward the fountain. Seeing the spired stone structure that covered the Buxton fountain, she hurried as fast as she could without someone taking notice of her. The last thing she wanted was to risk Lawrence's safety. As she reached the fountain, her heart sank when she saw no one near the structure. Phoebe slowly came to a halt as disappointment sped through her. He wasn't here. Had something terrible happened to him?

"*Bonjour*, my lady." The quiet greeting made her draw in a quick breath as she turned around to see a stranger standing in front of her. Disappointment made her sigh at the fact the man wasn't her friend.

"*Bonjour, monsieur*," she murmured with a polite nod. About to turn away, Phoebe stopped as the man chuckled.

"It appears my disguise is far more effective than I'd hoped."

"*Lawrence*," Phoebe exclaimed as she darted forward to throw her arms around him. As she clung to her friend, tears formed in her eyes. Lawrence gently pushed her back from him to stare down at her.

"I've missed you, my pet," he said in a reserved voice before he pulled her arm through his, and they walked toward a park bench that faced the Thames.

"Why are you here? You've taken a great risk returning to England—London especially. What if you're recognized?"

"When my dearest friend doesn't recognize me, then I

think it's unlikely I have any real fear of discovery if I limit my visits to places where no one knows me well." A small, wry smile tipped one corner of his mouth as he eyed her somberly.

"It is a brilliant disguise, but why did you come back?" Her friend winced as a look of sorrow darkened his features.

"My father died last week." The grief in his voice tore at Phoebe's heart as she caught his hand in hers.

"Oh, Lawrence, I'm so sorry." At her soft exclamation of sympathy, Lawrence shook his head.

"I was with him at the end and was at least able to say goodbye. He was an exceptional man, and I'll miss him very much."

"I know you will. I only wish things had been different for you. It had to have been difficult with Coombs determined to ruin you and Anthony."

"Actually, Coombs did us a favor. He forced us to make a choice between remaining in England or being together without fear in France."

"But the man was wrong to do what he did. I can't imagine how hard the whole affair was for you." She squeezed his hand in sympathy, but Lawrence shook his head.

"The only truly difficult thing has been my inability to see Father more often. Although I admit that telling him the truth before Coombs did was one of the hardest things I've ever done. But ironically, he already suspected the truth," Lawrence said with a sad smile. "When I told him about Anthony and me, he said he'd always known but that I was his son, and it didn't change how much he loved me."

"I'm so glad, but these past five years…" Phoebe's voice trailed off as her friend winced in pain. With a shake of his head, he patted her hand.

"I have actually managed to visit him two or three times a year since I left for the continent, but this is the first time I've been to London since I left England. I needed to speak with the family's solicitors to make financial arrangements for the estate until my cousin is old enough to take on the responsibility."

"I wish I'd known when you were in England. I would have found a way to come to Ashtead for a visit."

"Perhaps if you hadn't stopped writing to me, you would have known." The disappointment and chastisement in her friend's voice made her bow her head to look at her hands that were clutching her purse tightly.

"I…things were so bad when Alfred…I knew you wouldn't have hesitated to come help."

"You're right. I wouldn't have. I would have come and taken you to the continent to live with Anthony and me."

"I wasn't about to risk your safety." Phoebe shook her head fiercely. "There was far too much attention centered on me after Alfred died. Someone would have notified the police."

"Oh, my pet, do you really think me that dull-witted?" Lawrence sighed. "I suppose I was, but I've changed a great deal, Phoebe. Anthony and I are quite happy living quietly in the country. We have friends who visit regularly, and the rest of the time we spend enjoying life and each other."

"I'm so glad, Lawrence," Phoebe said softly as she grasped his hand and squeezed it. "You deserve happiness."

"And you? The last communication I had from you indicated you were going away. I assumed you meant America. I wrote back, only to have my letter returned with a terse note that your whereabouts were unknown." Lawrence frowned. "But what I've heard since I arrived in London two days ago has troubled me deeply. I cannot tell you how disappointed— and angry—I am that you didn't trust me to help."

"You had enough worries of your own. I couldn't thrust mine on top of yours."

"*Don't be absurd,*" her friend snapped. "From what I've gleaned from the gossip that's been relayed to me, Helstone's heir tossed you out on the street, and you resorted to working in a seamstress's shop."

"I needed to live, Lawrence."

"*No*, what you needed to do was write to your dearest friend and ask for help." Blue eyes flashing with disappointed, he eyed her sternly. "Especially when I consider the risk you were so willing to take to save me."

"I didn't do anything," she replied as images of Gideon caressing her flashed through her head. "You never came."

"No, because I came to my senses. I realized Helstone would have beaten you when the gossip made its rounds. *That* I refused to have on *my* conscience. Do you have any idea how hurt I was that you didn't ask for my help?"

Despite the anger in his voice, the disappointment and pain were equally prominent. Phoebe released a sigh and turned her head to stare out at the Thames. It was a bright sunny morning, and the sunlight bounced off the water as if throwing diamonds onto the water's surface.

"I'm sorry. I thought it best."

"*No*, you were too proud to ask for my help."

The sharp, piercing words made Phoebe flinched. He was right. She had always been too proud to ask for help. Even now, she didn't have the ability to tell Lawrence everything about her current situation.

"And now you're married to Chelmsford. Do you love him?"

"Yes." Her gaze still focused on the river, she nodded her head. "I love him with my entire being."

"And?" The single-word question indicated Lawrence knew there was more to her story than that.

"He doesn't love me. Gideon married me as a matter of honor."

"A matter of honor?" Lawrence's reaction was one of dark outrage. "Did he compromise you in some way?"

"I am just as much to blame for the incident. It was a moment….a passionate moment of indiscretion. He was insistent that we marry. I objected, but he refused to take no for an answer."

"That does not sound like a man who has no feelings for you."

"Gideon says he enjoys my company."

"Will that be enough for you to be happy, my pet?"

At the question, the memory of the last few days and nights she'd spent with Gideon filled her head. The nights of passionate lovemaking since their wedding night had been moments of ecstasy. Afterward, Gideon would refuse to let her leave him, and each night she'd fallen asleep in his arms. Then there was the laughter and teasing during the day. The evenings of companionship and his genuine interest in her thoughts and opinions.

Last night, her heart had soared with happiness when Gideon had said he was happy as he whirled her around the dance floor. It had given her hope that he might be developing deeper feelings for her. Even now, she realized how much she wanted to believe there was another explanation for Gideon's behavior last night. How could he say he was happy with her, yet moments later, enter a dark garden with another woman? Whatever his reason, she knew the only way would be to ask him for the truth.

"I don't know, but I know I would be miserable if I were not able to hear his voice or see him smile at me, even if it's only with affection and not love when he does so."

"I think I understand," Lawrence said with a nod. "I would feel the same way if Anthony didn't love me."

"When do you return to France?"

"I sail for Calais in two days. Will you at least come for a visit in the future?" he asked quietly. "I've missed you."

"Yes, I'll find a way to come visit as I've missed you too."

They sat in silence for a few moments, and when Phoebe heard the clock tower's bell echo in the distance, she rose to her feet.

"I must go. It will be close to lunchtime when I return. The fewer questions I'm asked, the better. I have no wish to lie." There were enough lies laying hidden between her and Gideon.

"Very well, but I'll have your promise that you will write me. Send it care of Freemont and Turner. I also expect you to come for a visit soon."

"That is a promise I can keep," she said with a smile as she kissed his cheek before she looked at her friend with sadness. Lawrence hugged her tightly before releasing her. He took a step back and returned her smile.

"Forgive me for not walking you to a hack, my pet. If someone were to see us, it would put both of us at risk."

"I would not have let you if you had tried to." With another hug, her vision grew blurry as tears threatened to fall.

"Now, now, no tears. We will see each other soon." At his gentle remonstration, she nodded.

Phoebe kissed her friend goodbye once more, then walked away. As always, she felt better after having shared her problems with her friend. It was the one thing Phoebe missed the most about Lawrence. He had been her confidant when she had nowhere else to turn. The thought made her wince as she feared she would need his counsel in the very near future.

Chapter 22

Gideon entered Chelmsford House with a spring in his step and a smile curving his mouth. Laying his hat and cane on the entryway table, he walked quickly toward the stairs, his gift for Phoebe in his coat pocket. Before leaving to visit his club this morning, Gideon had gone through the connecting doors of their rooms to check on her. She'd still been asleep, and he'd studied her as she slept, memorizing the softness of her profile and the full, lush curves of her beneath the sheets.

Eager to give her the present he'd bought for her and to gauge her reaction to his note, Gideon took the steps two at a time and strode down the hall to her room. He rapped on the door with his knuckles and waited a moment. When there was no response, he knocked again. Concerned when his second knock received no answer, Gideon slowly opened the door of her room.

As he stepped across the threshold, he frowned in puzzlement. Phoebe's chifforobe doors were flung wide open, and her peignoir hung haphazardly off of the bed. His wife was not overly meticulous, but he'd never seen her bed chamber in such a state of disorder. It was as if she'd ransacked the room looking for something. Gideon's gaze fell on the breakfast tray with its untouched meal. Slowly crossing the floor to the table, he saw his note to her was unopened.

A sense of foreboding swept over him as his gaze continued to survey the chaotic state of Phoebe's room. Everything about the scene in front of him said something was wrong. He knew it as surely as he knew how deeply he loved his wife. It was as if she'd received some terrible news and dressed at a frenetic, frantic pace to leave as quickly as she could.

For Phoebe to leave her room in shambles meant the news she'd received had been so momentous that it had thrown her into a state of mental distress. Gideon shoved his hand through his hair, and a sense of impending doom coiled its way around his chest. The invisible vise continued to tighten as his gaze continued to scan the room. There had to be some clue as to what had incited Phoebe's frenzied state.

Gideon quickly moved to her dressing table to see if she'd dropped something that would give him a clue as to what had happened. Her brush lay haphazardly near the edge of her dressing table while the box that held hatpins was opened, and two pins were thrown carelessly on the table. But there was nothing that might have been the catalyst for the havoc in her room.

Crossing the floor to the chifforobe, he briefly glanced at the row of drawers inside the furniture. One drawer was still open and hung at an odd slant as if Phoebe had tried to push it close, then gave up the struggle to adjust it. A dainty stocking dangled carelessly over the side of the drawer, but he ignored it. Instead, Gideon fixed his gaze on the dresses in the large compartment next to the tower of drawers. As if he would find answers to his questions, Gideon jerked two gowns apart. He saw nothing out of the ordinary, and with a sense of hopeless frustration, he shoved them aside and moved on to the next two. As he forcibly pushed one dress after another to the opposite side of the wardrobe, they created small blasts of air, and out of the corner of his eye, he saw something flutter down to the floor.

Gideon's gaze dropped to see a piece of paper that had danced its way under the chifforobe until only a small piece of it was showing. Tension surged through him as his fingers carefully pulled the paper out from under the furniture. The moment he read the first line of the note, he froze.

At first glance, it was impossible for him to comprehend the words written on paper, and he was forced to read the note again. Each time he read one of the endearments the sender had used, it was as if they were nails being hammered into his body. She had a lover. *No. He refused to believe that.*

Whoever Lawrence was, the man was important to her, but Gideon couldn't believe the writer of the note could be Phoebe's lover. She could never have responded to him the way she had in every passionate moment they'd shared since they'd exchanged their vows. Every time he'd claimed her as his, Phoebe had cried out his name with passion, desire, and need. It defied logic that she had a lover with the way she'd responded to Gideon's every caress.

Even before they were wed, she'd given herself to him with an abandon that made it difficult to believe she had a lover. In the back of his mind, a voice called him a fool to think otherwise. Gideon quickly crushed the voice into silence. Seconds later, the voice reared its ugly head to jeer at him for thinking he could rationalize the note. A damning note the voice used as evidence with every disavowal Gideon considered as he tried to rationalize and explain away the letter's meaning.

Worse, it had been this note she'd chosen to open first—not his. The knowledge cut so deep it was as if someone had gutted him with one stroke of a butcher's knife. His gaze returned to the endearments written on the paper he was holding. Words boldly declaring love and affection for his wife. Jealousy and rage erupted inside him as images he didn't want to consider forced their way into his head.

The intensity of the emotion was so great that if the writer of the note had been standing in the same room, Gideon would not hesitate to strangle the man. Every inch of him was tight and rigid as his hand crumpled the note in his fist. From deep inside him, a dark roar of anger rose in his chest and rolled out of his throat in a visceral response to the pain slicing into every inch of him.

The agony slamming into him was almost crippling as his gaze searched for something to vent his anger on. The closest physical object in reach to inflict his wrath was the chifforobe. Fury pounded its way through his muscles as he slammed one of the doors of the wardrobe closed.

It crashed violently into the frame of the furniture before it swung outward with equal force. The force of the door crashing into the chifforobe made the entire piece of furniture shudder. As the door swung outward again, it brushed against the open drawer with its feminine undergarments. Already three-quarters of the way open and at an odd angle, the drawer teetered for a moment from the force of the door hitting it before crashing downward.

The wardrobe door had swung inward again and knocked the drawer off its downward trajectory. In a loud crash, it landed upside down at an angle that propped it up against the bottom portion of the wardrobe and spilled its contents onto the floor. Gideon glared at the feminine garments peeking out from under the drawer before he whirled away and strode toward the door.

He was almost halfway out the door when something odd about the drawer brought him to an abrupt halt. Gideon turned around and studied the drawer for a moment, trying to determine what had made him hesitate to leave Phoebe's bedroom. Slowly moving forward, he tilted his head slightly as his brain registered that there was a bundle of papers lying beneath the garments that had been in the drawer. The papers were almost completely hidden by the frothy underwear, but it was the hard outline of their solid form that had caught his attention.

More letters? Without thinking twice, he bent to pull the papers out from under the clothing. The bundle was too large to be letters, and Gideon frowned as he turned over the top sheet of blank paper. The page beneath it was filled with line after line of blue ink. He began to read, and the anger he'd experienced only moments before evolved into a cold rage.

All this time, she'd been making him out to be a wastrel in the Currer Chronicles. *Christ Jesus*, even the bumblebees on the cake last night. The performance of regret and remorse had been remarkable. She'd actually convinced him that her regret for adding the bumblebees to the cake was genuine. Not even Edith had ever manipulated him as skillfully as Phoebe had.

"Damn her," he snarled. "Damn her to hell."

Whirling around on his heel, Gideon strode out of Phoebe's room. As he made his way downstairs to the library, the pain of her betrayal and lies intensified with each step he took. He'd been a fool, and worst of all, despite his rage, a part of him wanted to believe there was an explanation for the evidence in his hands.

Gideon tossed down a gulp of his third glass of cognac as if it were a beer he'd bought in a disreputable pub. Where was she? He had no idea what time Phoebe had left, but it was almost noon. Was she in her lover's arms at this very moment? Was Phoebe giving herself to the bastard as passionately as she'd given herself to him? A light rap on the open door of the library made him jerk in surprise, and he spun around to see his mother standing in the doorway. A frown of disapproval creased her brow as she arched her eyebrows at him.

"Is it not a bit early for that?

Lady Wrotham nodded toward the snifter in hand. Gideon tossed the remaining liquid down his throat in a defiant move, then walked to the liquor cart to pour more cognac into his snifter.

"Was there something you wanted, Mama?"

"I was wondering if you'd seen Phoebe this morning? I wanted to see how she was feeling." The marchioness's words made Gideon snort loudly with disgust.

"My wife is out at the moment."

"Whatever is the matter with you, Gideon?" His mother eyed him with annoyed puzzlement.

"Pendleton announced lunch was ready a few moments ago. I suggest you go ahead without Phoebe or me."

"Whatever is wrong—"

The sound of the front door closing interrupted his mother's words, and Gideon jerked violently in reaction to the sound. His mother eyed him strangely for a brief moment before she turned to greet Phoebe. Not about to let his mother delay his conversation with his wife, Gideon moved to stand in the doorway.

"Are you feeling better, dearest?"

"I'm feeling quite well," Phoebe replied quietly. Something flashed in her brown eyes, and with his gaze still locked with Phoebe's, he addressed his mother.

"Mama, I have a matter of some urgency that I need to discuss with Phoebe. I suggest you begin lunch without us."

"But, Gideon—"

"*Now*, Mama," he snarled.

Out of the corner of his eye, Gideon saw his mother recoil in surprise, but he ignored her reaction. Instead, he took a step out of the library and, with a sweeping gesture of his arm, silently invited Phoebe into the room. When she hesitated, he narrowed his gaze at her, and she flinched before complying with his inaudible command.

As she walked past him, the scent of roses filled his nostrils. Instantly, his body reacted to hers, and his inability not to let her affect him caused him to release a low growl of anger. Out of the corner of his eye, Gideon saw the marchioness staring at him in amazement and concern. Without a word, he stepped into the library and slammed the door closed behind him. Phoebe immediately jumped and whirled around to stare at him warily.

"Where have you been?" Gideon managed to keep his voice even as he eyed her with suspicion.

"I was with a friend."

Confusion furrowed her brow, and there wasn't a trace of guilt or trepidation in her voice. Gideon clenched his teeth in anger as a voice in his head tried to suggest he was wrong in thinking she'd betrayed him. The voice suggested everything about his suspicions might be wrong. Was that possible? Could there be a reasonable explanation for her behavior? Gideon almost snorted at the thought as he brushed it aside.

"And was this friend a man?" His question made her jump as she watched him with uncertainty and apprehension. She blinked and remained silent. "*Answer me*, Phoebe, and I want the truth."

"Yes."

Gideon stared at her for a long moment. At least she'd not lied, but she was clearly unwilling to explain any further unless pushed. He turned around and walked to his desk, where the note he'd found was lying on top of the chapter she'd written. The moment he picked up the note he'd found in her room, indecision grabbed hold of him.

What if he was wrong? Gideon stared blindly down at his desk and cleared his throat. An image of his unopened note lying on her breakfast tray constricted his lungs as a wave of desolation crashed down on top of him. His fingers rubbed over the fine linen of the note as he hesitated to turn around. The last thing he wanted was for her to see how deeply she'd injured him. As if determined to inflict more pain and humiliation on himself, Gideon asked the question he already knew the answer to.

"Did you read the note I left for you this morning?"

"No, there was no time, and…"

"I see," he murmured.

Gideon understood why she'd not bothered to find the time. The note in his hand had been of far greater importance to her than the one her husband had written. His gaze fell on the stack of papers sitting on his desk. The damning chapter only reinforced the pain that had been lashing at him for more than an hour now.

Gritting his teeth, Gideon struggled with the fact that she'd displayed no guilt in answering his questions. Nor had she lied when he'd asked for a truth he already knew. Yet, despite his best effort not to be swayed by her, he couldn't deny he was finding it difficult to believe Phoebe had gone to see a lover. A small bit of doubt rose in him.

"*Why* didn't you read my note?"

The question was met with silence, and he slowly turned around. The stark look of anguish on her face immediately twisted Gideon's gut into knots. Was she experiencing regret that she'd not opened his? Was it possible he was wrong—that this was all a misunderstanding? As if suddenly realizing he was studying her, Phoebe's expression became unreadable. Gideon extended his hand and offered the note to her with a sharp movement of his wrist.

"Was it because you found this one more important?"

Phoebe's hand trembled as she hesitantly accepted the wrinkled missive from him. She glanced down at the note before her head jerked upward. A flash of anger sparked the gold flecks in her brown eyes.

"Where did you find this?" she asked quietly.

"When I came home from several errands this morning, I went to your room to see how you were feeling. When you didn't answer your door, I became worried."

"And you thought it appropriate to search my room?"

The icy note in Phoebe's question made him stiffen. With a defensive gesture of his hand, Gideon narrowed his gaze at her.

"Your room was in complete disarray. It was obvious you had been in a great hurry to leave the house, and as I said, I was concerned." At his reply, the color drained from her face until it resembled a cold, porcelain figurine devoid of any emotion.

"You were *concerned?*"

The condescending note of disbelief in her voice angered him. Why would she question his for her safety? Even if she didn't love him, she should at least understand that as her husband, he was honor-bound to protect her. A second later, he realized they were no longer discussing the note in question. How easily and quickly she'd diverted the conversation from the note to his behavior in searching her room. The realization of how adeptly she'd changed the subject made Gideon grit his teeth.

"*The note*, Phoebe. Who is he?"

"Lawrence is one of my dearest friends. *No*, my only friend. He took me under his wing when I first came to London."

It was a response that held not one iota of guilt or trepidation. In fact, Phoebe's reply had been defiant and angry. It was precisely the reaction one might expect when an innocent party was accused of impropriety. Phoebe eyed him with cold outrage. The voice in the back of Gideon's head told him she was innocent of everything he'd imagined. Jealousy made him brush the voice aside.

"A friend who didn't bother to come to your aid when you needed someone the most," he sneered. Inside his head, a harsh voice reminded him of his own inaction in her hour of need.

"Lawrence was in France when Alfred's heir threw me out of my home."

"Yet for a man who addresses you with such familiarity, I would think he would come running at your first plea for help." Gideon tried to maintain his anger by confrontational manner of her indignation.

"You're correct, he would have, but I didn't tell him. If Lawrence had known of my plight, he would have risked his own safety to come back to London."

"His safety?" Gideon frowned in puzzlement.

"Suffice it to say that returning to London would have put his person in danger. Lawrence is the brother I never had, and I would do anything to protect him, just as he would me. However, I refuse to betray any of his confidences, and that is all I have to say in the matter."

Phoebe tilted her chin upward in defiance. Her soft lips were thin with anger, and her expression dared him to call her a liar or imply any other accusation where her friend was concerned. Her demeanor was enough to convince she was being truthful.

"Very well, I shall take you at your word with regard to the note."

The small bit of relief that surged through Gideon as he bobbed his head in a sharp nod was quickly crushed as he remembered the other discovery he'd made. Phoebe eyed him with contempt.

"Thank you for that *magnanimous* gesture in dismissing my guilt."

Sarcasm punctured Phoebe's biting tone, and Gideon scowled. He believed her. What more did she want from him? The real treason was yet to be presented. Gideon met her gaze, which was nothing more than an icy glare. The defiant, rebellious look aroused Gideon's anger again. He wasn't the one who'd done anything wrong. Muscles knotted with outrage at her righteous air, he turned back to his desk to pick up the offensive, loose-leaf papers.

"Since we've established your innocence about the note,

what explanation do you have for this?"

Gideon turned and offered her the chapter. Although he'd tried to convince himself not to read past the first couple of paragraphs, he'd read every single page. The vitriol her pen had spewed out had left him speechless with rage. Worse, it had ripped his heart out of his chest as he was forced to realize how much she despised him. Phoebe stared at the papers in his hand and became white as a sheet. She swayed on her feet, but he didn't move to steady her.

"Oh, dear God."

The words were barely a whisper as she stared at the pages in his hand before accepting them as if they were something unclean. That she might actually be appalled by the chapter would have been laughable if his body hadn't felt as if he'd taken a severe beating in the boxing ring.

"I take it this is your next chapter in the serial." The icy words made her jerk her gaze up to meet his.

"No," she exclaimed passionately. "I rewrote this chapter before I fell…after I realized you were nothing like the character I created for the Chronicles."

"And when did you come to this eye-opening realization? Before or after you accepted my offer of marriage?" Gideon didn't even try to keep the bitterness out of his voice.

"It was…I didn't…"

"I see. So this was *after* you accepted my offer. Then congratulations are in order, my lady. You achieved what you were after all along."

"I don't understand," she said with a look of bewilderment that he immediately discounted despite the voice inside his head beginning to challenge him and spread more doubt in him.

"In marrying me, you achieved your goal of another title and one with far greater influence than a mere viscount."

"Another…that's *not* true," she denied angrily as she shook her head and eyed him with scorn. "You seem to forget

I *refused* your offer of marriage."

"But you were easily convinced to accept my hand."

"That's unfair of you, Gideon." She glared at him as if he'd insulted her. "I tried to convince you to wait until we knew if I was…but you refused to listen to me. You didn't even try to consider my suggestion. *You* were the one who insisted we not wait."

"Yet all the while, you were spewing your venomous words onto the page to humiliate me."

"No, it wasn't—"

"*No more lies, Phoebe.* Either you did or didn't write that chapter with the intent to humiliate me, which is it?" he snarled as he pointed to the papers she held. The helpless look on her face only increased his anger.

"Answer me."

At his thundering command, she recoiled from him. Her reaction was a blow to every inch of his body. Did Phoebe really think so little of him that she might believe he was capable of harming her? The answer to his question was in the pages she held in her hand. The truth sliced deep into his soul until he wanted to roar at the pain it caused him.

Instead, Gideon allowed his anger to consume his agony as he eyed her with a scathing look of fury. Silence fell between them for a long moment until an icy bitterness made her pale features even colder. It was a look he'd never seen before, and it made his muscles tighten as he steeled himself for words that would no doubt emphasize the poisonous ones she'd written.

Dear God, he was furious.
Unforgiving.
Phoebe's fingers tightened on the papers in her hands.

Ink-filled pages of contempt, insults, and lies that she'd written in a fit of outrage and pain. Frantically, she tried to think of something she could say that would calm Gideon's anger. Helplessly she stared at him, and the depth of his rage made her stomach roil with a strong wave of nausea.

God, how she wished she'd never written the chapter in her hand. Then he wouldn't have found—something sent her brain careening in a completely different direction. How *had* he found the chapter? The note from Lawrence she understood. It must have fallen to the floor when she was dressing so fast.

But the chapter had been buried in one of her drawers beneath several layers of undergarments. A reminder of how much she'd misjudged him and what she could lose if he ever discovered she was P. Currer. A fear that had come to fruition. Now that he'd found it, she knew there was only one way he could have discovered the pages.

He'd spied on her.

It demonstrated his complete lack of trust in her. A trust he obviously thought unnecessary to reciprocate, given his behavior last night. Bitterness spiraled through her at the hypocrisy of it all.

"How did you find this, Gideon?" she asked coldly. A small nick in the armor of his anger appeared as he stared at her in surprise before narrowing his gaze at her.

"The drawer where you'd hidden it fell out of the wardrobe. It spilled out the contents onto the floor."

"Do you *really* expect me to believe the drawer fell out of its *own* accord?"

She could hear the ice layering her question. An emotion she didn't recognize flickered in his eyes, but he didn't flinch as he returned her glare. There wasn't even the tiniest bit of remorse or regret on his face.

"How I found it has nothing to do with this conversation."

"It has a great deal to do with it," she said fiercely. Anger made her muscles grow taut, and the tension added to the pain gripping her body. "You violated my trust in you."

"Trust in—" The laugh that blew past his lips was as if someone had taken an iron off the hearth and pressed it into her chest. It was a harsh, mocking sound filled with, God help her, loathing. "Phoebe, you don't know the meaning of the word."

"Considering how you humiliated me last night, I'd say the concept of the word is lost on you as well." The sharp condemnation and contempt in her words made him jerk slightly.

"What the hell are you talking about," he snarled.

His anger rumbled in his chest like thunder in the distance, but she saw the sudden uneasiness in him. If Phoebe didn't know better, she would have sworn he was experiencing pain and despair. She immediately berated herself for thinking such a thing. Instead, she sniffed with disdain.

"Don't you *dare* add insult to injury by pretending you *don't* know what I'm referring to."

"Does this have to do with the Duchess of Stockdale?" he bit out sharply. Phoebe glared at him as he asked the question. In the back of her mind, she noted the woman's name.

"Oh, so *now* you remember your little tête-à-tête with the woman."

"It was *not* a tête-à-tête, and if you had asked me about it, I would have explained everything."

The defensive note in his voice made her grow cold. *If she had asked him about his behavior?* Clearly, he'd thought it unnecessary to mention his intimate meeting with the duchess unless Phoebe had questioned him about it. The callous manner in which he dismissed his indiscretion made her take a step back from him.

The pain of his betrayal and cavalier treatment of her sent

an icy blast of air across Phoebe's skin. It seeped through her pores to work its way down into her bones. Bile rose in her throat until the bitter taste of it hit her tongue. Phoebe swallowed hard as she found her voice.

"And no doubt your explanation would have been a lie spoken as eloquently as all your other lies. You managed to fool me completely, *Lord Chelmbee.*" In a vicious movement, she flung the pages at him. The paper barely touched him as the sheets of ink-stained parchment fell and scattered on the floor. "You can lay no claim to being the injured party, my lord, when you simply prove the words I wrote."

"I've warned you before to take care when you choose to address me in that manner, Phoebe," he growled menacingly.

"As if there was something more you could to humiliate me, *Lord Chelmbee.* I should never have agreed to marry you. I should have followed my instincts where you are concerned."

The moment Phoebe addressed Gideon by the name she'd given him in the Chronicles, she was certain she saw a look of anguish slash across his face. It was gone instantly as a blazing fury glittered in his eyes, Phoebe didn't experience any fear as he took a step forward to tower over her. Determined not to retreat from the blatant act of intimidation, she didn't hide her scorn as she didn't retreat.

"You seem to take pleasure in provoking me, Phoebe."

"Then you need not worry about me doing so in the future," Phoebe snapped as she made a decision she knew would send her plummeting into a dark place she'd never been before. "Because I intend to end this farce of a marriage."

The speed with which Gideon grabbed her and tugged her into his chest caught her off-guard. Instantly, her body responded to his. Bergamot and leather scents mixed together to assault her senses, and she fought the urge to burrow herself into the heat of him. Instead, she struggled to free herself, but he easily restrained her. One arm wrapped around her waist, he held her fast against him while his free hand cupped her chin and forced her to look at him.

"Let me go, Gideon." Her demand echoed with staccato precision as she pushed against his chest.

"No, Phoebe. I have no intention of making it that easy for you."

"Making *what* easy for me?" she exclaimed as she braced her palms against his chest, trying to break free of his hold. As she stared up at him in anger, unwilling to cower from him, a alarm streaked through her as a cold smile tipped his lips upward.

"I have no intention of letting you go." For a brief moment she thought his voice echoed with pained regret. She quickly dismissed the possibility as she studied his hard, inflexible features.

"You cannot keep me here, Gideon. You signed a contract," she gasped as she stared up at him in horror.

An icy finger scraped down her back as she shook her head. *Dear God,* no punishment handed down from on high could ever equal the torment of being condemned to remain at Chelmsford House. The prospect of watching Gideon parade one mistress after another in front of her made her stomach roil. The humiliation at the hands of the Marlborough Set would be little more than a bee sting compared to how her heart would break with each new liaison he engaged in.

"A contract I can easily have discarded in court. Instead, I prefer you experience the full depths of Lord Chelmbee's depravity."

"Why in God's name would you want to do such a thing?" she whispered. At her question, Gideon's mouth twisted in another mirthless smile.

"Surely you should expect nothing less based on your words of condemnation and scorn. It's just the sort of behavior you expect from Lord Chelmbee. Since you despise me with such vehemence, I—"

"That's *not true*," she exclaimed in dismay as her heart stopped beating with a vicious twist at his declaration. Phoebe struggled to keep breathing and fight off the wave of panic threatening to take control of her body. "I *don't* despise you, Gideon. I could never despise you. I—"

"The words you wrote in that damn chapter, and all the ones preceding it, say otherwise, Madam Currer." Phoebe flinched at his icy words, then shook her head fiercely.

"I *do not* despise you, Gideon. I never have. I will not deny—"

"Haven't you lied enough, Phoebe? I confess I am growing weary of your protests. I'm not a fool, my sweet."

"I am *not* lying to you, Gideon. *please.* You must believe me. I could never despise you." A part of her demanded that she tell him how much she loved him, while the other half told her how he would use her confession against her.

"Very well, then you will have an opportunity to prove it as I intend to extract full payment for the title I gave you the day we married."

"Full payment?" she whispered.

"You're my wife, Phoebe. As such, you'll fulfill *every* aspect of your wifely duties. Especially when it comes to sharing my bed. It will be quite a long time before I'm willing to leave your bed in search of another flower."

"You told me you would never make me do something I didn't want to do."

Phoebe tried to breathe as she struggled to realize how fast her life was spinning out of control. Gideon hesitated for a short breath, and she thought she saw pain slide across his features before they hardened with a contempt that was almost a tangible blow. Narrowing his gaze at her, he smiled coldly.

"Despite your low opinion of me, my sweet, I always honor my word. But do not think for one moment that I cannot bend you to my will," he murmured.

The moment Gideon bent his head to brush his mouth across her lips, Phoebe drew in a deep breath of fear. Dear God, he meant to deliver her into heaven before tossing her back into the fires of hell. Every time he touched her, she was little more than clay in a potter's hands. She had to find a way to escape. If she didn't, she would be lost, and when that happened, he would know the true measure of her feelings, and he would use that against her as well.

"Please don't do this, Gideon. It's unworthy of you." Her quiet plea went ignored as his voice became a wickedly sinful caress on her senses.

"Do you know *how* I'm certain you'll surrender to me so easily, Phoebe? I know exactly what spot drives you wild with desire, my sweet. I know just how easy it is to make you whimper with delight. The way you writhe with pleasure every time my mouth teases that sensitive bud between your legs."

Gideon's hedonistic description made her shudder as her legs wobbled beneath her. His lips slowly blazed a trail of fire across her cheek and down to her throat. Unable to help herself, desire and need rushed through her veins. A shudder rippled through her as his hand slid up along her side to her breast. The warmth of his palm sent heat sweeping through her, and a second later, his fingers trailed a white-hot caress across the tops of her breast. It was a touch that illustrated he was in complete control of her pleasure and response to him.

"Gideon, please."

Her words were a mere breath of sound, and she didn't know whether her plea was for him to stop or to continue. Fingers digging into his shoulders, she clung to him while her body reacted to the fiery touch of his mouth against her skin. Desire became a stream of molten lava in her veins as she instinctively arched backward to let his mouth nibble its way across her skin.

The moment his tongue slipped between the valley of her

breasts, she uttered a soft cry of pleasure. The hot, wet heat of his tongue made another part of her ache for a different caress that was even more intimate. Trembling against him, her senses pulled her down into a wicked pool of fiery sensations that held her captive as his mouth worked its way up her throat.

Unrestrained need tugged at her as a voice of reason in her head fought to regain control of her body. The voice died as Gideon's mouth captured hers in a hard kiss. With a soft murmur, she parted her lips beneath his, and their tongues tangled with each other much in the same way she wanted her body entwined around his.

Desire pulsated through her as his mouth hardened against hers. A raw, primal sound rumbled in his chest, and she slid her hands around the back of his neck to spike her fingers through his silky hair. Eager for more of his touch, her body pressed even harder into his, and her hips swiveled against him and where the beginnings of his erection pressed into her thigh.

With each stroke of his tongue against hers, the rising tide of passion threatened to pull her completely under until she would be willing to do whatever he asked of her. His kiss teased, tempted, and tantalized her as she experienced a familiar pulse working its way down to the apex of her thighs.

A brief second later, frustration assailed her as he denied her the pinnacle he'd been drawing her toward. Phoebe released a soft cry of protest at being deprived of even a small piece of satisfaction. Her breathing frantic, Phoebe's mouth sought his, but he lifted his head and pulled away from her just enough to keep her from finding his mouth again. Her heart pounding wildly in her breast, a whimper of disappointment escaped her as her eyes fluttered open to stare up at the man she'd married. A man who'd become a stranger in the span of just a few hours.

"Tell me you don't want me right now, Phoebe. Tell me

you don't want me teasing those delicious nipples of yours," he whispered as satisfaction curved his lips upward. "They're hard right now, aren't they? They're aching for me to nibble and suck on them. Are you wet with desire? Are you craving my tongue on you, or are you aching for me to drive my cock into you until you shatter in my arms?"

"*Oh God*, Gideon, please…I…"

She knew the breathy sound of her voice revealed how aroused she was. The moment her body trembled against his, he smiled with triumph and bent his head to brush his mouth across her ear.

"Please what, Phoebe?" he whispered. "Are you asking me to take you upstairs where I can show you just how easily I can make you respond to me?"

She was on the verge of begging him to do just that when she saw the gleam of satisfaction in his gaze. Oh dear God, had Gideon felt nothing at all when he was caressing her only seconds ago? His breathing was steady, and he appeared as he was actually bored. The only thing that made convinced he was not as completely unaffected was the way his heart was pounding wildly against her fingertips.

Then there was the tic in his cheek that suggested his jaw was tightly clenched. Trembling like a leaf dancing in the wind against him, Phoebe's heart crashed into her chest at the cold, calculated triumph in the small smile that touched his lips.

"Now, do you understand, Phoebe? Do you see how easy it's going to be for me to have you in my bed anytime I want?"

Gideon released her and stepped back to narrow his gaze at her, and Phoebe's throat threatened to close shut. In the back of her head, she knew he was right. He would always be able to bend her to his will. It had taken only seconds for her to be on the verge of surrendering to him completely just now. Slightly dazed, she looked up at him and struggled to speak. Unable to bear his triumphant demeanor, Phoebe turned her head away from him.

The fact that he appeared completely unmoved by her made her sway on her feet. Gideon didn't bother to help steady her. Instead, he simply folded his arms over his chest as his eyebrows arched arrogantly. There was a cold insolence in his reaction, and tears threatened to spill down her cheeks. Swallowing the hard knot in her throat, Phoebe turned and stumbled toward the door. It was a short distance, but it seemed far, far away.

She'd known he would be enraged if he were ever to discover she was P. Currer, but somehow she hadn't expected him to be this angry. No, she'd known he would be furious, but she'd never dreamed he would be so angry that he would want to keep her here as a form of punishment. It made no sense. Gideon was not a vindictive man. What could be driving him to refuse to honor their contract?

The one thing she did understand was that it was unlikely he would ever forgive her. He would never trust her again. The knowledge was like shards of glass slicing into her. The moment Phoebe's hand touched the doorknob, Gideon cleared his throat. Phoebe paused, but she didn't look at him.

"That was just a taste of what to expect tonight, Phoebe. I intend to make you sob with pleasure, and by the time I'm done, you're going to be begging me to do it again."

As his quiet words drifted through the air and faded away, she bit down on her bottom lip until she tasted blood. Phoebe understood his determination—his need to make her pay a price for her offenses. She'd judged him harshly and unfairly. But Gideon needed to know she'd realized her folly long before today. She needed him to understand how deeply she regretted her actions. She needed to try and convince him of that fact. Slowly, she turned to face him.

"If refusing to honor our contract is your way of making me pay for having wronged you in the Chronicles, Gideon, then I'll gladly pay the price," she said softly. "The lies I wrote in that offensive chapter entitle you to that much."

Phoebe hesitated for a moment and saw Gideon frown as something similar to pain twisted his mouth in a grimace. Gideon's arrogant, dismissive posture didn't change, and her heart twisted painfully in her chest as she realized she'd been mistaken.

If he could find it in his heart to believe her, then maybe in time he might forgive her as well. Scornful laughter echoed loudly in her head. The harsh, unyielding planes on Gideon's countenance told her how hopeless that wish was. Phoebe bit down on her lip and bobbed her head toward the pages on the floor, then met his gaze again.

"I wrote that chapter in the heat of anger. I wanted to make you feel as small as you made me feel with your condemnation of me. It was only when I realized how much I…"

Phoebe drew in a sharp breath. God help her. She'd nearly confessed her love for him. She immediately dropped her gaze to stare at the pages on the floor. Why hadn't she simply burned the horrible thing? None of this would be happening now. Phoebe thought she heard a soft sound emanate from Gideon, and she jerked her head upward to look at him. The harsh, stony inflexibility of his expression belied the possibility he might have been experiencing a softening of his judgement of her. Phoebe looked away from him again as she continued.

"I did turn the chapter in to be printed, and I almost failed in my efforts to stop the Times from printing it. They were already setting the type when I reached my editor's office. He said it was too late and there was nothing he could do. That's when I began to beg, Gideon. I *begged* him to stop that chapter from being printed. I have *never* begged anyone so desperately before in my life. But I couldn't bear the thought of…"

Phoebe's gaze met Gideon's, but she saw no softening in his harsh expression. Tears pressed at the back of her throat.

It was becoming clear she wasn't reaching him, and she struggled not to go down on her knees to beg his forgiveness. Phoebe wanted to look away, but didn't. She needed him to see her face—to let him see her sincerity.

"You are nothing like Lord Chelmbee. I know I have taunted you with that name, and I am sorry for it. I wish with all my heart that you hadn't seen that abomination. I should have burned those pages the moment I returned home. I think I kept them as a form of penance. A reminder of how easily my anger could injure someone who didn't deserve to be judged harshly. Perhaps worst of all is that I've destroyed any hope of you ever…"

Phoebe paused as she studied Gideon's expression, hoping she might see a softening on his stony features. Some sign that might say he believed her. After a long moment, she swallowed hard and closed her eyes then looked at him again.

"I don't expect you to forgive me, Gideon. I'm not even asking you to try. I know how difficult forgiveness is. I simply wanted you to know that I realized my mistake in time and that I am glad—grateful I was able to save you any humiliation. I would never have forgiven myself if I'd failed. I truly am sorry."

Gideon jerked with surprise, and his gaze narrowed to study her closely. Phoebe didn't flinch beneath his gaze. When it became obvious she'd failed to reach him, she quickly turned away as her vision began to blur. Phoebe's hand fumbled to grasp the doorknob, and when she found it, she tugged the library door open to dart through it.

Phoebe closed the door behind her, and the sharp thud it made as the door clicked shut made her jump. A tear slid down her cheek. She wiped it away only to have another one wet her skin.

"Phoebe, dearest. Are you all right?" At the sound of her mother-in-law's voice, Phoebe quickly wiped another tear away and kept her head bent.

"I just have something in my eye, Mama. Forgive me. I need to change."

Without waiting for her mother-in-law to speak again, Phoebe hurried toward the stairs and ran upward as fast as she could. All she wanted was to reach the privacy of her room. The tears Phoebe had been holding back began to stream down her cheeks. No one was in the hall to witness Phoebe's sorrow and pain, for which she was grateful. Throwing herself through the door of her bedroom, Phoebe closed it behind her. Blinded by her tears, she stumbled to the bed, where she curled up in a small ball to sob quietly at what she'd lost. Now she would live in a purgatory of her own making.

Chapter 23

With a snarl of fury, Gideon's hand swept across his desk in a wide arc and sent several ledgers and a paperweight flying off the desk and into the wall with a loud crash. What the fuck was wrong with him? He should have let her go. What kind of man would insist she stay?

A desperate one.

Not once since he'd discovered that savagely written chapter had Gideon even considered the possibility she would leave him. In truth, Gideon knew he should not have been surprised by Phoebe's declaration, but he had. Stunned and desperate not to lose her, Gideon had blindly grasped at anything he could think of to keep her with him.

"*Fuck.*"

Gideon's hand struck out again and sent a small stack of books flying off the corner of his desk. He was a fool. What had he hoped to achieve by trapping her for a *second* time in a marriage she didn't want? Had he really thought she might come to care for him if he kept her with him? Gideon snorted with disgust before a dark groan rumbled out of his chest. His biggest mistake had been his failure to realize what it would cost him not to let her go.

That point had been driven home only moments ago. It had taken every ounce of willpower Gideon had possessed not to carry Phoebe upstairs and make love to her when she'd responded to him as she had. She might despise him, but her body responded to him like a violin did to the bow a master wielded. But if he had given in to his desire, he would have condemned himself for certain. Gideon had no doubt that in a blind moment of passion, he would have confessed his soul to her.

Hands braced on the top of his desk with his head bowed, Gideon remembered Phoebe's warmth as she'd pressed her body deeper into his. Her response had been a clear demand of need. It had been impossible not to become intoxicated by the scent of wild roses teasing his nostrils or the hot sweetness of her mouth. She had been a fire he'd wanted to consume and be consumed by.

When he'd finally managed to bring his desire under control and break their kiss, it had been difficult to keep breathing as he'd stared down at her. Eyes closed, desire had made her radiant. Her breathing had been ragged, and her lips swollen from his kiss. It was at that specific moment he'd understood the fresh hell he'd descended into and would experience every time he held her in his arms. God, how he loved her, and God, how much he wanted to make her pay for the way she'd cut his heart out with that damn chapter of hers.

Gideon turned away from the desk to stare at the sheets of paper strewn about the floor. He pinched the bridge of his nose as he remembered Phoebe's torment the moment he'd thrust the ink-covered pages at her. Her anguish had startled him, and Gideon was convinced she'd been deeply distressed knowing he'd seen the chapter. The pain darkening Phoebe's lovely brown eyes had made him want to pull her into his arms and tell her that even despite the vicious words she'd penned, he loved her.

A snort of contempt escaped him at how eager he'd been to console her. Then there was that pretty little speech of hers as to how she'd begged to keep the newspaper from printing the chapter. She'd even said she'd wronged him—declared he wasn't like the caricature in her serial. It was difficult to believe her when he remembered the scathing pages of ridicule he'd read.

And then saying she didn't expect him to forgive her. Why would Phoebe want his forgiveness? For that matter, why should he forgive her? She'd made her feelings quite clear with her words. Why should he forgive her for such a caustic attack on him? The question filled his head with an image of Phoebe's pale, drawn features, and Gideon remembered her saying that forgiveness was difficult. She hadn't mentioned him or Edith by name or what he'd done last night. But he had no doubts as to what she was referring to.

Never in his entire life had Gideon ever made a blunder of such monumental proportions as he had last night. He could have been accused of many things in his youth, but stupidity was not one of them. Yet the manner in which he'd confronted Edith last night had been something even a wet behind the ears schoolboy would have thought twice about doing. It had been the most ill-conceived, dull-witted act he'd ever committed in his life.

He should have sent Edith a note via a footman to have her meet him somewhere without the possibility of being seen. Gideon prayed Phoebe was the only one who witnessed his despicable behavior. Despite his wife's scathing words, he didn't want to see her hurt. He loved her, no matter how much she loathed him.

Another loud noise of self-disgust escaped him. Only a fool would love a woman who held him in such contempt. Gideon bent and angrily collected the papers Phoebe had thrown at him. The pages crackled as he picked up the offensive work in sharp, vicious movements, along with the note she'd received from her friend.

The last page scooped up off the floor, Gideon carried the sheaf of papers to the fireplace and tossed them onto the fire. As the flames danced around the paper, satisfaction swept through him. Finally, he was rid of the damn thing. Hands braced against the mantelshelf, Gideon watched the paper begin to curl up and burst into flames. The note took longer to catch fire, and as the flames licked at the stationary, he recalled Phoebe's reaction when he'd confronted her about the note.

Gideon hadn't known what to expect when he'd demanded the truth from her, but he'd been completely unprepared for her righteous indignation. Nor had Gideon expected to believe anything she had to say about the note or its author, but he did. He had no doubt that Phoebe's and her friend's relationship was purely platonic and nothing more. However, the Currer Chronicles was a different matter altogether.

Blue and yellow flames danced across the pages in the hearth as Gideon watched the vitriol burn. Although Phoebe had mocked him frequently in the Chronicles, being the target of her pen wasn't what Gideon had found irritating. Instead, it was Phoebe's satirical depiction of him that had always set his teeth on edge. Far too often, he'd actually seen himself in her droll, witty words.

Gideon dragged in a deep breath and rubbed his forehead. It was one thing to accept his own faults, but for someone to expose his flaws in such a droll and witty manner had not been a pleasurable experience. And Phoebe's pen had been exceedingly scintillating. He could not deny her skill at lampooning him, or anyone else for that matter.

A growl of anger rumbled out of him as Gideon began to pace the floor. What the hell was wrong with him? Was he actually feeling proud of the fact that his wife was the anonymous author of a popular satire? A satire in which she'd made him a figure of fun on more than one occasion. Worst of all, she'd written a piece designed to publicly eviscerate him. The voice in the back of his head reminded him that she'd not allowed the Times to print it.

Gideon looked over his shoulder at the fireplace where the flames were eating away at the last of the chapter's pages.

His jaw tightened as he turned away from the fire once more. Watching it burn didn't ease the pain Phoebe's words had inflicted. She'd spared him nothing in the chapter that was quickly becoming ash in the fireplace.

Her depiction of Lord Chelmbee choosing his liaisons with a mere flick of his fingers had made Gideon appear as if he was a man of few morals and obsessed solely with pleasures of the flesh. Perhaps worst of all, the words had made it clear how much Phoebe loathed him. But if she despised him, why had she stopped the chapter from being printed?

Phoebe had said she'd written the chapter because she wanted to make him feel as small as she had when he'd condemned her. Gideon uttered a soft oath beneath his breath. It was true he'd baited and taunted Phoebe from the moment he'd returned from Amsterdam. Could he really fault her for not wanting to strike back?

The memory of her apology a few moments ago made him frown in confusion. The regret in her voice had been undeniable, but there had been something more than regret in her voice. Another emotion had been threaded beneath her remorse. He drew in a deep breath of frustration and pinched the bridge of his nose.

"*Damn it, Chelmsford*, you're a Goddamn ass," he snarled.

"Yes, you are. You're an ass who doesn't deserve to have such a wonderful, loving wife." At the sound of his mother's angry voice, Gideon jerked his head up in surprise before he narrowed his gaze at her.

"I am not in the mood for one of your lectures as to my shortcomings, Mama," he growled with irritation.

"I couldn't care less about your mood given the current state of chaos in this house."

"I'm warning you, Mama."

"Do *not* take that tone with me, Gideon Alexander Lethbridge. If you weren't such a simpleton, we wouldn't be having this conversation."

"Then say what you wish and be done with it," he snarled.

"Did you take leave of your senses last night? Your brazen temerity in accompanying that Stockdale woman out of the ballroom was not only the height of stupidity, it was cruel."

The fierce anger and contempt in his mother's voice made him stare at the marchioness thunderstruck. The outrage in her voice was clearly visible on her face, and it made his jaw clench until it was painful. The fact that his mother had seen him lead Edith out of the ballroom meant that others most likely had as well. It emphasized just how disastrously he'd handled the matter. His mother was right to ask if he'd taken leave of his senses because, clearly, he had. When he remained silent, his eyed him with furious disgust.

"What in heaven's name is wrong with you, Gideon? Ever since you returned from Amsterdam, you've been acting like a snarling dog, particularly when you're around Phoebe. Are you deliberately trying to break her heart by renewing your acquaintance with the duchess?"

"*No.* I intercepted a note from Edith yesterday. She appeared to be hellbent on causing trouble," he snarled. "When I saw her heading toward Phoebe and me last night, I pulled the woman aside to issue a warning to stay away from Phoebe, or she'd regret it."

"Are you aware that Phoebe saw you as well?" His mother's icy words made him go rigid, and he nodded sharply. The marchioness glared at him with a contempt that slice through him. "At the moment, it appears no one else saw you. If they had, Lady Gresham and others would have been here first thing this morning to inform me, *and Phoebe*, of your indiscretion."

The marchioness's harsh words made Gideon grow cold. *Christ Jesus*, one of the things he'd promised Phoebe was that their marriage would be nothing like she'd endured with

Helstone. Yet, like a fool, he'd managed to humiliate her, whether he'd been seen by anyone in the Set or not.

Gideon's gut twisted viciously with regret and fear. In his effort to protect Phoebe, he'd caused her more pain than Edith ever could. But it was the thought that she might never forgive him that scared him the most. Still embroiled in his internal condemnation of his behavior, Lady Wrotham's deep sigh broke the silence. Jolted out of his thoughts, he met his mother's gaze and flinched at her obvious disappointment.

"I find it ironic that as a man renowned for your ability to charm the fairer sex, you seem incapable of doing anything except fall on your face where your wife is concerned."

"I'm well aware of my failings, Mama. I do *not* need to be reminded of them," he said tersely as he clasped his hands behind his back and turned away from her to stare down at the ash that was all that remained of the scathing chapter Phoebe had written.

"Do love her, Gideon?" Her blunt question startled him, and he jerked his head up to look over his shoulder at his mother. As if she could read his thoughts, the marchioness nodded with approval. "Thank God for that. I was worried you didn't."

"My feelings for Phoebe are none of your concern, Mama."

"For heaven's sake, Gideon, must you be so stubborn?" Lady Wrotham released a sound of exasperation. "Go to her, tell her how you feel."

"That's not possible. My wife despises me." The words hammered their way into his chest like an opponent who'd managed to gain the upper hand in the ring.

"What in heaven's name are you talking about? Phoebe doesn't detest you."

"Until a few moments ago, I could have shown you evidence proving otherwise," he said bitterly.

Gideon turned away from her to watch the fire burn.

How he wished his mother was right about Phoebe. The word why began to repeat itself in his head in a persistent demand for answers. Gideon already understood the reasons behind Phoebe's decision to write such a scornful essay. His mother was correct. He had been a snarling dog since coming home to find Phoebe here. He'd baited—insulted her constantly. How could he blame her for wanting to strike out at him?.

She'd said the chapter was her penance—a reminder of how damaging angry words could be to others. But what had stopped her from letting the Times print the chapter? He was missing something there, but what?

"Think, Chelmsford. Think," he muttered fiercely.

He closed his eyes and visualized Phoebe standing at the library door. As he remained completely still, he heard her voice echoing softly in his head. *Perhaps worst of all is that I've destroyed any hope of you ever...* Her voice had trailed off in to silence, and at the time, something in her voice had puzzled him.

It was as if she'd lost all hope. Had it been despair he'd heard? He repeated her words in his head again, and this time he was certain there had been a note of hopelessness in her voice.

What was it she believed she'd destroyed? What had she hoped for where he was concerned? As he tried to understand what she'd been referring to, something else she'd said pushed its way into his consciousness.

'It was only when I realized how much I...'

Realized what? What had she realized? A rush of hope crashed through him. Had she realized she loved him?

"Did you hear what I said, Gideon?"

His mother's voice barely registered with him as he whirled around and headed toward the door. As he brushed past Lady Wrotham, he heard her speak his name again.

"Not now, Mama. I need to see Phoebe."

His stride long and fast, he charged out of the library,

crossed the entryway, and ran up the steps. In less than a minute, he was outside Phoebe's door. Gideon raised his hand to knock, but stopped. What if he was wrong? A voice in the back of his head chastised him for wavering. Gently, he rapped his knuckles against the door's wood paneling and waited for her to answer the knock.

When the door didn't open, and there was no sound from within, his body tightened with fear. Slowly opening the door, he saw Phoebe standing at the window, which looked out over the garden that adjoined the solarium. As if suddenly sensing she wasn't alone, Phoebe looked over her shoulder. Her eyes widened in surprise before she turned to stare out the window again.

"Go away, Gideon."

The listless note in Phoebe's voice twisted his insides, and Gideon didn't move for a moment before he stepped fully into the room and shut the door behind him. At the sound of the door clicking shut, he saw her sag slightly, and a small sound echoed out of her. It was a soft cry of pain that tore into him with the savagery of a wild animal. He took a step forward, and the moment the floor squeaked beneath his feet, Phoebe whirled around. Trepidation furrowed her brow before her expression became cold and devoid of any emotion.

"Since you refuse to leave, am I to assume you wish to collect the first installment of my penance?" Her voice was icier than a winter's wind, and Gideon's gut knotted up at her question.

"I deserved that," he said quietly. Phoebe jerked slightly as her expression became one of humorless skepticism. Gideon winced at her disbelief. Once more, her features became devoid of emotion, and she turned away to stare out the window once more.

"If you're not here to demand your rights as a husband, then leave."

"I'll go if you answer one question and answer it truthfully."

Tension wound his muscles tight as he waited for her to agree to his request. After a long moment, she nodded but didn't turn away from the window.

"If I said I loved you, would you believe me?" At his soft question, she didn't move, but he saw her shudder. "Phoebe, look at me."

When she didn't turn around, he slowly closed the distance between them. Fear wrapped a vise around his chest as he halted a foot away from her. Afraid she might dart away from him, Gideon didn't try to touch her. Instead, he stood quietly behind her. Muscles knotted with tension, he cleared his throat.

"I love you, Phoebe. I have since that night at Montjoy's. I didn't understand what I was feeling, but the harder I fought it, the harder it was for me to deny that I loved you."

Phoebe didn't move. She simply stood motionless in front of him, so close and yet so far away. Gideon's stomach twisted viciously into knots as fear sent his heart slamming into his chest as if it were a battering ram. God help him. If he was wrong, he would be in hell.

"I said I would go if you would answer my question truthfully, but you've still not answered me." Gideon dragged in a ragged breath as dread wound its way through him. "*Look at me, Phoebe.* Do I go or stay?"

The words were barely out of Gideon's mouth before a quiet sob escaped Phoebe, and she whirled around to throw herself into his arms. Uncertain how to interpret her reaction, Gideon remained silent as he wrapped his arms around her and absorbed her violent trembling into his body. After a long moment, she lifted her head to meet his gaze.

"I do love you, Gideon. I love you so much."

Tears shimmered in her eyes as she pressed her body back into his. Relief surged through him, and he pulled her tight against him knowing her heart belonged to him. They stood like that for some time until Gideon gently pushed her away from him a few inches.

"I need to explain about last night."

At his quiet statement, Phoebe grew as still as a wild animal, sensing imminent danger. Panic and apprehension plainly visible on her face, he saw the color drain from her cheeks. In an attempt to ease her fears, he kissed her lightly.

"I told you before we married that our marriage would never resemble the one you had with Helstone. Unfortunately, last night, I made a grave error and unintentionally broke my word to you."

Phoebe opened her mouth as if about to speak, but he pressed his fingers against her lips and shook his head so he could finish.

"Before the gala, the Duchess of Stockdale led me to believe she intended to cause discord between us and attempt to humiliate you. When I escorted the duchess out of the ballroom last night, it was simply to issue her a warning. I made it clear that if she did *anything* to cause you pain or humiliation, I would make her pay a heavy price. But I was so intent on saving you from being hurt that instead of saving you pain, I inflicted it, and I deeply regret doing so."

"That is an error easy to forgive," Phoebe whispered as she pressed her forehead into his chest. "My sin isn't. I'm so sorry I wrote that terrible chapter, Gideon. I was hurt and angry. I know that isn't an excuse for what I did, but—"

"No more recriminations or apologies, my love." Gideon bent his head and kissed her. "I burned it. It's gone. I'm simply relieved to know it's not what you really think of me."

"And can you forgive me for mocking you in the Chronicles?" At the apprehension in her voice, Gideon frowned as if seriously debating his response.

"*Gideon,*" she gasped with a note of fear in her voice. With a grin, he kissed her.

"Forgive me for teasing you, my love. I merely wanted to be sure there wasn't anything I wanted P. Currer to apologize for publicly."

"I see," she murmured with a soft laugh. "Unfortunately, Mr. Currer is about to succumb to a terminal illness. I submitted the last of my chapters for the Chronicles the other day."

"When did you write them?" Gideon asked with a frown of curiosity.

"I wrote the last three chapters at Lyndham House. I knew I couldn't write them here. I was terrified you would never forgive me if you learned the truth."

"Are you telling me Constance and Lucien know you're Currer?" Gideon arched his eyebrows with a touch of pique in his voice at the possibility that his friends had known something about his wife that he hadn't.

"Only Constance." Phoebe brushed her fingers over his mouth. "Her gift showed her who I was when we met at Madam Sabine's."

"I don't know who I fear more, you and your wicked pen or Constance for her special talent."

"I think you might want to wait and decide when the last chapter is printed."

"And why is that?" Gideon murmured as he brushed his lips over her cheek to find her earlobe and nibble on it.

"I believe Mr. Currer gently points out in his final chapter that Lord Chelmbee, a man of fastidious tastes, appears to have hung up his wings for the time being as the rogue has suddenly and surprisingly acquired a countess of late. If I recall correctly, I also seem to remember a mention of bumblebees adorning a certain cake." The droll note in her voice made Gideon bite down lightly on her earlobe.

"You do like to test me, don't you, Lady Chelmsford?"

"It's a necessary requirement for the wife of *Lord Chelmbee* to ensure he never becomes too pompous or full of himself."

The light-hearted teasing in her voice made him chuckle as he lifted his head. No sooner had he taken a breath than the air in his lungs disappeared as he saw how radiant she looked. Gideon's heart slammed into his chest at the thought he might have lost her. When he didn't speak, a troubled look darkened her eyes.

"What is it?" She whispered. "Are you still having doubts? Do you regret—"

Gideon captured her mouth in a gentle kiss. There was still a hint of dismay lingering in her expression, and his arms tightened around her.

"I love you, Phoebe. I will never have any regrets about loving you. Never." Gideon caressed her cheek with his hand as the happiness he'd experienced last night returned tenfold. The rogue's countess was his until he drew his last breath. "Did I tell you how much I love you, Lady Chelmsford?"

"Not enough that I want to stop hearing it," she whispered. "I love you too."

# Epilogue

"**G**ood morning."

A warm mouth brushed across Phoebe's lips as the wickedly sinful sound of Gideon's voice echoed in the air above her. Eyes fluttering open, she saw Gideon hovering over her as a wicked smile of amusement curved his lips.

"Clearly, last night's activities exhausted you, my lady." A deep rumble of laughter rolled past his lips as she glared up at him, then slowly smiled.

"Hmm, is it any wonder? Although, as I recall, I did manage to make you plead for mercy. It is not an easy thing to make the Earl of Chelmsford beg for his release."

"And yet you did it so incredibly well, my love." Gideon kissed her quickly, then straightened upright. He was fully dressed, and Phoebe pushed herself up on her elbows to stare at him in surprise.

"*You're dressed.* Did I really sleep so late?"

"No, but as I recall, you were far from enthused about spending the morning in the Villa Borghese's gardens." Gideon's beautiful mouth twisted in a droll smile. "So I thought I would go alone and allow you to rest for this evening's events."

"You're correct," she said with a laugh. "I do not want to spend two hours listening to you and Signore Calabrese discussing how best to care for one plant or another. I politely, *and patiently* I might add, sat through an hour's discussion on the virtues of the lily the other afternoon."

"Forgive me, my love," Gideon grimaced with regret. "I should have been more thoughtful."

"I didn't mind," she said softly as she caught his hand in hers and kissed the inside of his palm. "I was with you, and it made me happy to see you happy."

Gideon leaned over her again and kissed her deeply. With a murmur, she wrapped her arms around his neck to pull him downward. Gideon resisted her efforts, and with obvious reluctance, he straightened upright again.

"At the moment, I am deeply regretting my having accepted Signore Calabrese's invitation." The indecision on his face made Phoebe scrambled up onto her knees and kiss him gently.

"Go, I know how much you have been looking forward to this. I'll enjoy a long bath, have breakfast in the courtyard, and perhaps take a walk down the Spanish Steps. Then, when you come back, you can tell me how much you missed me." Gideon appeared to be on the verge of staying, and Phoebe smoothed the lapels of his jacket before playfully slapping his shoulder. "Will you go? I really *do* want you to. I refuse to be the reason you missed the chance to discuss a topic near and dear to your heart, especially when I know how much you love puttering around in the arboretum."

"Have I told you how much I love you, Lady Chelmsford?" Gideon's voice was husky with emotion.

"Yes, and I love you too," Phoebe said as she kissed him gently. *"Now go."*

"Say that again." Gideon's arms wrapped around her waist as he pulled her into his chest.

"Say what? That I want you to go?" she teased him with a smile.

A strong hand smacked her bottom in a move that startled her. Phoebe gasped as she met Gideon's gaze. Eyebrows raised, his authoritative gaze locked with hers. With a laugh, she shook her head.

"You, my lord, are being a tyrant."

"A tyrant who's ready to stay here and torment his wife until she's begging me to satisfy her need, only for me to make her ache even more," he growled.

"I love you, Gideon." As she stared into his gray eyes, her fingers brushed across his sensual mouth. "I don't have enough words to say how much I love you."

"That's better," he murmured as he brushed his lips across hers. "However, I intend to make you pay a penance for being such a disobedient wife."

"Perhaps I need to be disobedient more often because the thought of such a punishment is delightfully pleasant." Her playful words tugged a dark groan from him.

"*Damn it, Phoebe.* Even though I know you want me to go, you're making it damn difficult for me to leave you," he muttered as he grabbed her hand and pushed it between them to press her palm against his hard erection. Quickly pulling her hand away from him, she shook her head.

"Go," she said firmly. "Enjoy your conversation with Signore Calabrese. Tonight I promise to apologize quite sweetly for having teased you."

"A promise I intend to hold you to, Lady Chelmsford." There was a wicked glint in his gaze as he smacked her bottom again.

"*Gideon,*" she protested in a breathless voice. A smile of satisfaction curved his lips as he kissed her again, then strode out of their suite.

The moment he was gone, it was as if the light in the room had somehow grown dimmer at the lack of his presence. But he would come back. The knowledge made her heart swell with happiness. Falling back into the mattress, Phoebe smiled happily as she remembered the past two weeks.

The first week they had only left their suite to have dinner downstairs in the hotel's courtyard. The rest of the time they'd spent in each other's arms laughing, talking quietly, or making love until they had fallen asleep fully satiated. Last week, they had emerged from their room and walked the streets of Rome. The city was a marvel of an ancient civilization mixed with new structures that reflected they were in the modern era.

While on one of their daily outings, Gideon had pulled her into the shop of one of the city's renowned jewelers, stating he'd not yet given her a wedding present. Although she'd protested, he'd been adamant and refused to be swayed. His only concession had been accepting her choice of jewelry.

She'd chosen a gold locket with a heart etched into the top of it. When opened, it was designed to hold miniature paintings, and when she'd asked Gideon to have a small portrait of him painted, his expression made her heart feel as though it would burst from being so deliriously happy.

The clock sitting on a nearby table chimed the hour of nine. With a leisurely yawn, Phoebe climbed out of bed and make her way to the bathroom. It boasted the latest in modern plumbing features, and Gideon had declared he intended to have Chelmsford House and the house at Lethbridge Farms outfitted with similar improved plumbing.

Phoebe bent over the tub and turned on the hot water faucet. While Gideon had arranged for a maid to assist her while they were at the hotel, she had chosen not to have someone help her. Phoebe had grown accustomed to fending for herself for the past several years. She tested the water's heat for a moment before turning on the cold water and pushed the tub's stopper into place.

As she turned to collect a washcloth, something wet slid down along the inside of her thigh. Heart sinking, Phoebe bent over and lifted her nightgown to see a drop of blood hit the bathroom's marble floor. A soft cry escaped her as an invisible vise constricted around her chest, and she stared helplessly at the floor.

She wasn't carrying Gideon's child. The onslaught of grief slicing through her caused her to stumble backward as she reached out to brace herself against the washbasin. On numerous occasions, Phoebe had contemplated what she would feel if this moment came. Her imaginings had done little to prepare her for what she was feeling now.

Tears rolled down her cheeks as she struggled to accept the inevitable. Although she'd known she would feel pain and disappointment, the intensity of the emotions assaulting her senses was overwhelming. Deep inside of her, a voice cried out in anguish, which made her tears flow faster.

For almost a month, she'd tried not to think about the possibility of being with child, but it hadn't stopped her from hoping. With each passing day, that hope had become a small flame that had begun to grow brighter. Now that fledgling flame had been snuffed out.

In one brief instant, the idea and hope that she was carrying Gideon's child had been swept away with a devastating finality. She'd been right, after all. It was unlikely she would ever be able to give Gideon a son. It was a fact she couldn't ignore, and it made every beat of her heart a painful one. The fears she'd tried to express to Gideon had come to pass.

The first week they were in Rome, Phoebe had tentatively brought up the subject, and Gideon had dismissed her worries. He'd reiterated several times that his nephew would inherit his title. Although he'd been emphatic that he didn't expect an heir, she couldn't help thinking he would be disappointed to learn she wasn't with child. Suddenly, her stomach lurched as a sickening wave of fear rolled over her.

Would he regret having married her now? She quickly rejected the thought. No, Gideon loved her. He told her so several times a day, and he demonstrated it over and over again. Whether a tender caress, a smile, or in a moment of blissful passion, Gideon loved her. Never in her life had she ever felt so cherished.

Despite her refusal to consider the possibility that

Gideon might experience regrets at having married her, she failed to stifle the fear slithering through her. Like a poisonous vine, it twisted its way through her veins as she wondered what Gideon's reaction would be to the news.

Wiping the tears off her cheeks, Phoebe swallowed her sadness and disappointment. Nothing was to be done now except wait and see what Gideon would say when she told him she wasn't with child. She could only pray he truly believed in his heart what he'd told her about not needing an heir.

Sorrow swept through her as she quickly undressed and sank into the hot water. It was a tad bit hotter than she normally liked her bath, but at the moment, she was cold, and the water helped to warm her. Phoebe didn't know how long she'd been reclined against the back of the tub, but a shiver rippled through as she realized the water had grown cold.

Reluctantly, she climbed out of the bath and dressed. A short time later, she was staring at herself in the mirror. Phoebe winced at how pale she was and pinched her cheeks hard to bring color into them. She met the brown-eyed gaze reflected in the mirror and glared at her image.

"Enough, Phoebe. You knew the chances of becoming pregnant, let alone carrying a child to term, were against you. Moping around like a sulking cat won't change anything."

With another pinch of her cheeks, she quickly rose from the dressing table's bench to collect her hat and place it on her head. When it was securely pinned in place, she gathered her gloves and parasol, then left the suite. As she made her way down to the hotel lobby, she passed a young woman holding the hand of a little girl. The woman smiled in a silent greeting while her daughter shyly waved hello.

Phoebe forced a smile to her lips, then increased her pace in an effort to put distance between herself and them. When she reached the lobby, she took a few steps toward the hotel's dining room, only to realize she wasn't hungry. Instead, she walked toward the hotel's main doorway and the sunshine beyond. The sun's warmth might ease the chill that still engulfed her.

Wrapped up in her thoughts, the sound of someone calling her name drifted close to the edge of her internal musing, and Phoebe paused for a brief moment to glance over her shoulder. When she didn't see anyone, she dismissed the soft echo as having come from her own imagination, and she continued toward the exit.

"Phoebe."

This time her name was a louder cry in the air, and it mixed with the fast, light clatter of shoes on the marble floor from only a few feet away. Phoebe stopped again and looked over her shoulder to see Lawrence and Anthony hurrying across the lobby in her direction. Stunned to see the two men, she stared at them with her mouth parted in amazement. The moment he reached her, Lawrence enveloped her in a warm, tight embrace and kissed her cheek.

"What are you doing here?" she gasped in bewilderment as she returned the gesture of affection.

"We're here for the annual *Palio Madama Margarita.*"

"The what?" Phoebe arched her eyebrows in puzzlement.

"It's a festival in Castel Madama where the entire town becomes a medieval village almost overnight. It's become a yearly destination for us. The last two days of the event are the jousting match, which Anthony participates in. Although I'd rather he not."

"You worry too much." Anthony Evans, Baron Siddall, arched his eyebrows at his partner before greeting Phoebe with a broad smile and a peck on each cheek. "How are you, my dear, Phoebe? It's been far too long since we saw each other."

"Hello, Anthony." She smiled at the man who was several years younger than Lawrence. "It's wonderful to see you."

"When are you going to visit us in France? Lawrence told me he asked you a few weeks ago."

"I don't know," she said with a shake of her head. "I…Gideon and I haven't been married very long, and I've not discussed it with him."

"And why are you here, my pet?" The question made Phoebe flinch as she tried not to think about her current situation. When she didn't immediately answer, Lawrence looked around with a frown of disapproval. "And where *is this* husband of yours?"

"He's meeting with a horticulturist."

"Are you telling me the man brought you to Rome simply to leave you alone while he dashed off somewhere?" The disapproval in Lawrence's voice was accompanied by a thinning of his lips and a flash of anger in his gaze.

"No. I encouraged him to go." Phoebe shook her head sharply as she corrected her friend. "We've been in Rome for the past two weeks. It's…it's our wedding trip."

"All the worse for leaving his bride alone," Anthony said with condemnation in his voice.

"Stop this." Phoebe eyed both of them with irritation. "I told Gideon to go. I know how much he enjoys puttering around in his garden at home, and I didn't want to sit through a discussion about plant soil and what flowers grow best."

At her fierce repudiation of their judgmental observations, both Lawrence and Anthony stared at her in surprise. Lawrence's amazement swiftly disappeared as he narrowed his gaze at her.

"Something's happened."

"Nothing has happened other than Gideon and I have confessed our true feelings for one another." Phoebe forced a smile to her lips and shook her head. "I am blissfully happy in knowing my husband loves me as much as I love him."

"Then why aren't your eyes shining with happiness, not to mention the fact you're as pale as a ghost."

"I am happy, Lawrence. I truly am," Phoebe said fervently.

"I don't believe you," her long-time friend said briskly. Lawrence raised his hand as Phoebe started to protest. "Don't say a word, Phoebe. We both know I can read you as easily as I can a book. Anthony?"

"Why don't we take Phoebe to that small café we found yesterday," Anthony suggested quietly. "Something tells me she's not eaten today."

"A capital idea," Lawrence said with a nod.

Before she could say another word of protest, Lawrence pulled her arm through his, and with a nod to his partner, her best friend guided her out of the hotel. As they stepped out into the sunlight, Phoebe blinked as she adjusted to the bright sunshine. His hand over hers to prevent her from escaping, Lawrence's expression was one of concern and a hint of anger.

Phoebe was certain the irritation twisting her friend's mouth was from his incorrect assessment that Gideon had made her unhappy. The three of them headed in the direction of the Spanish Steps in silence. When they reached the famous stairway, they descended the steps designed in the shape of a large butterfly.

Despite her sorrow, Phoebe couldn't help but find a small amount of pleasure in her picturesque surroundings. At the foot of the stairs, Lawrence drew her toward a small establishment that had outdoor seating. The three of them sat down at one of the tables, and Anthony waved for a server.

"Now then," Lawrence said in a no-nonsense voice. "Out with it, Phoebe. I know when you're unhappy, and if your husband has done anything to hurt—"

"Gideon would never raise a hand to me," Phoebe snapped. "He makes me very happy. *We* make each other happy."

"Then who or what has upset you, and no prevarications, Phoebe."

Faced with her best friend's demand for the truth, Phoebe shook her head in dismay. Lawrence used his fingers to tip her chin up until their gazes met.

"Out with it, Phoebe." At his matter-of-fact demand, tears welled up in her throat, and Lawrence uttered a small sound of anger and dismay. "Whatever he's done, I intend to make him pay."

"No, it's me. I'm the one who's at fault," Phoebe choked out. Beside her, Anthony muttered something beneath his breath.

"Lawrence, stop scolding her. Whatever's causing her distress, it's not her husband."

"Then tell us what has you so upset, my pet," Lawrence pleaded softly as he caught her hand and pressed his lips to the back of her hand. "I'm worried about you. You look as miserable now as you did the day we met in Victoria Gardens."

Phoebe stared at him as a wave of sorrow washed over her. Her friend knew of her past miscarriages, but this was different. This was Gideon. She'd lost Gideon's child. Deep inside, she'd prayed she was carrying his child, only to have her hopes and prayers crushed this morning. Even though she'd known it was a likely outcome, it had done nothing to ease her pain. She met Lawrence's worried gaze and shook her head.

"I thought I might be with child, but I'm not."

"Oh, my pet," Lawrence said tenderly as she suppressed a sob of disappointment. "It will be all right."

"But he married me because he thought I might be carrying his child, and now I'm not. If I can't give him a son…I know he says he loves me, but what if he's mistaken affection for love?" Phoebe choked back a quiet sob as she stared helplessly at Lawrence. "I don't know what to do. What am I supposed to say? How do I tell Gideon the truth?"

"And what truth is that, Phoebe?"

The harsh sound of Gideon's voice made her jerk away from Lawrence and twist around in her seat to stare at her husband in horror. Dear God, how much had he heard? Gideon's cold, forbidding look sent fear streaking through her. Clearly, he'd heard enough to consider the possibility she wasn't with child.

His stony expression was the same one she'd imagined he would have when he learned she wasn't pregnant. Harsh and immobile, his features revealed nothing except cold anger. As she met Gideon's icy stare, Phoebe tried to keep breathing as she struggled to think of a response to his question.

Gideon entered the Hotel Hassler's lobby and walked toward the registration desk. This morning's conversation with Signore Calabrese had been a pleasant and informative one. That Phoebe had insisted he keep his appointment with the horticulturist had been an act of love and he intended to make it up to her. As he reached the registration desk, he asked if there were any messages for him. The clerk shook his head, and Gideon wondered if Phoebe had come back from her walk.

"Have you seen Lady Chelmsford this morning?" At his question, the man's cheerful expression became one of discomfort, and he held up his hand.

"*Un momento, signore.*"

The clerk disappeared through a door behind him, and Gideon frowned at the man's odd manner. Gideon heard the murmur of voices, which grew louder as the clerk returned with a distinguished-looking man.

"Good morning, my lord," the man said quietly with the same uncomfortable expression as the younger man. "Luca says you were asking about Lady Chelmsford."

"Yes. My wife had said she was planning on having breakfast in the dining room and perhaps going for a walk."

"Luca says he saw her ladyship leave the hotel with two men about thirty minutes ago." Clearly disconcerted, the man shook his head as Gideon stared at him in stunned disbelief. "I'm sure it is nothing to be concerned about, my lord. Luca says she did not appear to be coerced in any way but seemed to go willingly with the gentlemen."

"Did you recognize these men?" Gideon turned his head and pinned his gaze on the young clerk.

"*Mi dispiace, signore.* I have not seen them before."

"Perhaps these are friends Lady Chelmsford encountered by chance, my lord. It is not unusual for guests to suddenly find themselves face-to-face with those they know at home."

What the man said was true. On occasion, while in different cities across the continent, he had run into people he knew, but Phoebe didn't know any men in London. It made no sense that she'd leave the hotel with two strangers. Fear suddenly stiffened his limbs. What if the men had told her something had happened to him? He had no doubt that Phoebe would have allowed strangers to take her to him. She loved him and would fear for his safety.

"Which way did they go when they left the hotel?" The terse note in his voice made both men behind the desk flinch before the man called Luca pointed to a spot behind Gideon.

"Toward the Spanish Steps, my lord."

With an abrupt nod, Gideon spun around on his heel and walked quickly out of the hotel. His stride fast-paced, Gideon tried to think of an explanation for Phoebe being with two strangers. Two *male* strangers. He muttered a harsh oath under his breath. God help them if they had done anything to hurt her.

The distance to the Spanish Steps was short, and he paused briefly at the top of the famous stone stairway to study the people climbing and descending the steps. When he didn't see Phoebe, his heart sank. Where the hell was she. Fear followed Gideon as he quickly descended the steps. At the foot of the stairs, he came to an abrupt halt in the Piazza di Spagna. Uncertain which direction to take, Gideon's gaze searched the busy square. He was about to turn left when he saw a woman sitting at a small outdoor café flanked by two men.

The woman's back was to him, but she was wearing a hat, just like the one Phoebe had worn the other day. He distinctly remembered it because he'd teased her about the hat's outrageously wide brim. Then there was the soft roundness of her curves beneath her dress. A second later, the woman revealed her profile as she turned her head to look at the man on her left.

Relief crashed over him. She was safe. Whoever Phoebe was with hadn't harmed her. Gideon made his way toward his wife and the strangers at a quick pace. The moment one of the two men rested his arm on the back of her chair and took Phoebe's hand in his, every last bit of air in Gideon's lungs was sucked out of him.

The man kissed Phoebe's hand with obvious affection, and an unspeakable rage exploded inside Gideon. He wanted to pummel the stranger until the man lay half-dead at his feet. An image swirled through Gideon's head of the man sprawled on the ground, unconscious, bloodied, and Gideon increased his pace as he strode toward the small party.

Gideon was still several feet away when he heard Phoebe mention his name, followed by the revelation she didn't know how to tell him the truth. Gideon's stride faltered as he tried to comprehend what she was saying.

What was she afraid to tell him? What was she hiding from him? Had she suddenly realize she didn't really love him? Gideon immediately dismissed the thought. Phoebe loved him. Of that, he was certain. A mocking voice in the back of his head asked him what he would do if he was wrong.

Anger and fear pounded through his blood as he fought off the urge to drag her out of her chair and shake the truth out of her. What could she so easily share with a stranger that she couldn't tell her husband? Closing the distance between them, Gideon came to a halt behind her and bitterly asked her what she found so difficult to share with him.

The instant Phoebe heard his question, she immediately pulled away from the man at her side. With a jerk, she twisted around in her seat to stare up at him in horror. The idea that she might be afraid of him twisted his gut. Hadn't he told her—showed her—how much he loved her? Had he failed to make her understand he'd never hurt her? He'd give his life to keep her safe. He loved her that much.

"I asked you a question, Phoebe," he growled softly. "What is it you find so easy to share with a stranger but far too difficult to share with your husband?"

"Lord Chelmsford, I presume?"

"I suggest you move away from my wife," he said coldly to the man whose arm rested on the back of Phoebe's chair.

The small smile twisting the man's lips made Gideon want to drop the man to the ground with a hard right jab. The bastard was laughing at him. As the stranger pulled away from Phoebe, she sprang to her feet. Anger darkened his wife's lovely features as she faced him with a look of disgusted irritation. Gideon narrowed his gaze at her, but her anger didn't abate.

"Gideon, I'd like you to meet my friend Lawrence Babcock, the Earl of Linshal," she said in an icy voice. In a sharp sweep of her hand, she introduced the man who had demonstrated an obvious affection for Phoebe. In another pointed gesture, she bobbed her head toward the man on her right. "And this is his friend, Baron Siddall. Gentlemen, this is my husband, Lord Chelmsford."

As he drew in his next breath, his gaze swung toward the

man Phoebe introduced him to first. Lawrence. This was the man Phoebe considered her dearest friend. The man she'd been trying to protect the night they'd met in Montjoy's garden. Almost as if he could see the puzzle pieces coming together in Gideon's head, Lawrence eyed him with amusement.

"So you're the man who stole my dearest friend's heart," Lord Linshal said with a cheerful smile in what was obviously a deliberate effort to ease the tension between Gideon and Phoebe. The moment her friend spoke, Phoebe jerked her head toward Linshal to glare at him. Her expression made Lawrence arch his eyebrows. "Are you going to deny you're in love with your husband, my pet?"

Phoebe didn't answer her friend, and she turned her head away to avoid Linshal's gaze. The earl's attention still focused on Phoebe, Linshal addressed Gideon.

"I confess I was uncertain whether I would like you, Chelmsford. When it comes to the woman who is the sister I never had, there are few men I would find worthy of her. But it's quite clear to me how much you love Phoebe, despite her stubborn nature," Linshal said with a smile.

At his cheerful statement, Gideon saw a fierce shudder rock Phoebe's body. Linshal's smile was pleasant as he extended his hand in friendship. Gideon didn't move for a moment as he studied the stiff line of Phoebe's back. Then, suddenly aware that he was being rude, Gideon accepted Linshal's hand in a firm handshake and did the same with the baron.

Polite greetings dispensed with, Gideon returned his attention to Phoebe. As the silence stretched out between the four of them, Lord Linshal uttered a soft sound of exasperation. The man leaned forward to whisper something into her ear. Whatever he'd said caused Phoebe's posture to sag as if in defeat. Slowly turning around, she drew in a deep breath.

"I need to speak with you, but not here," she said in a wooden voice.

"As you wish," Gideon said quietly. "Shall we return to the hotel?"

Something indescribable flickered in Phoebe's eyes as she looked at him for a brief moment. She jerked her head in agreement, then turned back to her friend. Phoebe kissed the earl with affection as she said her goodbyes. Phoebe did the same with Baron Siddal, then walked away in the direction of the Spanish Steps.

With a nod to both men, Gideon turned and followed his wife. He caught up with Phoebe easily, despite her quick pace. As he came abreast of her, Gideon saw her flinch, and she immediately widened the space between the two of them.

Frustrated, he extended his hand to brush his fingertips over hers. Phoebe's reaction was to jerk away from him and widen the distance between them even more. *Christ Jesus,* they'd only been apart for a couple of hours. Where had his sweet, loving, mischievous wife gone, and why? He was still asking that question when they reached their hotel suite.

Closing the door of their rooms behind him, Gideon remained where he was as he watched Phoebe cross the floor to the dresser. Her movements lethargic, she slowly removed her hat and gloves. It was as if he was watching the same woman who'd come to him that day in the arboretum and accepted his proposal. Then, as if a sledgehammer had hit his chest, Gideon's thoughts slammed into a wall.

Phoebe wasn't pregnant.

The sudden realization made his muscles knot with pain. The one thing she'd feared had come to pass, and it was obvious she was devastated. While he couldn't deny it would give him great pleasure to see Phoebe growing round with his child, it was not for the reason she thought. Carrying his child would make her happy, and that's all he wanted.

He wanted Phoebe to be happy. The fact that his wife

was afraid to tell him there would be no child meant Gideon had failed to make her understand the real reason he'd offered his hand to her that night in the library. Gideon inhaled a deep breath, then took a step forward.

"I love you, Phoebe. Nothing. *Nothing* will ever change that. With each passing day, I love you more than the day before. I can't imagine what my life would be like without you. No, I *can* imagine it. It would be a bleak, hellish existence."

Phoebe turned her head to look at him, and the sorrow and pain shadowing her brown eyes made him want to sweep her up into his arms and hold her close. Gideon cleared his throat as an invisible band wrapped around his chest, making it difficult to breathe. If he failed to make her understand him now, it would eventually cause a rift between them. A divide that might never heal. His gut twisted painfully at the thought.

"I'm fairly certain I know what's upset you." His quiet words made her eyes widen as she stared at him in horrified dismay. Gideon took another step forward. "You were happy when I left this morning, and there's only one thing I can think of that could have made you this miserable between then and now. So unhappy that you're afraid to tell me what's wrong."

A tear rolled down her cheek. It twisted his gut to see her so despondent. He took another step forward, praying she didn't retreat from him. Gideon saw her throat bob as if fighting back more tears, but she didn't move.

"I married you because I love you, Phoebe, not because a child might have been conceived that night in the library. I'll swear to it on the good book, in a public square, or to anyone who will listen. I might not have realized it at the time, but I married you because I love you, Phoebe."

Gideon took two more steps forward until there was hardly any space between them. He breathed in the soft scent of roses wafting off her skin. Every time Gideon smelled the roses in his gardens, he would envision Phoebe standing beside him. Their gazes locked, and he slowly reached out to stroke the side of her cheek.

"Why did you agree to marry me, Phoebe?" At his quiet question, she drew in a sharp breath. She hesitated for a moment before she exhaled.

"Because I love you," she whispered.

"Not because you might be with child, but because you loved me?" He studied her closely, and she slowly nodded.

"Yes."

"Then why can't you believe me when I say I married you for the same reason."

"I…because…that day in the arboretum…you…you said you didn't want any child to be born out of wedlock. You believed it was the honorable thing to do."

"I never said that, Phoebe. I said my behavior was dishonorable. I said I wouldn't shirk my duty where you and the babe were concerned if you didn't marry me, but that it would be for the best if you were my wife."

"Duty and responsibility are matters of honor."

"*Damn it, Phoebe*," Gideon said with frustration at her stubborn nature. "Was there any other argument I could have used that would have convinced you to marry me? Would you have married me for any other reason than the possibility of a child?"

"I don't know, I…" The moment he arched his eyebrows, she shook her head and turned her head away from him. "No. At least not then. But you were so adamant. You even refused to wait until…"

"Refused to wait until today to determine if you were with child?" he asked gently. Phoebe kept her face averted as she nodded abruptly. Gideon's fingers caught her by the chin and forced her to look at him. "Oh, my darling, don't you understand? Even then, I was willing to *do* anything—*say* anything to make you my wife."

"But—"

"If I hadn't truly wanted you to marry me, do you think

I would have willingly thrown myself into the fire by asking Mama for her help? Facing the full force of my mother's wrath and contempt is not an experience I recommend." Gideon grimaced as he remembered the conversation with the marchioness. "But I knew that if there was anyone who could convince you to become my wife, it was Mama."

Gideon stared down into soft brown eyes, glistening with unshed tears. Tension tightened his muscles at her uncertainty. Helstone had done his job well to make Phoebe was nothing more than an object to debase. Her father hadn't been much better. With a gentle tug, he pulled her into his arms to cradle her against him. A quiet sob escaped her as she wrapped her arms around his waist and pressed her body deep into his.

"No matter what I say, you seem hellbent on believing I need you to give me an heir. I don't, Phoebe, and you do me a disservice in your refusal to believe me."

"I'm so sorry, Gideon," she whispered against his chest.

"For what, sweetheart?"

"For not believing you…but I don't…I don't want you to regret…"

"*God help me, woman.* What do I have to say to convince you?" he exclaimed in a gruff voice. "I love you. Nothing, *nothing*, will ever change that. Any pleasure I might find in seeing you with child wouldn't be for my sake. It would be for yours."

She stiffened in his arms, then pulled away to look up at him. Eyes wide with surprise, she shook her head in bewilderment.

"My sake?" The puzzlement in her voice made him sigh with aggravation. Pressing his forehead against hers, he lifted her hand and pressed her palm over his heart.

"If a child would make you happy, then I hope for a child, but *only* because it would make *you* happy. There are only two things I want or need in life, Phoebe. Two things. Your love and the joy of seeing you happy."

"You really do mean that, don't you," she said with a soft note of awe in her voice.

Although her eyes still shimmered with unshed tears of sorrow, he saw a newfound trust glowing there as well. He'd won. Relief thundered through him as he tightened his arms around her and kissed her.

"I love you, Phoebe. I'll say it every morning when we wake up. I'll say it every night before you fall asleep in my arms. I'll say it so often you'll beg me to stop."

"No, I'll never beg you to stop, Gideon. I'll never grow tired of hearing you say it." Her fingertips brushed across his mouth as she pulled his head down and brushed her lips over his. Her voice was a mere whisper as she kissed him again. "My heart will always belong to you, Gideon."

Monica Burns Books

THE RECKLESS ROCKWOODS SERIES
Obsession #1
Dangerous #2
The Highlander's Woman #3
Redemption #4
The Beastly Earl #5

THE RECKLESS ROCKWOODS NOVELS
The Rogue's Offer
The Rogue's Countess

SELF-MADE MEN SERIES
His To Command #1 (Novella)
His Mistress #2

STAND ALONE TITLES
Forever Mine
Kismet
Mirage
Pleasure Me
A Bluestocking Christmas
Love's Portrait
Love's Revenge

THE ORDER OF THE SICARI SERIES
Assassin's Honor #1
Assassin's Heart #2
Inferno's Kiss #3

About The Author

Monica Burns is a bestselling author of spicy historical and paranormal romance. She penned her first romance at the age of nine when she selected the pseudonym she uses today. Her historical book awards include the 2011 RT BookReviews Reviewers Choice Award and the 2012 Gayle Wilson Heart of Excellence Award for Pleasure Me.

She is also the recipient of the prestigious paranormal romance award, the 2011 PRISM Best of the Best award for Assassin's Heart. From the days when she hid her stories from her sisters to her first completed full-length manuscript, she always believed in her dream despite rejections and setbacks. A workaholic, Monica is a survivor who believes every hero and heroine deserves a HEA (Happily Ever After), especially if she's writing the story.

Connect With Monica

Follow For New Release Alerts

BOOKBUB
www.bookbub.com/authors/monica-burns

AMAZON
www.amazon.com/Monica-Burns/e/B002BM7C5Q

Social Media

FACEBOOK
Monicaburns.net/readergroup

PINTEREST
www.pinterest.com/monicaburns

NEWSLETTER -COMPLIMENTARY DIGITAL BOOK
www.monicaburns.net/newsletter

WEBSITE
www.monicaburns.com

EMAIL
monicaburns@monicaburns.com